SHADOWS OVER KAIGHAL

BOOK 3 OF PACTS ARCANE AND OTHERWISE

JOANNA MACIEJEWSKA

ALSO BY THE AUTHOR:

Pacts Arcane and Otherwise

By the Pact

Scars of Stone

Shadows over Kaighal

Demon Siege

Shadows of Eireland

Humanborn

Myth-Touched

Snakebitten

Other books

Memories of Sorcery and Sand

Collections

Scourges, Spells, and Serenades

*To my dear beta readers: Mariusz, Kamil, and Mattheus,
who donated their precious time to this story.*

1

The initiation rite chamber had rarely been used, save for the annual initiation of the new high mage students who had successfully completed the first year of their training. Most of the time, it stood as empty as it was vast, with its circular walls, its tall windows, and its lush tapestries forgotten. Before Irtan became an archmage, he enjoyed both the solitude of that space and the view it offered. The crowd filling it now clashed with those memories of tranquility.

The assembly of most if not all High Towers' teachers and students filled the chamber, many of them standing in the wide door leading to it, and perhaps even in the stairway. The odd melody of their hushed conversations filled the air, and though most of them avoided pointing at the crystal in the middle of the initiation circle, their gazes constantly darted toward the motionless woman inside it. Irtan doubted they recognized her, except maybe for a handful of teachers... and his own student. Pelina stood by his side, wide-eyed and paralyzed.

Yoreus stepped out, and a smug smile curved his lips

when at his gesture all the whispers died out. Irtan refrained from chuckling. *He still savors the feeling of power like a boy given his first training sword.*

"Undoubtedly, many of you wonder about the reason for this gathering and the purpose of the crystal," Yoreus said. "Recently, the archmages discovered a plot aimed against the High Towers, and an arcanist you see here braved many dangers to warn us in time. A group which shall not be named schemed to destroy the High Towers. In the end, the arcanist sacrificed herself to avert the spell that could outdo the Cataclysm from centuries ago and gave the archmages a chance to deal with the unforeseen threat." Murmurs rose, and Yoreus let people stir for a while before speaking again.

Irtan had to agree that the story was good enough. The first archmage didn't have to get into details, allowing gossip and speculation and thus letting everyone choose their own most plausible version of the events. With the passing of months and then years, the truth would get buried so deep, it wouldn't even matter whether anyone doubted Yoreus's explanation. A decade later there would be nothing left but a vague tale of an arcanist who helped the high mages in the time of a great need.

"Kamira, which some of you might know as a former student, diverted the attack toward herself and let us encase her in the crystal to ensure the malicious magic would become trapped with her," the first archmage continued. "It's the highest sacrifice, and we're honored that, despite our differences, she was ready to give her life to save our home. And thus, in recognition of her great deed, from now on I wish to welcome any arcanist teachers and students within our walls. It's time we worked together and ensured proper education for all those who seek magic, be it the high or arcane one."

It seemed that Yoreus's offer to Kamira wasn't only a way to make her agree to what archmages had planned, but Irtan had no doubt that all arriving arcanists would be encouraged, more or less adamantly, to receive at least basic high magic schooling, thus bolstering the mages' numbers and strengthening Veranesh's prison. As boyish Yoreus was in his demands of respect and displays of power, he did know what to do to preserve his rule.

"I hope that all of you will work hard to be worthy of the high mage's title in the future," Yoreus said. "It's the best way to show gratitude for the sacrifice made."

A hesitant cheer rose above the crowd, and then people stirred, heading for the doorway. Irtan caught a glimpse of a Devanshari man rushing through the door, the protests of students pushed aside ignored. His face, frozen in horror, revealed his feelings, and Irtan arched an eyebrow. According to the gossip Pelina had gathered for him, Yoreus had a Devanshari in his services, pulling the strings through his own daughter, Atissa. But if this was the same man, it hardly seemed reasonable he would react so strongly to the news. Unless, of course, the first archmage had deceived him.

As others left, Irtan glanced at his student and leaned over to her. "Control your emotions. You look guilty, and you shouldn't."

When she looked back at him, Pelina's expression was that of a loyal and devoted person who'd discovered her ally's demise. "I've failed her," she confessed, taking advantage of the rustle accompanying others' departure.

This must be as close as Pelina would get to admitting she was doing Kamira's bidding all along instead of Irtan's, like she'd agreed. The feeling of all being lost must have pushed her into such a confession, no matter the consequences. The look on her face suggested she cared little about what was to come.

Ignoring the remark, Irtan turned his head toward Kamira. The crystal around her pulsated with energy. It stemmed both from the original circle and from the archmages' spell cast over it. Yet there was something more. The lines of the new symbols Pelina had secretly put in, distinct only for those who knew what to look for, seeped their own magic into the crystal. Power gathered around Kamira, but it escaped into nothingness before it could condense. Irtan doubted such flow was the result of Yoreus's spell alone.

"I don't think you did." He kept his voice down, but in the commotion following the announcement, nobody paid attention to one old archmage and his student. "Have a closer look at the crystal. And at the circle." She should have noticed it herself long before Yoreus finished speaking, but it seemed her emotions had affected the arcane perception he'd had her train for the past weeks.

At first, confusion flashed on her face, as if she was back in the high mage's mindset, but then Pelina focused on Kamira's prison. Irtan watched, amused, as she discovered all the energy fluctuations and distortions within its flow. He doubted she understood it all or could tell their origin apart, but even to a beginner arcanist like her, it had to be clear the magic energies within were clashing.

Satisfied, Irtan walked to the door, and his student rushed after him.

"How did you know?" she asked when they cleared away from the crowd.

"I watched you putting in these symbols, didn't I?" Of course, he'd only caught a glimpse of her work, but that was enough to suspect more. "You're still curious what's my play in it all, aren't you?" he asked. Pelina proved loyal to Kamira, which left little suspicion of her being Yoreus's agent. The first archmage wouldn't have allowed the new symbols in the circle. Therefore, Irtan could take a chance himself. Perhaps, in return, his student would share more, offering insights into what Kamira's plan really was. With all that transpired and all the things Kamira had said during the meeting with Yoreus, Irtan doubted it interfered with his own goals, but the more information he had, the better he could prepare for what was to come. Because one thing he was certain of: it wasn't the end yet.

He looked at Pelina.

"Let's go back to my quarters. I believe Kamira would be happy if you received a reward for your loyalty. Even as meager one as a handful of answers."

THE MAID REFILLED HIS MUG, but no amount of wine could ease Ryell's pain and erase the memory of Kamira's body encased within the crystal. With her eyes closed, the arcanist looked like she was only sleeping, and Yoreus insisted she was still alive, but Ryell couldn't bring himself to believe the archmage's words, not anymore. *They killed her, and I'm to blame for it.*

"Leave the whole jug," he said. At least he could hope that enough wine would bring dreamless sleep, allowing him to escape the consequences of his own actions.

The voice of reason told him that if he wanted to drink, he should have found a cheaper place than the Jagged Swordsman, but he had to talk to Veelk. No matter what Ryell thought of the mage killer, Kamira's friend deserved to know what happened. An ugly smile crept up on Ryell's lips when he thought that Veelk would likely take it personally and seek revenge. Perhaps he and Yoreus would end up killing each other, freeing the world of the two men who'd brought demise upon Kamira. One by not letting her seek the mage's counsel soon enough so the archmages had time to find another solution, the other by not even trying to help her. Besides, the mood of the Jagged Swordsman, with grim undertones and somberness hanging in the air, matched his own. Any port tavern would have too many cheerful people who would grate on Ryell's composure.

He downed another mug of wine, curling his other hand into a fist.

The maid's gasp made him look up. She was already running to the kitchen, calling out Opyr's name as Ryell looked at the entrance. Lefna walked in, helping a wounded man. A patron rushed to their side, relieving her of the burden and leading the man to the table while Opyr clutched his daughter in a tight embrace. Despite his own suffering, Ryell couldn't help smiling at the reunion full of tears and heartfelt whispers.

Opyr, with his arm still around his daughter, approached the wounded stranger. "Forgive me for not believing your words. You've saved my daughter, just like you promised. Do you need someone to look at your wound?"

The man shook his head. "It's fine now. It just needs time to heal." He looked around. "I'd have thought someone would already let Veelk know."

The joyful expression faded from the innkeeper's face. "Master Veelk left four days ago, in a great rush. He took a lot of supplies and said he won't be back for a week or two."

"And Kamira?"

Ryell twitched at someone speaking her name. Of

course, it made sense that if the man knew Veelk, he must have been acquainted with her as well, but a particular note in the stranger's voice struck at Ryell's jealousy.

"I haven't seen her since two days ago." Opyr spread his hands. "She didn't mention when she'd be back."

"She's at the High Towers, and she won't be back," Ryell said before his common sense advised him otherwise. Besides, that man seemed to know them both well enough, and perhaps was less secretive than Kamira herself and that wretched mage killer, so Ryell could gain some insights. Not that it made a difference anymore, but alone in his grief, he wanted anything that could ease the guilt or make him forget.

The man evaluated him with an inquisitive gaze, and subtle shifts in his expression suggested he was putting pieces of knowledge together. His moves stiff, he lifted from his table and walked over to Ryell's but waited for the invitation to sit down. Having enough time for second thoughts, Ryell would much rather send the stranger away, because talking meant revealing his own role in the events and Kamira's demise. Yet he was the one to have spoken first, and he couldn't back out.

Resigned, Ryell pointed to the chair in front of him.

The man sat down, his caution and slowness compensating for the injury, but he still carried himself like a man who knew how to fight. Ryell remembered Opyr mentioning a mercenary group that failed to rescue Lefna, and Ryell's respect for the stranger grew. Of course, there might have been less fighting, and more sneaking in and out, but even such a task required agility and skill. And the stranger's wound suggested he had to fight his way out anyway.

"You must be Ryell," the man said after the maid left food and drink at the table. "Kamira mentioned you."

That remark stung more than Ryell expected, and he grimaced. "I don't think she mentioned you." The way the stranger spoke about her indicated they were more than passing acquaintances. Ryell inspected the man's wiry muscles and brown skin. Was he one of Veelk's brethren? His outfit resembled more the local fashion than tribal attire.

"We've only met recently, so she might have had no chance. I'm Koshmarnyk." The man stretched his hand in a greeting. "So, Kamira went to the Towers?"

Ryell stared at Koshmarnyk's wrist and the crystal bracelet coiled around it. "She did," he replied after a long pause and finally shook the man's hand. "I thought she was attached to those." He pointed at the jewelry. "I've rarely seen her taking them off."

Koshmarnyk nodded. "She... insisted I take them. I think she hoped they'd bring me luck."

Ryell swallowed a ball of bile forming in his throat. Whoever Koshmarnyk was, it seemed that Kamira trusted him with her most personal possessions. Ryell drank from the mug, ready to walk away with any excuse, but his own curiosity was pushing him to stay. There might be an explanation to his relation to Kamira. "Are you Veelk's friend?" He forced his tone to remain polite. "Is that how you met?"

"Indeed I am. Kamira was in need of my skills, and Veelk got us acquainted." Koshmarnyk's lips curled in a half-smile. "But that's a story she probably should tell you herself if she chooses so."

From Koshmarnyk's choice of words, Ryell had no doubt that there were secrets involved, and his anger boiled within. Kamira had promised him answers, and the longer he looked at the man she had supposedly met only recently, who was speaking so casually about her and wearing her precious bracelets, Ryell couldn't help wondering what else she'd conveniently forgotten to mention. He was a fool for not having asked more questions and not pressing her more, but the circumstances were hardly suitable for lengthy discussions. Or Kamira simply had led Ryell to believe so.

"I don't think Kamira will be telling any stories... ever again." He let bitterness echo within the words. Anything to wipe the smile off Koshmarnyk's face. Anything to disrupt the connection that man had with her. "The archmages encased her in a crystal."

Pain or shock didn't appear on Koshmarnyk's face like Ryell had expected. Instead, the wiry man snorted. "So that's why she didn't tell us anything about her plan," he said. "She's worse than her demon." He shook his head.

"You don't seem upset by her death," Ryell prompted.

The man in front of him shifted, stretching into what must be a more comfortable position, as if the only thing bothering him was his wound. "Do you really think she'd plan everything for months just to die at the end?"

"Plan?"

"She planned for everything, including your betrayal," Koshmarnyk said without a trace of maliciousness. "If she's stuck in a crystal now, I think this is exactly where she wanted to be. Though, of course, you or I might question such a choice."

The mention of betrayal cut deep, and Ryell shook his head, trying to keep emotions off his face. "I've been deceived and unknowingly led her into a trap." His voice came weaker than he liked it, as if it belonged to a defeated man, not to a proud Devanshari and a confident royal guard.

"She couldn't have known what the archmages had prepared."

That remark resulted only in more amusement. "And the archmages couldn't have known what she'd planned, could they? I watched her preparations, and if I was to make a bet, I'd put all my money on her. She's neither defeated nor dead."

"What makes you so sure?" Ryell spat. With so little emotion Koshmarnyk showed, it was hard to discern whether he truly believed in what he said or simply tried to conceal his shock and grief behind a confident façade. "You admitted yourself that you didn't know the details of her plan. How can you tell she's still alive in there?"

A dry laugh shook Koshmarnyk's body, but he was serious again once he looked down at his wrists. "Because if she was dead, her bracelets wouldn't have saved my life."

Ryell stared at him, unable to find words. The claim seemed absurd, but maybe Koshmarnyk meant some sort of magic contained within the jewelry that wouldn't last after Kamira's death. Ryell clung to that thought. If she was still alive, he could explain everything to her and make her understand he'd been played by Yoreus as much as she.

Opyr approached the table, but he paid no attention to Ryell, fully focused on the other man. "I've prepared the best room in the inn. It's the least I can do in return for saving my daughter."

"There's no need for hassle," Koshmarnyk replied without the false modesty Ryell had seen so often among the Devanshari noblemen. "I'll sleep in Kamira's and Veelk's room, if you have a spare key."

The innkeeper nodded and rushed away.

Koshmarnyk stood up from the table, and a flash of pain was the only reminder of his wound. "You can keep lying to yourself that you did it for her." He was looking straight at Ryell. "But you did it for yourself. If you had accepted the way she is, an arcanist with a good—if grumpy—nature, things could have been different. She would probably tell me there was a Devanshari man waiting for her in Kaighal. Sharing all her secrets and hoping for her to succeed, not trying to change her into what he thought was best."

Ryell gritted his teeth. The words were like a slap, and he had to fight his own body to not run after the man who was allowed into Kamira's room while she was away. She had never extended such a privilege to Ryell. He took a deep breath, considering what he'd learned. Koshmarnyk claimed Kamira not only stayed alive, but that becoming trapped was a part of her plan. Perhaps Yoreus should know... *No.* He abandoned the idea when the memory of the archmage's deception resurfaced. It was time he made his own decisions and kept his knowledge secret.

The coins rang on the table as he threw them between the unfinished food and jug of wine and left. First, he had to know whether Kamira was indeed alive. Then he had to find a way to talk to her.

2

Kamira's lungs fought for the breath she couldn't take. Energy filled her nostrils and mouth, soaked through every part of her body, keeping her alive and refusing life at the same time. The magic also poured into her mind, flushing out thoughts and filling her head with images. Colorful but eerie vegetation and unknown animals flowed before her eyes, and she watched a landscape no human had ever seen before, mesmerizing and alien. Energy condensed in that world's clouds, filling the sky with purple and red, and winged creatures soared high above.

The crystal's magical structure seemed fluid enough to allow movement within, but even the slightest tremble brought pain, so she tried to remain motionless. The thought of Veranesh caught within a similar crystal made her wonder how he could move so casually within its cold embrace. She'd rather not twitch a single muscle.

With no need for food nor sleep, she hung suspended in her own suffering with the images of what had to be the demon domain as her only distraction, but she never ceased channeling Veranesh's magic, letting it enter the flow around her. The burn of the scars on her arms reminded her of her purpose.

She was Kamira. She was an arcanist. And she could endure the pain.

"You keep staring at her." A woman's voice traveled through the crystal, echoing within its eerily liquid structure. "It's not going to change anything."

"Maybe not."

That voice... It took Kamira a moment to realize it sounded familiar.

"Come to bed, then. It's the middle of the night," the woman pleaded. "You did what you could for her, but it's not your fault she served a demon."

"I betrayed her."

Ryell. That was his name. Kamira forced her eyes open, and the magic stung, but the vision itself remained clear, as if unhindered by her crystal cocoon.

Ryell stared at her. By his side stood a woman whose expression resembled that of Yoreus, cold and calculating, though the gentle jaw line made her face look more pleasant.

"Do you think your father will let you keep your toy now that all is done, mage?" Kamira's voice echoed within the structure, and its flat tone resembled the way Veranesh spoke: with no air to breathe, she relied on magic to execute her intention to speak.

The woman pouted, and her hand brushed Ryell's chest in an intimate gesture. "Spit all the bile you want. You've lost."

Kamira allowed herself a laugh. Yoreus's daughter must have been naïve to believe they were competing for a man's attention. Or, perhaps, the archmage kept her in the dark about what the stakes really were. "What makes you think I've lost?"

"Pathetic," the mage replied. "If you're done with your lousy tricks, I'll be retiring." She climbed to her toes, and her arms closed around Ryell briefly as she left a kiss on his cheek. A subtle aura of magic surrounding her enveloped the Devanshari as well. "Don't stay up too long. She's not worth it."

Ryell watched her leave and only then looked back at Kamira. "You played her, didn't you? To make her leave." He fidgeted. "But she's going to tell Yoreus."

"It doesn't matter anymore," she replied. "Yoreus is convinced he won, and he'll consider my state of awareness to be a minor inconvenience. He'll only want to ensure no one talks to me and learns the truth."

Ryell leaned forward. "About how he lied to you?"

"No, about how the archmages lie to everyone."

He took a step back, his face shifting from curiosity to frustration. "You're still full of hate toward them, aren't you?" A grimace spoiled his otherwise handsome face. "Even if Yoreus lied to you, he did it to protect people and to prevent your death."

Kamira sighed. "He didn't do it for the people, let alone for me. He did it to protect himself and the power he has."

"What do you mean?"

She caught a hint of doubt in his voice. Finally, Ryell was starting to listen and question. If only he had done so earlier... The energy waves flushed the bitter feelings from her thoughts. Within the crystal, no emotion survived long —only pain lasted.

"High magic is a lie. It always was," she said. "They steal their power from the very demon their predecessors trapped in the old Towers. And if he gets out, they'll lose it all."

"That's absurd!" Ryell raised his voice. "Who told you such lies? The demon? Veelk?" He watched her intently after each question. "Or maybe that Koshmarnyk?"

Her eyes opened wider, and she smiled gently. It brought a feeling of razors against her skin, but she relished the news. Ryell mentioning the adept's name could mean only one thing. "Koshmarnyk returned? Did he save Lefna?"

Ryell didn't reply. He fought to keep his face straight, but muscles played under his skin when his teeth gritted, revealing a reaction she was certain he wanted to hide. "He did," he said in the end. "He said your bracelets saved him."

"I appreciate you telling me," she said with all honesty.

His expression shifted, turning into sadness. "I did betray you, didn't I? Not because I led you here, but because I did it for the wrong reasons." He paused as if considering. "That man, Koshmarnyk, told me so."

It sounded as if he wanted her to deny it. "Do you think he was right?" Curiosity surged before being flushed away by waves of magic.

He hesitated. Biting his lip, he looked away. "I think that what happened in the Devanshari capital... What the queen did... I think it blinded me." He let out a short, bitter laugh. "I wanted to save you from the evil I saw in everything demon-related, and I missed... all the other evil. And the good, too, I suppose."

His words might not be an admission, but they seemed like a step in the right direction. At the same time, she couldn't help her disappointment. In the past, Ryell seemed eager to listen to her, but in the end, at one of Yoreus's lies or the flick of his daughter's hand, he always shifted back to his blind hate. Stuck in the crystal, she neither had the means nor will to try to make him see the truth again. The prolonged conversation already enhanced her pain and made channeling magic difficult. Yet there was a way that perhaps would help him. "I need to rest, but before you go, I want you to chip off a piece of the crystal."

"What for?" Suspicion flashed in his eyes.

"It will help you contain your hunger for magic. And if you ask Koshmarnyk to blend it with your skin, you'll never need to depend on anyone to give you magic." This was all she could offer him, but at least it would cut the thickest string that tied him to Yoreus and his daughter. If he still decided to side with them, it would be by choice, not out of addiction-driven desperation.

"It's not a cure."

"No, it's not. But it would give you your free will back." She didn't hold back, and he squirmed. "Be warned, though: Gildya condemns blending stones with demon power with the human body. I'll understand if you'd rather not do it."

His eyes widened. "D-demon power?"

She held off a sigh. One word and he was back-pedaling into the embrace of his hate and fears, but venting her frustration wasn't worth the pain. "There's no other magic but the one that comes from demons."

To her surprise, Ryell offered no argument. The expression on his face suggested his deeply ingrained prejudice fought with reason. Then he pulled out a dagger and worked the blade into the crystal, chipping off a piece. The missing part grew back in an instant, but Kamira paid no attention to it, focused on Ryell. The relief on his face when he closed the tiny shard in his fist reminded her of the short time when she was pact-less. The void, the desperation... In a way, she was as addicted to magic as he was.

"Thank you," he whispered.

"Find Koshmarnyk. Tell him I asked him to do the blending for you. And stay away from the Towers for a while. Take Yoreus's daughter along if you must, but leave. It's not going to be safe here."

He narrowed his eyes. "You didn't bluff, did you? When you said you didn't lose."

"No."

A mixture of relief and guilt was in his smile. "I wish you could tell me of your plans, but I think it's better I don't know them. I'm still tangled in the web of commitments. But I hope whatever you're about to do, it'll free you from... your prison."

Kamira didn't waste her strength on telling him she hoped so as well. The conversation was becoming too much of a distraction. Her task was to channel energy, not to help Ryell find his way. "Go now. Yoreus will be here soon, and I do not wish to be awake for that."

Her own voice sounded distant as the images of another world poured into her mind, blurring all that was beyond the crystal. Ryell's response drowned in the magic wind whistling in her ears, and Kamira sighed, closing her eyes. The pain eased when her body froze, motionless, and though her scars burned, they brought no suffering anymore.

She let the energy flow into the world and toward the other circle. Before her mind drifted away, a shift in magic streams told her of a change.

The first crack appeared in the other crystal, hidden under the desert.

～

KOSHMARNYK SQUATTED OUTSIDE A WINDOW, pressing his fingers against the brick wall and balancing on the narrow ledge. The night concealed him from any prying eyes, and though he didn't enjoy the climb, risking it was a better choice than causing a bloodbath if he decided to simply enter Gildya Magna. As soon as he had his footing, he peeked inside, but the dark room gave no indication of who its inhabitant was. *I wonder if he still lives here?* Any changes in the adepts' structures could have had his former colleague moved to another quarters, but Koshmarnyk counted on Gildya's laziness and attachment to tradition. For the fearless inventors and explorers of reality they were supposed to be, they surely loved their conventions. At the same time, any adept would do to pass the message, even if it would take a bit more convincing.

He inspected the window. Up on the fourth level of the building, the adepts must have felt safe enough to refrain from installing shutters and traps. The reinforced crystal panes rested in metal frames that relied on a simple mechanism to keep the window shut. If needed, he could get inside within a heartbeat.

"It would be a waste if you fell and broke your neck." The nightfly hovered by.

Koshmarnyk refrained from reminding Veranesh that he'd gone to Gildya at the demon's very request. "I don't suppose you have news from either of them?" He thought of the note from Kamira he found in the tavern room that confirmed the Devanshari man's revelations about the mages' trap. It explained where both Kamira and Veelk disappeared to and why.

"You needn't worry. She is still alive, and the energy keeps flowing." The nightfly shifted, and the sound of its wings cutting the air was the only sound for longer than

Koshmarnyk liked. "I know nothing of the mage killer, save that the dagger I gifted him is destroyed."

Koshmarnyk could swear concern rang in the demon's voice. He might have been fishing for an emotion that wasn't there, or perhaps Veranesh preferred Veelk alive simply because the mage killer was Kamira's friend. He sighed. Kamira claimed they could trust Veranesh, but Koshmarnyk still had his reservations. Even Suzhaul's actions weren't always what his people considered just or honest, and Veranesh wanted his freedom above all. He was so close to regaining it, he might care less about those he used to get it back.

"I'll look for him once I'm free," Veranesh said, to Koshmarnyk's surprise. "If he went after the people sent to seal the ruins, they have to be somewhere between my prison and the city." The nightfly flew down to his arm and coiled around it. "Call for me again when you're done with that human."

Inside, a man entered the room, and Koshmarnyk focused his attention on him. The warm glow of an imbued lamp lit a tired face surrounded by a stub of a beard and graying hair. Years certainly hadn't been merciful to Adept Davshil.

Koshmarnyk knocked on the crystal pane.

The adept inside flinched, and his eyes widened when he recognized his guest. Hesitating, he glanced at the door, but then walked over to the window.

"Glad you're still alive," Koshmarnyk said as soon as Davshil let him in.

"Are you here for revenge?" The tired voice belonged to a man accepting his fate.

"If you think so, why did you open the window?"

Davshil snorted, and for a glimpse his face lost all the

years, reminding Koshmarnyk of the much younger and more energetic man. "With all those demons you had put in your body, I wouldn't be able to run fast and far enough. I'd be just living in fear trying to postpone what would come anyway."

"You seem more solemn than I remember." Koshmarnyk couldn't help a quick inspection. Davshil looked healthy enough, so it likely wasn't an ailment of the body, and they weren't close friends even before Davshil and others had betrayed him. "I'm not here to kill anyone. I bring a message to Gildya."

"A message? From whom?" Curiosity brought liveliness to the adept's face.

"In days to come, a demon will pass over Kaighal," Koshmarnyk said. "He's after the high mages and wishes no harm to the people in the city, so it's best if Gildya stays out of his way."

Davshil stared at him. "That's rather... unexpected." He took a deep breath. "Is he one of those who attacked the overseas kingdom?"

Koshmarnyk offered him a half-smile. It was so like Davshil to fish for information, but Koshmarnyk wasn't about to give him any openings for more questions. "No."

"And you're involved with him?" the adept pressed.

"I'm but a messenger, and all I ask you is to pass the word to the council."

"You've changed." Davshil shook his head. "I'll deliver your message, but I can't promise they will listen. And they might choose to warn the mages."

"Warnings won't change anything." Koshmarnyk mustered confidence, wishing he had the demon's certainty. It was Kamira's fate at stake, after all. "The high mages will fall, and if the council wants to see Gildya still standing on that day, do your best to convince them to keep everyone out of that demon's way." He let a note of concern to ring in his voice, hoping Davshil would conclude that Veranesh was indeed a threat better avoided.

Davshil sat heavily in the chair. "But how can we be sure the demon won't take advantage of our doing nothing?"

Of course, more questions. Koshmarnyk grimaced. Gildya might consider him a rogue adept dabbling in forbidden experiments, but had never given them a reason to doubt his truthfulness. "I told you, he'll be here for the mages. Give him no grounds to attack, and everyone else will be safe." Koshmarnyk sighed. As much as questioning of his word irked him, in a way, he could relate to his former colleague's doubts. He himself was not quick to trust Veranesh. "Arm and prepare if it makes you sleep better at night. Just don't be fools to attack first."

"And what about you?" Davshil asked. "When I heard news of your escape, I thought you'd be far in the south now, or sailing for Juamha."

"I had some debts to pay first."

"I see." Davshil shifted uneasily in his seat. "The Gildya will want to know who brought the message. And if they learn you're still around, some might think it would be best to get you back where you were for the last ten years. Or find another, final solution."

Koshmarnyk first tensed at the hidden warning but then relaxed. Whatever threat would come, it wouldn't be Davshil's doing, and it wouldn't be now. "Back then, they only succeeded because I was foolish enough to believe they wanted to talk. If any troublemakers get the wrong ideas, be sure to remind them of it." Issuing threats wasn't his way, but he'd rather make Gildya back away than waste time and energy on fighting them. He just had to ensure they left him alone.

Davshil narrowed his eyes. "I never considered you a killer. Would you really turn against your former colleagues?"

"If they attack first, I won't stand idle," Koshmarnyk said coldly. "I won't let them drag me back to another prison over their childish fears."

"Childish fears? I'd consider attaching imbued stones to a living body a serious concern," Davshil said.

Koshmarnyk knew better than take the bait. He'd had enough similar pointless discussions before Gildya turned on him. At the same time, ignoring such a remark felt like giving it credence. "I'm a living proof against your serious concern." He walked over to the open window before the shortsighted adept could draw him into a pointless argument. "Be well, Davshil."

"You too, Alluvendran."

Koshmarnyk looked over his shoulder. That name was everything he had left behind. Everything that made him doubt Gildya—politics, backstabbing, jealousy, secrecy... The list went on longer than he cared to recall. Perhaps Davshil and others were right, and binding imbued stones with flesh posed unknown dangers, but for the inventors and explorers to give in to their fear and give up learning the answers meant going against everything Koshmarnyk used to believe Gildya Magna stood for.

Without hesitation, he descended the wall. At least Davshil had the decency to allow him to leave instead of raising the alarm. It seemed that threats, no matter how petty Koshmarnyk might consider them, worked well on people eager to subdue to fear, any fear.

Landing nimbly on the street's cobblestones, he had a

notion of severing the last ties with the place that offered little beyond disappointments and betrayals. With the message delivered, Koshmarnyk had no reason to go near there ever again... Even the revenge he had considered so often during his imprisonment faded in comparison to everything else the world of the free people had to offer. And the best payback he could possibly imagine for his former colleagues was to let them stew in their own inability to think beyond safe and comfortable ideas.

As soon as the shadows of a nearby alley offered him shelter from any prying eyes, he focused on the stone linked to Veranesh. The nightflies uncoiled from his arms in an instant.

"I've reached the surface. I'll arrive in the city soon," Veranesh said.

Koshmarnyk glanced back at Gildya's building for the last time. He could only hope those thick heads would make the right decision. Otherwise, Kaighal's streets could change into rivers of blood.

Freedom tasted different than he remembered, but everything in the human world seemed to taste different. Veranesh scoffed at the memory of himself, so eager to be the first one to cross, and so confident humans and their realm posed no threat to him. Always staying one step ahead of all the other yalari, he truly believed it. And he got to pay for such carelessness dearly.

The sand still poured into the hole he climbed out of, but Veranesh paid little attention to it. Instead, he spread his wings, enjoying the sensation. After centuries of nearly motionless existence, every free move was worth savoring, and he indulged in a long stretch, ignoring all the pressing issues. Yet when he lifted into the air, nothing remained in his mind but matters of importance.

The moonlit desert below him looked serene with its dunes gently brushed by wind, creating peculiar ripples in the sand. Veranesh cared little for the view itself, instead searching for tracks of people. He didn't expect to find much, though he never doubted what the adept had relayed to him from the letter Kamira left. The destruction of the dagger he'd gifted to the mage killer suggested the confrontation with whomever the high mages sent out had already happened. Wind could have pushed sands over any trace of human presence, and Veranesh would never find anything. Yet he searched. His plans would be easier to carry out if Kamira trusted him, and that required some effort. As much as he longed to crush the mages, he could wait a day or two longer if it meant ensuring he reached his other goals as well.

His eyes caught nothing, so he focused on energies instead. An insignificant item like the lizard-shaped dagger wouldn't be enough back in Yalarethe, but human world was so devoid of magic that the tiniest trail teased Veranesh's senses and pulled him to the north. He followed it with caution. Kamira might have trusted the mage killer, and in the past Suzhaul had never acted against Veranesh, but centuries of imprisonment demanded healthy distrust toward everything.

Contrary to his expectations, the battlefield was clearly visible once he got closer. Human bodies and their belongings lay scattered across a small area, and their wounds looked like they were inflicted by the mage killer's weapon, but otherwise Veranesh could make little of the scene before him. As much as he tried to study humans and their habits, the way they fought each other barely made sense to him. All he could conclude was that none of the bodies resembled that of his pactee's companion and his weapon wasn't in sight.

Traces of magic lingered in the area. Most of it he recognized as the high mages' spells—his own energy stolen and twisted. But there was something else...

He drew the air deep, catching a scent too familiar to be comfortable. Another yalari had been to the battle scene. Veranesh tensed, but no immediate threat presented itself, and the scent was too faint to be recent. At the same time, he couldn't tell whether the yalari was present during the skirmish or arrived later, to investigate. He decided on the latter. If a yalari was present, the mage killer wouldn't have stood the chance in a fight, and his body would be among others.

Unless... Unless his brethren was cunning enough to take the mage killer with him and interrogate.

Now that Veranesh was back in the game, he had to consider enemies old and new. His pactee's cunning gave him a few names to be wary of, but there had to be more, and with so much time having passed, he had to assume that his old allies could have turned against him or new players had joined the game. His instincts itched for him to take off and search for his adversaries, in this world or in his own. He lifted in the air, hovering over the battlefield, though the bird's-eye view offered no more insights.

In the distance, odd shapes of human dwellings stood against the starry sky and dark ground. Within his sight, there were at least three or four, but one surpassed all of them in size. A faint trace of magic pulling him toward it confirmed this had to be Kaighal—his destination. Before he went after other yalari, he had to teach human mages a lesson and then see to his pactee.

That thought gave him pause. He had never considered her an ally, and several times she'd openly admitted to doing his bidding only because of the spell he had on her. Yet she never acted against him, and in the end, she'd agreed to the plan that put her own life and freedom at risk. At the least, she deserved to keep the pact he had made with her, but perhaps there were other possibilities. Yalari had always considered humans to be mere tools, useful but inferior in every way, and hardly any would stoop to making actual alliances with them, only beneficial pacts that required little of them. But the plot that brought together high mages and Veranesh's enemies proved there could be more to gain, and his own agreement with Kamira brought unexpected knowledge that he couldn't have easily gathered if he had killed her to gain his freedom.

He smirked at that. His pactee's distrust surpassed that of many yalari, making her a perfect ally, but at the same time, her loyalty to the few other humans could cause rifts. He'd already witnessed how her friendship with the mage killer dimmed reason, and he had to consider that Suzhaul could try to use his servant… to what ends? During their brief conversation, Suzhaul seemed his usual self, but even if the hermit yalari cared little beyond his experiments, when anything threatened his solitude or his work, he proved as ruthless as any other of their kin. It would be beneficial to see him as an ally again… Veranesh shook his head. He couldn't soothe himself with such hopes. He had to be prepared for any outcome. On the other hand, his own pactee was willing to defy Veranesh in the name of her friendship with the mage killer. If Veelk survived the battle in the desert, it would be interesting to see whether he would also be willing to defy Suzhaul for Kamira, should the circumstances require it.

But first, the mages. And once it was done, he'd see if his own experiment survived in the crystal. If his pactee was still as sane and strong as the pact bond between suggested, possibilities would open, and perhaps she'd even prove worthy of the secrets he'd kept from her.

Without any more delay, he flew toward Kaighal.

3

Night was Mizena's friend. Not only did it conceal her from prying eyes, but it also provided opportunities. Under the veil of darkness, all ne'er-do-wells of Kaighal conducted all sorts of shady activities, from smuggling to murder, and a spy who knew what kind of information traded well could earn a week's or even a month's worth of coin in just one evening. And Mizena needed coin. Giving up spying for the archmage, or rather for the people he employed to deal with spies, meant giving up the generous payments he offered for knowledge hidden in the city's dark alleys. She had enough to get by, but none of her other patrons could match the archmage.

Mizena chewed on a piece of a dried meat as she waited near one of Gildya's lesser-known stockpiles. Some gossip she'd picked up in passing suggested that it was worth a closer look, but after almost an entire night spent in an uncomfortable position, squatting between barrels and crates by a merchant's store, she still had nothing. It seemed her famed luck that allowed her to always get the best information before anyone else was waning.

The night was already receding, giving way to the first sun's rays, and even if the bowels of Kaighal still remained awash in shadows and darkness, the closer to morning, the more passersby. No one in their right mind would do any underhanded business so close to daylight.

Careful not to cause any noise, Mizena stretched her body limb by limb. Perhaps she'd try again the next evening.

A muffled rumble in the street adjacent to the stockpile put her on alert. Her clothes were a bit too good to be those of a beggar, so if someone saw her hiding spot, questions would follow, and Mizena liked questions as little as she liked any other trouble. *Time to go.*

She remained in her spot when a hushed but heated conversation reached her. An argument among workers wasn't anything unusual, but no one in the middle of a disagreement would bother to keep quiet... unless they had something to hide.

Mizena peeked out.

Two men stopped a small hand-drawn cart by the stockpile's side door. Slight jitters in their behavior made it clear they weren't Gildya's workers. They were still arguing, and the few words she caught suggested it was about a delay caused by one of them. The angrier one knocked on the door, and it opened immediately.

Mizena couldn't quite make out the face of the man who appeared, but his voice left no doubt about his emotions.

"'Ere now, what took s'long?" he asked the others with clear ire. "Waited all night, and on the double they almost found me!" He waved his hand when another one started to speak. "Never mind! I ain't wantin' to hear it. Get the goods, and get to movin'."

One of the two rushed inside, while the other kept a worried eye out. Mizena huffed, displeased at the sight of the man's weariness that would only alert him to someone who approached openly, if even that much. These men were not skilled... Likely hired thugs, the cheap kind, and that could mean that whoever had planned the theft wanted to remain unknown. Her curiosity surged. It seemed that her luck had not run out after all.

The crates they carried were small but heavy, judging from the huffs and strained walk. Other than that, nothing betrayed their contents. She'd have to follow the men to wherever they intended to bring the stolen goods, and doing so at the break of day would be difficult. Shadows would already be receding, and there wouldn't be enough people to blend in with the crowd. Yet, if she wanted to learn more —to learn something that would bring coin—she had no choice.

"Hey, what are you doing here?" a woman called out.

Mizena flinched, but a glance around reassured her that she wasn't the one drawing attention.

The three men by the stockpile tensed as a pair of city guards, a man and a woman, approached. Their lantern swayed to the rhythm of their steps, sweeping shadows to and fro, even though the sky above was already brightening.

If the thieves could come up with even a moderately convincing story, they had a decent chance of getting away, especially since Gildya didn't like the city guards meddling in their affairs. Even on the spot, Mizena could come up with several excuses, including that they weren't taking out Gildya's possessions, but delivering the goods. As the guard asked them what they were doing, Mizena strained to hear the response. Good lies could always be reused, and she could also learn something useful from their explanation, if they mentioned the person who'd hired them.

She definitely didn't expect one of the men to lunge at

the guard. Before anyone reacted, he dug a knife deep into the guard's chest.

The female guard dropped the lantern. "Over here!" she shouted, as she used the butt of her sword to knock the attacker down.

In the distance, more voices rose as the nearby guards responded to the woman's call.

One of the two remaining men forced the crate open and fished an item out of it. Mizena caught the glow of an imbued stone on it as he threw it at the remaining guard. Then a fiery explosion lit up the night, consuming the guard, her dead companion, and the unconscious thief. Her scream, if there even was one amongst the roaring of flames, died quickly.

The men didn't wait for the fire to burn out. They took off. One of them passed by Mizena's hiding place, and she got a clear glimpse of his face. *Cranwy?! What is that fool doing here?* Without hesitation, she jumped out and dashed after him. Behind her, at a distance too close for comfort, guards called out to each other.

Cranwy ran through the narrow alleys, knocking down anything in his way and jumping over piles of garbage. He was a burly man, and not trained at all, so Mizena had no trouble following him, but at the same time, it meant that neither would the guards. He was smart enough to take turns rather than running along the same alley, but his chaotic route suggested no specific destination. If he kept at it, he could well run straight into another group of guards.

"Stop!" a man called out behind her.

Mizena cursed. The last thing she needed was for the guards to think she was involved in the theft. But to stop following Cranwy meant no information, and therefore no coin. She had to take the risk.

She sped up to catch up with him, but in a narrow alley filled with obstacles to avoid, it was hard to get beside Cranwy or in front of him.

"Cranwy! It's me! Mizena!" she called out in a hushed voice.

As he slowed down and turned, looking over his shoulder, she made it past him, tugging on his sleeve. "This way!"

If he stood his ground, she'd never be able to pull him along, but her promise made him follow without hesitation.

He could barely keep her pace, his broad chest heaving more and more the longer they went.

A woman guard stepped into the alley right in front of them. Mizena dove to the side to make it past him, all too late considering that she wasn't alone this time. Cranwy rammed into the guard, knocking her down. As soon as she was out of the way, he started running again.

Mizena knew this part of Kaighal well, but with more and more guards closing in, likely drawn to the explosion she'd witnessed, the usually friendly alleys were beginning to feel too much like a maze without a way out. Cranwy was already struggling for breath, so he wouldn't be able to run much farther anyway.

With no other choice, she led him down another alley, straight to a safe hiding place she'd used several times in the past. To share it with someone else grated on her nature, but it seemed a better way than getting herself caught along with Cranwy.

The small shed, nestled between two buildings, looked as abandoned as the last time Mizena saw it, and without hesitation, she opened the door. Cranwy made his way inside without an invitation, and she followed. In what seemed only a moment later, the heavy boots hit the cobblestones outside. The guards didn't stop to inspect the shack, and soon the sound of their footsteps and voices faded.

Mizena leaned against the wall, and Cranwy relaxed too. It would be a while before the guards stopped searching for the thieves, so they both remained silent.

The sun was already up when Mizena finally gave Cranwy a sign and they left the shack. From a distance, merchants were already calling out their wares and prices, and a low murmur of conversations carried through the streets.

"I owe you for saving my skin," Cranwy said.

Mizena nodded. Such a debt was a given, but she appreciated when others acknowledged her efforts, no matter what they were. "What were you doing there, anyway?" she asked, taking the opening. "I didn't take you for someone who'd get mixed in thievery and murder."

Cranwy was one of the lowlifes haunting the port district. Burly and strong, he made his coin as a carrier for the ship captains and local merchants. On occasion, he'd intimidate other lowlifes when they owed money to someone willing to pay to get it back. Such a heist, even if a simplistic one, was not Cranwy's regular work.

"Lacca needed a someone to carry crates, and the pay was good." Cranwy shrugged. "We were to pick up the goods and bring them to a place Lacca knew about. Said some Gildya woman wanted it moved, that's all. He said no word of thieving Gildya's stock and killing. I don't know who the third man was."

"You should probably get back to the port district," Mizena replied, though her mind wasn't on Cranwy's wellbeing, especially that he hardly had any useful information. "A Gildya woman" was too little to go on, and there were countless reasons why some adept was stealing from her fellow inventors. Though—Mizena's stomach twisted when she thought of it—these weren't some valuable resources. The woman wanted devices that could kill a lot of people, judging by the size of the crates.

They walked onto one of the main streets, mixing with the early-morning crowd. People were already buying goods, selling them, or rushing to other parts of Kaighal, and two more passersby drew no attention.

"I'll see you there?" Cranwy asked.

"I'll be around," she replied absent-mindedly. They were never friends, so she cared little for him or his debt. If she ever needed a favor, she'd seek him out, but until then, Cranwy could just disappear.

As they parted, Mizena checked her surroundings out of habit. After a night of keeping watch and an unexpected chase, her body was demanding some rest, but if a good opportunity waited around a corner, rest could wait a little longer.

Someone shouted in the distance, pointing at the sky, and Mizena looked up. A dark, winged silhouette was gliding above the city.

"A demon!" someone shouted.

A woman screamed, and a few people turned and ran, knocking down a merchant's basket or two. Others—Mizena among them—were watching, some with curiosity, some with concern. The creature, no matter how fearsome it looked with its black wings and what must be massive claws, seemed uninterested in the people below. Instead, it headed straight for the High Towers.

Mizena couldn't help the nagging feeling this had something to do with the odd duo she used to spy on, the demonologist and her tribal companion, and a shiver ran down her spine when she realized her own actions might have become part of that plot.

The demon landed on the hill, looking around with caution and curiosity, and for a glimpse Mizena considered that it might be the high mages' guest. Then, in a rush of magic, a barrier rose around the High Towers, sealing them from the city and making it clear archmages did not consider the creature friendly.

Mizena swallowed, starting to make her way down the street, away from the Towers. She could only hope that any battle that followed would not reach the rest of Kaighal.

THE FOURTH ARCHMAGE Varessa listened to Yoreus's speech with growing ire.

Woken up early in the morning, she hadn't expected the news of a demon arriving in Kaighal, and even though she had to praise the first archmage's prompt response in raising a barrier to provide immediate protection for all the teachers and students, she'd expected to be summoned to a war meeting, not to a one-sided oration by the most pompous man Kaighal might know.

Varessa fought to keep a sigh from escaping her mouth. She'd have even settled for being overlooked when it came to making decisions about the threat, since she had little knowledge or experience to contribute, but if the first archmages didn't want anyone's advice and insights, he should have presented something more elaborate than a speech with little detail and way too much rushed reassurances. The sighting of a demon in Kaighal was hardly a commonplace occurrence and deserved a swift and decisive measures. Yet their leader offered nothing but empty promises of stopping the threat by any means possible.

Not to mention that the way the three first archmages exchanged glances suggested they knew more than they let on, and Varessa couldn't help wondering how this event was linked to the crystal that had grown overnight in the initiation rite chamber, and the woman encased in it. Secrets might be the daily bread in the High Towers, but until now Varessa had wanted to believe that, for the good of not only the students but all people in Kaighal, they would set aside internal politics and intrigues. She might have swallowed the brief explanation of how an arcanist uncovered some sinister plot and how the first archmages decided to deal with it, but a demon circling over the city was not a matter they could conceal and deal with quietly, so the least Yoreus could do was offer some truth.

"...Therefore, we will do anything in our power to bring the demon down." Yoreus's voice brought her back to reality.

That pompous, arrogant hoyve! He'd have them all die in a blaze of magic only to match the grandeur of the founding archmages who defeated Veranesh centuries earlier. And— she looked around the room—it seemed no one was going to say a word about it.

She stood up. "That's not acceptable. We're responsible for everyone, including the apprentices who can barely summon a lumisphere and all the people in Kaighal. We can't gamble with their lives." Biting her tongue might have been a better option, but she took pride that no insulting— even if truthful—remarks made it past her self-restraint.

"Haven't you heard, fourth archmage? A demon seeks to destroy the Towers!" Yoreus raised his voice, his face emanating anger. "There's no bargain, no pleading. We fight, and we do it like the high mages of old did."

Except that, if tales were to be believed, the high mages of old didn't have to actually face Veranesh, fighting him from afar. Such magic was lost to the ages, unless Yoreus and others were hiding a lot more than she suspected.

Varessa gritted her teeth. Instead of indulging in teaching, she should have pushed for her own advancement more. Third archmage Kerl was hardly a challenge to begin with, and his drinking habits and lecherous tendencies, which he wasn't smart enough to hide, made him even an easier target. But, of course, when Irtan stepped down, she had settled for the title of the fourth archmage and returned to the classrooms.

Yoreus's insistent stare made it clear that it wasn't the time for recollections or analyzing her past mistakes. She steeled herself. Secrets or not, she would not give up so easily. "Every sentient creature, human or demon, can be reasoned with. I'm sure he is willing to negotiate."

"What makes you think so?" Loktra's mocking voice made her thoughts clear. "Because he demanded our barrier down and gates open?"

Varessa snorted. "No." The reason Loktra had climbed so far in the High Towers' ranks had always remained a mystery to Varessa. The woman had little knowledge and even less ambition, but perhaps other players saw her as malleable and therefore useful, or a minimal threat in a position of power. "It's because we haven't received a word from Gildya yet." This once, Varessa savored using the tone she reserved for the most wisdom-resistant students. "If they aren't concerned about a demon circling over Kaighal, it means he struck a bargain with them. And if that's true, perhaps so could we."

"It also means that we're alone," the seventh archmage added. Until now, the middle-aged man had always remained quiet in the gatherings and seemed uncomfortable with his title, but when he spoke, he had insights to offer, contrary to his many bickering colleagues.

Yoreus looked around them, and Varessa could swear he felt like his control of others was slipping. If only Irtan was still in charge... The old archmage was always more concerned about solving the problem than taking care of his appearances.

"If you want to fight, then do." She took the chance to speak before he made any final decisions. "But let me first speak to the demon and try to save our students. Their lives mean that even if we fail, there'll be another generation of the high mages."

Kerl let out a short laugh. It hushed under Yoreus's gaze, but it was enough to prove the first archmage was hiding something. Varessa glanced at Irtan sitting to the side, a pose of a jovial old teacher not interested in the youngsters' squabbles and the troubles they brought upon themselves, but she could hardly believe he had no knowledge of others' secrets. And the demon's sighting was not a coincidence either. She swallowed, but she didn't allow a bitter smile to spoil her neutral expression. If she couldn't learn the truth from her colleagues, perhaps the demon would say something to lead her the right way. Assuming she survived the meeting.

"Very well. Suit yourself." The first archmage waved his hand impatiently. "Just make it quick."

Her jaw clenched so hard, she heard her own teeth gritting. As she was heading out of the room, Yoreus was already drawing battle plans.

Before she left, Irtan put his hand on her arm in a reassuring gesture. "Keep your mind focused and heart calm, and you'll be fine," he whispered.

He said it with such certainty that she had to take it as confirmation that he knew more than he was letting on. But then, it wasn't the place and the time to share secrets, even if she allowed herself an illusion that the most powerful and cunning man in the Towers would be willing to impart some of the hidden knowledge to her. A fourth archmage, and one whose ambition focused on teaching, was not a partner for plots and intrigues.

"Thank you," she muttered, and rushed outside.

The Towers' corridors remained empty, with all the students gathered in study halls and given menial learning tasks aimed to keep their thoughts away from bigger concerns. Varessa took breaths as long as her strides, fighting to keep her own fear at bay, but when she reached the terrace overlooking the entrance to the Towers, she hesitated. All the tales she'd been fed told of demons as vicious and unreasonable creatures, but arcanists dealt with them all the time and made beneficial pacts. If they could speak with demons, so could she. Hushing the voice that whispered arcanists rarely dealt with demons present in the flesh, she whispered a spell that allowed her to cross the barrier protecting the Towers.

The creature waited by the entrance, and from the height of the terrace, he seemed much smaller than the menacing, dark shadow in the sky above mere hours earlier. He still stood taller than humans, and his wings, though curled, reminded her she was not safe up above. He looked up but didn't attack on sight, and she took it for a good sign. When she looked at his face, so humanlike and at the same time otherworldly, with its sharp features and beak-shaped nose, she found no signs of rage or other beastly qualities. Intelligence shone in the demon's eyes, and the way his thin mouth curled revealed a cunning opponent, ruthless and cruel perhaps, but one that could control himself to achieve his goals.

"I'm Fourth Archmage Varessa, and I wish to speak with you."

Within a heartbeat, his wings shot open, and he was hovering in front of her. "Fourth archmage?" The demon's voice was deep but lacked emotion, and his long nose, shaped like a crooked beak, gave his face a sinister look. "Did they send you as an insult to me?"

"You don't expect the first archmage be a fool enough to step out, do you?" She couldn't resist a jab. Then she offered the truth: "But he won't speak with you anyway. I came out because I wish to bargain for the lives of our students."

A sly smile stretched the demon's mouth. "A bargain indicates you have something to trade."

Varessa considered her next words. Unless she was willing to offer her colleagues' lives in exchange, and thus become a traitor, she had nothing that could possibly interest a creature like that. Yet, so far, he'd turned out more reasonable and calmer than she expected, so a little reasoning couldn't hurt. "You don't care about all of them, otherwise you wouldn't demand our surrender. Allowing those whom you do not wish to fight out of the Towers would make your goal... free of disruption. Easier to find the ones you desire to kill."

The demon's expression changed, and she could swear he was bored. "So far, I don't see any reason to keep you or your students alive, fourth archmage. You'd better give me one soon, because after centuries of entrapment, I'm not the most patient of yalari."

Entrapment?! If there was time, she would cling to the scrap of information the demon divulged, asking questions and prompting him to tell more, but knowledge was useless if she died trying to obtain it. "I didn't come to bargain for my own life. I'm assuming that, as an archmage, I'm among those you wish dead. I only want to ensure safe passage for the students. Then I'll be at your disposal."

The mask of boredom faded from the demon's face, and he inspected her with renewed interest. Her instincts tugged at her, urging her to flee, and even though nothing in the demon's posture suggested immediate danger, Varessa had a hard time keeping the appearance of a confident and composed mage.

"Very well," the demon said all of a sudden. "I'll allow safe passage for anyone who wishes to leave the Towers, but all who exit will be stripped of their magic. They won't be stealing it anymore."

"Stealing?" Varessa said.

Without warning, the demon lunged forward. His clawed hand shot at her neck. Varessa's heart tripped in its rhythm. The grip turned out gentle enough to leave her skin—and everything under it—intact, but she had no doubt death was lurking within his claws. With the speed the demon demonstrated, she wouldn't be able to utter a single spell, if any could even prove useful in such circumstances.

"Yes, stealing." With his face close to hers, he inspected her. "But you didn't know, did you?"

He released his grip, and Varessa locked her knees to avoid collapsing. At the same time, her mind was too busy to give in to the wave of relief washing through her body. The longer the conversation with the demon lasted, the more interesting tidbits she gathered, but time was running short, and so could the demon's patience.

As much as she wanted to ask questions, she said, "Your condition is accepted. If that's all, I'll go back inside and let everybody know. Expect the students to depart soon through the main gate."

"Go. Tell them there will be a circle outside," he replied. "Once they step through it, they are free to leave."

Varessa walked back to the terrace's door. The demon's words sparked her curiosity. He mentioned entrapment, and his demands suggested the high mages might have had something to do with it. A thought, a ridiculous thought, made her stop in her steps and look back. She might as well take the opportunity to prove herself wrong, since the demon still stood on the terrace. His eyes were on her as if he expected foul play, but he did not move.

"Do you have a name you wish to give us?" she asked.

A smile crept up on his face, wider and wider. "Do you really have to ask, archmage?"

It would be pointless to conceal the trembling of her hands as the truth dawned on her. Had she been anywhere else, she would have sought the support of a wall or a chair, babbling a single word: *Impossible!* Perhaps she would cling to hope that the cunning demon alluded to the one name that would bring fear. But Yoreus and others had been keeping secrets, and neither seemed shocked enough by a demon's presence, so no matter how many excuses and arguments she could conjure, she couldn't discard the truth:

That the creature who stood on the terrace, too composed and calculating to match the idea of the violent and unpredictable demon who had destroyed the kingdom of Zemarion, had to be Veranesh himself.

At that thought, her own mind was ready to slip away from sanity, so she wasted no time. The demon seemed satisfied enough with her silence, and she retreated inside, a cloak of spell allowing her to pass once more.

If they survived all that was to come, First Archmage Yoreus and others would have a lot of questions to answer.

~

A STEADY STREAM of humans trickled from the Towers' entrance. Their faces, full of uncertainty, turned toward Veranesh, and fear widened their eyes when they hastily looked away as if afraid to draw his attention or wrath. Fourth Archmage Varessa corralled them all toward the circle... toward his smoke screen. He could sever the connection with the mages as soon as his prison crumbled, but keeping the archmages unaware was more valuable than petty demonstrations of power. For the same reason, he'd agreed to Varessa's request. Killing a bunch of helpless humans would hardly bring any satisfaction anyway, and could cause a rift between him and his pactee.

The fourth archmage was still watching him, her brown eyes wary and focused. Even when half of the students had already left, she was still expecting foul play. The people in the line stepped into the circle one by one and stood there for three heartbeats as he instructed them, none the wiser that their access to magic had been broken as soon as they stepped into his view. Unlike arcanists who were sensitive to the flow of magic and nurtured the connection with their yalari, high mages only took what they needed, when they needed it, remaining oblivious to the energies around them and their currents.

A familiar face flashed among the mages, and Veranesh took a step forward. Of course, before he reached the brown-haired female surrounded by a familiar aura of a pact, Varessa threw herself between them in a foolish gesture of self-sacrifice.

"You said everyone will be allowed to leave!"

He had to admit, he hadn't expected her to be so demanding, as if she wanted to remind him of the word he had given instead of pleading like any reasonable human would do in the presence of a powerful yalari.

"Arcanists of the past knew I always keep my word. Step aside, fourth archmage."

"It's fine, Archmage Varessa," the woman behind her said.

Reluctantly, Varessa moved to the side, still tense and ready to act.

"You are Pelina, aren't you?" Veranesh had only seen her for a brief time, before Kamira forced him out of the nightflies, but a mistake was unlikely.

"Yes." Pelina looked at him with no fear. The magic surrounding her was that of a pact, but her yalari didn't count among the higher ones. Sufficient power for an apprentice pactee, but nothing Veranesh would concern himself with.

"Archmage Irtan hopes to have a word with you in the Towers," she said.

The name sounded familiar, and he recalled Kamira's remark. An old archmage whose play remained unclear. A conversation with him could be quite an interesting one— unless, of course, sending a messenger served only as deception.

"And what of my pactee?"

Confusion flashed in her eyes, but with the speed she pieced the information together, Veranesh had to give a nod to Kamira's choice. This young pactee had proven loyal and smart, and the risk of trusting her, though he'd still argue it as unnecessary, paid off.

"She's imprisoned within a crystal in the initiation

chamber. If you lift in the air, you'll see its large dome," Pelina said.

"Thank you. You may go now."

The way she bowed brought satisfaction. Whoever had been training her to be an arcanist certainly knew how to appease a kanyalari and had passed that knowledge on to her.

As she walked away, Archmage Varessa called out after her, "You must go through the circle!"

Pelina paused and inspected the circle with interest and a hint of amusement. Then she smirked at Veranesh. "Whatever he is doing, it has nothing to do with the scribbles on the ground," she said to Varessa. "It's not even a proper circle."

Veranesh couldn't help laughing. In a way, this young woman reminded him of his own pactee. "Such knowledge for someone who is only starting on that path."

Her face brightened. "Master Irtan is not forgiving to students who don't learn quickly enough."

"I see." The tidbit of information kindled his curiosity. An archmage teaching arcane arts had to be something more than just a coincidence. "You can go now." He waved her off and turned to Varessa. "Fourth archmage, I think it's time you rush your precious students to leave the Towers at once. As entertaining as this farce was, it's time I took care of more serious matters."

"So the circle...?" Varessa gave it a glance, but her furrowed forehead suggested she had less understanding of it than the student who'd called him out.

"A mere spectacle I couldn't resist." He spread his wings. "I wouldn't recommend reentering the Towers once you're done here, archmage."

As he lifted into the air, he caught surprise in the

archmage's eyes. To the very last moment, she must have been expecting to die. Veranesh let out a short laugh, ascending to the Towers' highest levels. Killing humans unaware of the past was unnecessary as long as they stayed out of his way, and he entertained the thought that she would take it as mercy. Kamira would immediately question what gain he had in leaving the archmage alive, and she would be right to do so. Those of the yalari who vied for the most power always acted with a goal in mind, and any pactee worth their salt would know it. For a pawn found by chance, Kamira had proven both more resourceful and more insightful than he could have hoped for. The more he thought about it, the more he became convinced that one day Kamira would stop being an object of his games and become a partner in them. Unless, of course, all she sought was to be free of Veranesh's power over her.

High in the air, he looked down at the High Towers. The crystal dome arched below his feet, familiar power within.

The mages who'd devised the plot with his enemies among the yalari died centuries ago, but a few mages within the Towers clearly knew of his prison and helped to maintain it. Dealing with them could slake some of his thirst for vengeance, and depending on the circumstances, it could provide other benefits as well. Maybe he would even learn the names of those who had sided with humans against him. Any knowledge would be useful in dealing with his true adversaries.

With his leg stretched to strike, Veranesh folded his wings and let his body descend to the crystal dome.

4

Kamira didn't have to channel energy anymore, and with that purpose gone, pain was all that was left. As time passed, she indulged more and more in a lethargic state that offered a scrap of comfort. Any presence within the chamber stirred her back into consciousness, but she rarely revealed it to visitors, mostly curious students and teachers who wanted to have a glance at the peculiarity she must be to them. Ryell did not return after their last conversation, and she hoped this was a sign that for once he had listened to her advice.

This time, though, it was Yoreus himself who paid her a visit. In the distance, Loktra and Kerl lurked by the massive door, and by the way the energy in the chamber flowed, there had to be one more archmage around—likely Irtan, since she hadn't seen any other archmage back that night when they encased her in the crystal.

"I've been told you are awake," Yoreus said. "Enjoying your prison?"

"It served its purpose. Nothing else would have convinced you to let me stay in this circle so long. I'm also glad you figured it out on your own and tried to play me. I wasn't sure if you would have believed that I offered to self-sacrifice." Now that all was done, she could allow herself honesty.

"Atissa told me of your pitiful attempts to sow discord," Yoreus replied. "Whatever you might have planned, it failed. We're still in control."

"But the demon is free, isn't he?" Not only was Veranesh free, the pact she still had told her he was nearby. Yet what the demon intended or why the high mages still had their magic remained unclear.

"It doesn't matter. We still have his magic and we can bind him again." Kerl stepped closer, vicious satisfaction clear on his red face when he stared at her. Despite all the years that passed, the public insult she had served him must still be hurting the pitiful drunkard. "And he'll never get through the Towers' defenses."

Kamira shifted, ignoring the accompanying torment, and looked up beyond the crystal and past the dome over the chamber. A black shadow against the bright sky hovered just above it.

"Defenses relying on the magic you steal from him?" She couldn't help her amusement. As the dark silhouette descended, her emotions resurfaced. Excitement and hope ran through her veins as if her blood fueled them.

Yoreus's face froze in shock when he followed her gaze. He had only enough time to shield his face from the rain of shattered crystal and retreat to the edge of the chamber before Veranesh landed by the circle.

Kerl and Loktra began an incantation, and Kamira felt the energy they pulled to enact their spell.

"No," Veranesh said, and their magic stopped flowing.

The archmages stumbled backward with wide eyes

focused on the demon. His moves almost escaped Kamira, as if four centuries of motionless captivity within the crystal hadn't any effect on Veranesh at all.

One quick swipe of Veranesh's claw and Kerl's scream shifted into the gurgling sounds of his ripped throat. Kerl slumped to the floor, grasping at his neck in a frantic attempt to stanch the fatal wound causing him to cough blood uncontrollably as Veranesh's fist closed around Loktra's face. The crack of her skull muffled Kerl's last whimpers, and Loktra's arms, thus far frantically slapping at the demon's grip, fell limp along with the rest of her body.

A stream of fire shot through the chamber, and ignoring the restrictions of her prison, Kamira lunged forward, pushing through the crystal. Her scream of warning turned to a shriek of agony when the energy tore through her body and violently pushed her back in place.

The crackling flames caught only the edge of Veranesh's wing as he sidestepped the assault. "At least one of you is prepared." The chill-inducing grin of a demon surfaced as he turned.

Kamira's attention shifted to Yoreus standing by a pillar, his composure unshaken. His lips kept moving, and a barrier rose around him before the demon reached him.

"You've found another source of magic, but it's not a pact," Veranesh said. "I take it this is not the first prison you've created. How many minor yalari did you have to trap like that to match what you were stealing from me?" Without turning his head away to look at it, he pointed at the crystal.

Yoreus's gaze remained focused, and he kept muttering words. Kamira struggled to hear, but the archmages often altered common incantations, making them into new spells, and she couldn't guess what he intended.

Veranesh approached the crystal and looked at her, ignoring Yoreus. "How does immortality feel? You're as close to a yalari now as any human ever was."

She couldn't help thinking of their first meeting, when she was the one walking freely, and he remained encased in magic and crystal. He could have tried to regain his freedom back then, and even if he didn't succeed, he would have likely weakened his prison enough to break free in time. Yet he decided to let her find another way. With the pain lingering in her bones and flesh, she couldn't even imagine having half his patience and perseverance. "Free me or kill me," she said. "You owe me that much."

"I do."

Another stream of fire shot out, striking Veranesh from behind, but the lashing tongues of flame slipped off the obsidian leather of his interposing wing.

"You'll have to try harder, mage," he called out, but his eyes remained fixed on Kamira. "You did well, pactee."

Only four words, but they sounded like the highest praise, and the unexpected softness in his voice promised that Veranesh wasn't about to leave her to her fate. He tapped at the crystal with his claw, and magic hissed like a sandstorm forcing its way through a tear in a tent. The way its structure cracked into pieces reminded her of ice sheets on Tivarashan lakes in springtime, and her prison collapsed into shards all around her.

Kamira fell to her knees, greedily taking in the air and forcing her muscles to stop shaking, but when the cracking of flames reached her ears, her instincts took over. The incoming fire assailed the barrier she brought up instantly. Magic flowed through her, stronger and easier to control, and as she forced her body up, she smiled. No matter how

Yoreus might have prepared, the battle that was about to start would not be a fair one.

Flames shot toward them once more, and Veranesh grimaced as they tried to envelop his body. With no apparent damage to his skin or dark leather outfit of otherworldly make, his expression must be the result of discomfort. He looked at Yoreus. "What now, mage? Will you chant your spells until your throat runs coarse?"

"What other choice do I have? Surrender?" the archmage replied.

Kamira sighed. Against her own better judgment, she had hoped Yoreus would see reason. "You could be the one who ends the centuries-old lie."

"Or we could have a real duel," he replied with confidence. "Unless, of course, for the lack of that dumb muscle of yours, you'll use the demon to kill me."

She narrowed her eyes. The provocative remark about the time when she and Veelk schemed to kill the archmage hardly moved her, but if Yoreus wanted a duel, he must be planning something. "Conditions?"

"If I win, you and your demon let me leave, demanding nothing," he said in an instant. "If you win, you get what you always wanted: a public apology and recognition of your skills. I'll also reveal the truth about events from the past."

She scoffed. He was a fool to believe she really wanted an apology, but if he was the one to speak to teachers and students, it would be easier to convince them of the truth. "Very well."

"I want the demon's word too," Yoreus added.

Veranesh looked down at him. "Defeat my pactee in a duel, and I might consider you worthy of talks, mage." With that, he spread his wings and lifted toward the decorative ledge that once supported the crystal dome above the chamber.

"Quite quick to abandon his lackeys, isn't he?" Yoreus remarked casually.

Kamira couldn't blame him for trying to sow doubt. After all, she'd used it too, against the fool who thought a pact with a higher demon was enough to take her and Veelk on. But dwelling on the demise of her teacher's student was not worth a breath, and two could play the game Yoreus started. "Or he's confident in my victory. After all, I did dispose of Uganel."

The warm brown of the archmage's face paled only by half a shade, and nothing else suggested the news shook him. "I'm sure it was quite a feat." Without stopping for a breath, his mockery shifted to an incantation, starting the duel without warning.

Except for stabilizing the flow of magic to her barrier, Kamira didn't react. With all the power at her fingertips, she could go for the kill, but that meant exposing herself to whatever deception her opponent was preparing. If he insisted on the duel, he had to be hiding a trick or two.

Flames erupted all around her, slithering and sliding over the barrier, searching for a way in. Loktra's and Kerl's bodies caught on fire, and so did several tapestries on the walls, but it wasn't enough to breach her defenses. Yet Yoreus kept chanting as if keeping the spell longer would make a difference.

Magic flowed through her as easily as a gentle breeze, and Veranesh's nearby presence invited her to make use of it, all of it. Energy was malleable and obedient as it had never been before; it promised ultimate control. In the past, she could hold two spells at the same time. Now it seemed like she could channel many, many more. She didn't fall for the allure of power, as no matter what else she did, the barrier had to stand if she wanted to survive.

The heat around her surged, but Yoreus couldn't have meant to roast her alive. The temperature would rise in the whole chamber, and his barrier wouldn't protect him either... and she could bet that the archmage was not one to sacrifice himself in order to defeat her. The duel's conditions suggested he was playing for his life.

With caution, she channeled more magic, thickening her barrier as she let the outer layers change to water. It hissed as it evaporated, but she didn't have time to cherish the diminishing flames. She had to figure out his plan quickly. With nothing much to go on, she listened to Yoreus's chant. His voice was quiet enough to conceal his words, but the rhythm of the spell was familiar. High mages wove incantations together to create complex effects—a lengthy process, but it was the only way high mages could cast more than one spell at once. Most of the knowledge from her days in the High Towers had long since faded from her memory, but the barrier spell was easy enough to recognize. It seemed that, like her, Yoreus reinforced his protection every once in a while. The other part... She squinted, tugging at the forgotten teachings... At the core it had to be the spell calling upon flames with all the additions needed to enhance them into a fiery storm.

That couldn't be all. The water evaporated quicker as she stopped channeling more magic and instead focused on the faint sounds of Yoreus's chant. There had to be more! Syllable by syllable, she ignored pieces of his incantation until only the unknown remained. She hummed to that rhythm, letting her mind wander.

And then the words arrived.

Yoreus's version had been altered, but she knew that odd melody well. The same chant saw her locked in the crystal.

The surge of magic within her was in response to her emotions, but no matter how much she didn't want Yoreus to imprison her again, she would not lose the duel by succumbing to her own fears. Instead, she wove them into her magic, and the water burst out from around her barrier, drowning the chamber and quenching the raging fires.

The steam grew dense, giving her several moments of needed concealment. Yoreus would never expect she'd risk her own protection for the ability to move freely, and he couldn't know that arcanist barriers took a while to fade entirely, such that she'd have time to raise another one should he prove quicker with rekindling his flames.

Running through a chamber full of broken crystal and rubble could hardly be stealthy, even under the veil of steam, so she called upon her magic. Several lightning arcs danced through the fog. She hoped they'd draw Yoreus's attention away from her silhouette moving closer and conceal the sound of her footsteps. The electricity dispersed, fizzling closer to her than comfortable, but if Veelk could withstand a whole storm, she could surely endure a small jolt. Perhaps the scars on her arms would shield her as his did him.

She made it all the way behind Yoreus, and the moment he called back the flames, she brought her barrier up. Of course, he didn't even notice the change in where the energy flowed, too convinced that she must have still stood where he saw her last. She smirked. High mages could surely do with some more practical expertise. Memorizing spells was useless if one couldn't think on their feet.

But the duel was far from over if she couldn't get through Yoreus's barrier. Channeling pure magic could help her break it, but the blast would likely level the chamber, if not the whole Towers. As much as she hated that place, she couldn't risk innocent lives.

At the same time, she didn't have to crush his whole barrier. High mages summoned them with a spell, but since they were unable to channel energy, they couldn't feed it with magic constantly, instead relying on reinforcing incantations whenever it was necessary. If she timed it right, all she needed was a small crack.

The heat in the chamber rose as the flames continued to roar, and Yoreus was halfway through the binding. She channeled all the energy her body could handle and focused it into her hand. Then she waited through the cycle of Yoreus's complex incantation, and before he finished reinforcing his protection, she changed her own barrier into water and struck.

Steam billowed around her with more violent hissing as the flames consumed the water she shielded herself with. A few more heartbeats and she'd have to bring her barrier back up or risk roasting alive.

But with one forceful thrust of her hand, sheathed in condensed energy in the shape of a stout spike, Yoreus's protection cracked.

Triumphant, she called upon more magic and let loose a torrent of water around her, quenching the fires.

At that, he finally turned. The disbelief faded from his face quicker than she'd expected. "I should have known that what they said about arcanists was true," he said. "Congratulations. You deserve this victory." He stepped forward and stretched his hand out, as confident in defeat as in everything else.

"You admit to being beaten so quickly?"

He might be hoping to save his life and maybe slip away

before or after he addressed the students, but she couldn't help suspicion.

Yoreus gave her a disarming smile. "You stand two steps away from me. I'd never finish the barrier spell in time. I'd be dead." He took another step forward, his hand even more invitingly stretched. "Or perhaps this is what you really want? To see me dead?"

She didn't miss the challenge in his voice, as if her hesitation could prove him right. So she extended hers, and their hands locked.

Yoreus yanked her toward him, in what he must have thought to be an unexpected attack. His other hand rose to strike, a dagger's blade catching a flash of the dying flames around them. Kamira didn't try to dodge. So close to her and holding her hand, Yoreus wouldn't let her escape. Instead, she used magic, as she always did.

A barrier rose around her, catching the blade before it struck. She looked into his eyes, wide and frozen. And if she were a woman who prided herself on higher morality, this would be the time to show her benevolence, but since the first archmage of the High Towers was foolish enough to use deception after losing a fair duel, he didn't deserve mercy. They had never agreed that the duel had to end with both of them alive, and given the dagger in his hand, Yoreus clearly didn't expect it to be so.

Magic still flowed through her, and she channeled it all through her hand, the one still within his grasp.

As soon as he realized what she was doing, Yoreus fought to pull away, but his hand and arm were already frozen. She grinned. He could be desperate enough to sever his now-useless arm, but arcane magic didn't need physical touch anyway.

In moments, his whole body was frozen, the terrified expression forever etched upon his face.

She stared at the icy corpse, trying to conjure some appropriate feelings, but the only one to manifest was relief. So much planning and so much pain, but the long plot had finally ended.

A whoosh of wings announced Veranesh's descent. "Well done, pactee," he said casually, as if he was a teacher praising a student who'd performed a minor spell. "You succeeded."

THE INITIATION CHAMBER was quiet and brought the inevitable question of what to do next. Throughout the months of searching, fighting, and planning, Kamira's thoughts had never ventured beyond that point. With so many unknowns and things that could go wrong, she didn't dare to indulge in any plans for the future, and the presence of the demon by her side, calm but with his goals concealed and actions unpredictable, would affect that very future.

"What of Veelk?" she asked the most important question. It was unlike her friend to never join her, even if he would have to run through the whole Towers or convince Veranesh to carry him up in the air.

The demon's expression changed, and she could swear it showed concern and sadness. "I know not of his whereabouts. The battle site I found suggests he caught up with the mages and adepts he was pursuing. All I could tell is that he didn't die there."

She narrowed her eyes. So far, Veranesh had not hesitated sharing knowledge with her. "But there was something else."

"A yalari. Perhaps he or she arrived later, once the mage killer had already left," he replied.

That Veranesh seemed more concerned about another demon than Veelk made it clear she shouldn't expect more information... or help. Their mutual agreement and support only lasted until he was free, but before they parted ways, she had to make sure he kept his part of their deal. "You're freed now. You don't need the spell you put on me."

Veranesh cocked his head like a curious bird. "Indeed, I don't."

He made no gesture, and she felt no difference, but to express distrust clashed with her pride. Besides, even if she asked, and the demon reassured her the spell was gone, it would bring no more certainty than she would get remaining silent. Apart from their first encounter, when Veranesh cast the spell that was meant to kill her and unleash destruction, not once had she sensed any unfamiliar magic around her that would prove the demon's claim. Perhaps there was never a spell, but she couldn't have afforded such doubts, not after he had severed her old pact. She almost smiled at that. Just like she had to believe he had means to kill her even from afar, she had to trust he gave up such power over her. And, in the end, even Veelk's demon, Suzhaul, said that Veranesh always kept his part of any agreements.

Footsteps echoing within the ruined chamber made her spin in place, with magic at the tips of her fingers.

"The first archmage of the High Towers beaten in a fair challenge by an arcanist." Archmage Irtan stepped forward from behind the columns at the far end. "It's not something I expected to see in my lifetime."

Despite his rather casual stride, Kamira eyed him with suspicion. Veranesh might have taken away magic from the mages, but it had hardly stopped Yoreus from finding other means, and she had to expect Irtan wouldn't approach her unprepared either.

Irtan lifted his finger. "I'd rather not fight," he said in an amiable manner and glanced at Veranesh. "With neither of you." He kept his distance, and his moves revealed readiness to defend should it become necessary... or to attack sneakily despite his reassurances.

Kamira tensed, anticipating a much harder battle to come. Yoreus had been predictable in his pride and desperation, and he had never tasted a real fight, but Irtan remained an unknown. With his knowledge and experience, he could have many tricks up his sleeve.

Veranesh, on the other hand, showed no concern. "And who you might be, mage?"

"Honorary archmage of the Towers, Irtan." The old man regarded the demon with curiosity and nothing more.

"You're the one who sent the message through the young pactee." Veranesh returned the gaze.

"I'm but a messenger myself."

Magic swirled in the chamber, though its flow remained neutral, and Kamira followed its strings to the source. Once she found it, her eyes shot wide open. "You're an arcanist!" The thought, when she spoke it out loud, sounded ridiculous. The longtime first archmage of the High Towers who had mastered all aspects of the high magic could not possibly have had a pact.

"For over a decade now," he confirmed with a hint of amusement. He looked at the demon. "I was hoping that removing one of the pillars on which your prison stood might give you enough freedom to act. I suspected it might take a long time... What I didn't expect, though, was that

Yoreus would send someone into the ruins... and all its consequences."

A bitter chuckle was her first response. "It would have been easier if you had told me the truth." Had she known there was an ally in the Towers, perhaps much trouble and death could have been avoided. Her thoughts drifted toward Cahala's entourage, all those innocent deaths, but even with Irtan's help, she still would have needed her scars and Koshmarnyk's skills. Those people would have died either way, and their death would forever be on her.

"I'm sure it would." Irtan remained unmoved. The demeanor of the jovial old man was gone, and his posture emanated confidence. "But I hardly could trust a rebellious former student with a secret I hadn't shared even with my closest friend. Should you have been captured and questioned, my name could be revealed. I couldn't take such risk. Especially not with... other parties involved." He stared directly at Veranesh.

"You know of other yalari," the demon said. "I take it you have a pact with someone significant."

His posture changed, as if he sensed something, but Kamira couldn't tell if it was just the response to Irtan's revelations or if there was real danger. She tensed.

"Significant enough." A deep male voice echoed within the chamber. The sound of wings beating the air accompanied the words, and another demon descended through the shattered dome. "It's been a long time, Veranesh." He was smaller in frame, and his claws weren't as impressive, but his wings spanned wide.

For a heartbeat, Kamira hoped he was an ally, with his greeting more respectful than threatening and facial features carrying an odd, otherworldly friendliness, but one glance at Veranesh made her step back. A human had no place in a fight between demons, and one had to be coming.

"I didn't take you for a fool, Fyertash." Veranesh's expression could freeze the air around him. "And confronting me alone is more than foolish. I destroyed Uganel, and you aren't even a match for him."

"I didn't come to confront you." The other demon's lips curled in a smile, but his eyes remained focused. "And I count on you not being keen on destroying me while your pactee is right beside you."

Veranesh stared at the other demon. "What makes you think I care?"

Fyertash pointed at the crystal's remnants. "Why free her if you don't?" he asked. "Until now, I suspected another yalari's involvement, since you've never made a pact. And that Suzhaul's dog was adamant in keeping information from me. But if you made a pact, it would be one to be remembered, not forgotten, and for that, she must live."

"Veelk," Kamira said when the meaning of Fyertash's words dawned on her. He must have been the one whose presence Veranesh sensed in the desert battlefield. A sudden rush of blood and a clenched throat made it hard to say anything else, so she stood, waiting for the demon's reply.

"Yes, I think that is his name. When I was leaving his village, he was still alive, pactee," Fyertash offered in an almost comforting manner, as if he cared about her wellbeing. "Though even Suzhaul himself might not be able to heal his wounds."

She narrowed her eyes. The demon had no reason to help Veelk, let alone carry him all the way to his tribe. Unless he had hoped to come across as benevolent and get information he needed through means of deception. The corner of her lip curved in a snide smile. A wasted effort, because Veelk would much rather pay such a debt back by saving the demon's life in return than willingly share any of her secrets.

"Even if you're telling the truth, it's not enough for me to consider you an ally." Veranesh moved his claws with anticipation. "Not after Uganel cried your name. Stop wasting my time, or I'll rip you to pieces."

Friendliness ebbed from Fyertash's face. "Others are coming through the sea. You can confront them here or go back to our realm, but either way, you'll need someone who has been around for the last centuries, watching and gathering information." He spread his arms in a gesture of peace. "If I played against you, I wouldn't have made a pact with a man whose magic was supposed to keep you imprisoned."

Veranesh watched the other demon in silence before speaking again. "You wouldn't risk coming here if there wasn't something in it for you."

Without hesitation, Fyertash nodded. "There's one thing worth such risk, isn't there?" His voice became quiet. "We both want revenge on the same yalari. I don't care what happens to me afterward as long as I can see them fall."

Kamira might not know her demon all that well, but even to her it was clear that Fyertash had failed to convince him.

"Very cunning," Veranesh replied. "Appeal to something I can relate to."

Fyertash let out a short laugh but shook his head. "You were never sentimental, so I doubt you would. Your revenge is reason-driven. You want to put them in place and teach them a lesson, so no one ever threatens you like that." He looked around the chamber. "Someone like Uganel would level this place out of sheer rage, even though most people here were not directly responsible. You did only what was necessary. But I have nothing more to bargain with, and nor would I care to try. Your choice."

Kamira glanced at Irtan, who, like her, stood silently through the demons' exchange. The worried expression on his face made it clear that he believed Fyertash's claims.

Swallowing sudden bile, she took a step forward. Without a circle, she was defenseless if Veranesh chose not to protect her against the other demon. "How many yalari are coming?"

Fyertash glanced at her, and his curiosity carried a hint of respect, as if he hadn't expected her to have enough courage to interrupt their conversation. "Three that I know of, but they aren't fools. With Veranesh free, they'll bring more in."

She drew a sharper breath when the meaning of his words sank in.

"You shouldn't concern yourself with matters of yalari," Veranesh remarked.

"Shouldn't I?" she fired back. Wrapped up in finding a way to free Veranesh, she never paid close attention to what had happened in Devanshari, relying on scraps from information she got from Ryell and others. Kaighali people might not be addicted to magic as the Devanshari were, but the city also lacked a magical artifact that would shield it... Not that the artifact sufficed. "We stripped Kaighal of its defenses. If not the demons, then Tivarashan or the Western Kingdom will claim it. With no mages around—"

"We do have the first archmage," Irtan interrupted, gesturing at her. "And I'll gladly join her as the second should the demon I have a pact with be still alive." He gave Veranesh a telling glance. "Master Tijhran wouldn't refuse the title of the third in such circumstances."

The prospect of three arcanists, with the titles of archmages or not, facing an army led by demons could evoke a dry laughter at best, but it was all they had. Unless Veranesh agreed to spare Fyertash and helped protect the city... which she saw no reason for him to do.

Her demon regarded her as if he knew what she was thinking. "I could dispose of that pathetic yalari, sever our pact, and be on my way."

"That changes nothing. Unless you dispose of me as well, I'll simply make a new pact." She held her chin up, though it did cross her mind that Veranesh wouldn't be a fool to leave her alive. Any higher demon who wanted to play against him or simply gain insights would offer her a pact in exchange for any knowledge she might have. There was also the matter of the powdered stones in her body that likely forever tied her to Veranesh and his magic. For a moment she pondered whether she'd be able to draw energy through them even if the pact was gone, but she'd rather not be forced to sate her curiosity.

"Careful, pactee. The secrets you know might make me tempted." Veranesh's voice carried both amusement and a warning.

Before she could find a reply, Fyertash burst out laughing. "A pactee worthy of you. Who would have thought?" he remarked with casual amusement, as if the situation wasn't dire. "So, shall we?"

Kamira looked between them, and Fyertash smiled at her confidently.

"He's made his decision. If he wanted to be gone or to

see any of us dead, it would have happened already," he said.

Veranesh grunted, but he gave the other demon a nod of appreciation. Yet, when he spoke to Fyertash, his voice remained cold. "I don't consider anyone an ally until they prove their worth, and as of now, you're worth to me less than a mere human pactee. So you and I will talk until you sate my need for knowledge. In the meantime, our pactees will take care of the disorder among humans and muster whatever meager defenses they have." He glanced at Irtan. "The woman who braved speaking with me earlier. Varessa. I'd consider keeping her around, should she be willing to make a pact."

"I'm sure she can see reason," Irtan said.

Veranesh paid no attention to his response. His wings shot open, and he left the chamber through the shattered dome, with Fyertash following him at a distance.

Pieces of the dome crunched under Irtan's feet as he approached Kamira. "Quite a pair you are, you and your demon. Come, let's see how much we can salvage to make your title something more than an empty word."

He headed for the exit, but Kamira still stood in the middle of the rubble, thoughts racing through her head. Her title... The title she'd once coveted and dreamed of, and the title she gave up in exchange for freedom from the Towers' politics. She did not care for it anymore. But she was the reason Kaighal remained mostly defenseless, and she would not turn away from the city that was her home more than Tivarashan ever was.

At the same time, she couldn't deny that the possibility of changing the history and repairing the past held a lot of appeal. The first archmage having a pact with one of the most powerful demons could restore the old glory of arcanists. She could make things as they should always have been.

That was, if Veranesh survived the confrontation with other yalari—and Kaighal along with him.

5

Ryell stood among the students and listened to Fourth Archmage Varessa's speech. Behind her, a demon watched the gathered with a mixture of curiosity and caution, and whenever Ryell glanced at the winged creature, his vision blurred, and he had to fight the urge to unsheathe his sword and charge the monster before it could destroy this city just like its brethren destroyed his home. If he could, he'd shout at the people around him to wake up, to flee or to stand up to an uneven fight, because trusting a demon was a path to certain death. It might have kept its distance and acted harmless, but he'd seen what a demon could do and how little human lives mattered to those despicable beings.

Yet, in the moments when his rage subsided, he couldn't blame those students for returning from the town at Varessa's call. Many of them probably had no other home than High Towers, and Kaighal itself wasn't prepared to defend against such foes. They didn't have an artifact to protect them from an intrusion, so they had to negotiate with the demons, even if Ryell considered such a choice foolish.

In the distance, some townsfolk had also gathered, their curiosity—or perhaps their need for reassurance—stronger than fear.

Atissa shivered and moved closer to him. With no magic, she lost her confidence, and Ryell enclosed her frail body within his arm's embrace, letting her head rest upon his chest.

"The recent events in the Towers are the consequences of the betrayal high mages committed centuries ago." Varessa's clear voice carried over the crowd. "More, we all have been betrayed as the foundations of high magic were laid on deception and destruction. Today we had to pay the price for our predecessors' misdeeds."

"One would think she rehearsed this speech for weeks," Atissa muttered. "For someone who supposedly learned the truth just now, she doesn't look too shocked."

"Do you think she knew?" Ryell picked his words carefully.

As much as he was willing to see lies and deception in anything demon-related, he did notice the archmage's stiff posture. The way she spoke, quick enough to sound confident but slow enough to control her own voice should it betray her, suggested Varessa put on a brave face for the students' sake, but he kept the observation to himself. Atissa was too bitter and shaken to listen to a voice of reason, and in a way, she reminded Ryell of himself, of the way he acted shortly after the Devanshari capital fell. Atissa was the one to save him back then, after he landed in the foreign lands struck with grief and hate, and now he had to save her in return.

"Maybe not," Atissa replied. "But I'm sure that power-thirsty gaharra already saw the opportunity for herself. Bargaining with demons, maybe claiming leadership for herself." She went silent when a few other students threw curious glances at her.

Meanwhile, Varessa continued her speech. "First Archmage Yoreus has been defeated by an arcanist in a fair challenge, and with him died the last person to keep the lie alive."

Atissa stiffened in Ryell's embrace, her eyes wide and breath held, but otherwise she kept her composure. No tears showed, and no words of denial slipped from her lips. She must have been expecting such news after Yoreus told her to leave the Towers with other mages, and even if some hope for a different ending might have lingered, she knew better than to bet on it. But Atissa's neutral expression didn't mean the public announcement hadn't shaken her, because fears hurt deeper when someone dressed them in words and presented them as truth. Ryell pulled her closer, offering comfort.

"The new first archmage of the Towers, arcanist Kamira, asked former Archmage Irtan to rejoin the ranks, and they intend to bright the Towers back to their grandeur from centuries ago." Varessa paused and looked around. "All of the former students and teachers are welcome to return, but the easy days of high magic are gone. Everyone will have to master arcane knowledge and skills, and prove themselves by earning a pact."

"Is high magic forbidden now?" a man in the crowd dared to ask.

Varessa shook her head. "It is not. But high magic as you know it, easy and powerful, was a lie. We all stole it from the demon who claimed it back today. The high magic in its true form, the one from before the Cataclysm, isn't outlawed, and anyone is welcome to study it if they choose so. Be warned, though, that it's not an easy path, and the power you might attain will most likely not rival the benefits of a pact even with a minor demon. I myself decided to stay in the Towers and make a pact. There is news of a demon army traveling across the sea, so Kaighal is going to need arcanists' help soon, and I won't let prejudice keep me from protecting our home from demons and those humans who might wish to claim it."

Former students stirred as the archmage's words sparked multiple discussions, shock, disbelief, hope, and sarcasm on their faces and in their words. Undoubtedly, some would decide to go back to the Towers, even though they would be taught demon magic. Others, perhaps, would do so in hopes of finding a way to restore high magic.

Ryell's thoughts turned toward Kamira. According to Varessa's words, she was not only free of her prison, but also the new first archmage of the Towers. A crooked smile spoiled his face. Of course she would want everyone to become arcanists and let demons dwell in the city. Until now, he'd wanted to believe all the things she had told him, but he couldn't help doubts when he considered all that he knew. Around Kaighal, Tivarashans were perceived as crafty and deceptive, and the way Kamira played the archmages— a sudden twitch shook his body, as she had played him as well—made it clear she was no stranger to manipulation. Perhaps there never was any danger to her life and no trapped demon forcing her to do his bidding. Instead, she'd crafted a sinister plot along with demons to get the High Towers for herself.

"Will you be going back there?" he asked Atissa, mostly to take his mind off Kamira.

Atissa pressed her lips in a thin line, and her stern face

made it clear she despised the sheer thought. Then her expression softened. "There is a place my father wanted me to go to. A family home where I would be safe. It's to the west, in the woods." She looked him in the eye. "I have no magic to share with you anymore, at least not until I figure out how to get it back."

He recognized the unspoken question. She must have worried that now, when she had nothing to offer, he'd leave her in search of someone else to sate his hunger. But he didn't need mages or arcanists anymore. The skin on his chest, right above his heart, still itched from the blending of the shard Kamira had told him to take, but magic flowed steadily, reminding him of the times when Hajihali's power reached throughout Devanshari lands, touching every single man, woman, and child. He was finally free of the hunger and its consequences.

Kamira was free too, and he could try to mend things between them. They could forgive each other and perhaps create a better future that wasn't built on secrets.

Yet a glimpse of a man walking with confidence toward the Towers' entrance, and the way he spoke with the demon barring the entry, made Ryell reconsider. Kamira didn't need or want Ryell. She'd trusted a stranger, that Koshmarnyk, with secrets she had never shared with Ryell, and even though she might have had reasons to keep things away from him because of his ties to Yoreus, not even once had she tried—really tried—to build trust between them.

Besides, even though she might be free from her crystal prison, she was still wrapped up in whatever plots the demons were involved in, and that was the last thing he ever wished to be a part of.

Atissa's anxious expression tore him away from unpleasant thoughts. There he was, torturing her with silence she didn't deserve. Her father might have double-crossed him, but Atissa had never lied to him, had never deceived him. No matter how his heart felt about Kamira, perhaps it was time to hush it and search for the future in a place that wouldn't have the shadow of so many lies cast over it.

He gave Atissa a comforting hug. "I promised your father I'd protect you. If you would like me to, I'll go with you." It might have been a meager offering with no promises, but it seemed like a good start. He would see to Atissa's safe journey to her new home, and perhaps that would be enough time to figure out his own feelings.

Her face brightened, and before they walked away, she kissed him. He held her close on the way down to Kaighal, desperate in his hope that this one tidbit of deception, his real reasons to accompany her, wouldn't be enough to spoil whatever they could possibly build together.

As STUDENTS GATHERED at the entrance to the Towers, with Archmage Varessa preparing a speech, Koshmarnyk weighed his chances of getting inside. He'd had enough of waiting and gossip that painted unappealing scenarios. He needed real information, not scraps that circulated around Kaighal, more ridiculous the more ears and lips they passed.

A demon landed nearby. He looked smaller than Koshmarnyk had imagined, but it mattered not. Without hesitation, he approached.

The demon turned his head toward him, his beak-shaped nose pointing directly at Koshmarnyk, but no recognition flashed in his eyes.

"You're not Veranesh," Koshmarnyk said.

"You know of him?" The demon cocked his head. "Another friend of his pactee?"

Koshmarnyk tensed. Playing word games with a demon would risk revealing something that could harm Kamira or Veranesh. Without hesitation, he rubbed one of the stones in his skin, ignoring possible onlookers. A flying bracelet would not be the biggest oddity of their day. The magic within the stone stirred. The crystal creature uncurled from his forearm, its wings beating the air silently, and for a heartbeat Koshmarnyk wondered whether Veranesh was even controlling it.

"Fyertash," Veranesh said through it. "Let him in."

The demon inspected the nightfly. "Cunning. I'd like to learn the trick one day."

"Of course you would." Veranesh's voice was cold, and Koshmarnyk couldn't help suspecting the demon named Fyertash wasn't an ally. The nightfly darted toward the door. "This way, adept."

Unwilling to engage with the unknown demon any longer than necessary, Koshmarnyk followed the nightfly inside.

He'd thought the High Towers would resemble Gildya Magna, but apart from the opening area by the entrance, the Towers lacked vast halls and tall ceilings. Led by the nightfly that seemed to know its way around better than he'd expected, Koshmarnyk passed multiple study halls and what seemed to be dormitories, all spacious enough to accommodate people living there but missing the exuberance and vastness the adepts preferred. Instead, he climbed countless narrow stairways and couldn't help wondering whether they served the purpose of providing the students with physical exercise.

On the other hand, space must have been quite limited

if the high mages wanted to contain all their activities to the Towers, unwilling to search for additional buildings in Kaighal like Gildya did. It didn't surprise him. After all, they had the best spot, on the hill overlooking the city, and they likely wanted to keep distance between themselves and commoners. High magic was quite elitist for something supposedly available to anyone. *But not anymore,* he corrected himself.

"So, what happened?" he asked his crystal guide.

"Kamira fought the first archmage and emerged victorious, so she's now considered the first archmage," Veranesh replied.

"And the other demon?" Koshmarnyk asked. "Fyertash?"

"He's not significant in any way," Veranesh said. "But there are other concerns."

Koshmarnyk didn't like the sound of it, but as he walked past a half-open double door, his attention shifted toward the black-winged creature standing inside the chamber. In person, Veranesh turned out quite imposing and intimidating, but his relaxed posture suggested he wasn't a threat, nor did he expect one. The nightfly darted toward the woman who stood by his side, small and fragile in comparison, and coiled around her wrist in a way Koshmarnyk had witnessed so many times before.

Kamira turned around, and a smile warmed up her serious face. He made it to her with several quick steps, and without a word, he enclosed her in his embrace. He might have trusted her plan would work and was confident in her ability to see it through, but to finally learn she was indeed alive and safe came with a bigger relief than he'd expected. He buried his face in her hair, inhaling the familiar scent filled with notes of her magic. No matter how much he wanted to believe otherwise, he cared more for her than his own wellbeing. But now, she was the archmage and likely had no need for a rogue adept by her side.

"The first archmage, eh?" he teased. "I hope that doesn't mean Veelk will be hunting you now." He looked around in search of his friend. Surely Veelk would have made it back from the desert already and beaten him to the Towers.

The shine in Kamira's eyes dimmed, and she tensed in his embrace. "He's not here. I was told he might be still alive, but it's all in his people's hands now."

Veranesh looked at her. "I could have Fyertash carry the adept over there. It wouldn't take long. And he can keep one nightfly to communicate."

Kamira's forehead furrowed. "We will need him here. Unless you don't trust him enough."

"He'll do what he's told," Veranesh replied.

Someone on the other side of the chamber called out the demon's name, and Veranesh walked away. Koshmarnyk eyed the old man in a high mage's outfit with caution, but neither Kamira nor the demon seemed concerned by his presence.

"Fyertash brought information of the other yalari's moves and agreed to help with Kaighal's defense." Her eyes flashed with amusement. "That was enough for Veranesh to keep from killing him, but not enough to gain trust."

"Defense?" Koshmarnyk asked with rising concern. He'd heard Varessa mentioning it outside but paid little attention to it, busy trying to get in instead.

Her expression became grim. "Other demons are coming, and they are bringing an army along. With the high mages gone, we have but a few arcanists to organize everything. I need to contact Gildya, the council, city guards, and Devanshari refugees, then send out letters in hopes of getting more arcanists in here before the siege starts." A heavy sigh left her. "To think I believed it was all going to be over when I freed Veranesh..." She shook her head as if disappointed with her own naivety.

He looked her in the eye. He might have hoped that once her obligations to the demon were fulfilled, Kamira would welcome his company in her travels with Veelk, but his personal desires could wait. Ten years of Gildya's imprisonment might have weakened his own ties to Kaighal, but it was the city *she* considered home. "How can I be of service, then, first archmage?" he asked with all seriousness.

Kamira's expression changed, relief flashing on her face, as if she'd feared he might have decided to leave.

"I was hoping you'd ask that. I could use the company of someone more levelheaded than two demons and an old arcanist." She rolled her eyes. "Their company really makes me think Veelk is not half as bad."

He let out a short laugh. Demons, invasion, siege, and becoming a leader of the place she had brought down... and Kamira still managed to keep her acrid sense of humor intact. She pulled him toward the table by the wall, where Veranesh was engaged in a discussion with the old mage. "Come—I'm sure they could use the knowledge of a man who actually knows how to make use of imbued stones instead of simply creating them."

6

Prince Jalyn, the fourth child of Queen Andalisha and insignificant in any other matter, stepped onto the wide, sun-kissed terrace. As everything in the palace, it was made of sky marble, remarkable for its blue tint, and it always reminded him of calm, cold lakes. Perhaps this was why his mother liked the terrace so much: a private oasis of tranquility in the constant buzzing of the Tivarashan Southern Palace.

She was sitting at a small table in the middle of it, far enough to not see the gardens stretched below as if she wanted to create the feeling of solitude, but then, it was his mother. She may have only wanted to make Jalyn think she desired such alone time. This way, he would be flattered all the more that she'd granted him an audience during her most precious moments of the day. He allowed himself a small smirk. With his mother, everything was a game, so no matter her reasons, all he could tell for certain was that she wanted to speak with him alone.

Without looking up, she gestured for Jalyn to approach. She wore a sky-blue dress with an intricate pattern of lace and sapphires decorating the neckline, and matching white-gold jewelry, including a circlet with a single large jewel in it, a sapphire to put all others to shame, and the outfit alone told Jalyn his mother intended to discuss something more serious than his fencing progress that she, in fact, cared nothing about. His heart skipped a beat, but to allow himself any hope would be foolish. Whatever the queen wanted from him, it would serve her goals, not his.

"Have a breakfast with me, my son." Her voice might be soft, but she still didn't grant him even one glance.

He sat down. There was no servant to assist him, so he poured himself caffra juice and inspected the pastry selection on the platter between them, as if the decision what to eat had any significance. At least it served to conceal the mixture of emotions ready to boil over within him.

"You've heard about the changes in the High Towers in Kaighal," she said between bites.

It might be a lure to check how involved he was in politics, but Jalyn had to take that chance. If he never showed any ambition, his mother would either get suspicious or lose any scraps of interest she might have in her fourth child.

"The new archmage comes from Tivarashan blood, from noble descent," he offered a piece of information he considered crucial.

When he thought about it, he understood why in the recent weeks the queen had decided to move to the Southern Palace. Her spies had likely informed her of the turmoil before it happened, or she anticipated it from whatever meager information they provided, and she wanted to be as close to the events as possible without being exposed to its possible dangers. Of course, even if another Cataclysm-like event was about to happen, the Four would protect her within Tivarashan lands, so the threat was minimal, and being almost at the border meant she could receive news quickly and act on it in an instant.

She finally looked up at him. Some poets said the night sky hid under her eyelids, but Jalyn would say her eyes were bottomless pits and danger lurked in there, waiting for all those fools who came looking for stars.

"You will go to Kaighal," she said. "You will act as my voice and work on an agreement that would open Kaighal's port to Tivarashan ships and merchants... without restrictions or tolls."

He couldn't hide his surprise. "Me, Mother?"

For her to make such a decision was unreasonable. Both Mefina and Hyuleen were not only older, but had received far more thorough education in politics and history—after all, one of them would rule Tivarashan in the future. It seemed wiser to send either of them, to entice the new archmage with the attention of the most important women in the royal family, to present her with prospects in the court that would come from her cooperation, and at the same time give one of the royal daughters an opportunity to gain experience she'd need in the future.

"Have I not made myself clear?"

"You have, Mother, but I can't help wondering why you would not send Hyuleen, whose lips change words into pure honey and could lure a rabbit into a drakkat's paws."

Her eyebrow arched slightly, but her face remained devoid of emotion. "I don't want your sister to make mistakes that wouldn't be easy to fix. And in a confrontation with another woman of power, who in her eyes is nothing more than a noblewoman—but almost equal to her, given the circumstances—such mistakes are possible. You're more composed than her, and your presence will make the archmage feel like she has the upper hand." She leaned forward, her smile inviting, as if she was once more a proud mother of a five-year-old boy who'd completed a difficult task. "And then you'll play her, won't you, my son? You'll win Kaighal for Tivarashan without a single drop of blood spilled, and in return, I'll ensure your life at the court will be everything you desire."

He restrained himself from grimacing. Her reward meant a position of some significance or lands at his sole disposal. Or an uninterrupted life of pleasure and leisure. This was all that his mother would give him, and not what Jalyn desired, but her offer was still more than he could dream of as a fourth child, a male child, in the kingdom where royal mothers passed the crown to their daughters.

Yet there had to be more to his mother's generous offer. Hyuleen might be proud, but she would know better than to act upon emotions even if a new situation challenged her composure. For her, the stakes would be even higher, and the reward ultimate. A woman who won unrestricted access to Kaighal for the Tivarashan, a first step in annexing the unruly city for the kingdom, would secure the crown for herself, no matter how many military successes her sister Mefina could boast.

He couldn't simply ask Mother for the real reasons—nothing to be gained by revealing his confusion and suspicions—so he took time to re-examine what he knew. His personal resources were meager in comparison to what his mother had at her disposal, but a clue might be hidden within those tidbits of knowledge. He considered the magical explosion in the desert to the south of Kaighal and the mention of war preparations, which couldn't be directed either against Tivarashan, which had made no move so far, or against the Western Kingdom, which wouldn't have even received the news yet.

Jalyn shivered, remembering the other bit of gossip he'd heard, the one of demons in flesh circling Kaighal. Like everyone else, he'd heard of what happened overseas, in the kingdom of Devanshari, and even though the Four would shield their followers from any demonic intrusion, they likely wouldn't extend such protection to Kaighal citizens who cared nothing for the protectors of Tivarashan.

With such consideration, the answer to his unspoken question became clear, and he looked his mother straight in the eye. The queen was silent so far, as if she wanted to give him time to think.

"You're sending me there, Mother, because I'm expendable."

The queen leaned back in her chair, looking calculating and, oddly, satisfied. If it was a test, he'd passed it.

"Prove me wrong, my son."

THE LARGE TABLE looked too empty and too pristine to belong in the initiation rite chamber, which still bore all the marks of Kamira's battle with Yoreus, but she cared little for appearances. With its crystal dome already shattered, it was a perfect place to allow the demons to participate in any meetings, and she hoped that the battered chamber would also serve as a reminder of the events that brought the end of the high mages and, perhaps, save the new arcane Towers from a similar fall... save her from suffering similar pride and corruption.

She closed her fingers on the edge of the table. She hadn't asked to become a leader, and in any other circumstances she would have laughed Irtan off and left him to deal with the aftermath, but with demons coming, she couldn't leave Kaighal at their mercy. Yet planning a defense of the whole city was different from making sure she and Veelk survived, and it'd been a long time since she had even dreamed about leading. Over a decade ago, the title of the first archmage was everything she'd desired. Now, older and more experienced, she'd give it up in a heartbeat in favor of a strenuous journey west just to learn whether Veelk was still alive.

The whoosh of wind brought her back to reality, and she looked up at the two demons making their landing. Fyertash kept to the side and at least several paces away from Veranesh, and Kamira narrowed her eyes. As proud as those creatures were, it was hard to believe that a higher demon would accept an inferior place so willingly. Yet Fyertash seemed content with his role, obeying Veranesh's directions. That worried her. The new demon might be less imposing than Veranesh and less threatening than Uganel, whom she'd faced in the desert, but the way he acted reminded her of the duplicitous Pardayi. At the same time, the sly demoness might prefer indirect manipulation to raw power, but even she was prone to outbursts of anger. Fyertash's composure suggested he was an experienced and cunning player, one who would submit himself to humiliation only to strike at the opportune time. And the way he turned on his former demonic comrades, siding with Veranesh, made Kamira wonder how quickly he'd be willing to swap his allies again.

Kamira hid her grimace. It also didn't help that Fyertash had a pact with Irtan, and she still wasn't certain how much she should trust the old archmage. If there was a man to match demons in their games and deception, it had to be

Irtan. Yes, until any of them showed their hand, all she could do was deal with threats as they came and hope Veranesh would not allow himself to be blindsided.

"Others?" Veranesh said.

Before she could reply, the door to the chamber opened. Archmages Irtan and Tijhran walked in, deep in conversation. Kamira smiled at their engaged and amiable discussion. Now that they were on the same side, they would likely keep very little from each other, and she hoped that it would help the arcane arts grow. At the same time, their slow pace didn't escape her. Tijhran walked with difficulty, his body balanced unevenly between his healthy leg and his walking cane. Kamira's hand moved toward her own leg as the memory of the battle with Uganel resurfaced. She was lucky he'd wanted her to suffer rather than die quickly; otherwise his claw might have dug much deeper into her calf, causing damage that would leave her crippled forever. A little pain while walking was not too high of a price to pay, especially not after what she'd endured within the crystal. Come to think of that, both her leg and once-broken arm hadn't bothered her since Veranesh freed her. Perhaps the pain was still there but imperceptible after the torment of being encased in pure magic.

She focused back on the approaching archmages. The time for reflection would be later.

Behind the men walked two women. Archmage Varessa was one of the few other archmages who'd decided to stay in the Towers, but since Veranesh had mentioned her by name, and Irtan spoke highly of her teaching skills, Kamira let her keep her title and included her in the meeting. Even if Varessa had little knowledge about how arcane magic worked, she excelled in scholarly matters and overseeing tasks—the very skills that the new Towers would desperately need.

Next to Varessa walked Pelina. The young woman's eyes darted between the archmages, and Kamira wondered whether Pelina would rather dash out of the chamber instead of attending the meeting, but after all her help, she deserved to be a part of it.

The last person to enter was Koshmarnyk. He rushed in, carrying several rolls of paper. As he closed the door, Veranesh gave Kamira a nod. The meeting was about to start, and she was to lead it. She kept her face neutral, but she couldn't help grim thoughts. Six people and two demons were not enough to defend the city against an army of demonlings, arcanists, and higher demons, but with a good plan, they could prepare Kaighal for the siege. She sought comfort in the city's past when it held against Tivarashan armies and the Four's priests, who wielded powerful magic not once but twice, and it fought off the Western Kingdom's invasion as well.

"Any word from Gildya?" she asked when they'd all made it to the table.

Irtan and Varessa shook their heads.

"They are likely waiting for the turmoil in the Towers to pass," Koshmarnyk said. "The council of adepts is not willing to take sides. They will speak with the winners only, and I'd wager they see none just yet."

Varessa huffed. "It's so like them to risk the city's safety just to make sure nothing threatens their position."

Kamira found Varessa's open disdain for politics appealing, though she couldn't ignore the possibility the fourth archmage was being deceitful about it. "Then perhaps we should make them aware that if they wait, the arcanists will be the ones to take all the glory of repelling the demon army."

"But will we?" Tijhran asked.

Kamira had to appreciate that her teacher, despite bleak prospects for the future, still looked at her with that spark of pride in his eye.

"I have a plan. Whether it succeeds..." She shrugged. "Our most important task is to ensure people's safety, so I asked Adept Koshmarnyk to create a blueprint of a device that would allow us to create a protective barrier around the city."

"That didn't help the Devanshari," Irtan remarked.

Koshmarnyk looked at Kamira, and when she gave a nod, he said, "They had only one device, and they didn't even know its workings. We will have as many as we can create. This way, if one fails, the breach should be easy enough to contain until we can fix the device or replace it."

She kept to herself that the Devanshari also had a traitor in their midst. Such knowledge would betray how close her ties with Ryell truly were, and if someone ever learned of what happened to their queen, Kamira's involvement would come to light. The first archmage of the Towers taking part in arranging Cahala qi'Devanshari's death would destroy the shaky trust people had in arcanists and bury any hopes for saving the city.

"If we have enough arcanists with basic training completed, they could also create barriers to ensure no demonlings get into the city while the repairs are carried out," Kamira added.

Tijhran rubbed his chin. "And what of the higher demons? We don't know if it'll work against them."

"The kanyalari will not engage in the battle directly,"

Veranesh said. "They won't risk it with me and Fyertash nearby."

Everyone looked at him, likely expecting an elaborate explanation, but Tijhran's eyes remained focused on Kamira, and she knew that inquisitive expression. Undoubtedly, her former teacher remembered that she'd admitted to having knowledge of what transpired in the desert, and even though she'd told him little of what really happened during the battle with Uganel, he was wise enough to make guesses at the missing pieces.

Cautiously and slowly, she nodded. It was better to confirm what he already suspected than to risk his asking questions that would force her or Veranesh to reveal too much. With sudden interest, she shifted her attention to Fyertash, but his face was inscrutable, and he wasn't watching her, so he likely didn't suspect she had knowledge of what Veranesh was talking about. And Archmage Irtan's curious expression suggested that the smaller demon didn't share anything about the destruction spell with his own pactee.

"If possible, I'd like Archmage Irtan to help Adept Koshmarnyk in his efforts," Kamira said once it became obvious Veranesh didn't intend to say anything else. "And let's hope that Gildya will put the politics aside. Perhaps another message, one that would make them worry the Towers will gain too much influence and power if the adepts decide to wait?" She turned to Irtan.

"I can make it happen," he said with a mischievous expression. "Perhaps they need to be reminded that the new first archmage comes from Tivarashan."

Kamira bit her lip before protesting. The last thing she wanted was to be perceived as yet another ruthless archmage who cared only about her own ambitions and goals, but if that made the adepts desperate enough to come to her, even if only to ensure their influence remained as strong as before, and convinced them to join the defense of the city, she'd not let her pride get in the way.

"Very well," she said. "Archmage Tijhran, I'd like you to focus on teaching. Pick the most promising students who could be trusted to make the pact soon." She turned to Pelina. "I need you to help him. I know your own training is far from finished, but you can share the knowledge you already have."

Pelina straightened her back, confidence emanating from her posture. "Whatever you need from me, first archmage."

Kamira swelled with pride. Theirs was a chance meeting and a chance taken, but Pelina had turned out to be a loyal and valuable ally, and she deserved recognition. Besides, she was the only other true arcanist in the Towers—if not one fully tutored yet, still one with great promise. Kamira had no doubt that Master... no, *Archmage* Tijhran would go out of his way to provide additional guidance to Pelina despite his other obligations.

"Archmage Varessa..." Kamira turned to her. "I've heard of your dedication to teaching, and it pains me to ask you to oversee the more mundane side of the Towers' activities. You're likely the one with the best knowledge of what our teachers and students need, which would help us ensure the teaching resumes quickly and smoothly."

"I understand," Varessa replied, "and I'll gladly take on such responsibilities. I'd rather not return to the classrooms before I have mastered what I'm supposed to teach. With my new duties, it wouldn't be a surprise if I don't have time to show others how to use magic I can hardly control myself."

"Then it is settled," Veranesh said. "Fyertash and I will keep scouting the seas."

Everyone else stirred, sensing the end to the meeting, and relief washed over Kamira. At least no one seemed to favor empty speeches or games. Once the tasks got divided, each of them was ready to leave.

"I'll be here." Kamira stepped to the side as Koshmarnyk rolled out papers onto the table. "There are still parts of the plan I have to figure out." And, perhaps, she should also consider alternate plans... So many things could go wrong, and if Gildya refused to help, it would be much more difficult to get everything done on time.

Varessa glanced at the chamber. "Do you want me to send someone up here to clean up the rubble? It will take a while, but if you're also going to receive guests here..."

"No," Kamira said firmly. "We have the city to defend. The time for cleaning the Towers will be later." By then, perhaps she would also have a clearer vision of what she wanted the new Towers to become.

"As you wish."

The three archmages and Pelina left. Veranesh gestured at Fyertash, and they took off through the shattered dome. The silence around her was like a sigh of relief.

Koshmarnyk smiled. "It went well, don't you think? I somewhat expected much more squabbling and arguing."

"So did I."

He probably read concern on her face, but he didn't ask any questions, with his eyes already at the blueprints, and Kamira allowed herself a moment of reflection.

Perhaps the unexpected had indeed happened, and a common goal united all of her allies, no matter how reluctant they might be, but the cloud of old ways still lingered in the Towers, and she'd be a fool to believe that the death of a few corrupted archmages was enough to make a change. And then there was Irtan. Such an experienced player as him would rather act complacent than stir the pot and bring attention to himself. She'd noticed the smirk that passed over his lips at her remark of having time to do cleaning later. Irtan wasn't expecting her to stay in the Towers for that long. Even if he was genuinely interested in defending the city, she had to watch her back. Once Kaighal's safety was reassured, her own wouldn't be anymore.

Kamira rubbed her temples in a vain attempt to ease the tension in her head. Days of organizing former students and teachers of high magic made her regret once more that she didn't walk out of the High Towers the moment Yoreus fell. If only the demons weren't coming. If only she hadn't made the city vulnerable with her actions. If only she cared less about Kaighal and people who lived in it. But she didn't have only one friend and no obligations anymore, and she had to clean up her own mess. Even if it meant performing all the duties of the first archmage and dealing with people she'd rather avoid... Like the two men and a woman who were approaching her. She forced a courteous smile as they stopped in front of her.

Gildya members wore matching robes, as ornate as they were impractical, and in comparison, she must have looked underdressed. Still wearing one of her traveling outfits, she stood in the ruined initiation chamber like she didn't belong here, and to her brief amusement, the adepts looked around in search of someone else to address before they turned to her.

"First Archmage Kamira?" asked the one in front. His tone suggested he was hoping she'd deny it. "I'm Adept Ervan. We received your message."

She caught their curious glances at the pile of crushed crystal in the middle of the chamber and shattered dome above.

"I appreciate Gildya's response, adept." She knew better than to mention that Gildya had taken its time responding. "I hope together we can prepare for the upcoming threat."

"Indeed. The news we've received is quite disturbing," Ervan said. "The gossip of demon sightings in Kaighal in addition to the turmoil in the Towers... and now the supposed invasion."

Kamira's lip twitched in a constrained expression of disapproval. It would have been hard to miss the demons above the city during the past days, and questioning whether other demons were coming was nothing but an attempt to undermine her confidence or position. Her Tivarashan blood demanded she treated them as they deserved for such pettiness, but to indulge its call meant to stoop to their level. "I understand the balance between the High Towers and Gildya Magna was always overshadowed by a struggle for dominance," she offered with as much neutrality as she could, "but I don't believe this is the time to engage in games and squabbles. I'm sure Gildya already knows demons are very real, and can hardly question the possibility of an invasion when refugees from Devanshari gave us all the details of what happened to their kingdom."

Adept Ervan shifted uneasily, but kept a confident expression. "Archmage, adepts and high mages have always had a mutual understanding of... the limits of their influence. We've found ways to share the responsibility for the wellbeing of Kaighal's citizens and—"

"Then we can as mutually agree that petty politics can be left for later." Kamira gave him a cold stare, her patience wearing down fast. "Since the very wellbeing you mention is at stake. After a successful defense of Kaighal, we can discuss... influences for as long as Gildya wishes. Assuming that the adepts pull their weight in such efforts, of course."

Ervan offered an apologetic smile. "Your adamant stance puts us in a difficult position, first archmage. We understand that now might not be time for detailing new arrangements, but without any discussion, it seems that you want Gildya to submit to High Towers' orders. In the past, any crisis would be resolved by the highest members of both Gildya and Towers."

Kamira swallowed a word or two before the frustration got the better of her. After a slow, deep breath, she looked Ervan in the eye. "How much do you know of demons? Has Gildya studied them more extensively than I'm aware?" she asked calmly. "Do you know how to best kill them? How to keep them from entering the city?"

Ervan grimaced but didn't say a word.

"I understand Gildya's concerns, but let me assure you that any arrangements we agree on now will be temporary." It seemed that she had to convince the adepts she wasn't making a play at power, but at the same time, they chose what they wanted to believe, no matter what she said. "Arcanists are better suited to tackle demon-related aspects of the looming threat, and I believe that with our help, Gildya would be capable of creating devices that could protect Kaighal from intrusion, both physical and magical. Yet no arcanist, myself included, will be dictating your adepts how to proceed. We will provide suggestions for the workings of such devices and fine-quality imbued stones to power them, but the mechanical side of the construction would remain solely in Gildya's adepts' hands."

"That's... reasonable." Ervan's stiff body and voice said otherwise. "I'm sure we can discuss other arrangements after the invasion is stopped, but unfortunately, one requires your attention immediately."

"And that is?" If he was to bring up some political trivialities again, the next time she'd have him negotiate with Veranesh instead.

"We've been made aware that a felon took refuge in the Towers," Ervan replied. "The man called Alluvendran has recently escaped from our prison, and it would be a truly appreciated gesture of your goodwill, archmage, if you surrendered him into our custody."

She should have known. Koshmarnyk had warned her that although he was willing to help as much as he could, Gildya would likely fuss about his presence. "I could say no one by the name Alluvendran is here and that would be true, but I know the man you have in mind. Regretfully, the answer is no." She held her chin high. The whole Kaighal could be doomed, but she would not betray the man who was her ally... and more. Even if she had to compromise on many of her rules, loyalty was not one of them. "Not only will I not allow Gildya to impose any unlawful imprisonment on him, but I'll make it clear that should any underhanded actions be taken against him, there will be consequences."

Ervan's face reddened. "Alluvendran committed crimes against Gildya. It's only just that he pays for it. If word gets out that the first archmage of the Towers gives shelter to a law breaker—"

"Did he murder a fellow adept?" she said, cutting him off without mercy. "Did he steal from Gildya? Sabotage his colleague's works? Claim someone's invention as his own?" If Ervan thought she was unprepared for this discussion, he was wrong. Koshmarnyk had told her enough about what happened ten years earlier, and she had no reason to doubt his words.

"No." Ervan took a step back under the barrage of her questions. "He pursued forbidden research."

"Then I figure ten years of prison and expelling him from Gildya's ranks would be enough punishment for such a crime." Kamira arched her eyebrow. "Or does your council intend to keep him secretly confined forever?" She let the threat hidden in her words sink in. If Ervan was about to stir the waters, claiming she sheltered a felon, she would not hesitate to expose Gildya's unlawful practices in return. No one would like the idea that the council of adepts made people disappear without proper judgment.

All the adepts stirred, and Ervan lost his confidence. "I'll pass your words to our council, first archmage. I'm sure this matter can be resolved to everyone's satisfaction. Until then" —he met her eyes—"Gildya is ready to support the High Towers in all their efforts to defend Kaighal and will await the design details and the stones."

"I'll have them delivered to you shortly," she replied. "I hope that both adepts and arcanists will benefit from working together."

"I'm sure of it, first archmage."

He offered a slight bow before turning away, and Kamira responded with a courteous nod, but her attention was already on Varessa, who'd entered the chamber. The middle-aged woman passed the leaving adepts halfway but didn't stop to exchange courtesies, and Kamira smiled. The fourth archmage, though still hardly an arcanist, despite a rushed pact, was exactly the kind of person Kamira wanted to keep around.

"How did it go?" Varessa asked, her posture making it clear she was not fond of Gildya. Likely no high mage was.

"They reminded me why I was happy to leave the Towers in the first place," Kamira replied. "We have a demon invasion at hand, and they still wanted to engage in petty politics."

Varessa gave her a knowing look. "Yoreus and others got them used to it. One more reason I preferred to focus on teaching."

"I appreciate you still do," Kamira said. Even if Varessa wasn't exactly teaching anymore, without her it would be much more difficult to organize the students and the few teachers they had. "Do you know how they are doing so far?"

"Confused and lost, but I can't blame them. You've shattered all they knew about magic, and they're starting over. Some of the teachers who stayed adapted a bit quicker, but they need practice and can't pass on knowledge they haven't mastered themselves. The only ones worth anything at the moment are Archmage Tijhran and that girl Irtan taught. I wish Irtan could lend a hand too, but I understand he's tied up in setting up the defenses." Varessa let out a heavy sigh. "But that's a discussion for another time, and I came with a different matter." She glanced at the double door. "There are people waiting to see you."

"Can't you tell them to come another day?" The last thing Kamira wanted was to deal with another petty group like Ervan and his colleagues. "Or have someone else talk to them?"

Varessa's sigh might have been an unspoken apology, but her eyes remained unmoving, and Kamira could see that, despite all her caring for the students, the fourth archmage was likely a demanding teacher. "I think it's best if you receive them," Varessa said. "They wear noble outfits, and they come from your homeland."

~

PROVE ME WRONG, my son.

Jalyn clenched his fists. The queen's words echoed in his ears again as he climbed the stairs of the High Towers. People accompanying him exchanged glances, but all knew better than to mention anything, so their ascent was silent. Jalyn couldn't help cherishing it. He might have been insignificant back at his mother's court, but here, in Kaighal, his word mattered the most among the delegation sent from Tivarashan.

Three people wearing exquisite robes came from the opposite direction, and as they rushed down the relatively narrow stairwell, Jalyn indicated for his entourage to step aside, onto the balcony overlooking the chamber below. Back in Tivarashan, people would rather throw themselves over the railings than stand in his way, but the citizens of Kaighal, independent and wealthy, held no such sentiments for a man of a foreign look whom they couldn't recognize as royal blood. Demanding respect would not only be a waste of time but could earn him enemies in his already difficult mission.

"That Tivarashan gaharra..." one of them muttered in the passing, throwing a displeased glare at Jalyn and his companions.

The prince allowed himself a smirk. The three words he'd caught from a Kaighal commoner told him more of the new archmage than any detailed letter would, but then, he didn't expect anything else from a Tivarashan woman of a noble descent, especially one of the older houses. It meant she would be hard to manipulate, but when it came to playing games with his compatriots, Jalyn was confident he could emerge victorious.

As his group resumed their ascent, he entertained himself with guesses which of his sisters the only daughter of Lord Altrainne was like. Brusque and abrupt like Mefina, a warrior ready to fight everyone and everything, or sly and evasive like Hyuleen, cunning with her words and avoiding honesty as if it could stain her honor.

They stopped by massive double doors at the top of the stairwell. No man stood guard in front of them, and no doorkeeper waited to announce their arrival, though the mage who sent them on their way had reassured them that a message was sent upstairs to let the archmage know. Jalyn hesitated. Lacking the knowledge of the Towers' protocol meant the risk of insulting the one they wished to appease, but waiting could result in the same. He regretted not taking time in the city to learn more about how things worked in the Towers, but if he wanted the advantage of leaving the archmage no time to prepare, he couldn't have risked that someone would let her know a Tivarashan prince was in Kaighal, asking questions. He hid his reaction from his entourage as his own mistake dawned on him: he was so steeped in the ways of Tivarashan court, he'd failed to consider that things in Kaighal could be much different.

A middle-aged woman in a teacher's robes stepped out. "The first archmage will receive you." She gestured toward the half-closed door and left without any parting words or courtesies.

"Such impertinence!" Priestess Bayena huffed, though Jalyn would bet her gray face wasn't darkened from rage but the strain of their climb. Bayena might look healthy and young, but servants of the Four rarely had to exert themselves in such ways. "This city needs to be reminded of how civilized people act."

"Kaighal is not under Tivarashan rule and has no reason to love Tivarashan royalty." Jalyn couldn't help his ire that he had to remind her of such a simple truth. At the same time, he understood all the better why his mother had chosen him for the mission, regardless of whether he was expendable. He was so used to lack of respect back home, he wasn't about to lose control over such a minor insult. "That's why we're here. To warm the relationship," he added, hoping that Bayena would take the hint and behave accordingly.

The priestess's narrow lips twisted, but she resumed control over her manners. "We should be here to accept their subjection."

"Now that didn't work too well in the past, did it?"

Jalyn didn't wait for her response and headed for the crack in the door, thankfully wide enough for him to go through without having to open them himself. Bayena could argue all she wanted, but Kaighal had held off three sieges in the past, from both Tivarashan forces and the Western Kingdom's armies. The combined power of the high mages and Gildya adepts, along with Kaighal citizens' determination, had proven enough to ensure Kaighal remained an independent port. If there was a way to annex the city to Tivarashan, it wasn't by the means of war, of that Jalyn was sure.

They entered a round chamber, supported by columns and crowned with a mostly shattered crystal dome. The room was empty, save crystal rubble across its floor and a table by the wall, where a lone woman stood. Her simple traveling outfit suggested one of the arcanists who were said to have recently arrived in the Towers, and Jalyn took a step forward, hoping she'd direct him to the archmage's reception area.

She turned, and her black eyes, set in a gaunt, gray face, inspected him with intensity he didn't expect.

The Four's blessing! She's the archmage? He froze, as confused as the rest of his entourage, but was quick to regain his composure. The woman in front of him resembled neither of his older sisters. No smug expression, no elaborate makeup that would conceal her reactions, and no expensive dress that would make her status clear—just dark circles under her eyes speaking of lost sleep and hard work.

"I'm Prince Jalyn of Queen Andalisha's blood." Jalyn offered a slight bow, but the woman didn't reciprocate the gesture as she should. His mother had been right about not sending Hyuleen. He was so used to dismissive treatment back at home, he could swallow an open affront... his sister wouldn't. "Lady Altrainne, it's an honor and pleasure to meet you," he added to make it clear that he'd chosen to ignore her lack of courtesy.

"In Kaighal, my title is the first archmage, prince," she replied, her voice carrying no warmth. At least she didn't sound hostile. "The noble title, to which I'm not sure I'm still entitled to, has no meaning here."

Before Jalyn could stop her, Bayena stepped forward with a stern face. "Title or not, a woman of fine Tivarashan descent should know how to carry herself in the presence of Her Majesty's blood." Her voice vibrated with anger.

The archmage gave her a calm look, and nothing in her posture suggested the outburst bothered her. "As soon as I cross the border, I'll be sure to express all due respects, priestess. But this is Kaighal, and a noble title is worth only as much as the coin its owner spends. To merchants and tavern keepers, all generous patrons are lord and ladies."

Jalyn arched his eyebrow at her response. Had he chosen to take offense, he could demand she be punished or exiled, so she'd risked a lot on the assumption the Tivarashan delegation wanted to negotiate. Unless... He kept his face straight as a new thought struck him: she didn't care. From what little information Jalyn had, Kamira Altrainne had spent years away from Tivarashan and maybe didn't intend to come back at all. They held no power over her in Kaighal, and if they threatened consequences back in Tivarashan, she'd likely laugh at them and send them away. His mission would fail before he even started it.

With that in mind, he put a hand on the priestess's shoulder before she barked a response that would become their ruin. "You must forgive our brash behavior, first archmage." He hoped that using Lady Kamira's chosen title would reassure her that he was willing to play by Kaighal's rules... by *her* rules. "We should have known better than come in here shortly after our arrival, with the journey's strain dictating our words." He looked at Bayena. "Priestess, if you'd be so kind and see to our people's accommodation, I'd appreciate it. We could all use a good rest now that we've paid our respects."

"If I may be so bold to recommend a place, I'd suggest the Spinning Maiden," the first archmage said in *almost* courteous manner. "Their rooms should suffice for the needs of the royal entourage."

"Thank you," Jalyn replied politely, but when he looked back at Bayena, his voice was cold. "Can I trust it to be done?"

Bayena bowed. "Of course, my prince," she said through

a clenched jaw. "If you wish to wait here, I'll send a servant with a message once we've found appropriate lodgings."

Her eyes barely skimmed the first archmage's face as she left, and Jalyn gestured at the rest of his companions. "Go with her." To his relief, no one dared object, and soon he stood in the chamber alone with the first archmage.

Amusement flickered in her eyes. "The Four's priestess running a servant's errand. Quite an unexpected sight."

Her voice had lost the cold edge, giving him hope that he could turn that near-defeat into a victory... or at least a draw.

"I'm sure I'll suffer the consequences later," he replied in a lighthearted tone, though they both knew he spoke the truth. The Four's priests enjoyed privileges that even the royal family didn't dare to challenge. "Although to Priestess Bayena's dismay, by my mother's order, I'm the one in charge."

The first archmage made an inviting gesture then poured wine while he approached the table. "The queen has heard the news of the Towers' fall and saw opportunity to gain influence in Kaighal?" she asked. "It's been merely a week or so since the... changes."

His outfit must have been a clear giveaway that he and his people had traveled at the fastest pace possible, and she should have expected Tivarashan would not be idle in the light of what happened, so he ignored the last remark. "We've heard the city is to be invaded." He accepted the cup. Like everything around the archmage, it had a practical shape and was made of wood instead of crystal or precious metal. "My mother is ready to offer help."

"I don't doubt she is. But Kaighal has been independent for centuries, and we aren't quick to accept foreign rule." She dipped her lips in her wine in that particular way

Tivarashan women did when they were carefully playing their game, yet it might have been a game itself, steering him to believe that she was like her compatriots. "If anyone in the royal court is under the impression that my ancestry constitutes Tivarashan influence in Kaighal, they're wrong."

It didn't escape Jalyn how she used the word "we," making it clear that Lady Kamira Altrainne considered herself a Kaighal citizen, not a Tivarashan noblewoman—but he still could use the pride that came with her heritage.

"If anything, first archmage, your ancestry would make it more difficult to negotiate," he offered with a hint of amusement. "Tivarashan women are known for their adamant attitude."

She nodded at his veiled stab. "Let me adamantly state it, then, Prince Jalyn. As much as the High Towers appreciate the Tivarashan offer, Kaighal will deal with its problems without foreign help."

"Surely there is some room for negotiations." Jalyn took a sip of his wine, never letting his eyes off the archmage. The sweet taste of the surprisingly fine vintage teased his tongue. "Agreements to be made that will satisfy both sides while Kaighal's status would hardly change." He took a step forward. "I don't have to say that a woman with noble blood and the title of Kaighal's first archmage could achieve a lot in Tivarashan."

He did not expect she would burst out laughing at that, especially not in a way that indicated genuine amusement rather than mockery.

"I haven't visited my homeland in quite a while," she said when her laughter died away, "but it's a relief to learn things haven't changed much there. Go home, prince. Your talents will only go to waste here. I'm not interested in politics, neither here nor in Tivarashan, and I won't submit

Kaighal to your mother's rule, not even in the slightest of ways."

All he could do was take another sip of wine while he frantically searched for an explanation. She'd clearly fought for the first archmage position, and if the destroyed chamber was any indication of her efforts, she'd risked her life for it—nearly bringing the Towers down in the process, as the gossip had it. Why would she then not want to reach further than governing a single port, forced to share her influence with Gildya and the city council?

"Your Tivarashan blood speaks through your words, first archmage." He put the cup down. "Adamant and unwavering... You can say whatever you want, but you can't pretend you aren't one of us. I'm sure we're going to have many interesting conversations that will eventually lead to an agreeable conclusion."

She sighed and shook her head. "Kaighal is soon to be besieged, prince. I can't guarantee your entourage's safety."

"I know the risk. I'll stay," he replied. "And should it come to the worst, Priestess Bayena can send a request for help."

"I will not ask for Tivarashan's help."

"And I will not leave." To return home without Kaighal in hand would be the end of his dreams. He weaved that sadness into his next words: "We're both bound by our duties, aren't we?"

Her face softened, and for the first time since entering the chamber, Jalyn felt he'd made progress.

"Please, call me Kamira when there's no one around to frown at it," she said with a sincerity that made him doubt her previous behavior. "I can't force you to leave, prince, and to my regret, you seem more levelheaded than your royal sisters, if what I've heard about them is true."

Jalyn's eyes widened, then he laughed. Of course—she must have expected Tivarashan would make a move and had prepared herself for the arrival of Queen Andalisha's envoy. The only thing she couldn't have predicted was that Jalyn would keep his composure. He shook his head in disbelief, because Archmage Kamira had played him, though not to the end he'd thought she would. "This whole reception was meant as an insult. You wanted to make us leave, enraged."

"I do not want to see my compatriots die in a war that is not theirs," she replied.

"Die?" He searched her face for clues. "You expect Kaighal to fall, don't you?"

"I'll do everything I can to defend it. But Kaighal is not ready for such a siege, likely even less than the kingdom of Devanshari was."

Grim understanding dawned on him. Even if in the darkest moment Kamira caved and asked for help, Tivarashan forces would likely arrive too late. Besides, Tivarashan soldiers weren't equipped to deal with demons, since, with the protection of the Four, they'd never had to even consider such threats. Jalyn couldn't help wondering whether his mother cared about the state of the would-be annexed Kaighal to begin with. The army protected by the Four could force other demons to retreat, but if they ravaged the city before leaving, Queen Andalisha would laugh it off and order the rebuilding of the port... this time to be more Tivarashan-like.

Kamira must have caught his reaction. "That's not your concern, prince. If you insist on staying, I hope your time in Kaighal will be as pleasant as possible, considering the circumstances."

"I appreciate it... Kamira." He offered a bow. "May I be

hopeful that the first archmage will grant me another audience?"

Her lips curled in a smile. She didn't miss how he balanced flattery with playfulness. "There are no audiences here. Everyone comes and goes as they see fit, and I do my best to ensure they receive answers they seek." She rubbed her temples, and he could swear it wasn't a calculated gesture. Perhaps, after the private conversation, she'd opened up a little. "I hope that soon other archmages will take some of the meetings upon themselves, but I'll try to find time for you, prince."

"Jalyn," he said. "My title is not worth much even back in Tivarashan, so there's no need to burden a casual conversation with it."

Surprise flashed on her face, but she nodded, and that was all Jalyn needed. "As you wish."

He hid his satisfaction. He would cherish his small victory later. The two of them, bonding over mutual contempt for politics and etiquette... It seemed like a good start, and that connection gave him hope that, in the end, he would succeed.

The woman in a teacher's robes he'd seen before entered the chamber and headed straight for the table. "Looks like it's nobility day. The Devanshari have just arrived. What did the Northerners want?" She looked at Jalyn, and only then did she recognize him, but she didn't lose her confidence. "Still here?"

"Prince Jalyn is waiting for his companions to find suitable lodgings in Kaighal," Kamira said.

The teacher looked him up and down. "In that case, let me find you some more comfortable place to wait... prince."

She gestured toward the door, and Jalyn had no doubt that his meeting with the first archmage had concluded, no matter what protests he could conjure. He offered a quick bow and rushed after his guide.

On his way out, Jalyn passed a young man, not even in his twenties yet. His fair skin revealed Devanshari origin, and he wore simple clothes. Yet a gold circlet rested on his blond hair, and Jalyn caught a glimpse of a royal crest on the chain resting on the newcomer's chest. *A messenger from the Devanshari queen?*

"Your Majesty, it's a pleasure to meet you again! I'm glad you found time for me," Kamira said.

"It's the least I could do in return for the help you've given us, First Archmage Kamira," the Devanshari replied.

Jalyn looked over his shoulder at the sound of Kamira's warm tone, so different from the one she'd greeted his entourage with, while he pondered the title she'd used to address the man. It seemed that the Devanshari were led by a king, not a queen... When Kamira offered a courtly bow to the man, frustration stabbed Jalyn. She bent her head for a man with no kingdom, a throneless refugee, but refused the same courtesy to the royal blood of her own land.

The taste of the earlier victory vanished, and as Jalyn left the chamber, he couldn't help thinking that, in the end, he hadn't achieved anything during the meeting.

IF THERE WEREN'T MORE PRESSING matters, Kamira would be sure to express her gratitude to Varessa for taking Prince Jalyn away. His gray face and black eyes, and more so his words, reminded her of everything about Tivarashan she would rather forget, and even though some of his replies rang with sincerity, the presence of the Four's priestess and his royal blood made it clear that Tivarashan was ready to make a move on Kaighal. Not that she hadn't expected it, but her plans she didn't take into account that the queen would send someone resilient instead of one of her hotheaded, proud, and ambitious daughters. She gritted her teeth. Just what she needed right now—more politics! Any Tivarashan woman of notable stature would have taken offense to everything that she experienced, from a ruined chamber inappropriate for receiving royalty and nobility to Kamira's deliberately discourteous behavior, but the stubborn prince endured it all.

She forced herself to respond to King Allyv's greeting and offered a bow, both out of courtesy and to conceal the frustration that still tainted her thoughts.

"The news you mentioned in your letter bothered me greatly," King Allyv said. "I dread to think we've brought danger upon Kaighal."

Kamira shook her head. "The demons came for other reasons, and I'll do my best to ensure no one here blames the Devanshari. I was also hoping your people could lend a hand in preparations and share their experience with us, but if you wish to leave before the siege, I understand."

"Citizens of Kaighal welcomed us and offered us a new beginning. We won't turn our backs on them." Allyv's eyes dimmed, as if he was reliving a memory. "Maybe we shouldn't have run from our homeland in the first place."

"By retreating, you ensured your people's survival, and maybe one day you'll be the one to reclaim your lands," she said. If only there was a way to know whether the demons had fully abandoned the kingdom of Devanshari. His people could return home and start rebuilding instead of fighting all over again, this time in foreign lands.

Allyv gave her a bitter smile. "It's a beautiful sentiment, but at the moment we struggle to even survive. Our addiction makes us pay more and more with each passing day."

The Tivarashan in her demanded she remained silent, because no one made better cannon fodder than people with nothing to lose who were on brink of death already, but she would not allow the recent meeting with Prince Jalyn to influence her mindset. She still remembered how, back in the asylum, Allyv greeted her with courtesy while others had only hate for her. "I might be able to remedy that."

His eyes lit up, but the expression on his face suggested he wasn't ready to allow himself hope. "Do you know how to cure it?"

"I'm afraid not," she replied. If the cure was the only thing he was after, he was chasing a dream. "But I do have a way to sate your people's hunger. As generations pass, time itself might become the cure. You'll never be free of your addiction, but your children and their children might be." She pointed at the crystal rubble in the chamber. "These pieces are more powerful than any imbued stones you know. If your people were to carry even a small shard close to their skin, they should emanate enough magic to keep hunger away."

His eyes fixed on the crystal, and the very hunger she'd mentioned flashed in his eyes. He must have sensed the power, even from a distance, and when she made an inviting gesture, he rushed over to the rubble.

"They're truly powerful." When Allyv stood up, only his eyes betrayed his longing. "I'm afraid we have very little to offer in exchange. Most Devanshari lost their wealth already in vain pursuits of alleviating the hunger, and others weren't rich to begin with."

Kamira joined him at the rubble and picked up a shard. "You misunderstood me, Your Majesty. This is going to be a gift." She put the crystal in his hand before he could move away or object. "To all of the Devanshari who need it. More so, Adept Koshmarnyk offered to blend the stones with the owners' bodies, should they fear losing their shards. Be warned, though, that Gildya frowns upon such practices, and as much as I can vouch for the safety of the process and stand in defense of anyone who pursues it, the adepts will condemn it." Once Koshmarnyk was done with his blueprint, he'd have enough time to see to blending the stones.

Allyv stared at the shard in his hand, and Kamira didn't have much trouble envisioning the storm that went through his head. She didn't press for an answer, though if some Devanshari decided to proceed, it would help to hush Gildya's complaints about Koshmarnyk. They couldn't persecute a whole nation just to get to one man.

A shadow crossed over the chamber, and Allyv's eyes widened as the huge, winged creature descended through the shattered dome. He gestured as if he was ready to run or call for help... Perhaps his guards had accompanied him all the way to the chamber and he left them outside to have a private conversation.

"It's fine, Your Majesty. He's an ally," Kamira said, though with little hope to dispel the horror of Allyv's memories, probably still as vivid as on the day his kingdom fell. Instead of more reassurances, she excused herself and rushed to Fyertash as soon as he landed. "Any news?" If there was nothing demanding her attention, the demon could wait above the chamber until Allyv departed.

Fyertash shook his head. "They're not to the northeast, but I expected that much. They're more likely to land south, in the desert." Even with his wings folded, he still towered over her.

Allyv took a step forward, his eyes fixed on the demon. His hands were both curled into fists and shaking, as if he found courage in anger. "I've seen you before."

The way he said it made it clear he didn't mean recently, and Kamira drew a sharp breath. Wrapped up in the preparation for the siege, she'd never bothered to consider Fyertash's position among his kin. Even though Uganel, before Veranesh destroyed him, had revealed Fyertash as one of the demonic conspirators, her own demon seemed to trust him enough. Not once had she stopped to consider that some of the Devanshari could recognize him from the siege.

Fyertash looked down at Allyv, unmoved. "You're the queen's child from the overseas kingdom," he said, and looked at Kamira. "Get rid of his people. They had a traitor among their own who allowed us the victory."

"You were there!" Allyv trembled. "You slaughtered innocent people!"

To Kamira's relief, Fyertash didn't react to the open display of aggression, though his cold demeanor wasn't helping either.

"I was there to ensure a task done," he replied. "Had you destroyed the artifact as we demanded, no blood would have been spilled."

"So you say." Allyv's face expressed only anger.

"Fyertash brought us the warning, Your Majesty," Kamira said. "Without him, Kaighal would have no time for preparations and would fall. But if you and your people wish to leave, I understand. My offer of the stones remains unchanged, and I could also draft a letter to some Tivarashan nobles, asking them to offer you shelter."

Allyv didn't reply, exchanging glares with Fyertash.

"It's better if they leave," the demon remarked. "Or

Myrkan will reach out to the traitor again, and the defenses will be at risk."

The king tensed. He was ready to defend his people or throw more accusations, so Kamira threw him a warning glare. No matter how much he might have hated Fyertash, they both were her guests in the Towers. "There's no need for concern. From the little that I know, the traitor is dead. Of course, that doesn't mean Myrkan won't seek out another one, maybe even someone from the Towers. There are always people who'll fall for the promise of power, and I won't refuse refuge to everyone simply because one of them did."

Fyertash arched his eyebrow. "You know who the traitor was? Myrkan didn't tell us."

Allyv looked at her with desperation. "Please, first archmage. If this is true, you need to tell me where you learned about it."

Kamira pressed her lips together tightly. With the situation as tense as it was, it seemed foolish to even try convincing the new king that his own mother was the reason his people suffered so much. Not to mention that if she told him, it could lead to admitting her own involvement in Cahala's death. "I know little, Your Majesty, and it's not my story to tell. I believe Ryell qi'Teshari might know more."

He stiffened. "Nobody has seen Ryell since"—he glared at Fyertash with poorly concealed hatred—"since the turmoil in the Towers. Considering his ties to the former first archmage, I can't help wondering if he's still alive."

The challenge in his voice made Kamira narrow her eyes. She hadn't expected the Devanshari king to be less composed than a spoiled Tivarashan prince, but then, Jalyn didn't have to face a nightmare from his not-so-distant past.

"Last time I saw Ryell was before Veranesh and Fyertash arrived at the Towers," she said coldly. "Yoreus's daughter, Atissa, did not return to the Towers after the events, and I wouldn't be surprised if he left with her," she added with more confidence than she felt. The last time they met, she had offered Ryell a solution to his hunger, so he didn't have to keep around a magic-less woman whose father manipulated him, but if not with Atissa, Kamira had no idea where he could be. It seemed that revenge had been fueling him ever since he arrived in Kaighal, and once he got it... he might have had no other goal in life. At the same time, she couldn't suggest that Allyv's people looked for Ryell in Kaighal's many taverns.

Allyv remained silent, as if considering the information. "I wasn't aware Atissa was an archmage's daughter. Perhaps I owe you an apology, first archmage." His voice remained cold, but it had lost its hostile edge. He looked down at the shard in his hand. "Do you mind if I take a few more? There are many in the asylum who suffer more than I do."

A gentle smile couldn't hurt, so she offered it. "Take as many as you need, Your Majesty. And don't hesitate to ask for more. The small shards will be useless to Gildya, but should be more than enough to ease your people's pain. It's the least I can do in gratitude for your patience and understanding."

He shifted, avoiding looking at Fyertash again. "I'll pass the message to my people. They won't be happy with the news of a demon nearby, but some might join the defense."

"Thank you, Your Majesty." She bowed slightly.

Allyv grunted something that, with a dose of goodwill, could have been taken as acknowledgment and left.

Fyertash watched after him until Allyv was out of the

chamber. "Are you sure the traitor is dead? If Myrkan gets a hold of her again..."

She glared at the demon. If Myrkan could manipulate humans and make them do his bidding, it didn't matter whether one traitor lived or not. "I watched her die. Is that good enough for you?"

To her surprise, Fyertash's long face stretched in a grin. "So that's why you wouldn't say much to that child king. Cunning, pactee, very cunning." He leaned forward. "No wonder Veranesh decided to keep you around." Without warning, he squatted, dropping to her eye level. "But cunning pactees are often tempted to play their own games toward their own ends. Are you playing against Veranesh, pactee?"

She scoffed, keeping her composure, though her instincts demanded she move away from the demon. As much as Veranesh's presence tugged at her primal fears, it was bearable due to their mutual agreements, while being so close to another demon screamed of hidden dangers. She looked Fyertash in the eye. "Maybe I should ask you the same. I was there, by Veranesh's side and doing his bidding while Uganel revealed *you* as one of his allies."

A wave of warm air hit Kamira as Fyertash burst out laughing. "Pactee, I'll certainly enjoy your presence for as long as Veranesh keeps you around."

He stretched his wings abruptly, making Kamira take a step back, and launched into the air. Soon, he was sitting perched at the crushed edge's dome, a place she suspected to be his favorite. The stare the demon gave her, both evaluating and calculating, woke her instincts, and she hesitated before turning her back to him. Fyertash was bound to stir trouble.

8

Being an archmage meant Kamira couldn't go back to living at the Jagged Swordsman. As little as she cared for meaningless traditions, she hadn't objected when Irtan insisted she live in the Towers. In the inn, everything would remind her of the simpler life she had enjoyed—thus, also of Veelk. No matter how much she tried to chase the thoughts of her friend away, throwing herself into the whirlwind of countless problems to solve, the images of his smirks and grins plagued her nonetheless. Every now and then, she was ready to abandon Kaighal to its fate and set out on a weeks-long journey to find him, but duty demanded she stayed. It was her fault that the city was in disarray, and she couldn't leave it at the mercy of its many enemies to satisfy her own selfish need for knowledge. Veelk either was already dead, and her presence wouldn't change anything, or he was alive and maybe already making his way back to Kaighal. The comfort of this realization lasted but a heartbeat when another thought plagued her: Veelk could also be dying, clinging to life only in the hope that she would make it there in time.

She huffed. Her own mind was her worst enemy, and it didn't matter whether she was staying at the Jagged Swordsman or not. Nevertheless, she couldn't return to the inn. The idea of receiving the Tivarashan delegation, or even Gildya representatives, in a comfortable but small room was a ridiculous one, and no matter how much she'd rather change how things were done around the Towers, the first archmage had to evoke respect and authority with her presence. An inn's room was not a place she could achieve that. In the Towers, even the burn marks and crystal rubble in the initiation chamber served to reinforce her image as a powerful woman who wasn't afraid to get what she desired. Nobody had to know that her desires were quite different from what she had now.

Irtan suggested she move into his quarters, a courtesy that—as she'd been told—he didn't offer to Yoreus, but she hated the thought of forcing the old man out of his longtime lodgings. She also loathed the thought of taking the former second archmage's chambers. She didn't want to be seen as his successor. If something was to improve in the Towers, she couldn't let people believe the only things that had changed were the name of the first archmage and the kind of magic practiced.

In the end, reluctantly, she took Archmage Loktra's quarters. With the departure of many of the Towers' former students and teachers, there were many empty rooms, but Kamira had neither time nor desire to search for something suitable and then have it furnished. The former archmage's chambers already had everything she needed, and as soon as the students carried out all Loktra's personal belongings, Kamira could move in. Koshmarnyk, of course, declined Irtan's offer to have his own lodgings, and she couldn't help smiling at that. Like her, he needed little—a bed, a table, and a chest to store his meager possessions. And there was also the unspoken promise in it, that he was willing to share more of his life with her.

The thought that at the end of the day she could find solace in his embrace helped her carry on through the days, instead of succumbing to dark thoughts.

When she entered her chambers, Koshmarnyk was sitting by the table, sorting through papers and taking notes. She sent him a tired smile. He was working as hard as she was, and without his help, she would have to resort to trying to summon a barrier that could envelop the whole city—a feat that Veranesh's power would undoubtedly allow, but hardly a solution if Kaighal's protection relied on her being able to stay awake for days, if not more.

"I've heard you had quite a day," Koshmarnyk said. At her inquisitive stare, he added, "Students gossip, and you might be their favorite topic." He pointed at the empty plate. "One of them brought me food at midday and lingered for a while, sharing news, though I do suspect he was trying to find anything new to gossip about. Like you, or us."

The playfulness in his last words suggested he didn't mind being on other people's tongues. "Or the demons," she added. "I ordered most teachers and all the students to stay away from the initiation rite chamber. I'd rather not test Veranesh's patience by having crowds of former high mages gawk at him."

"Perhaps you could put Fyertash on display, then," Koshmarnyk offered.

She chuckled. "I'd rather not test him either."

Koshmarnyk nodded. "There's something sly about him. He seems friendlier than Veranesh, but I can't shake the feeling it's only meant to put us at ease. Do you think him and that old archmage, Irtan, are playing some game?"

"Irtan's been playing games long since before I was even born, but I don't think he'd sacrifice the city... or his own position. He'll help for as long as there is a threat to Kaighal. After that..." She shrugged. After that, if Veelk hadn't returned, she would be leaving anyway, and she had no illusion that Irtan would be more likely to take power for himself again than preserve her seat. "The first archmage isn't a position in which you make friends."

"And that's why you didn't agree to Gildya's demands?" he asked. "To uphold appearances by making more enemies?"

Kamira looked at him, startled. She'd quickly gathered that the student who brought him the meal must have blabbered about it too, but the casual way he was discussing the possibility of her turning him over to Gildya unsettled her. She already felt like she was sacrificing everything she believed in by accepting the archmage's position and agreeing to engage in political games with both Gildya and Tivarashan.

Her thoughts must have shown on her face, because Koshmarnyk stood up and offered his embrace. "If I knew they were coming, I'd tell you myself to give me up," he said. "It would make the adepts more agreeable, and I could handle them."

They sat on the bed, and though she enjoyed leaning against his side, with his arm around her shoulders, her thoughts were focused on problems, not on the comfort his presence offered.

"It would only make them think that they can make even more demands. Things in Gildya have to change too, and I will not let them think that they can imprison you again, regardless of whether they'd actually succeed or not. Besides, I know you prefer to avoid pointless bloodshed."

"If that's what it'd take to show the council they can't have their way, I won't hesitate," he replied. "Otherwise they will just think I'm hiding under your protection and plot behind your back."

She refrained from reminding him that Gildya would plot either way. The subtle balance of power between them and the high mages, with both sides attempting to tip the scales in their direction, meant endless games and plots beneath the surface of amiable cooperation for the good of Kaighal. "I think that if you want to confront them, you should be in a position of power and free, not their prisoner who's fighting against their rules."

He frowned. "That's not going to happen, unless you plan on bringing Gildya down next."

"Tempting," she replied playfully. "But I had something else in mind, if you agree."

That got his attention. He let her go and indicated for her to continue.

"I was thinking of making you my... representative to Gildya. I understand little of how adepts work and how they create their devices, and I should focus on the arcane part of the protection anyway. With your knowledge and insights, you're the perfect person to talk to them."

"And the worst person too," Koshmarnyk said. "You're risking a lot hoping that they will listen. If they won't, there might be a bloodbath after all, and no matter how annoying Gildya's games are, Kaighal needs adepts' skills."

Kamira thought about it, but she knew he wouldn't go about killing every single member of the Gildya. For a man putting a lot of time into his martial prowess, he was surprisingly peaceful in his ways. She could only guess that his past had made that choice for him, but he didn't talk about it much. She knew he used to serve in the Western

Kingdom's army, so training was a part of his life. And the betrayal he'd suffered at Gildya's hands must have made him determined to fight back. Still, he never came across as someone who reveled in mindless slaughter.

"The ones who weren't determined enough to claw their way to the top are usually less... argumentative," she said. "They're also more inclined to do actual work instead of engaging in petty games. If the council decides their pride and old ways are more important than anything else, we'll discuss the defense of Kaighal with those that are left once you're... done." Even with all his resolve to find peaceful solutions, she had no doubt Koshmarnyk would show no mercy to whomever threatened him.

"Or dead."

"I'd rather not see you die a heroic death," she used his own words. A memory of their time in the cave flashed in her head, a reminder of what seemed another lifetime. "If you can think of another way, I won't insist. Perhaps you could sway a few adepts to come work in the Towers, and we'll deal with Gildya some other time."

"No, I'll go. You're right. If I want them to stop going after me, I have to show them I'm not afraid to stand against them." He brushed her forearm. Magic within her scars stirred upon his touch. "This way I can ensure you'll be safe too, should adepts learn secrets not meant for them."

"And maybe things will really change in Kaighal." She let that sentiment linger, bringing comfort.

～

Though Jalyn wouldn't admit it out loud, he appreciated that Priestess Bayena waited for servants to leave before she spoke. Even if they likely didn't miss the black fire burning in her eyes, at least they would not witness the confrontation... or rather, the humiliation that he was about to suffer.

"I believe I deserve an explanation, *my prince*." The last two words sounded like mockery in her mouth, as if a mere male child of the queen was worth less respect than the elevated servant of the Four. "To allow some overambitious noble insult us in front of everyone and then you punish me with a maid's task..."

Jalyn endured her glare—it was nothing in comparison to the way his own mother looked at him when he disappointed her. Bayena, a woman in her late twenties, who cared for her grooming a little too much, might have had all the power and respect as a priestess of the Four, but as long as they stayed in Kaighal, Jalyn remained in charge. Another reason to not leave the city until he had no other choice.

He took his time watching Bayena in silence. The corners of her eyes trembled in barely suppressed anger. Of course, once they came back to Tivarashan, the vengeful woman would pay him back for every single insult, unless he returned victorious. At the same time, with the siege about to close around the city and the risk of the demons' victory, Jalyn might never see his home again. After all, that was why the queen had chosen him for the mission in the first place. As grim as such a prospect was, it also meant he didn't have to hold back.

"I wouldn't have to send you away if you knew when to keep your mouth shut," he said, imitating the cold voice Hyuleen often used, and the sense of power rushed through his veins. "We're not here to prove our superiority to the archmage. We're here to make Kaighal part of Tivarashan. If I have to listen to the archmage's insults for the next month to make it happen, I will." He looked her in the eye. "And so will you."

The downward curve of her lips was the only sign of her emotions. "You're pathetic, prince. Your sister would have this outrageous woman begging for mercy within moments of walking into the chamber."

He almost grinned at her pitiful attempt at throwing him off balance. She couldn't have truly believed that it would have worked after he'd endured the archmage's calculated insults. "Hyuleen would fall for the same trap you did, priestess. Demanding respect and threatening consequences, likely exile." He snorted when the image of all of Kamira's possible reactions came to mind, none even close to begging. "Did you see the archmage's clothes? Did she wear any jewelry, including her family crest? Did she have a row of servants ready to guess her every wish?"

With each question, he took a step forward toward Bayena. He'd seen Mefina do it with some of the rowdier captains, and such a combination of questions and physical intimidation worked well for her. The priestess's flinch suggested that Jalyn had succeeded as well.

"She doesn't care about our homeland," he added. "She might be Tivarashan by birth, but she's of Kaighal by heart. So if we want Kaighal, we need to appeal to that heart, not to her ancestry. Do you think you can do it, or should I ask Her Majesty, my mother, for a replacement?"

Bayena watched him with narrowed eyes and a stiff face that suggested she'd taken affront, but then a sly smile stretched her lips. "Replacing me is the last thing you should want, my prince, if appeasing the archmage is your plan."

No matter how vulnerable her pride might have been, he had to give it to her that she thought of solutions as new information arrived. "You're right. I don't." While Bayena would continue to act in the way the archmage must have expected from a Tivarashan woman, her demanding and unyielding behavior would contrast with Jalyn's willingness to compromise. In no time, the archmage would be drawn to him, perhaps ready to commiserate and confide.

Yet he couldn't forget how Kamira greeted the Devanshari envoy: as someone who deserved a bow and manner of address that was the privilege of kings and queens. For all Jalyn knew, the path he was choosing was the one the archmage herself had prepared for him, with carefully picked words and behavior making him believe that this was the way to gain her trust. At the same time, he could use her game to his own advantage. Keeping Bayena around and pretending he'd fallen for the trap she'd set up would give him more freedom to act. As his own mother had said, convince the archmage she had the upper hand and win Kaighal... *No,* he corrected himself, *if I play it right, I could win much more than an unruly port.*

"Her Majesty, your mother would be proud, my prince." Bayena gave him a nod of approval, and anger faded from her voice. "She made the right choice sending you on this mission. Even Princess Hyuleen couldn't have done better."

He acknowledged the compliment, likely empty words anyway, but he was still focused on the archmage. The information they had about Lady Kamira Altrainne hadn't proven useful at all, and he couldn't help questioning the skill of his mother's spies. A nobleman's daughter, educated and dutiful, one day left to study in the High Towers in Kaighal. He considered such a step to be a cunning one: make magic available to her family without the obligations and ties the priesthood brought while building much-coveted connections in Tyorane's biggest port. Yet, contrary to expectations, she returned home only for a brief visit, as an arcanist. Little gossip circled about that event, each piece less plausible than the previous one. The court considered news of Kamira Altrainne refusing a gainful union with another noble house absurd, and the whisper of her father publicly threatening to disown her to be insanity. Yet it was Kamira Altrainne's cousin who'd married Lansar of the Wynarians, giving credibility to the gossip and speculation. People at court suspected that after making young Gyera Altrainne replace her in a beneficial but not ambitious marriage, Kamira Altrainne had set her eyes on a bigger prize. Some speculated about a path to priesthood, with her eyes on the Temple's highest positions, since she was already trained in the arcane arts, while others made lists of eligible bachelors among the most powerful families she might have been trying to lure in with her power and position.

"We need to know more," he said. "Whoever gathered information about the archmage for my mother failed miserably and almost cost us everything. We need answers. How and why she became an arcanist? Is the tribal warrior who supposedly accompanied her in the past important? Who are her allies? What was she doing before she claimed power in the Towers? Where did she travel?"

"I'll sent people to gather gossip," Bayena replied.

"No. We need more than gossip and speculation. Pay what you must, but get us the truth."

Bayena bowed.

"One more thing. When I was leaving, she had another guest. A young man from Devanshari kingdom... their king." He had no certainty about it, but this should get Bayena's attention.

The priestess stared at him, confused. "But the

Devanshari refugees are led by a queen. Cahala qi'Devanshari, as I recall." Under his unwavering glare, she nodded. "I'll find out about this too."

"Very well." Jalyn waved her off, and to his surprise, the priestess left without a word of protest. Perhaps the day was not as wasted as he had initially thought, and although he was not where he'd intended, he had won a small victory after all.

He sat on a cushioned chair by the window, comfortable but meager in comparison to what the royal palace offered. While his eyes traveled aimlessly along the walls and furniture of the supposedly most expensive room in the Spinning Maiden, or perhaps even in all of Kaighal, skimming past the canopy bed and the table covered with white cloth, he couldn't help conjuring the image of the archmage greeting the man from Devanshari.

The way she'd addressed him and treated him suggested that he indeed was their king. Perhaps the queen had fallen ill, or their information was wrong to begin with. But such a possibility posed even more questions. Was the Devanshari king trying to take over Kaighal? Was he courting the archmage? Or did gossip at the Tivarashan court have it right, and Kamira Altrainne was aiming high after all? Her clothes, her lack of interest in titles and politics, her casual tone when Jalyn was alone with her... The more he thought about, the more plausible it seemed that it was all nothing but a façade to convince everyone she didn't care, giving her freedom to make her moves unwatched.

Jalyn pressed his fingers to his temples. At their arrival in Kaighal, he had considered himself both well informed and well prepared to handle the archmage, but one conversation had proven him wrong. He needed to learn more before he went to talk to the archmage again... Before another mistake could ruin everything.

He pressed his lips together, and his fingers curled into fists. He would come back home victorious or not come back at all.

MYRKAN'S CLAWS curled into fists and then uncurled, over and over again, as he perched on the rocky island. Around him, sea stretched in all directions, and on a stony beach below him a handful of pactees worked on fixing the leak in one of the barges. With all the magic yalari provided them through pacts, the humans still were unable to handle such simple task with the speed and efficiency Myrkan expected, and he couldn't help wondering whether summoning all of their asayalari army before traveling across the waters was the right choice. At the same time, he understood it had become a necessity after Veranesh broke free. They couldn't arrive with no minions to keep all the possible enemies at bay.

He gripped the rock underneath at the very thought. They all felt the collapse of his prison, and Myrkan could swear that even Arujhan's face expressed concern... or fear. The most powerful yalari among them might have been a match for Veranesh, and squabbles or not, all other yalari would support him in a fight, but since Fyertash had failed to return, they were going to arrive blind and clueless. With the way the trap had been devised, Veranesh couldn't have escaped on his own, which meant allies... likely yalari allies, because humans were too weak and clueless to be of significance. But the question remained: who'd decided to meddle? The yalari who contacted human mages and devised the trap made sure no one else knew that Veranesh was still alive, and the humans did their part, announcing Veranesh's destruction, but there were enough powerful yalari who could see through such schemes. *Powerful and patient,* he thought, because they didn't do anything for long centuries until an opportunity presented itself. *But who? Who?* The Four cared little about anything but their own domain in Yalarethe and their little human kingdom. Suzhaul, although in the past amiable toward Veranesh, didn't seem interested in games other yalari played, and given his power and unforgiving nature, all other powerful players agreed he was best left alone, and in return, he did likewise. And everyone knew that Veranesh had no allies who would be powerful or dedicated enough to risk their own lives and domains to help him. Yet someone did so.

"By the fires of Inihul, where are you, Fyertash?" Myrkan muttered.

They didn't sense his destruction, but so far he hadn't come back. He could have been killed and returned to the yalari realm, but in that case, one of the pactees would have been able to attempt summoning. They wouldn't be able to communicate with him so soon, but a human would at least sense Fyertash's immaterial presence. Failure to do so suggested he was alive and in this world.

"I wouldn't count on Fyertash anymore." Arujhan landed behind him but spoke soon enough for Myrkan to not feel threatened. "With Veranesh free, he might have decided his chance of survival is away from us."

Myrkan spat. "That worthless hoyve. I shouldn't have considered that coward worth our time."

"Fyertash used to be powerful, and he never lacked wits to get what he wanted without going the obvious way about it." Arujhan rubbed his chin. "It might be that he didn't flee."

"Then what? Confront Veranesh on his own?" Myrkan shook his head. Even if Fyertash was foolish enough to face the other yalari, such a battle would have ended in his death or destruction. Unless he fought and fled, too wounded to make it back.

"He might have sided with Veranesh."

The idea sounded so ridiculous that Myrkan couldn't help bursting out laughing. Whatever Arujhan meant to achieve by making the remark, he couldn't have possibly been entertaining the idea being true. "If he was as cunning as you claim he is, he would know better than to do so. After centuries of being trapped, Veranesh won't consider anyone an ally unless they broke down his prison with their own claws, and Fyertash would have been unable to do so. Besides, I wouldn't be surprised if Uganel begged for his life and revealed our names." Although Fyertash wasn't among the yalari who'd made the deal with humans centuries earlier, and he joined the covenant later, Veranesh was not likely to care.

Arujhan nodded in silence, as if all those arguments mattered little. Myrkan controlled his frustration. An outburst would prove him unworthy of an explanation.

"Then what makes you think Fyertash could have betrayed us?" he asked. No matter how powerful the other yalari was, Myrkan would not be kept in the dark. "The moment he approached Veranesh would have been his last. Besides, the agreement we've made allows him to gain more than he could ever gather on his own. A strong domain and your protection..."

"Are you sure this is what he wanted?" Arujhan replied. "Even you have desires other than that, and Fyertash..." He narrowed his eyes and fell silent, considering. "After all these centuries of his servile obedience, I almost forgot he has a reason to hate me and Derazin. And the more I think about it, the more I believe we've been played."

Myrkan shook his head. "By a yalari as powerless as him?" While all the concerns about Veranesh and his possible unknown ally were reasonable, to worry about one treacherous but weak yalari seemed unlike Arujhan.

"You didn't know Fyertash before his exile. Before Renalea's rebellion fell."

"That was nearly five hundred years ago. Twice as much if we use human measure. No one even remembers it anymore." At least Myrkan didn't, but at the time when Renalea made her bold play at power, he was clawing his way out of hordes of other insignificant yalari, too focused on his own survival and advancement to bother with what the greatest kanyalari did. Now, older and stronger, he would know to pay attention to such events, as they always brought waves of opportunities and threats, and if one was not careful enough, he would miss the first one or be swept away by the other one.

"And what if Fyertash still does?" Arujhan asked casually.

Myrkan considered that. Some yalari cared less about power and more about grudges, and someone as pitiful as Fyertash could have been among those too feeble to let go of past slights. And a yalari with thirst for revenge could be just the one to convince Veranesh to make an alliance, no matter how shaky it would be. "I should find that coward and bring him back," he muttered.

Arujhan narrowed his eyes, but nothing in his posture spoke of mistrust, and Myrkan took it as a good sign. "Go. Utanarra should arrive soon enough, and we need information. If you find Fyertash... don't turn your back to him." Arujhan unfurled his wings and took off into the air.

Myrkan watched his departure in silence. Arujhan might have been powerful and cunning, but the fear of someone as insignificant as Fyertash suggested he had a weakness. Myrkan sneered at that. Veranesh was still outnumbered, but with the rift between Arujhan and Derazin, and possibly Fyertash's betrayal, the odds were becoming more even. In the end, all the yalari could destroy each other in a bid for power... and Myrkan would be the last one standing, alone in a world hardly any other yalari cared for.

9

It quickly became obvious during their journey that Atissa had never set foot outside Kaighal, and with each passing hour, Ryell regretted not insisting they prepared better, stopping to pick up something more than a handful of travel rations. Not knowing where they were headed, he'd instead trusted her to make that decision and was paying for it now. Atissa could hardly walk on the unpaved merchant roads, and weariness quickly took her, so they'd made more rest stops than Ryell liked. That, in turn, led to two nights spend on the ground, by the fire, with little comfort or safety.

Even the sight of the woods they entered by the end of the first day didn't ease his mind. If anything, the forest reminded him of the home he'd lost, bringing back all the memories of the war with demons. Especially in the night, when he expected demonlings to swarm them, and his sleep was shallow and interrupted.

"I think it should be this way." Atissa's voice pulled him out of his grim thoughts.

The path that led away from the merchant road was

narrow and, as much as Ryell could tell, hardly traveled. They'd passed several similar ones that must lead to small hamlets or hunting lodges, and he reserved his doubts about Atissa's decision. She might have been following instructions from a letter—one he understood her father had left her—but if she'd never traveled in the woods before, she was likely to misread or miss the landmarks.

Yet he followed her without protest.

Their supplies were already running low, so it didn't matter which way they went. If at the end of the narrow path was a settlement, at least they could buy some more supplies and maybe even get directions... Though for all he knew, Atissa's home could be farther than they could travel anyway, and that brought the question of what to do next. They couldn't wander the forest aimlessly forever.

Atissa must have sensed his tension, because she glanced back at him. He forced an expression of reassurance and confidence onto his face. After all she'd been through, it would be unkind to put the blame on her. Kamira's schemes had pushed Atissa into this situation, leaving her no time to prepare, and with strong emotions following the loss of both her father and her magic, he shouldn't have expected calm planning.

"I'm sure we'll get there," he said despite his doubts.

She gave him a weak smile and continued on, her steps showing the growing struggle of a prolonged journey. Yet she didn't ask him to help her walk, and Ryell beamed. The grueling experiences of the last days were shaping Atissa into someone new. She'd lost a lot of her pride and childishness, and even though she seemed more vulnerable and innocent, at the same time he sensed inner determination growing within her. The spoiled child she had once been was vanishing before his eyes, replaced by a woman he could admire.

Following an impulse, he matched his pace with hers and took her hand. As they walked, Atissa's expression softened, losing the desperate edge, and Ryell couldn't help wondering whether it was his presence alone that put her at ease or the faint magic that emanated from his body. The thought of the crystal shard being a part of his body still unsettled him, especially when he remembered that its power came from demons, but that was a small price in comparison to suffering the excruciating hunger for magic.

They walked in silence, and Ryell allowed himself to daydream. Even though the forest was different from the vast woods of his homeland, with its shades of green deeper and birds singing different songs, he could at least pretend he was back in the Devanshari. Maybe one day his people could return there and start rebuilding, creating a better nation. He would be a royal guard again, serving the young king with his sword and experience, and he could take Atissa with him... He strained to picture the splendor of the royal palace, the always-blooming gardens, and the capital's busy streets, but all his mind could conjure were images of carnage and destruction. The heavy smoke from fires started by both demonologists who threw their magic indiscriminately and by people running for their lives when the barrier fell. The harder he tried to chase away those memories, the more vivid they became, and his good mood vanished. Even if they ever returned to Devanshari, even if they rebuilt it, nothing would ever be the same. The hunger still tormenting his compatriots and the shadow of the lives lost would make the new kingdom a very different place. A place that, perhaps, Ryell would not want to return to.

"I think we're here," Atissa said all of a sudden, full of anticipation.

Her voice pulled him back to reality. The trees surrounding the path ahead became scarce, and as the path curved, a wall and a gate appeared. And beyond it—Ryell's eyes widened—stood an old but well-preserved two-story building that could be a proper seat for a wealthy family back in Devanshari. When Atissa had mentioned a family home to him, he hadn't expected to see a place suitable for noblemen. It seemed that even without her magic and position, she was wealthier than he had ever been.

Yet she stood on the path as if sudden fear took her.

Still holding her hand, he said, "Let's go, then." Wealthy or not, she still needed him, his protection and support, and that reassured him he'd made the right choice. Maybe the Light had led him to her so that he could start over. With Cahala qi'Devanshari dead, he could forget about the past and build a new life with Atissa.

She sent him an excited smile when they approached the gate, but it faded at the sight of the guard posted in front of it. The man's posture was hardly appropriate for someone tasked with the house's safety, but as Ryell and Atissa approached, he put a hand on his sword.

"My name is Atissa." She clenched her map as she spoke, and her other hand squeezed Ryell's fingers tightly. "I'm Archmage Yoreus's daughter."

Ryell expected questioning or demand of proof, but the man just leaned to the side and pushed the gate open. As it squeaked in protest, the guard resumed his previous, lazy position against the wall. Atissa hesitated, but Ryell rushed her along the path. It was better if they spoke to someone at the house instead. If the guard changed his mind, they would have a hard time convincing him, while whoever took care of the building, even if he or she didn't believe Atissa's claims, might at least let them spend the night under the roof instead of camping in the woods.

A single person waited at the steps leading to the front door. An older man in a servant's attire bowed at their approach. "We've been expecting you, Miss Atissa. I'm Dynar, your father's and grandfather's butler. It's a pleasure to finally meet you."

Atissa blushed. "H-how did you know?"

"Your father informed us that you would be coming, and we don't get many visitors here, especially not young ladies in high mages' attire." His jovial expression faded, replaced by a solemn one. "Since you're here, I take it the archmage is dead?" Before Atissa could reply, Dynar straightened himself up and indicated the door. "My apologies. I shouldn't have started with questions. Why don't we enter, and I'll make preparations for a hearty meal and a warm bath for you and your companion..." His eyes narrowed ever so slightly.

Ryell bowed. "Ryell qi'Teshari. I'm Atissa's guardian."

"Ah, yes, I believe the archmage mentioned your name. Please, come in as well."

As they entered, Ryell couldn't shake the feeling that Dynar had disliked him from the first moment. Perhaps it was mistrust toward strangers, or maybe the old man, having likely lived his whole life in such a remote place, had never met anyone from the other continent. But, in the end, Dynar's attitude mattered little. Atissa was the rightful owner of the house, and she wanted Ryell here, by her side.

The building's interior was clean and well kept, with paintings and draperies indicating the subtle wealth of an old family. The lamps—traditional, not powered with imbued stones like in most places in Kaighal—were scarce, suggesting most of the rooms and corridors were unused, but nowhere within their reach did Ryell spot dust or wear. Dynar must have taken good care of the place. The entrance hall was vast enough to become a reception area if needed, and broad stairs led to the second level of the building.

"This way, please." The butler led them into one of the rooms to the side. "Please, get comfortable, and I'll have someone bring caffra juice and candied fruit while the meal and bath are being prepared."

The room was cozy, with comfortable, cushioned seats and low tables, perfect for an afternoon of leisure in pleasant company. As soon as Ryell closed the door behind them, Atissa spun in place, facing him. Her eyes shone with excitement, and a broad smile brought innocence back to her face. For that moment, no matter how brief it would be, she was a happy young woman, unburdened by her parent's death and harsh experiences.

As he embraced her, Ryell promised himself he'd do everything in his power to make those emotions last.

THE TALL HALL of Gildya Magna reminded Koshmarnyk of his past more than he liked. Back then he'd often sneaked through the servants' door, rushing to a lecture or a workshop, avoiding his teachers. This time, he used the main entrance, and a passing-by adept's startled expression brought a half-smile to his face. His sleeveless vest exposed gems in his forearms, and although he wasn't one to provoke, Gildya had made the first move ten years ago.

Kamira was right—if he wanted to change things around Kaighal, he had to do it from a position of power and confidence. Otherwise the adepts would once more coddle him with empty promises while preparing the knife to go in his back.

As he walked across the polished marble, its geometric designs once fuel for ideas and now nothing but pointless shapes, another adept gasped. She took off, running in the direction Koshmarnyk headed, and sure enough, six heavily armored guards stood in his way at the end of the hall. He stopped, anticipation like a rush through his veins, but they didn't make a move, as if his capture wasn't their goal.

Another man approached. "It's wise you've decided to turn yourself in, Alluvendran." Adept Ervan wore a rich robe and a smug sneer.

Koshmarnyk stared him down, unmoved. "I'll have to disappoint you. I'm here by the first archmage's request."

"I'm glad she saw reason, then."

"I'm afraid she didn't," Koshmarnyk replied, and the look on the other adept's face was enough of a reward. "The first archmage decided I'm best suited to speak with Gildya regarding the supply of imbued stones and the devices to be constructed, since I've already been drafting their blueprints with the help of the second archmage."

The usual brown hue of Ervan's skin gained reddish undertones, and the adept took a deep breath. "That's unacceptable."

"I'll be sure to pass your sentiment to the first archmage," Koshmarnyk replied dryly. "She'll be delighted Gildya is wasting her time... again."

Ervan's narrow lips twitched like a trapped worm. "I could have you imprisoned, and she wouldn't do anything about it. Don't you think it's the reason she sent you here? She wants to save face, but she needs us. She'd make a fuss, demand we free you, but that's it."

Were it someone else Ervan was talking about,

Koshmarnyk would nod to such logic. But not Kamira. That stubborn arcanist of his was more loyal than any of the self-absorbed adepts could ever imagine. Nevertheless, Ervan believed what he wanted to believe, and Koshmarnyk looked him straight in the eye. "Then I trust you have more men than these six for the task?"

Ervan's fists curled. "Don't be so confident. We've improved many things since the last time."

Koshmarnyk gave the motionless guards a quick inspection. "The new dart throwers look effective. I see you found a way to improve the reloading mechanism. And the darts' tips are poisoned, I presume?" The confidence in his voice never faltered. No matter how fast the projectiles became, they were no match for the speed he'd needed while sparring with Veranesh. Koshmarnyk might have had to deal with only two nightflies back then, but unlike darts, their flight was unpredictable and harder to dodge. "Placing the stones in the new pattern protects the armor's weak spots. Well done. I see Gildya didn't waste the last ten years... entirely." With their outdated and stiff approach to research, they couldn't have progressed much further. Even reinforced, armor still could be broken and penetrated, and the humans beneath the steel and leather were as vulnerable as always. "So, are you really prepared to make a scene before I go back to the archmage to tell her you aren't happy with my presence here, or shall we start working on the shielding devices she asked for?"

Ervan didn't conceal his displeasure. "I'll take you to the council, and they'll decide. Can I trust you will carry yourself with dignity and honor?"

"It's an odd question coming from a man who ten years ago delivered a knife to my back," Koshmarnyk replied coldly. "I'll not attack anyone unless they attack me, but if you're under the impression I'm going in to be judged, you're mistaken."

The other adept avoided meeting his eyes. "Very well. Let's go." He waved at the guards, and they parted, letting Koshmarnyk through, but fell in behind as soon as he passed them.

Koshmarnyk held back a sigh. Gildya might have improved their inventions and devices, but other things seemed to never change. He wouldn't be surprised if he had to fight his way back out—an outcome he wasn't looking forward to, but unless he was ready to leave Kaighal forever, he needed to ensure adepts changed their stance on blending flesh with stones. Besides, it wasn't only about him anymore. If someone noticed that the marks on Kamira's forearms were more than scars and started asking questions, she could be in trouble too.

They walked past the great hall and the reception area, and up the winding stairs, then through a short, straight corridor to another stairwell—just like Koshmarnyk remembered. He ran his hand along the polished wood of the railing as they ascended, like he had many times in the past, but he didn't let memories swarm his thoughts.

"I can't help but wonder what you offered the archmage to make her protect you so fiercely," Ervan spoke for the first time since the great hall.

Koshmarnyk offered a half-smile. "Hoping that Gildya could come up with a better offer?"

"I'm simply trying to understand her motives." His tone made it clear he didn't consider Koshmarnyk worth an offer.

"I didn't promise her anything. She asked me for help."

"Word is you warm her bed at night."

Koshmarnyk held his face straight. Not that he'd expected it to remain a secret, but the speed with which the news got to Gildya suggested they had someone inside the Towers. He made a note to speak about it with Kamira. The adepts might have offered reluctant help, but by no means were they allies. Given a chance, they'd deliver a treacherous stab or turn their back on the Towers. He cringed at the thought. In a way, Gildya posed a bigger threat than any traitor that demons could find and use.

Ervan kept glancing at him, so Koshmarnyk said, "All for naught, I'd say. Most nights she doesn't even make it to bed. But I'll be looking forward to see Gildya's counteroffer. Might be quite amusing."

"I must admit, I find it surprising a woman like her would care so much for you," Ervan delivered another stab. "Gildya can wait until she gets bored with you... or is done using you."

Koshmarnyk stopped and looked him in the eye. "You speak as if my freedom hinges on her whim, so let's make it clear. I won't make the mistake of trusting Gildya again. Any of you try anything and this ends in blood."

"Bold words, Alluvendran. Especially for a man who spent the last ten years chained to a wall."

Koshmarnyk didn't take the bait. With a warning delivered, there was no point in engaging in a squabble. If Ervan was fool enough to believe that the last time the adepts could have succeeded without deception and poisoning, reality would teach him what Koshmarnyk's words would not. Koshmarnyk resumed his climb up the stairs, leaving the other adept behind, and before the guards caught up with him, he walked alone into the council's chamber.

Six pairs of eyes turned to him. He recognized their faces, and memories resurfaced, reminding him of their sly words when they lied about their peaceful intentions.

Perhaps Kamira was wrong after all, and even making a stance would not change anything: Gildya would agree to tolerate him only to brew more treachery as soon as his suspicions waned. Their gazes fell on him, and the echo of the chains' rattling filled Koshmarnyk's ears as he recalled the cold metal closing on his neck and wrists.

Yet he would not allow them to see doubt or weakness, and he returned the evaluating stare to each and every of them.

Arrogant Hybal, whose once-handsome face bore the first marks of age. Gray-skinned Zaveshan, as sly as most Tivarashan nobles Koshmarnyk knew. Yinka, who lacked both spine and brain but had other things in the right places... Was she still sleeping with Hybal? Koshmarnyk held off a smirk. Even if she wasn't, she must have already found someone else to secure her position in the council. His eyes slipped toward the next council member, Loyuwan. Another one gossiped to have gained his influence through his bed in the past, but at least Koshmarnyk could recall some of the sleek adept's inventions. If he was more interested in research than in fellow adepts, he could achieve a lot. And perhaps, in the end, he had. Ten years was enough time for one to prove their worth of a place in the council.

"Alluvendran." An old man stepped forward. His hair, the same gray shade as a decade ago, was now longer and braided, but other than that, Adept Yzeth hadn't changed much. "Are you here for revenge?"

They must have really thought him a fool to walk in openly if he intended to kill them. "I come at the first mage's request. She chose me to be her voice in all matters between the High Towers and Gildya Magna."

"That's unacceptable." Filidana stepped forward.

It took him a moment to recognize her within the plump body and sagging chin. How had she managed to change so much in as little as ten years? Her strong makeup couldn't conceal her overindulgence, and the elaborate hairdo added years to her looks rather than subtracting them.

"Adept Ervan already expressed Gildya's disapproval," Koshmarnyk replied, glancing at Ervan, who'd entered the chamber and made his way to the rest of the council. "He was also foolish enough to make threats. If the council has nothing to add, I'll leave now and inform the first archmage of the High Towers that Gildya refuses to cooperate."

"I'm afraid we can't allow you to leave," Yzeth said, though without hostility. "You still are an escaped felon, and the deaths of the adepts who guarded your prison are now added to your crimes. In due time, we will also investigate what the first archmage had to do with your escape."

Koshmarnyk narrowed his eyes. Revealing that it was Cahala that arranged the slaughter would cause even more problems if they questioned what happened to her, or if the new Devanshari king protested such an accusation. Ultimately, Kamira and Veelk's involvement could come to light. "Their blood is on your hands. If you hadn't kept me prisoner, they wouldn't have died when the killers tried to get to me. Or maybe... the council is the one who sent the killers in the first place?" Even if he knew they hadn't, such a suggestion could make the adepts suspect each other and create a rift that would serve him if some sided with his cause. Not the most honorable way of doing things, but better than more bloodshed.

"You don't get to blame us!" Filidana's high-pitched voice echoed within the chamber, and several council members cringed. Some things, indeed, didn't change. "Having you imprisoned was an act of mercy. Gildya should have you killed for pursuing illegal knowledge."

Koshmarnyk stared her down. The knowledge was only illegal because Gildya said so. No laws of the land explicitly forbade it, and the Free City of Kaighal cared little for what people did as long as they paid their taxes and didn't steal from or murder their fellow citizens. Yet he refrained from arguing. Filidana's claim that he deserved death added credibility to his accusations of the council's underhanded dealings.

"Enough, Fili." Yzeth gestured at her and then looked at Koshmarnyk. "The council decided that for now we'll respect the archmage's wish, but in return, we expect you to pull your weight. You'll be here, working with our adepts, not just passing vague suggestions."

Such a concession was quite unexpected and too quickly made to be without hidden motives, even if they'd discussed it at length before he arrived. But Kaighal needed Gildya and the Towers cooperating, so Koshmarnyk nodded. "I think it's best if I worked alone, in the Towers. Of course, I'll share my knowledge and any blueprints or sketches. This way the council won't have to suffer my presence in Gildya." And he would avoid any plots or assassination attempts.

Yzeth thought about it. "That's reasonable, and we'll agree to such terms. In return, when Kaighal is safe again, the council expects you to hand yourself in instead of hiding behind the archmage's back."

Koshmarnyk's laughter filled the chamber. Of course Gildya had planned on keeping him around only to seize the opportune moment to imprison him again. His cheerful reaction faded, and he looked Yzeth in the eye. "When the fight is over, we'll discuss it again. This much I can promise you." He put no threat in his voice, but the confidence was enough reassurance that he didn't intend to surrender. "As for the first archmage's involvement... She does what she wants and when she wants."

The doors opened behind him, and Koshmarnyk exercised self-control when his instincts demanded him to face a possible threat.

"Ah, the eighth council member is finally here." Yzeth's voice, though seemingly friendly, carried a reprimand. He gave Koshmarnyk a nod as if appreciating the basic trust he'd displayed through his lack of reaction.

The woman who walked in ignored the remark. Instead, she stopped by Koshmarnyk and looked him up and down. "Alluvendran unbound in the council chamber. It's not something I expected to see in my lifetime."

The auburn locks around her peach-hued skin and her deep brown gaze were as Koshmarnyk remembered, but wrinkles now marked the corner of her lips and eyes.

"Mayetti. You've aged well," he said with a hint of amusement.

"Not exactly what a woman wants to hear from her lover." Her lips curled. "Former lover," she added when Koshmarnyk stared at her.

Yzeth walked over to them. "Mayetti, Adept Alluvendran will be working in the Towers. You'll keep Gildya informed of his progress and pass him messages from other adepts assigned to prepare defenses as needed."

She gave them both one of her stunning smiles, but her eyes were focused solely on Koshmarnyk. "I'm looking forward to spending more time with you... again."

He ignored the remark. Back in his youth, he might have been infatuated with Mayetti, but such feelings didn't fit a seasoned man, one who had firsthand experience of both her feebleness and manipulative nature. Given a chance, she'd likely put many Tivarashans to shame with her schemes. If he was a fool to fall for her charms again, she'd use him and leave him like she did the last time. He narrowed his eyes. Mayetti's presence in the council could complicate things even more. Though oldest among them, Yzeth seemed open-minded enough and was Koshmarnyk's best chance at resolving the matter of his own future in both a peaceful and satisfactory way, but if Mayetti interfered...

He snapped out of this thoughts, as everyone was looking at him.

"If everything is set," he said to Yzeth, paying no attention to the woman standing beside them, "I'll return to work now."

"We'll be looking forward to progress," the old man said with sincerity.

Without bothering to address the rest of the council, Koshmarnyk turned his back on them. The guards between him and the door stood motionless for a heartbeat with their crossbows raised before they parted. He made it past them at a deliberately slow pace. His delayed departure might have irked the adepts behind him, but he needed to be sure they wouldn't try anything. In the silence disturbed only by his own footsteps, no sound of betrayal came, and he made it outside.

10

Cool night air seeped into the chamber through the shattered dome, but neither of the yalari cared. Veranesh studied the map they'd etched onto the wall, a detailed bird's-eye plan of Kaighal and its surroundings, while Fyertash perched at the edge of the dome. He flicked his claws and looked toward the sea every other moment. The prospect of meeting those he had turned on must have been a source of anxiety, even if the cunning yalari never showed any emotion.

Veranesh scowled. It was time to stop pretending he had any interest in the map, to stop pretending he and Fyertash were allies. With the night late and humans already seeking rest, no one should interrupt them for long.

"You've been most helpful so far." Veranesh didn't look up at the other yalari. "Accepting every petty task I give you and every humiliation without even the slightest protest."

"I'd rather not test the boundaries of your mercy." Fyertash's wings spread, and a quick dive had him landing in the chamber. "I'm no match for you."

Veranesh looked at the other yalari, who kept far

enough away to show unwillingness to provoke any confrontation. "Too helpful."

Fyertash snorted, his posture changing from servile to confident. "I should have known I wouldn't be able to play you for long." The smile never faded, but his eyebrow arched slightly when no reaction came. "I expected you to be at my throat by now."

Veranesh took several steps toward him. "I'd start with your limbs. You can't speak without a throat."

The other yalari returned his stare without fear. "Few have your control," he said with respect that didn't carry any notion of desperate flattery. "And since humans aren't around, let's not waste time on games and talk trade instead."

Veranesh took another step, but Fyertash didn't flinch. He was bold enough to reveal himself instead of resorting to deception, so his offer had to be worth it. "Do talk, then."

"I know your secret," Fyertash said. "I know why you're still here, defending the human settlement you find of no worth. You help me get my revenge, and I'll ensure your secret... stays safe."

Veranesh drew a sharp breath, and his fists curled, claws digging into his skin. Others often overlooked Fyertash, considering him weak and insignificant, but Veranesh knew better than to discard the risk... Yet, even in his own plans and schemes, he hadn't expected the other yalari would find out what Veranesh was willing to protect, and at the same time, not for a moment did he doubt that Fyertash knew what he claimed to know.

"Well played." Veranesh's instinct urged him to attack and destroy the unexpected threat, but resorting to the destruction spell meant risking the very city he'd pledged to defend. And if he only killed Fyertash, thus allowing him return to the realm of yalari, the secret wouldn't be safe anymore. As much as Veranesh hated it, trade was his best choice. "If we're to have an agreement, you owe me the truth."

"Do I, now?" Fyertash asked, then inspected Veranesh's face. "You'll risk it, if I don't give you answers, won't you?"

An ugly grimace twisted Veranesh's mouth. His opponent might have gained an upper hand in discovering what was meant to remain concealed, but it didn't mean Veranesh would allow it to stay that way. "You either give me a good reason for your revenge, or I'll assume you're doing Arujhan's bidding."

"Fair enough," the cunning yalari said. "It's for Renalea."

Not an answer Veranesh had expected, and a strange one that suggested deception. "I find it hard to believe you still hold a grudge for that failed uprising—" Veranesh cut himself off and stared at Fyertash. "No... Not for that. For her." He let out a short laugh as Fyertash's reasons became clear. "I always thought she gave up other leaders' names too quickly." For everyone else, it was anything but too quickly, and even Veranesh hadn't been certain about his suspicions that Renalea was protecting someone until now. After months of torture and humiliation, after multiple cycles of ripping that stopped short of Renalea's destruction and allowing her to regenerate... Even centuries couldn't wash this memory away. "But then, aren't you helping the wrong yalari? Or will you claim you've forgotten who destroyed her?"

Fyertash looked him in the eye. "I watched you back then. I know you suspected she lied, but you still let her go."

The memory of Renalea's determined gaze flashed in Veranesh's head. Back then, he couldn't believe there would be anyone or anything worth protecting through so much pain. Now, after watching how his pactee fought for the mage killer's survival, he had a better understanding, even if he still failed to relate to such notions. "She wouldn't have told us even in a thousand years, and without her, the uprising was crippled." The strength in Fyertash's gaze reminded Veranesh of the female yalari who'd endured so much to protect him. Now, it seemed, Fyertash wanted revenge for her—not for her destruction that was indeed an act of mercy, but for what had led to it. "You're after the traitors, then."

A slow nod was the only reply.

Veranesh considered his choices. As unlikely as the tale was, it rang true. Even before Renalea started a rebellion aimed at throwing the whole of Yalarethe in turmoil and ending the most powerful kanyalari's rule, Fyertash always excelled in long-running plans that required patience and secrecy. If he really had a deep bond with Renalea, waiting centuries for an opportune moment to act while everyone else had already forgotten, the events would have been a child's play to him.

"Very well, we'll make a trade, but on my terms," Veranesh said. "I'll help you get your revenge. I'll make sure Derazin and Arujhan suffer before they're destroyed, and I'll pass your regards to them as well. In return, my secret becomes yours to guard until the end. You will die for it, if needed. As many times as needed."

Fyertash huffed, his thin lips twisting. "You ask for a lot. What if I refuse?"

"I'll make your worthless hide into a peace offering to Arujhan," Veranesh replied. Even if such a move required adjusting plans he had for Kamira, at least he'd buy time by making a bargain with his enemies. If Arujhan acted swiftly enough giving in to his anger of having been betrayed,

Fyertash would die before he could divulge too much. "I'm sure he'll see reason."

The other yalari burst out laughing, but the display of amusement faded quickly. "I missed your presence in the game. Sharp, composed, and unyielding as always." He took a step forward, casual enough to pose no threat. "I'll accept your terms."

He stretched his clawed hand forward, squinting at the effort of gathering magic around his fingers and palm. Veranesh took notice of the display of skill few would be able to repeat, and only in their own realm. His thoughts wandered toward the uprising once more. Had Arujhan and Derazin not betrayed Renalea—and Fyertash as well, as it appeared—the two yalari would have amassed impressive power and influence. Veranesh's own domain would have remained intact, save some borderlands, but the balance among kanyalari would have shifted. He almost sighed. Such a magnificent plan, destroyed by two cowards. Yet it made the deal with Fyertash worth all the more.

He extended his hand, with the energy already enveloping it, and when their palms met, magic crackled around them.

"It's done," they said in unison.

Fyertash smiled. "Should you survive the confrontation... will you be coming after me?"

Veranesh had to appreciate the question. The other yalari was not foolish to believe Veranesh would forget being played. "I wouldn't tell you if I would. But the trade we've sealed binds you longer than it binds me."

"The price is still... acceptable, even if it will be a nuisance to fulfill," Fyertash said in a jovial manner. The shine in his eyes suggested he cared little for any burden as long as he got his revenge.

"Before that, we have to ensure that the city survives." Veranesh glanced at the map. Strong walls surrounded Kaighal from all sides but the sea, and his concern grew as his eyes slipped past the port, the weakest point of defense. At the same time, battlements that held off human armies could mean little against yalari's power, and he had to trust that his pactee and her adept would come up with solutions. At least the kanyalari would keep away, unwilling to risk their own destruction, so humans would only have to deal with asayalari, and even the hordes of them would not breach the thick stone around the city. But the port... They needed a solution.

"My guess is that they'll make their landing at least a day or two away from the city." Fyertash pointed at the belt of shrub land separating the city from the sands. "Maybe farther if they start being concerned about what could have happened to me." A smirk flashed on his face—he cherished the success of having played them, of that Veranesh was sure.

Veranesh narrowed his eyes as he considered possibilities.

If Arujhan caught on to Fyertash's deception, and Veranesh had no doubt he eventually would, they would change whatever plans they might have made in Fyertash's presence. It seemed almost better to risk his return to his former comrades, but Veranesh discarded that thought. With the trade they'd made, trust wasn't an issue anymore, but as unnerving as he was, Fyertash was more useful to Veranesh alive than dying.

"I'll go scout, then," Fyertash offered. "Into the sea and to the south."

Veranesh shot him a warning glare. His benevolent mood only lasted so long, and no matter what agreement they had made, he would not stand his authority being challenged if it happened again. "Very well. If you get caught, I expect you to play Arujhan at least as well as you played me."

"For someone who's been played, you gained quite a lot." Fyertash looked Veranesh in the eye. "Don't worry. I'll keep your secret safe like Renalea kept ours." With that promise, he took off.

Veranesh watched Fyertash's silhouette until it was one with the black sky. The determination in the weaker yalari's eyes reminded him again of the power of Renalea's gaze, and it reassured him that Fyertash spoke with sincerity few of their brethren would ever have. Shaped by love and betrayal, he was an odd yalari. Yet so was Veranesh—trusting humans more than his own kind and making those weak creatures his allies.

Two odd yalari against all others. Possibilities would open, should they both survive and Fyertash was willing to continue their peculiar alliance.

Should they both survive... Even if unlikely, it was a pleasant sentiment, and Veranesh allowed himself the joy of pondering it for a while.

RYELL FINALLY FELL ASLEEP, and Atissa sneaked out of the bed. The same thing that made him look so peaceful in his slumber grated on her nerves. A small shard of an imbued stone within his skin brought relief to his hunger, but it also reminded her of what she had lost. Ever since the demon cut off her tie to magic, the nagging longing had destroyed all her focus. Even the sight of her family home, one she never knew, didn't ease the turmoil within her. So far, nothing did.

When they'd first arrived, the few servants her father had kept around served food and prepared baths for both her and Ryell. She allowed herself to indulge in rest after days of straining travel, even if her mind circled things her father had mentioned in the other letter, the one she hadn't shown to anyone.

There was a promise in that letter... At the same time, it made her wonder whether her father had truly cared about her, or was hoping to shape her into a tool of his revenge. She always knew that he'd groomed her to be a part of his schemes, but it came with all the benefits and privileges of being an archmage's daughter.

She shook her head. She was supposed to have a great future and a position of power. To abandon her father's plans meant settling into the house that might have been comfortable, but offered no opportunities or power. To stay here meant to wither. Even if in the end she was nothing but a tool in her father's hands, at least the rewards for doing his bidding were all that she'd always believed worth desiring.

Ryell stirred in his sleep but didn't wake up. Atissa slipped on a robe and tiptoed out of the room. Thankfully, the door didn't creak as she closed it.

"Is there any way I can help you, my lady?"

Years of sneaking about the High Towers, sometimes at her father's request, sometimes on her own, made her resistant to jumping when surprised, and when she turned, her face was calm and moves composed. Dynar stood in the corridor, a small lantern in his hand, with a polite expression.

"I'd like to see my father's study," she said.

Dynar nodded. "Of course. I would have offered to show

it to you sooner, but I thought it prudent to wait till your companion retired." He indicated down the corridor. "This way."

The letter mentioned that although Dynar had no in-depth knowledge of her father's secrets, he was aware of them, and she could trust him. He led her through the maze of corridors, often odd in their irregular shapes. She only glanced at the tapestries and paintings decorating the walls. Her family wealth, her own wealth mattered little in comparison to the promise her father's study had. Later, when all was done and settled, she would take a closer look at her material inheritance.

Dynar stopped and opened the door. "I'll be in the kitchens, my lady. If you need me, there's a bell to the side of the door." He handed her the lantern.

She almost refused, out of habit. Mages didn't need lanterns. But the thought of summoning a lumisphere that followed became only another reminder of what she'd lost. Concealing her emotions, she accepted. "Thank you."

As he bowed and left, she walked in. The room didn't look much different from her father's study in the High Towers, though it lacked the bed in the corner. A desk, bookshelves, and thick curtains to protect the room from any curious eyes, as if someone could spy on her father in the middle of a forest. She smiled. Habits nurtured in the Towers never died, and she had no doubt that whenever he visited, he ensured the curtains were drawn.

She locked the door behind her and rushed over to the window. It took her a moment to feel the lever hidden in the wood. Her heart skipped a beat when the secret door opened. Her hand sweaty on the lantern's handle, she entered the passage within and descended the stairs at its end. The steps were steep and narrow, with enough space for only one person to get through. They led her down to a cellar that looked like an underground workshop. She paid little attention to the worktables and their content. What she needed was at the end of the room, and she rushed there without hesitation.

When the lantern's lamp scattered the shadows, illuminating three massive crystals, for the first time since her father's death, Atissa's heart sang with joy.

11

Kamira helped Master Tijhran to the chair. His chambers were suitable for a teacher, far less extravagant in both space and furnishing than those available to the archmages, but they also were closer to the teaching rooms. With his injury, walking must have been enough of an ordeal without adding several flights of stairs. Guilt jabbed at her, because even with all the duties, she should have found more time to talk to him and ensure his comfort.

Tijhran waved her off. "You don't have to treat me like a frail spider web. After all, I survived a battle with a higher demon."

With a sigh, she put his walking stick by his chair. That battle was her fault, and no matter how much Tijhran insisted on helping her, she shouldn't have made her problems his... And yet she did so again, this time asking him to join the defense. On the other hand, if her teacher learned what was going on in Kaighal, he'd come on his own anyway. At least by sending a letter she avoided complaints of keeping things from him, and she was able to ensure he was carried from Gaunash. She almost smirked. Knowing Tijhran's resolve, once he learned about the demon threat, he'd have been ready to walk to Kaighal on his own.

"I appreciate you coming over, master," she said. "The first arcanists in the new Towers will receive schooling from the best tutor they could have."

He laughed, a dry, coarse sound in his throat. "How could I miss being called 'master' by the first archmage herself?" Despite his playful words, she caught genuine pride. "But she better watch her tongue around students. The first archmage of Kaighal doesn't bow to anyone. No adept, no foreigner, and definitely not to her teacher."

She became serious. "Speaking of students, how are they doing, master? Any chance some will be able to make a pact soon?"

The old arcanist sighed. "I can certainly pick at least a few, though if the situation wasn't desperate..."

"You'd make them sweat for at least two years before even admitting they're worth anything."

Tijhran mocked offense. "I let you make a pact after a mere year."

"It's because you made me work twice as hard," she retorted.

"I should do so again, since no one's watching." He gave her a shameless grin. "Would you be so kind and pass this old man a mug of caffra juice?"

She rushed to the table before he changed his mind. No matter what he said about being fine, his leg deserved some rest.

The sound of the door opening surprised her. No student nor teacher would be so rude as to forget to knock. She looked over her shoulder, a reprimand ready, but no one entered. Instead, she caught a glimpse of a small object rolling onto the floor. Pulsating stones clanked against the wooden floor.

Kamira froze, her eyes widening.

The stone's light died, and green smoke seeped through the device's gaps. At the same time, the door shut, a wave of magic flowing around it. Kamira and Tijhran exchanged knowing glances: a locking seal had cut their way out.

Instinctively, Kamira channeled magic, and a burst of wind hit the device. The green cloud swirled, then parted, circling within the walls. In desperation, she moved her hands to the sides, trying to keep the smoke away, but it was already filling the room, and the device kept spitting out more.

Tijhran was on his feet, but coughing. He pointed at the window.

With the green poison already teasing her nostrils, Kamira woke up the nightflies. If they broke the crystal panes, maybe she could manage to push the fumes out of the room... The creatures hovered in the air. She stared at them, her vision blurred with tears. Desperately, she was mustering enough focus to make them do her bidding, but before she succeeded, Veranesh took control. The nightflies spun in the air as if the demon was familiarizing himself with the situation through their eyes, and then they darted straight for the window.

Glass shattered as they made it outside.

Kamira channeled magic once more, her focus failing, and the weak gusts of wind seemed to only nudge the green poison into swirls.

With his bent arm to his face, Tijhran took several steps forward, his lame leg slowing his moves as much as the poison, and he collapsed by it.

The scream that rose in Kamira's lungs died in a series of coughs.

Her teacher looked at her, pride in his gaze, and grabbed the device. His hand was trembling as he lifted it to throw, but then his body went limp.

Once more, Kamira forced magic to flow, but she was already succumbing to the poison. The breeze that she summoned did nothing more than stir the thick green cloud. With her mind drifting off, she stopped fighting and the last breath escaped her mouth. Any help the nightflies could get would arrive too late.

But then, no one ever survived when Tivarashan assassins came for them.

Kamira lay on the floor with nothing but green smoke in her lungs, and she couldn't resist the thought that dying was much like being imbued into a crystal. Same motionlessness, same pain... Only this time blackness would follow instead of visions of the demon world.

The room's violent tremble helped her refocus. The window's frame shattered along with the wall surrounding it when Veranesh forced his way in. The green smoke scattered and swirled, but the demon wasn't bothered by it. As he picked up the device, crushed it, and tossed it out of the window, no signs of poisoning showed on his face or body.

He rushed to her and knelt. "Fight it. Fight it."

She wanted to tell him it was too late, but her body was shaking with violent coughs. With no words at her disposal, she had to hope the demon would stay to defend Kaighal after she died.

Veranesh's clawed hand covered her mouth and nose. "No, don't breathe in more."

With half of her face under his rough, leathery skin, all

she could do was to stare at him. The amount she'd breathed in already was enough to kill her, and suffocating her would not help either. Yet, with every rapid heartbeat counting the passing time, her body relaxed and the burning in her lungs subsided.

"Good," Veranesh said. "Keep fighting." He ignored heavy pounding and shouts coming from the other side of the door and kept his hand over her face. "When you can focus enough, get rid of that poison. It's not pleasant to inhale."

She gave him a confused glance, but the energy flowed, obedient to her will, and light, controlled gusts of wind chased the remainder of the green smoke toward the broken window. Only then did Veranesh remove his claw, and Kamira took in air with a loud wheeze.

"I..." Her eyes fixed on the demon as he helped her up. "I didn't die."

Veranesh arched his eyebrow as if the situation amused him. "Are you disappointed?"

"I know you came too late."

A poison orb, a Tivarashan invention and favorite tool of Darethal's Thorns, an elite assassin group, left no survivors. It killed its victims within moments of inhalation... Just like it had with Master Tijhran. No matter how much she wanted to not look, her eyes kept drifting toward the body in the middle of the room, its motionless shape crushing any hope she might have had. But if Tijhran died, so should have she.

Veranesh cradled her in his arms. "Questions will have to wait. You mustn't tell anyone what really happened." He hesitated. "Tell the adept, if you really have to."

His voice rang with odd satisfaction, as if he had reasons to be happy about her survival, and Kamira opened her mouth. No matter what he said, questions couldn't wait.

Then the door broke apart, and Koshmarnyk stormed into the room.

~

KOSHMARNYK POINTED at the blueprints and went over the details of the device for the meager audience of an old archmage and two demons. They seemed to follow his explanations, and he caught some curiosity on Fyertash's face.

"A barrier didn't help Devanshari much," the demon said, his deep voice echoing within the initiation chamber they used for meetings. "Their device was much more powerful, with an unlimited flow of magic, and we still wore it down."

Koshmarnyk looked up at him. "That's not the story I've heard. You had a traitor inside working for you."

"We did," Fyertash admitted without shame. "The supply of foolish humans willing to exchange their services for their lives or some other rewards is never short."

The suggestion behind his words was clear enough: demons would find people to do their bidding in Kaighal as well, and the city would fall. Koshmarnyk offered him a crooked half-smile. "Therefore, we won't repeat their mistakes. Even if some traitor destroys one of the devices, it won't affect all the others, and a small breach will be easy enough to defend." At least, he hoped it would be. In the past, Kaighal had survived sieges and pushed enemy armies away, but that was when high mages were in power, and Gildya was pulling its weight as well instead of calculating how to do the least amount of work for the highest possible gain. With only a handful of arcanists to provide magical protection, the city would have to rely on Gildya's mechanisms and common people's bravery to fend off the invasion.

"Clever," Fyertash replied, though his tone revealed doubts. "Once you're done with the construction, I'll test the device's power myself."

Irtan looked up at the demon. "It would help if you shared what you and others did in Devanshari."

Koshmarnyk could swear there was a reprimand in the old archmage's voice. The demon must have not been as forthcoming as Irtan hoped for.

Silent so far, Veranesh said, "You do that. Tell humans all the details and all the tricks you know of. The less we have to concern ourselves with the safety of this place—" He froze and tensed. "Kamira." His wings shot out, and he left the chamber through the opening in the roof.

Koshmarnyk shivered at the tone of his voice. The demon rarely used Kamira's name, so it had to serious. "Where is she now?" he asked Irtan, ignoring Fyertash's curious glance that followed Veranesh's departure.

"She mentioned something about checking on students' progress... likely with Archmage Tijhran."

Koshmarnyk darted out of the chamber and down the stairs. Startled students stepped aside as he passed by. He didn't bother to slow down at any obstacle, and as he burst into one classroom after another, there was no sign of either Kamira or Tijhran. A nightfly caught up with him. "Tijhran's chamber," Veranesh said through it. "I'm with her now."

The vagueness of the demon's remark promised nothing good, and Koshmarnyk dashed through the corridors, hoping he remembered the way to Tijhran's quarters. A group of students gathered around one of the doors told him he'd found the right place, and he pushed his way through the small crowd. A smooth barrier barred the way, and a single device clung to the wood in the middle of the door. Imbued stones pulsated on in it in a steady rhythm, but Koshmarnyk didn't recognize its make.

Against his desperate desire to get in, he didn't attempt to remove it. He grabbed an onlooker. "Get Archmage Irtan." If the device was Gildya-made, the old man would not be of much help, but at least magic could help in breaking through it.

"I'm here." As the archmage stepped through the crowd, heavy breaths lifted his chest. "I could barely keep up with you."

"Do you know how to remove this?" Koshmarnyk pointed at the device.

Irtan inspected the door with caution, and Koshmarnyk bit his lip before demanding the old man rush his examination.

"It's what Tivarashan people call a seal," the archmage said. "I could remove it, but going inside might not be safe. It bears the mark of Darethal's Thorns, and they're famous for using poison orbs in their assassinations."

Blood left Koshmarnyk's face, and a cold shiver went down his spine, but he didn't hesitate. "Open it." His thoughts raced around Veranesh's remark. He didn't say Kamira was alive, and given how quickly the poison would have filled a closed room... A sharp pain pierced his heart.

"Move away from the door," Irtan said, then glanced at the onlookers. "Everyone leave."

His authoritative voice made people retreat in a hurry. Irtan focused on the seal.

An imbued stone in Koshmarnyk's body reacted to the flow of magic. The seal glowed white, and as it melted away, the door shattered into pieces. Koshmarnyk pressed his sleeve to his face and rushed inside.

A motionless body was the first thing he saw upon entering. It took him only a heartbeat to recognize Archmage Tijhran, and his heart pumped icy blood through his veins as he searched for another corpse. Instead, his eyes stopped on Veranesh. The demon was kneeling on the floor by the window, cradling Kamira.

"She'll be fine," Veranesh said, though his attention was still on the woman in his arms, and Koshmarnyk could swear the demon genuinely cared about her. "She didn't breathe enough of it."

"What happened?" Irtan walked in cautiously.

Kamira rushed to reply, but a violent cough shook her body.

"The old pactee." Veranesh pointed at Tijhran. "He threw the poisonous device out before he died."

The archmage walked over to the corpse, but Koshmarnyk kept his eyes on Kamira. Even a whiff or two of the poison orb's smoke was said to kill, and her cough suggested she'd had more than that. She hacked, and green phlegm appeared in the corner of her lips. Koshmarnyk's eyes widened.

The demon wiped it off with a swift move and sent him a warning glare. Whatever had transpired, he didn't want it discussed in front of Irtan.

"Take her. She needs to rest." Veranesh rose to his feet, though the ceiling forced his tall frame into a hunch, and passed Kamira to Koshmarnyk. "And you, Irtan, find out who did it."

"The seal used outside and the poison orb are how Darethal's Thorns work." The old archmage looked up from

Tijhran's body. "The question would be who paid them, and that's not an easy answer to find."

"Darethal's Thorns?" Veranesh asked.

"Tivarashan assassins," Kamira replied, her voice still coarse. She shifted in Koshmarnyk's embrace, and although he wasn't keen on letting her out of his arms, he helped her stand on her own. "They'll kill anyone if the pay is good enough. Their marks never survive."

"One did." Irtan eyed Kamira. "And that means they'll come back to finish the job. We need to double the guards and check everyone coming in. And you'll stay in your chambers, protected all the time."

As Koshmarnyk expected, she shook her head. "They won't come back," she said. "One failed assassination, should any gossip spread, can be blamed on someone pretending to be them. If they try twice and fail, their legend will crumble. They will not take that risk."

Irtan gave her a stern look. "I'm not willing to risk the first archmage's life and our only hope of defending Kaighal on that assumption. We've already lost one arcanist."

Kamira snorted, but her laughter turned into a violent cough. "Then you shouldn't have been so quick to give me the title," she replied once the attack subsided. "I won't show weakness now."

Contrary to her own words, she wavered in Koshmarnyk's grip.

"But you do need to rest," Koshmarnyk said. "Other things can wait, or Irtan will handle them."

"Go, have some rest." The old archmage's expression softened. "I'll keep this all a secret, and we will see if anyone's tongue loosens when they learn the first archmage is... unavailable."

Veranesh walked over to the shattered window. "Very

well. See what you can learn and let me know later. I have other matters to tend to."

As he squeezed through the opening, Koshmarnyk could swear he saw the other demon's shadow on a nearby tower. At least he could trust Veranesh to deal with whatever trouble Fyertash was stirring.

"Go," Irtan said as people started gathering in the corridor again. "I'll see to things around here."

Koshmarnyk nodded and led her through the Towers, not concerned students would see Kamira. Undoubtedly, Archmage Irtan didn't want to cause chaos and panic, spreading news of her death, only cause enough uncertainty with her absence to stir the perpetrators into action. Some of the teachers slowed down at the sight of Kamira, but one look at Koshmarnyk's face told them they should seek whatever they needed elsewhere, and he made it with Kamira back to their chambers uninterrupted. She wasn't coughing anymore, and he took it as a good sign.

As soon as he closed the door, he turned to her. She needed time to rest and grieve, but he had to know first. "What really happened in there?"

"I..."

For all he could tell, her hesitation stemmed not from mistrust but confusion, so he exercised patience, ignoring his own growing concern. He walked over to the window and let the fresh air in. Kamira still stood in the middle of the room, and he had to lead her to the armchair and force her to sit down. At least she didn't protest.

"I should have died, but I didn't," she said. "Veranesh lied back there. Tijhran's sacrifice didn't save me."

Her face changed, and her lips trembled. She must have been pushing away the thought of her teacher's death until now, but to his surprise, she didn't collapse in tears. Instead, her expression hardened.

"Veranesh wasn't surprised I survived." Once more, coarseness roughened her voice, and a shallow, short cough followed.

Koshmarnyk had no trouble guessing what was going through her head. As reluctant to trust as she was, it took her time to accept that the demon could be an ally. To discover that, in the end, he *was* hiding things from her must have damaged the amiable relation they might have been building.

"Whatever it is, it saved your life," he said. "And he did rush to your aid as soon as he learned you were in trouble." It stung to know that the demon was more efficient in protecting her than he was, but all that mattered was that she'd survived.

Kamira clenched her fists. "I've been too trusting."

"If anything, you haven't been trusting enough," Veranesh said all of a sudden.

Both their heads turned, but instead of a demon, a nightfly hovered in front of the open window.

"I don't blame you, given the circumstances of our agreement. But you shouldn't be surprised I wasn't willing to share all *my* secrets with you."

The glare he received in response made it more than clear what Kamira thought about it, but she still nodded. "You said you would defend this city, and as long as those secrets don't affect that promise, that's all I care about."

"I keep my word just like you keep yours, pactee. As for the secrets... I wish to speak about *some* of them." The nightfly shifted and looked straight at Koshmarnyk. "With her alone, adept. It's for my pactee to decide how much she's going to tell you."

"I must admit it, demon, you do not encourage trust," Koshmarnyk replied. At least Veranesh was willing to share those secrets with Kamira, though if he was reluctant to include anyone else, their nature could be dangerous. Either way, Koshmarnyk would likely know soon enough, because Kamira shared with him everything, not bothered whether such knowledge could be a threat to him... or her. No matter what issues she might have with trust, she'd decided to include him in her innermost circle. A circle, Koshmarnyk realized, that had only two people in it: himself and Veelk. He doubted that the demon had as much of her trust.

"No yalari ever does," Veranesh remarked dryly. "Seek me out later, pactee, once you've rested."

The nightfly coiled at her forearm before either of them replied, and Koshmarnyk looked at Kamira. "You want to go now, don't you?"

"I need answers."

"More than rest?" He couldn't resist. "More than time to grieve?"

With a sigh, she lifted herself from the bed. "I feel fine now. And as for Master Tijhran..." Her fists closed. "We don't have time to grieve."

He knew better than to argue, even if what she said was only half-true. Kamira was choosing to not grieve, instead occupying her mind with immediate tasks and future consideration. She'd done so even with Veelk...

Koshmarnyk frowned at the thought. Fyertash claimed Veelk was gravely wounded, though he insisted he'd found the mage killer like that. If what the demon said was true, he'd brought Veelk to his tribe to die, yet Kamira refused to acknowledge her best friend was dead or dying.

With a sigh, he said, "Go. I'll see if Irtan needs any help."

Kamira smiled with gratitude, but when she walked past him, he enclosed her in his arms. She returned the embrace.

"I don't care what those secrets are. I don't care whether you decide to share them with me," he whispered. "I'll stay by your side, no matter what."

Surprise flashed on her face, and her expression softened as she looked at him longer than necessary before she left. He stood in the middle of the room, realization dawning on him. Until now, he'd never made any promises, and neither had she. With the future uncertain and their relationship stemming purely from opportune circumstances, it seemed better to leave things unvoiced. Yet there he was, having made such a promise without doubt and hesitation.

He huffed, amused.

The lone adept he used to be truly was no more.

12

Mayetti marched out from the council chamber, not bothered to conceal her ire. Other adepts would talk about it, but if speculation and gossip helped her to deepen the rift within the council, perhaps she would find a way to get the majority of Gildya to support her cause. Loyuwan rushed after her in that servile manner that enhanced her fury. The more openly he showed his support, the less she could use him to sway others, and reassurances or compliments he could offer would not help her get what she needed. The more time she spent in Gildya Magna, the less worthy it seemed, but before the high mages fell, the adepts had a lot of influence in the city. Now, with each day the new archmage reigned in the Towers, the adepts' council seemed to lose their footing, and the cautious and diplomatic bastard Yzeth wasn't willing to take risks to restore Gildya to its past power. Former first archmage Irtan was said to be the same, and in the end he had to step aside, giving his position to a younger and more ambitious man, so if she played it right, she could also replace Yzeth with someone more... understanding. A quick examination of all the council members presented the answer she sought.

With that, she stopped and turned to Loyuwan, her smile sweet. "Do you think you could work your magic on Adept Hybal? Make him see our perspective?"

The sleek adept replied without hesitation, "I'm sure he's as tired of giving up ground as we are. If you don't need my company, I'll go now to see him while all emotions are still fresh."

Mayetti waved him off. Loyuwan had all the mental faculties but mostly lacked spine, and she always considered him someone more interested in his own pleasures than politics. Yet his ability to seduce anyone and everyone came in handy, and she could trust he would play Hybal right. As he rushed off, her frustration eased. In the past, she'd faced and conquered bigger obstacles. If the council was too stubborn and cautious to act, instead she'd sent them at each other's throats.

"Adept Mayetti... A word in private, if you please."

Ervan's voice behind her back was unexpected, but she kept her composure. He might have overheard her quick exchange with Loyuwan, but if he wanted to talk away from others, it meant politics and trade rather than lecturing her. She gave him a glance. He stood calm and composed, his eyes focused and no emotion revealed, but at the same time, his posture was casual enough for someone feeling comfortable in the situation.

"Of course," she replied amiably. Although an obvious first choice, perhaps Hybal wasn't the best one after all. If Ervan had enough ambition and determination, he could be the one to take control of the council... with enough of her help to make him obliging later.

They walked without hurry, and neither bothered making small talk. Adept Ervan led her through Gildya's corridors until they reached his office, and that alone told her he wasn't about to waste her time on idle or vague conversations.

Mayetti glanced over the room, not expecting to see anything beyond what other offices had, though contrary to many adepts, Ervan kept his space clean and free of distractions. Whatever projects he might have been working on, they weren't stacked in messy piles an intruder could peruse, but tucked away on shelves and in drawers. A man that organized must have had clear plans as well, no matter how well hidden they may be.

"You were quite vocally against Gildya's leniency toward the High Towers," Ervan said as soon as they both were seated. "At the same time, you are aware that in the current situation, we have no leverage."

She allowed some of her curiosity to show. "You have something in mind. Something that would give us such leverage." The fact that he didn't offer it to the council meant either underhanded dealings or inner politics she wasn't aware of.

"Perhaps," he replied in a dismissive tone. "I'm more interested why you didn't speak up about a rogue adept walking freely in the city. One would think this undermined Gildya's authority even more, and taking action would be in line with your other demands." He looked her in the eye. "Yet you didn't even mention his name. Sentiment? Or something else?"

"Common sense." While she spoke, her mind was already exploring all the angles. Ervan was one of the adepts who, ten years ago, apprehended Alluvendran, and when the council discussed the rogue adept's return to the city, he demanded taking decisive action. Since he always exercised restraint in supporting or speaking against other matters Gildya discussed, there had to be a personal history between him and the rogue adept. Alluvendran had never mentioned anything to her, so it could have happened while she was back home. "Adept Yzeth has assigned me to be the intermediary between Gildya and the Towers. Previous archmages had spies in Gildya, so we can assume the new archmage does too, and given the gossip of her... close relationship with Alluvendran, I thought it would be better if they didn't learn of my views on the matter." She chose her words carefully. If she played it right, Ervan would read what he wanted to read and at the same time get no proof he could use against her.

Interest sparked on his face. "So you are of the mindset that not only is he a danger but he also undermines Gildya's authority?"

"Adepts died during his escape," she said, playing the emotional card. "And his reluctance to provide details makes me wonder what his real role in it was. Nevertheless, it's hardly a topic worth discussing when Gildya is so powerless," she added, steering the conversation where it was meant to go.

At that, Ervan offered a sly smile. "Quite the contrary—it's a perfect topic for the situation."

With a neutral expression and a wave of her hand, she encouraged him to continue, hiding her excitement. Ervan had an idea, and he was willing to share it with her.

"The archmage holds all the best cards at the moment." He leaned forward, focus on his face but little other emotion, as if he wasn't discussing the man whom he likely despised. "Not only has she powerful magic, knowledge of demons, and demonic allies at her side, but she also has her own inventor to prepare any blueprints she might need. Thus, all she needs Gildya for is actual manufacturing of the protective devices, and if Alluvendran is as secretive as he used to be, we won't even see the actual designs that would allow us to study them and offer improvements. And if the archmage got desperate, she could find skilled craftsmen to work under Alluvendran's direction, ignoring us altogether." Ervan's voice carried no emotion. "While without him around, the High Towers will have to turn to Gildya and rely on our support."

"It's a vicious circle, then." Even though she could guess where Ervan was going, she would force him to voice his thoughts. "Alluvendran's presence is Gildya's weakness, but Gildya is too weak to do something about his presence."

Ervan must have figured out she wouldn't take the bait. "An esteemed inventor like you is surely aware that there's always more than one way of handling a problem. All I'm saying is that with Alluvendran out of the way, and with your... connections, Gildya's position in the city would become much stronger."

Mayetti kept her face straight while her mind raced. "Are you seeking to relieve Yzeth in his leadership duties?" The question served only to mask her own reaction. For an adept who was only interested in research, or so she and others had thought, Ervan knew a little too much of Mayetti's ties. Unless it was a mere shot in the dark stemming from her reputation. At least she could be certain that he knew nothing of her involvement in the failed attempt to steal Gildya's explosive devices. Hiring lowlifes for the task had turned out to be a good choice, as it convinced the council it was nothing more than accidental thievery of Gildya's property rather than an elaborate plot. Now, with the changes in the Towers and Alluvendran's presence in the city occupying the council's attention, likely no one would ever look closer at it.

He shook his head. "I think Hybal is better suited to represent Gildya's interests. And you and I could ensure that he has the council's unanimous voice to act upon."

With that, his motives became clearer. He wouldn't risk putting himself out in public, but he did want to have control over Gildya's moves. While maintaining the façade of a man focused on research, Ervan must have been craving power and influence like many other men convinced of their own grandeur.

"Thank you, Adept Ervan, for your insights. You gave me a lot to think about." She stood up, and left after exchanging empty pleasantries neither of them cared about.

Her earlier frustration faded, and even though Ervan's possible knowledge of some of her secrets could become a concern, the conversation itself had offered her the solutions she sought. For the first time in days, Mayetti knew exactly what to do.

WHEN KAMIRA WALKED into the chamber, both demons were at their usual spots, engaged in a quiet conversation. Their body language suggested they were at ease around each other, and Kamira couldn't help wondering how much of it was a game between them. Veranesh might have had the upper hand, but she doubted that after centuries of being imprisoned he'd turn his back on any other demon, and Fyertash might have been setting up his own game in which gaining Veranesh's trust played an important role.

As she approached, Fyertash took off without a word.

"Pactee," Veranesh said.

He landed softly in front of her, but the wind still hit her, and she fought for balance while her lungs fought for breath all of a sudden. As soon as she ensured her footing, she stood motionless, controlling the air she took in and letting her body recover from the spell of weakness.

Veranesh watched her with his eyes narrowed.

In a way, she preferred him up above. They were never equals anyway, and the distance between helped her forget how big the demons were, and how one swipe of Veranesh's claws could be her undoing. At least from afar, his massive dark wings and wiry muscles seemed less imposing.

"You should be resting." A statement, nothing more, as if he was certain she wouldn't listen.

Yes, she should be resting, but answers were more important. "What's happening to me?" Her voice came out weaker and raspier than she'd hoped for, as if confirming that, indeed, she should have seen to her body's demands first.

Veranesh squatted down, his eyes closer to her level. "You have changed. Your time in the crystal had brought that about."

The way he spoke left no doubt he knew that it would happen. Kamira's body trembled at the thought, and she had to ask: "How much? To what end?"

"A human would not survive a prison meant for a yalari," he replied. "Our kind takes in what you call magic like you take in air. The crystal would have smothered you the very moment it closed on you, and you would have died. I'd have loved to see the surprise on the high mages' faces when they realized they were their own undoing... But needless to say, it would have rendered all your prior efforts pointless. With your death, the city you wanted to save would be no more. All I did was ensure you survived."

Kamira gave him a solemn nod. "And you failed to mention it."

"You might have decided to trust me, but such a revelation could cause a rift to grow between us," Veranesh said without a hint of remorse. "Had I told you, you'd either search for another way, suspecting deception on my part, or deem it too risky... and search for another way. We'd waste time we didn't know we didn't have."

A huff of dissatisfaction was her response. To argue the past choice with the knowledge of what happened next was absurd. On the other hand, she couldn't be sure Veranesh didn't predict his kin would be heading for Tyorane. He had a better understanding of what other demons would do. Had she dawdled back then, they could have been facing a demon invasion with Veranesh still in his prison and high mages in power.

"You mustn't worry, though. The change makes you no less the human you were... perhaps only safer. As long as you can reach the energies in the yalari realm, your body will never need air again, and it will resist any poison, ingested or otherwise taken in." He gave her a wave of a finger. "You'll still bleed and die like any other human, so do avoid those assassins who prefer blades."

She would have appreciated the attempt at humor if not for the revelations shared. No matter what Veranesh claimed, the time she'd spent in the crystal had affected her body more than anything she'd ever heard about. Even Veelk, who enjoyed the gifts of a powerful demon, could not shrug off poisons so easily, and pouring magic into his scars only did so much to keep him alive. The thought of her friend soured her mood further. Invoking her arcane training and discipline, she forced her focus away from the fact that she'd heard nothing about Veelk's wellbeing. There were problems she couldn't solve and there were the ones she *could* deal with... and the way Veranesh watched her tugged on her instincts.

"I feel like there's more than you're telling me." No matter what he said about the beneficial nature of the change, no matter how human she might have remained, magic like that had to have more effects, even if Kamira herself felt hardly any different.

"There are things which will bring you ease of thought and help you make better decisions. You don't have to be concerned about poison anymore, and that lack of fear will show the first archmage's power, which in turn will solidify trust and willingness of other humans to follow your lead," Veranesh replied. "There are also other things. Things that are of no consequence now and will matter not until you succeed in defending this city. But if your mind is preoccupied with them, you might fail to repel my kin."

She should have expected that no matter how forthcoming Veranesh chose to be, there was always more he would keep hidden. But in the end, he did say he wanted to discuss *some* secrets. At least the demon was forthcoming enough to admit there was more for her to know. "Fair enough," she muttered.

"Conceding so soon?" Veranesh arched his eyebrow. "I expected at least some insistence."

Kamira responded with a snort that turned into a cough. "No matter how I go about it, you'll only tell me as much as you want and when you want," she said once the rasping in her throat subsided. "Besides, you're right. All that matters now is keeping the city safe. My curiosity can wait." Of course, she'd kept to herself that her own body was still rebelling, and a prolonged conversation strained it even more. With no hopes of making Veranesh talk, whatever strength she had left could be better used elsewhere—likely on getting to bed, as much as she'd hate to admit it out loud.

The expression on Veranesh's face changed, showing satisfaction. "You've come a long way... Kamira. I still remember when you were ready to second-guess my every word. I promise you that when the threats are dealt with, if we're both still alive, I'll give you all the answers."

It didn't escape Kamira that he'd used her name, a rare treat, or perhaps recognition that she had become something more than another human, more than a tool to be used. Or maybe, as her suspicious nature demanded, it was a trick to ensure her trust. She almost snickered at the prospect of sharing that consideration with Veranesh, but the mention of their possible deaths brought grim thoughts.

"That's quite a promise."

The grin on the demon's face was shameless—and almost playful. "I'm a yalari. I might keep my word, but what comes with it is sometimes worse than not knowing. I'm quite certain that once we're done, your feelings toward me won't be warmer than they were when we first met. But, perhaps, you will become willing to participate in the game you've been tangled in instead of resisting it."

A grimace came to her face uninvited. It seemed that in the end, all that was happening was but a game to him. "So much for saving me concerns."

"As if you didn't have any before I spoke." Veranesh was still smiling, but his tone had a serious ring to it. "I promised you the truth, so the truth you get. We've learned each other enough by now. I have my own reasons to help you with the defense, and you have your rebellious nature that will oppose any attempt at manipulation, mine or anyone else's.

So far, neither has stopped us from finding enough trust and understanding to work toward our goals. I do not expect that to change."

To know that Veranesh understood the complicated nature of their relationship, if she could even call it such, brought some relief. The demon knew the limits of mutual trust and wasn't about to hold it against her. "You're here, no matter your reasons, helping with the defense, though you could have left," she said. "And I haven't forgotten that you saved Veelk's life."

Veranesh let out a chuckle. "And here I was, beginning to believe our relationship was becoming something more than what's owed. That, perhaps, you started seeing more in me than a mere source of your power."

There was a tease in his words, as if he knew that, indeed, she'd grown attached to his presence, advice, and even secrets and games, and Kamira gave him a smile. No matter what he kept from her, no matter what dire consequences her time in the crystal might have had, one thing seemed certain: just like she could trust Veelk with her life, she could trust Veranesh would not turn on her.

"Perhaps I did," she replied. "But until the city is safe, until we've both survived, and until secrets are properly shared, such thoughts are a waste of time, aren't they?"

Veranesh's laughter echoed within the chamber, its strength knocking off forgotten pieces of the crystal dome. "A pactee worthy of me." He stood up, stretching his wings. "Go now and rest. You'll need your strength. It'd be shame if the city fell because the only reason that keeps me here got herself killed through her own carelessness." He hesitated, then looked her in the eye, all playfulness gone from his expression. "One more thing. I know you're fond of the adept, and he seems like a trustworthy ally, but it'd be better if you didn't share with him what we've discussed... or anyone else, for that matter. Once people learn about it, it won't be much of an advantage anymore. No matter how much the adept might be willing to die for your secrets, there are ways to extract them."

All she gave him was a defiant stare. Even if she understood Veranesh's reasoning, she also understood trust, and as reluctant as she had always been in giving it to anyone, she would never back out from the trust once given without a good reason. At least the demon didn't go as far as suggesting Koshmarnyk wasn't trustworthy. "I might tell him that the secret is dangerous," she replied, "and he'll decide for himself whether he wants this burden or not."

She expected Veranesh to express his displeasure, especially that he was right in his insistence, but his scowl was as passing as a bird in flight. "A pactee worthy of me, indeed. I suppose it's my turn to concede rather than engaging in an argument that will lead nowhere."

"I appreciate it."

Veranesh took off, but Kamira still stood in the chamber.

No matter how rebellious she might have been, it was Veranesh who had the upper hand... in everything. From his sheer physical strength to providing her with magic to offering his knowledge and power for Kaighal's defense. For him to not play those cards, one by one until she yielded, was an act of benevolence she didn't expect from a demon. At the same time, he made it clear there was more than benevolence behind his decision to aid Kaighal. If she was to make a guess, Veranesh needed her for something, after the city was safe.

She smiled. Perhaps, when the secrets were truly shared, they could become friends, as the demon had implied. Until then, she'd better act with caution, no matter what unexpected gifts or benefits Veranesh's goals might bring, because they were mere allies bound not even by their goals but only by the path that led to them.

IF THERE WAS something good about the time of Koshmarnyk's imprisonment, it was the lack of concerns. Back in the prison, it was only in the beginning when an adrenaline rush accompanied Koshmarnyk each time he heard the sound of footsteps, but as time passed, he understood that Gildya's council was content with keeping him confined and no executioner would come to end his life. Given they offered him little water and almost no food, perhaps they'd hoped he would die on his own, and the ten years in a dark cell turned out into an experiment to determine how long the power of the imbued stones would keep him alive.

Koshmarnyk doubted the adepts were satisfied with that experiment's outcome.

Now, when he was free and part of the world again, concerns returned. Not even for the city he ultimately cared little about, but for the woman who was trying to save it. The thought of Kamira facing Veranesh and his secrets on her own grated on his composure more than the prospect of fighting against a demon army. When he listened to his voice of reason, he knew she would be fine, because the demon wouldn't have had torn through the Towers' walls to save her if he wanted to see her dead. Unfortunately, his instincts also had a say, and the green phlegm she coughed out raised the very concerns Koshmarnyk had tried to hush. If there was even a grain of truth in what they said about Tivarashan assassins, Kamira should be dead. The demon knew why she wasn't, and if Koshmarnyk was patient enough, soon he'd likely know too.

He grimaced. Patience and concerns weren't a good match. As always when he needed a distraction, his eyes and hands wandered to blueprints and schematics. The design of the device was ready and in the hands of Gildya's adepts, but Koshmarnyk could still have a look at the details. Perhaps there was something he could improve or alter, should it turn out necessary. His own experiences were full of circumstances when things didn't go as perfectly as they should.

The newfound focus chased concerns and other thoughts away, and he clung to it, so when someone knocked on the door, he hardly bothered responding.

"Enter!" he said, his eyes still on the work.

Over the last days, he'd gotten used to students bringing him meals and fishing for gossip, to teachers in need of Kamira's assistance, and to strangers looking for the first archmage's help in their usually trivial matters. Upon entering, most visitors realized that Kamira wasn't in the room and left with as little disturbance as their rushed apologies required, and students were often too timid to engage in a conversation, so Koshmarnyk didn't even lift his head to greet the person entering. He wouldn't risk losing his focus to provide courtesy toward someone who would care little about it. After all, in people's eyes, he was a mere adept working for the archmage. Others, those even less willing to acknowledge his position, considered him nothing but Kamira's toy.

"Working. Always working."

At the sound of Mayetti's voice, he flinched and finally looked up. He had been hoping for a distraction, and instead, as it seemed, he'd invited frustration... and trouble.

Mayetti stood by the door, and her pose was what he considered relaxed and slightly seductive, but after all, she rarely did anything without attempting to stir the desires of both men and women. Once, he'd fallen for those false charms too, and it took a bitter lesson to realize that for her, passion was a tool.

"Is Gildya having any problems with my blueprints?" he asked, hoping that bluntness would discourage a lengthy conversation.

Mayetti pouted, but he paid no attention to it. What had made the twenty-something woman look innocent and adorable changed the mature woman's face into a childish mask. She should be wiser, using her charms in subtler ways, showing her experience and wisdom. Even if it served only her machinations, she'd catch many more people with them.

"I come with another matter." Her tone made it clear she took offense to the lack of courtesies. "One that would be best discussed in private." She looked around the room, undoubtedly taking in the comfortable but meager furnishing. "Is your archmage around?"

"It's as private as you can get in the Towers," Koshmarnyk replied. "Why did you come?" His patience was already stretched thin. If Mayetti had come with nothing but games to waste his time, he'd speak with Archmage Varessa to find someone else to take Mayetti's inquiries before she bothered him again.

She curled her lips displeased. "I don't remember you being so jaded. You used to know how to treat a woman. But fine, I can see you're busy. I wanted to warn you that there's conspiracy among the adepts. If what I've heard is true, some people in Gildya are hoping to ask the Western Kingdom for assistance."

"The Western Kingdom?" Koshmarnyk furrowed his brow.

"Perhaps they fear that an archmage coming from Tivarashan means tightening the relationships with the Northerners, which nobody in the city wants. After all, the queen's envoy is already here. Or maybe they just want their own foreign leverage." Mayetti shrugged. "I don't know the details... not yet. There's a meeting happening tomorrow, and if I'm lucky, I'll know more. You're welcome to join me, if you aren't too busy. Meet me at Gate of Northern Winds tomorrow, past noon if you choose so."

He kept his expression neutral. Mayetti herself came from the Western Kingdom, but given her opportunistic nature and penchant for making enemies, she might have decided to throw her lot in with Kaighal. Or there was no conspiracy except the one that sought to see Koshmarnyk once more at Gildya's mercy—if the council wanted him to lower his guard, they would definitely have sent someone like Mayetti and concocted a false conspiracy to draw him out. Either way, at least some of the adepts weren't as focused at preparing the city's defenses as they should, and Kamira had to know the truth. Otherwise the consequences of Gildya's schemes could surprise them in the worst possible moment. So he had to play along, even if he was risking playing into the council's hand or walking into a trap.

"I'll let the first archmage know and meet you there," he said.

Her expression shifted, and Koshmarnyk expected a remark about his being under Kamira's thumb, but apparently, she wasn't willing to push her luck. "Don't be late." She sent him a charming smile and walked out of the chamber.

Koshmarnyk sighed. This wasn't the kind of distraction he was looking for. If only Gildya could wait with their plots until after the city was safe.

The door opened once more, and he turned his face away from it for a moment long enough to hide his grimace.

"Did you forget someth—"

He didn't finish, as it wasn't Mayetti who entered the room, but Kamira. She leaned heavily on the doorframe, and Koshmarnyk rushed to her side. A glance was enough to reassure him she wasn't wounded, and her relaxed posture suggested no new dangers. He shut the door and helped her to a chair.

"I see you had visitors," she said. "Of the annoying kind, I take it?"

Weak and likely still suffering from the poison's effect, she'd picked up on the ire in his voice nevertheless, and the thought that she paid attention to him brought warmth. "It's nothing that can't wait. Judging by the look on your face, the demon gave you enough to think about." He hesitated. After being on his own for so long, he wasn't sure he knew the difference between offering support and prying. Even if he did, that line might have been different from Kamira's perspective. "You should rest," he said, settling for the neutral choice. Whatever the demon had told her, she might not want to talk about it.

Kamira leaned back in the chair. "Aren't you at least a bit curious?"

He hesitated. Despite the dramatic entrance, it seemed like she was regaining her strength, and the earlier rasping was gone from her voice. She needed to rest, but it didn't have to mean sleeping. "I suppose I am. I've got a possible conspiracy among Gildya's adepts and a trap that is set to spring tomorrow. What have *you* got to trade?"

"Nothing too exciting, I'm afraid. Just dangerous secrets of a demonic nature if you're brave enough to learn them," she replied playfully. "Will that be good enough for you?"

He pushed the blueprints to the side and poured Kamira some water. Then he pulled another chair closer and made himself comfortable. "You go first."

13

So early in the afternoon, the little square by the Gate of the Northern Winds was still full of traders, farmers, and occasional travelers, few of them expressing any concern over the news of demons.

Koshmarnyk took a deep breath, waiting in the shade of one of the run-down buildings. His instincts told him he was walking into a trap, but he couldn't turn away Mayetti's offer. Her news of Gildya conspiring to turn on him and Kamira had to be checked and confirmed. If the adepts were desperate enough to turn to the Western Kingdom for help, Kaighal could lose its freedom before even the demons made the landfall.

At least he didn't have to worry about Kamira. When he'd shared the information with her, the expression on her face was clear. She wouldn't let him go alone. And then the archmage in her took over.

"I want to go with you"—the pain in her voice was clear, too—"but I can't take that risk. If something happens to me, the defense preparations will fall apart in the squabbles for power."

That memory brought a sigh. She played her role well, the authoritative Tivarashan woman who had all the power and never asked anyone for advice. With Veranesh at her side, people feared her enough to not oppose her ideas and not waste too much time on pointless discussions. After the siege, a new way of governing the city had to be forged, of that neither he nor she had any doubt—but until then, Kaighal needed an unyielding leader and someone who understood the gravity of the threat.

A sour half-smile crooked his lips at the thought that some people would not believe in any danger until demonlings clawed at their very doorstep, even though there were already two demons around. At the same time, the way both Veranesh and Fyertash provided assistance might have convinced the Towers' opponents that demons could be reasoned or bargained with. There were always those who put profit before reason. The people Mayetti had mentioned might have been like that.

As if called by his thoughts, Mayetti emerged from the street leading into the city, her stride confident and ever so subtly seductive, turning heads of workers and traders. She carried a basket with her, and her casual clothes that mimicked the outfits of Kaighal's wealthy class suggested she didn't want to be recognized as a Gildya member.

"It's a strange place to meet," Koshmarnyk muttered when she leaned forward to kiss him on the cheek. Her flowery scent enveloped him and her locks teased his face, but he doubted Mayetti would do something crude if she was trying to charm him. It was likely to deceive anyone who might have been watching.

"We'll be heading out. A nice meal in the meadows." She showed him the basket and lifted her arm in a clear cue for Koshmarnyk to hold it.

In the meadows, outside of the city walls' safety, wasn't exactly where he wanted to be. The show Mayetti had put on so far suggested she was worried about spies, and if he refused, he'd learn nothing more from her. So he took the arm offered. If her deception was something other than a way to lose any curious followers, Mayetti was in for a nasty surprise. He might have been a naïve fool a decade ago, but ten years in prison was enough of a lesson to teach him to keep his guard up all the time.

That thought gave him pause, and he reevaluated it. No matter how much the betrayal of his fellow adepts taught him not to trust anyone, there were still those with intentions he could be sure of. Mayetti simply was not and would never be one of them.

Together, they passed the gate and walked in silence, Mayetti leading them down the road. At some point, she burst out laughing, arching her head back as if the amusement controlled her body, but in doing so she managed a glance over her shoulder before looking back at him. "It seems that no one is following us." With the weight of her body pressing on his side, she jostled them off the road and into the meadow. "We should make for the trees quickly."

The forest was at least half a day's walk away, if Koshmarnyk recalled correctly. He arched his eyebrow.

She rolled her eyes. "They'll be meeting in the clearing there. You don't think anybody would risk inviting Westerners into the city? They want to keep it secret until they're ready to make a move."

"We could have followed them," he said, though he expected Mayetti to have an answer ready.

"And risk being seen?" She pursed her lips. "I don't think you understand how much I'm risking by simply associating with someone shunned by Gildya and who has rather... *intimate* ties with the archmage."

He couldn't help wondering whether that note of jealousy in her voice was genuine, or if she wanted to make him feel desired. Probably the latter, seeing as everything else matched exactly the way she acted when she tried to manipulate people. There must have been no one to tell her some tricks worked only once. Or maybe, like him, all those other men she was playing had reasons to not mention it. Until Koshmarnyk knew whether she only played her little games out of habit, or if she had ulterior motives to keep him satisfied and complacent, he would allow Mayetti to think her tricks still worked on him.

"So, is the first archmage really worth the confrontation with Gildya?" she asked in a playful manner. "Is it the power she holds over the city? Or something else?"

He couldn't help wondering if Mayetti would even understand if he tried to answer honestly. Kamira was worth more than that, more than even having to confront an army of demons, but such confessions belonged between friends, not potential enemies. "Don't you think that I have my very own reason to stand against the council?"

Mayetti furrowed her brow, her head slightly cocked to the side. "You're right. They'd never agree with your presence," she said. "But you still could have left. Juamha might be a place of barbaric ways and an occasional demon army, if the news of Devanshari is true, but an inventor like you could do well there, unrestrained by Gildya's rules. The Western Kingdom would welcome you too..." She gave him an evaluating glance. "And I wouldn't put it past you to go far south, beyond the desert, and make your home in the jungles' solitude. But no. You stayed." With a charming smile, she asked again, "So, is the archmage really worth it?"

To show discontent with her insistence meant to give her both information and more ammunition. In the past, he would have wrapped his arm around her waist, pulled her close, and, with perfect compliments, make her forget what she was asking about. But after he had walked in on her in the embrace of some Westerner noblewoman, even if such strategy was still an option, the mere thought of it brought a vile taste to his mouth. "I suppose you'll soon know for yourself. We will have to speak with her after we confirm this conspiracy exists."

A shadow passed over her face, and she looked over her shoulder. The meadows behind them were as empty as before, but she picked up her pace nevertheless. "Come. I'd rather be in the woods before the nightfall."

He did not object, though the prospect of lying in wait, alone with Mayetti, made him regret he had agreed to be the bait in this trap. At least, no matter which way the evening went, it all would be done by dawn, and he'd be returning to Kaighal.

Thankfully, Mayetti stopped talking, and they made it to the forest at a good pace. The sun was already setting when she led him among the trees, seemingly with no path to follow. Before he could doubt her sense of direction, they walked into a small clearing.

"We're here, aren't we?" The question was nothing but a distraction. Even without any visible cue, he sensed tension in the quietness of the forest meadow. Or perhaps it was the fragments of demons spelled into the imbued stones he'd willingly blended with his own flesh, echoing their owners' stirred instincts, reaching beyond their own world. Either way, danger was gathering thick like an evening fog.

"To be honest, I wasn't sure if you'd come." Mayetti took

a step to the side. "Haven't you for a moment considered it could be a trap?"

Her confident and ever-so-slightly condescending tone told him more than enough.

"I knew it was a trap. But we needed to know who in Gildya is conspiring against the Towers." He looked her in the eye. "I would have been disappointed if it turned out it wasn't you."

Mayetti looked at him in that condescending manner she reserved for people not worth her effort. "So, where's your aid? The archmage didn't come to ensure her precious lover stays out of harm's way? Perhaps she cares less about you than you dare to admit."

"Or she wouldn't insult me by offering to help deal with a lousy adept and a handful of henchmen." With a fight looming over him, his mind was too focused on it to bother with Mayetti's games. "I hope you have an escape route prepared, because if you're still here when I'm done with your thugs, I'm taking you back to the council."

"It will not get you in their good graces. They will condemn me, that's certain, but as soon as their judgment is done, they'll turn their eyes back to you."

"But before they do, they'll have to stop their foolish power plays and do what everyone expects them to. They'll help defend their home from demons." As he spoke, he took a step forward. As much as he wouldn't mind testing himself in a fight, he first needed to ensure Mayetti didn't flee.

At her gesture, seven men and women stepped out of the bushes, all of them burly and rough, and their mismatched weapons and armors befitted robbers, not mercenaries. Without hesitation, they made their way toward him, tightening the circle with every step.

Koshmarnyk didn't wait. He lunged, knives readied. The

first to taste his blades was the largest, approaching from behind and wielding an ax. Koshmarnyk hopped backward directly toward the brute, which moved him to draw his weapon high in the exact manner one would chop wood, and that of course left his entire belly and throat exposed. The head of the ax dug deep into the ground, and the man stumbled backward, clutching at the blood pumping from his neck.

Sensing opportunity, the two closest lunged as their ax-wielding friend fell to the ground. Koshmarnyk moved with his momentum toward the lithe, thin assailant, his short sword recently cleaned of rust, and away from the mountain of a woman armed with an ornate staff. The key to fighting with knives was to get inside the reach of the opponent's weapon, and Koshmarnyk was almost hugging the wiry would-be swordsman when he caught his opponent's sword arm under his own and plunged his dagger rapidly into the thin man's chest then spun away to avoid the staff.

A slight misjudgment ensured a nasty bruise on Koshmarnyk's arm later, but the hefty swing of the staff was not that of a trained fighter, so no bones broken. Koshmarnyk lunged, scissoring his blades across her neck and thrusting his knee into her gut.

The others had to make their way around Mayetti, and Koshmarnyk caught a glimpse of fear on her face as she backed away. Things weren't going according to her plan.

"Attack!" Her voice was a notch too high-pitched to sound confident.

More thugs emerged from behind the bushes and trees, and Koshmarnyk had to commend their discipline, keeping that quiet until now. None of them wore any imbued stones either, which meant that even if Mayetti had underestimated his strength, at least she remembered he could sense the magic within them.

The remaining four of his first engagement swarmed, but they were clearly unaccustomed to fighting in close quarters, especially with allies. They were hesitant to swing their weapons, and Koshmarnyk made swift use of their ineptness.

As the last of the four fell, Koshmarnyk readied his bloodied daggers, eagerly awaiting the second assault.

A shadow passed over the clearing. Too large to have been that of a bird, it made Koshmarnyk tense. Kamira trusted him, and if she'd intended to send one of the demons, she would have told him. Or perhaps she'd learned something.

The men and women circling him paused in bewilderment, so he risked a glance upward.

Something large and clawed was all he made out before his consciousness was taken from him.

As eager as he was to reach land, Myrkan changed his route as soon as the wind brought the scent of familiar energy, heading to the southwest instead. Soon enough, the shoreline that stretched with bright sand and little more appeared in his sight. His primal instincts still fought against getting closer to his enemy, but at least the wind brought nothing more than salt, so the fear that caught him in its claws would soon subside. Myrkan gritted his teeth. The emotion reminded him of how helpless he felt against the most powerful kanyalari. They might have treated him like he was one of them, but in the end, he still had to bargain for what he desired and remained at the mercy of Arujhan and his equals.

To be away from those hoyve, even in an unfamiliar world, made Myrkan feel like he was in control again. Fyertash must have felt the same, and thus never bothered returning.

Myrkan narrowed his eyes, and the salty wind had nothing to do with it. Opportunities that human lands offered must have been clear to a cunning yalari like Fyertash, so if he'd decided to defy Arujhan and others, he could also become Myrkan's rival.

Against the urge, he didn't rush to the shore. Arriving exhausted would leave him vulnerable—something he couldn't afford. Instead, he glided through the air as much as he could, beating his wings only when he had to.

He made landfall hours later, when the sun was closer to setting behind the mountains far in the distance. The air smelled dry, and he caught the distinct trace of familiar magic, but it was fading instead of intensifying, and his aggravated instincts eased. It must have been near where Veranesh's prison used to be, and the magic that held him captive, his own magic—the irony of which Myrkan savored whenever the thought returned—still lingered within the place.

He took deep breaths, and even though Veranesh's ghastly presence grated on his composure more than he'd like to admit, Myrkan caught faint notes of Fyertash as well. Yet it didn't mean the other yalari had anything to do with their enemy's release or that he had even met him. He might have simply arrived like Myrkan had, far enough into the sand-filled lands—deserts, as humans called them—to remain unnoticed until he chose to reveal himself.

Unable to determine neither threats nor tracks, Myrkan

took off in the air again, heading west. Once he got deep enough into the land to stay away from the city where Veranesh's presence seemed the strongest, he turned north. Even if he wasn't and never would be strong enough to confront the once-imprisoned kanyalari, the answers had to be close to where Veranesh dwelt.

The desert below slowly shifted into shrubs and bushes, and farther to the north, forests stretched. From beyond those trees, a powerful wave of energy emanated, bringing a shiver to Myrkan's spine. He'd rather face Veranesh on his own than venture deeper into the lands that four kanyalari called their own.

Yet there were fluctuations other than the power of his enemy and the energy of the Four who, a long time ago, had made an alliance in a bid to win the worship of a nation. Myrkan flared his nostrils, catching traces of other magic in the wind. From what he could tell, three yalari, much weaker than him, lurked to the northwest, and his curiosity spiked. Yet the other scent of magic won the battle for his attention. If Myrkan didn't know better, he could swear Veranesh was out of the city and weakened significantly. His magic was faint, but unmistakable. A trap of sorts? Likely. But Myrkan had to know.

Without hesitation, he followed the trace.

It led him all the way to the forest's southeastern edge, too close to the city where Veranesh resided, and too close to the border of the Four's lands, and Myrkan slowed down, bringing himself to a hover over the trees. Nearby, in a clearing, eight people stood, five males and three females. Myrkan knew enough of human habits and behavior to recognize a fight was to ensue. The man, the one who carried Veranesh's power within, stood in the middle, turning his head as if he was trying to keep an eye on everyone else. A fight lost before it started, if Myrkan was correct, but he couldn't let the man die before getting some answers.

The humans below advanced, but to Myrkan's surprise, the man held his ground. He lunged first, and at least one strike of the tiny blades landed a fatal blow, and more slashes kept other opponents away. He moved fast for a human, and Myrkan sniffed the air. More magic swirled around the stranger, all originating from different yalari but none strong enough to tell him more.

The fight in the forest continued, and more bodies fell to the ground. The rich scent of blood reached even Myrkan's nostrils, and his claws moved in anticipation. One of the women, so far keeping away from the fray, called out, and more people rushed out from among the trees. From what he'd seen so far, the man below could likely take them on, or at least die trying, but Myrkan needed him alive. And the woman... her too.

Without hesitation, he swooped down. His first strike knocked down his target. Others dispersed, gasps and shouts like waves among them, their eyes wide and hands on their crude weapons shaking. It would hardly be a fight, but blood spilled in a fray always tasted the best, and human flesh had softness and sweetness no yalari's carcass had.

A grin wide on his face, Myrkan attacked.

They scattered like a flock of frightened birds. He plucked them one by one, cherishing each kill. If only he had more time to instill proper terror... But the smarter ones were already fleeing among the trees, and though their bark was hardly a barrier for him, he couldn't sow too much distraction unless he wanted to draw attention. He didn't sense Veranesh nearby, but it didn't mean that sly yalari wouldn't soon return to the city that had his stench all over it.

The woman, his target, was already at the edge of the clearing, so he ignored the remaining groups of other humans and lunged for her. She screamed and kicked as he lifted her in the air, closing his claws around her arms, just enough to savor her terrified face.

As much as he wanted the moment to last, he had to be quick. "Silence, or I'll crush you."

To his surprise and satisfaction, the scream died out in an instant. The woman's eyes narrowed, and he already recognized that calculating expression. She'd figured out in no time that he wanted her alive, and she would be obedient —at least until she found a way to leverage what he needed from her.

Myrkan smiled maliciously. "Good human. You'll give me what I want, and I might consider leaving you alive. I'll need cunning servants."

If the remark offended her pride, she didn't show it. Her only response was a slow nod.

"Good. If you run, I'll chase you down." As he released her, part of him wanted to see her run, to taste the fear, but he needed information. "You'll tell me everything you know. Of the yalari that resides in the city, and of any humans that serve him." He glanced back at the motionless one in the grass. "And you'll tell me everything you know about this one." The way he moved and carried yalari power within and at the same time still had a weak human body had to be a part of Veranesh's plan.

The woman relaxed. "Now that would take the better part of the night."

He caught an unusual note in her voice, as if she shared something with that man. Yet he had no doubt that she'd orchestrated the attack on him. Humans were so strange in their ways, but he could understand betrayal and greed, and though they lacked the finesse and brilliance of kanyalari, they weaved their own crude schemes.

He looked down at the unconscious man. Back in Yalarethe, he could simply lift him up in the air with the woman in the other hand, but this world was devoid of magic that supported his body, and he would need the full range of his wings for stable flight. Two burdens by his side would see him too clumsy in the air.

"We have time." He slung the man across his shoulder and pointed toward the trees. Since he was grounded for the time being, he could chase down the other oddity he'd sensed earlier. "Walk this way. And talk."

THE HOUSE WAS large and mostly unused. It was in a good shape, but as Ryell ventured down its countless corridors, he discovered many nooks that could use a bit of restoration... or at least a dust cloth. He couldn't blame the servants. There were but a few of them, too few for the place this size. Perhaps Yoreus's wealth had been less impressive than his position might have suggested, or the late archmage simply didn't care about the house he must have visited only on rare occasions. According to Atissa, Yoreus spent most of his time in the Towers, and he never even bothered to bring his own daughter here.

The thought of Atissa made him frown. While he'd taken took a few days to relax and enjoy the peace the secluded place offered, she'd disappeared for long hours, avoiding both his company and his questions. At first, he thought that perhaps she wanted to familiarize herself with the place that was now hers and inquire Dynar about the state of her father's wealth, but the longer it took, the more suspicious Ryell grew. There could be more to the house than a shelter. After all, despite never bringing Atissa here before, Yoreus had left her a letter with instructions...

Ryell grimaced. It seemed that there was more to it than mere directions. During their journey, Atissa had guarded the piece of paper like a treasure, and back then he'd considered it an emotional reaction—her father's last words, meant just for her, and possibly the only keepsake she had of him, since she'd refused to reenter the Towers after his death. Now, having spent days of wandering the house alone, Ryell wasn't so sure.

"There you are!"

The sound of Atissa's voice surprised him. It had been a while since it carried so much excitement and joy, as if the burden of the recent events had disappeared and she was back to being a cheerful and innocent woman. *There's something more...* he realized as he turned to face her. The subtle aura surrounded her and teased his senses. Ever since Koshmarnyk had blended the crystal shard with Ryell's skin, he didn't experience the hunger for magic anymore, but his long-starved body became more sensitive to it.

"I got my magic back!"

Instinctively, he took a step back. He remembered the speech in front of the Towers all too well. High magic was a lie, stolen from an imprisoned demon, and even if the demonologists colored the truth to paint themselves in a better light, their explanation made it clear why even high mages couldn't escape the clutches of corruption. Everything coming from the demon world was tainted, but at least high magic didn't require a personal bind with a demon. With it gone, Atissa had only one way to getting magic back.

Some of his thoughts must have shown on his face, because she laughed and shook her head. "I didn't make a pact, silly! I never would."

"But high magic is gone," Ryell said. If she wanted him to believe her, he needed more than vague remarks.

She became serious. "The one from the Towers is, and maybe it's better this way... It was all stealing. But high magic wasn't always like that. Back before the Cataclysm, it might have been less powerful, but it was pure. My father..." Her voice broke, and her lips trembled. "He was working on a way to bring the old high magic back. To make it as it used to be, and maybe even succeed in ridding the Towers of the corruption that was eating the archmages." She looked down. "He just never got to achieve his goal, because that vile woman killed him and destroyed all his efforts."

The longer she spoke, the more her expression changed, shifting from the excitement toward hate. Ryell pressed his lips together before any words in Kamira's defense slipped from them. "But you can continue his work," he said instead.

Atissa nodded, her emotions shifting once more and determination taking over. "I will. Once we're ready, we will return to Kaighal and throw all those treacherous demonologists out. They don't belong in the High Towers." She clenched her fists.

His heart sank. "So, you're after revenge?" he asked quietly.

"I'm after justice! She doesn't deserve the first archmage's title! She murdered my father and spun lies to convince everyone she wasn't just a jaded student who wanted to get back at the archmages for expelling her. And she claims there is an invasion coming, but she's the one who brought demons into Kaighal!"

Ryell could relate to the need for revenge. After all, he had sought it as well when he arrived in Tyorane. But he also had already tasted the bitterness of success. The memory of the events in the dark clearing in the forest carried no satisfaction, only emptiness. Atissa would not get her grand return to the Towers. Instead, she would have to fight Kamira, and even if she won... "You'll turn into her. Obsessed by revenge and blinded by it," he said before he could think the words over.

"What am I supposed to do, then?" she fired back. "Congratulate her? Allow her to go unpunished for what she did?"

"You could start a new life. One that wouldn't be marred by the war your father and Kamira waged for years."

Atissa stared at him, wide-eyed, leaving no doubt that she felt betrayed. Ryell sighed. Looking back, perhaps he should have shared with her his most guarded secret, the one of Cahala's death. Had he done it, maybe Atissa would already know that revenge brought no satisfaction, and could make wiser decisions than he did. If he brought it up now, she would only see it as an attempt to manipulate her. And—a bitter smile lurked in the corner of his lips—she would not appreciate that he'd kept it from her for all that time.

"I thought you were on my side!" Her lips trembled, but her voice never wavered. "I thought you came here because you wanted to support me. To help me!"

Her accusatory tone grated on his composure. She was so blinded by her hate for Kamira and thirst for revenge, she refused to see that he'd been supporting her ever since they left Kaighal. She'd relied on him all the way to the house, but as soon as she got her magic back, she forgot all about his efforts.

What a fool he was to believe she cared for him! Atissa was just like her father, seeing only a tool in him. It was time he stopped being so naïve, falling for lies and manipulation over and over again as if he was a gullible child, not a Devanshari royal guard.

He looked her straight in the eye. "Then maybe I shouldn't have come."

The surprise on Atissa's face brought unexpected satisfaction.

"It's that corrupted demonologist magic, isn't it? She managed to poison you with it." Atissa pointed at his chest. "I should have known you're really on her side."

Ryell clenched his fists. This once he would not fall for her manipulation. "Think what you wish. I won't stay to watch you two destroy each other, nor will I lend a hand to either of you." While she stood motionless, he walked past her. "Have a good day, *my lady*."

Atissa didn't chase after him, and Ryell took it as confirmation that she'd never really cared. His thoughts were drowning in bitterness, but he didn't allow himself to dwell. Instead, he made his way down the corridor, his back straight and chin high—a proud royal guard once more.

It was time he took the very advice he'd given Atissa. It was time he started a new life, away from all those who had betrayed him, one way or another.

14

Kamira stared at Kaighal's plan, marked with countless black lines. No matter how she adjusted them, the port remained the planned circle's weak spot. Going along the shorelines would allow for tightening the energy flow, but meant giving up part of the city along with its walls that provided a more physical defense in case magic failed. Even if stone couldn't keep the higher demons away, at least it would stem the wave of the demonlings she was certain would come with them. But to preserve the walls meant stretching the magic defense thin between the ends of twin crescent piers that guarded the port like stone jaws.

Yet her mind was not on the task, and lack of focus kept her from making a decision, any decision. *Nyk, where are you?* It'd been already a day since he set out to uncover the truth behind Gildya's machinations, and even though she knew he could handle himself, she couldn't help worrying. The caring man hidden behind the wiry adept with a dry smile had grown on her more and more. His absence also reminded her that she hadn't seen her closest friend for weeks now, and his fate remained a mystery. Even the demons had disappeared, scouting away from the city, so she couldn't seek comfort in discussions with Veranesh, whose unemotional approach to everything provided a mental ointment for her own concerns.

Focus! She pulled a fresh map from underneath the pile. If she was to worry, she should worry about the things she could fix, like the circle that would protect the city.

"It's not how I expected the first archmage to spend her time." Prince Jalyn approached, a jovial expression on his royal face. "I thought you'd be making decisions, giving orders, and not"—he glanced at the papers on the table—"doing a scribe's work."

"It seems that I live to disappoint you, prince," she replied dryly. She made no explicit demand to not be disturbed, but whoever was granting visitors access to the Towers should have been more concerned with letting Tivarashan royalty roam freely through its corridors. "Is there anything I can help you with?"

"I'd appreciate if you spared a moment of your time, that's all."

A moment of her time was the last thing she was willing to spare. As much as she hated stepping onto the path that could lead the Towers back to the habits that prevailed under the high mages' rule, it was time to put someone at the door who would keep guests and petitioners out. She could hardly focus as it was; she didn't need others piling on more distraction.

"Of course." She forced a smile. Maybe a break from her task would help in finding a solution. "Something in particular you wish to discuss?" She led them toward the windows overlooking the city.

He hesitated, and as far as she could tell, it wasn't a

staged reaction. "Yes, there is," he replied with caution. "I would like to make an offer... But the offer would be for Lady Kamira of the Altrainne family, who happens to also hold the title of the first archmage in Kaighal."

"There's no Lady Kamira of the Altrainne family. My father, Lord Altrainne, made it quite clear the last time we spoke." The memory of their meeting, though it carried the satisfaction of a rebellious act against the man who'd tried to manipulate her, was hardly a pleasant one.

"Lord Altrainne should have known better than speak words of anger publicly," Jalyn replied, "but I'm sure everyone knows he didn't mean them. You are, after all, his beloved daughter. His *only* daughter." He leaned closer, a feverish shine appearing in his eyes. "Your family is counted among the powerful ones in Tivarashan, and with your noble blood... All you'd need is to become a part of the royal family. Why play a leader of one city when you could have the whole kingdom?"

His intentions became clear, and Kamira burst out laughing. "You flatter me if you believe I could compete for the crown with Princess Hyuleen," she replied between chuckles. "Even without following court politics, I know she's the queen's favorite."

Jalyn smiled, seemingly unmoved by her amusement. "It's not hard to be favorite when there's no equal match. A woman of the finest ancestry who took the first archmage's title for herself, and who successfully defended Kaighal from demon invasion..." He lifted his hand when she gave him a dubious look. "It *will* be successful when you have a Tivarashan army and the Four's priesthood at your disposal, and I can make that happen. Finally, a woman who annexed Kaighal to the kingdom... That's someone who'd outshine Princess Hyuleen and win the queen's favor."

As he painted his vision, she had to appreciate his cunning. The ambitious prince craved the power that Tivarashan traditions denied him, and he found a way to fight for the crown. Queen Kamira of Tivarashan... Would any noblewoman from her homeland be able to refuse such an offer?

The intensity of Jalyn's stare and the hope poorly concealed on his face demanded a reply, and laughing him off would not bring her any gain. "Such an offer leaves me nearly speechless, but I can't help wondering... Is this your plan, prince, or your mother's?"

"I doubt my mother is aware of my... desires, but I wouldn't put it past her. If she sent me here considering such an outcome, it only means we have a chance to succeed."

Kamira gave him a sober stare. As cunning and ambitious as he might be, he lacked experience. Not that she had more insights on that matter, but at least she'd seen enough back at home and during her time in the High Towers to know better than to blindly hope for the best. "Or she's using your dreams to make Kaighal part of Tivarashan at minuscule cost: one marriage of a child she has no other use for anyway." Perhaps the words she chose were too harsh for a spoiled prince, but if he wanted to play games with the best of Tivarashan, it was better he heard them from her, not them.

To her surprise, Jalyn didn't snap. There was more to that young man, early in his twenties, than she'd expected, but the grin he gave her was nevertheless boyish. "I'd still consider such a game worth playing. Wouldn't you?"

She couldn't help laughing again. In one way, Jalyn was right: she couldn't escape who she was. A Tivarashan woman of a noble house. Yet he should have remembered such women weren't easy to sway. The echo of her laughter faded from the chamber.

"You give me the answer to that question," she replied with a serious expression. "I turned my back on my father when he threatened to disown me. I spent the last five years exploring half-crumbled ruins and crawling through underground tunnels," she continued, watching his face drop. Clearly whatever spies he had, they'd failed to find out the truth about her, and she couldn't help wondering whether Jalyn thought she'd spent the last five years in comfort, hiding, planning her grand revenge on the high mages. "And I sleep with a man Gildya Magna considers a felon."

The smile faded from his face, but she didn't catch any glimpse of displeasure at her blunt words. "Tivarashan would welcome a skilled inventor like him. And I wouldn't mind. After all, our history is full of marriages for political gain, and royal consorts have been commonplace as well."

"I would mind," she replied coldly.

Emotions flashed on his face: surprise and probably hurt pride at her turning down an offer many Tivarashan women would beg to receive. Yet he regained his composure quickly and lifted his chin. "Well played, first archmage." He offered a bow. It didn't escape her that his voice had the slightest tremble to it, and he'd resorted to her official title. "You might have won this game, but I won't withdraw my offer. Should you decide to call for help, I'll have the Tivarashan army obey your every order."

Kamira arched an eyebrow, once more taking in his posture and expression. He meant it, and it seemed he was ready to risk that he'd gain nothing in the end. Perhaps he could be made into an ally. "What about you, prince? Would *you* obey my order?"

She must have caught him by surprise, because he hesitated before replying.

"As long as you don't order me to leave Kaighal or go against my nation." His eyes searched her face for a clue. "You have a role for me to play, haven't you?"

She allowed herself a smirk. Queen Andalisha knew what she was doing when she sent her son to Kaighal. The young man had promise and could have made quite a name for himself back in Tivarashan... if he abandoned the ludicrous dream of being crowned a king. "I'm an arcanist, not a tactician. I'll need someone to work with the city council on organizing the guards and the militia, on overseeing non-magical defenses and coming up with battle plans, should they be needed. With so many years of peace, the city has hardly any experienced officers to turn to, yet I trust that the finest Tivarashan schooling still includes a lot of military knowledge. I've invited King Allyv to share his experience, and I see no reason to not issue you the same invitation, if you're interested."

Jalyn gave her a nod while he watched her as intently as she watched him. "Another good move. You flatter both him and me, get yourself tacticians you need, and by having both of us involved, you would avoid accusations that you're selling Kaighal to a foreign power. But tell me, why would I agree if it's not in my interest? It should be clear to you that I'd rather wait for you to be in a situation dire enough to ask for Tivarashan aid. Then I wouldn't have to share the victory with a so-called king who ran away from his own land."

"Maybe because the alternative is risking going back to Tivarashan empty-handed?" she said. The way he'd berated Allyv deserved some bluntness. The Devanshari king was young, but he was already dealing with more problems and responsibilities than Jalyn likely ever would. "As a son who failed his mother performing one simple task... Who got outmaneuvered by a mere noblewoman."

Jalyn shifted uneasily. He must have been picturing his return and disappointment on Queen Andalisha's face. Kamira had never met her in person, but back in the day, when she was still growing up, tutored and groomed to become the Altrainnes' heir, she had learned enough about the woman who held the ultimate power in Tivarashan.

"Perhaps it is time you stopped chasing childish dreams and carved out an ambition that serves you, not your mother," she added. "And contrary to many Tivarashan women, I don't forget those who help me."

He looked at her, fire in his eyes, as if the insult of being the queen's tool hurt him more than anything else.

The sound of the door opening distracted them both. Kamira could hardly contain her hope it would be Varessa with something that demanded the first archmage's immediate involvement. The prince and she were done, having exchanged offers, and she had no desire nor patience to suffer through his tantrum.

That hope was enough distraction to put her at a disadvantage. By the time she recognized two gray-skinned assassins darting across the floor, they were already halfway through the chamber. Jalyn watched them with wide eyes, which suggested he hadn't been the one to send them to the chamber, and with no weapon by his side, he'd be of no use. Without hesitation, Kamira stepped forward, shielding him with her own body. Contrary to her expectations, the assassins didn't charge straight at her. Instead, they split, cornering her and the prince against the window.

It suited her well.

The assassin deeper in the chamber threw an object at her, a metallic sphere, from what Kamira could tell. She was ready. Obedient to her will, magic flowed in a steady and powerful stream, creating a barrier. The device clanked against it and erupted into flames, showering the floor with sparks. The other one lunged forward, her forearm raised to her face. As she slammed against the barrier, its magic wavered, and the assassin pressed. Kamira's eyes widened at the shine of spiky imbued stones under the woman's clothing.

A triumphant grin stretched across the assassin's face as she pushed through the barrier, her eyes full of predatory hunger.

The waning barrier was not worth sustaining, so Kamira allowed its demise and created a new one instead. Then, with more magic channeled from her body, she thrust it outward. The force slammed into the assassin, pushing her backward. Taken by surprise, the woman lost her footing and got caught between the expanding barrier and the nearby wall. The assassin made no noise as the barrier compressed her lungs, and then bones cracked until the body hung limp between the barrier and the wall.

The other assassin had kept his distance, and so had time to withdraw to the far end of the chamber.

Kamira turned to him. To extend the barrier too much could mean weakening it or exposing herself to other possible dangers, so she had to deal with the man some other way. It was one thing to defend herself from pitiful thugs, especially with Veelk around to come to her aid if needed, and another to face a skilled murderer with a plethora of tricks, and her with nothing but a useless prince behind her back. That thought made her step to the side and bring him into her peripheral view. With the Tivarashan crown so interested in bringing Kaighal to its knees, Jalyn could see his own chance in the turmoil. It would be foolish to survive the assassins only to leave her guard down and end up killed by a mere boy.

Yet Jalyn stood in the same spot, as motionless and wide-eyed as when the assassins first arrived.

Relaxed but keeping him at the back of her mind, Kamira focused on her true opponent.

His dark eyes watched her intently with the experience of a veteran who knew better than to rush in. He'd wait for her to lower the barrier to throw magic at him. She *could* risk it. Even if he threw a weapon, he might miss, and even if a poisoned blade grazed her, she should be fine… at least according to Veranesh. Kamira grimaced. It wasn't the best time to test the demon's claims.

"In the name of Queen Andalisha, I order you to cease this assault." Jalyn walked past her toward the assassin, his expression stern and authoritative.

The barrier separated the two, yet the man on the other side rushed into action. Using the wall behind him like a springboard, he launched himself into the air, with his forearms crossed to protect his face, straight at Jalyn.

Against her instincts, Kamira remained motionless. Impromptu barriers wavered when their creators moved, and even though years of practice allowed her a few steps, they wouldn't suffice in getting to Jalyn in time if the assassin got through. But any attack would mean taking their protection down, and their opponent might have been counting on it. With little choice, she poured more magic into her barrier.

Her protection sparked with magic when the assassin's forearms connected. The power in the imbued stones he carried was immense, and it took all her focus to keep the barrier from cracking. Such magic could only come from one source, and it meant the Darethal's Thorns had the Temple's favor in this task.

"Jalyn, move back!" she shouted.

He was already scrambling backward, and her order added urgency.

As soon as the prince gained distance from the cracking barrier, she removed it. The assassin fell through, maintaining his balance, but before he could redirect his weight, Kamira brought another barrier up.

Her triumphant feeling faded as her shoulder stung. Hurriedly, she brushed the needle off. If the assassin had chosen such a small projectile, it must have been poison. At least the throw was off balance, and the metal hardly penetrated her skin. She'd worry about it later, if she felt any effects.

"What now?" Jalyn asked.

The assassin offered a confident grin. He must have been chosen because of his skills. He knew how to fight arcanists.

The door to the chamber swung open. Irtan rushed in with Varessa in tow. The assassin gave them one look and darted toward the nearest window. Kamira smiled. If he thought he'd escape, he was wrong. He slammed against her barrier before he got there. It required a bit of a skill to cast it at a distance and around a moving target, but with all the magic at her disposal and the space of the chamber, she could afford making his trap bigger.

In an instant, the assassin paused and looked at her, his expression full of cold fury and... determination, which she noticed too late. As she took a step forward in a vain attempt to stop him, he slammed his forearms together. A fiery explosion engulfed and consumed him nearly instantly, and her barrier wavered under the storm of flames. Once it died out, only ash and twisted pieces of metal were left.

Irtan took his own barrier down as soon as the unexpected flames burned out, proving once more that, despite his old age and sheltered life, hardly anyone or anything could catch him by surprise, and she herself should have paid more attention. With her attention on the obvious, she'd missed when he raised the barrier... and could have missed an attack, too, if Irtan turned against her.

The old archmage looked around, taking in the smoldering pile, the dead body of the other assassin, and finally Prince Jalyn, who stood nearby shivering. With a soft shake of her head, she let both archmages know the prince was not a threat.

At that, Varessa left immediately, and soon her confident voice sounded outside as she gave orders to students and guards.

Irtan approached, glancing at the dead body. "You said they wouldn't try again."

"I was wrong." It seemed that someone in Tivarashan really wanted her dead. Darethal's Thorns might have taken work offered by outsiders, but if they were using imbued stones of such power, the Temple of the Four had to be involved, or at least giving its silent approval. Tivarashan priests rarely did anything without the queen's knowledge, but Kamira had to consider that they simply wanted the new first archmage gone because of her pact with Veranesh. Even if the Four were powerful and nearly unconquerable together, another demon's presence so close to their lands might have felt threatening enough.

"Again?" Prince Jalyn approached, and although his face remained pale, focus returned to it. "You mean they attacked before?"

She replied with a short nod. The prince had to draw his own conclusions: that his mother was possibly involved, and that she'd made no provisions to ensure her son's safety. And that her actions were jeopardizing Jalyn's own mission, since an archmage assassinated by Darethal's Thorns, should she happen to survive, would be much less willing to negotiate with any Tivarashan envoy.

"I see," Jalyn said slowly. "I should leave you to your matters, first archmage." He offered a half-bow. "As for the topic we were discussing before being so rudely interrupted... You've convinced me. Please feel free to message me with the details of how I can help at your earliest convenience."

Kamira glanced at him, concealing her surprise. He'd made his decision quicker than she expected. Regardless of his shortcomings when it came to experience and skill, Jalyn had a swift mind, and she might have mistaken his earlier shiver: instead of shock from a brush with death, it could have been the realization of how little his own mother cared about his life.

"I appreciate it," she said. "I'll send a messenger shortly."

Irtan waited in silence until Jalyn left. "Are you sure he has nothing to do with it?"

"As much as I can be. Though there's little doubt *someone* from the Tivarashan court is involved." She massaged her forehead. So many years away from her homeland had left her with few contacts, and none close to royalty, but perhaps she could gather information locally instead. "You still keep spies to bring you news, don't you?"

The wrinkles on the old man's forehead shifted as he arched his eyebrow. "You would trust me enough to use my spies?"

Kamira couldn't help a burst of laughter. She couldn't

blame the old archmage for asking the question. After all, her distrustful attitude must have been famous by now. "I trust your spies are good enough to find someone for me," she replied. Remembering the story Veelk told her when they were traveling back to Kaighal made her believe there could be a spy, one she might be able to trust.

There were also other precautions to be taken. Master Tijhran used to say that only a fool attacked arcanists in their own homes, and it was time that she started treating the High Towers like her home, taking the necessary steps to keep it safe. Her teacher's house was covered in convenient circles that stabilized arcane magic, offered better protection, and even served as traps or defenses when constructed properly. She hardly had a time to run around the Towers with Hauhans's Graver in hand, but such tasks could be delegated to promising students, and Second Archmage Irtan wouldn't mind supervising it.

If any assassins were to try again, they would be in for a nasty surprise.

15

Atissa paced back and forth, gravel gritting under her feet in unison with the grinding of her teeth. Her blood was still boiling from the confrontation with Ryell. How bold had he become to say so many scathing and unjust words! There were times when she'd comforted him with her magic and given him all her attention, and he repaid her with such cruelty. Of course, she might have been a bit too focused on finding a way to exact revenge on her father's killer, but he should have understood! If he was, like he claimed, willing to support her in her grief, he should have applauded her determination instead of calling her obsessed.

She huffed, but it only stoked the flames of her anger. Back when she was still the first archmage's daughter, no one would ever dare to insult her. Yet Ryell went even further. He had the audacity to leave! Wrapped up in her anger and pain, she noticed too late that he'd taken all his belongings with him, and now, with the sun having already set, it seemed foolish to count on him to return. She shouldn't be waiting anyway. With nowhere else to go, he likely planned on spending the night in the woods to grate on her composure.

Fine! She almost stomped her foot.

An ungrateful refugee like him would not get any more of her attention. At least not until he came back and apologized properly. Then she could grant him forgiveness. That thought brought a smile to her face. Instead of pacing outside and looking all distraught, making it clear Ryell's words hurt her deep, she should head back inside, have a delicious dinner and the hot bath Dynar likely had ready for her. She should act like a daughter of an archmage and not like a foolish, betrayed girl.

Besides, she needed a distraction. Underneath the layers of anger, doubts were taking root, and if she allowed them to grow, she'd lose her purpose, and the last thing she needed was a painful reminder that without her father, without his power and his plans, she was nothing. The grimness of the approaching night only helped such thoughts to fester. She rushed back toward the building. The sooner she found something pleasant to occupy her mind for a while, the better.

She'd already made it back to the entrance when a noise caught her attention. First, the birds took off into the sky. Then treetops at the edge of her land wavered too much. As they parted with loud cracks, a creature walked out.

Atissa's eyes widened, and the beating of her heart drowned out all other sounds. *That Tivarashan gaharra sent a demon after me!* Instinct demanded she seek shelter inside the house, but the ease with which the demon crumbled the stones of the border wall to pass through made such a thought pointless. Atissa lifted her chin. If she was to die, she'd do so as her father did: with pride and composure. She would fight until the end.

The guard who stood by the gate chased after the demon, but the malicious creature turned to him only long enough to deliver a kick. Atissa almost screamed as her servant's body flew through the air, landing limp on a surviving piece of the wall, leaving little hope that he survived. Her thoughts raced, bringing images of herself soon sharing the poor man's fate.

Her voice trembled, but the well-rehearsed incantation flowed from her lips nevertheless, and soon magic followed. Fiery projectiles launched from her hands like flaming hounds searching for their mark. The demon smirked. With a slight move of his body, he shielded himself with his wing. Atissa's magic splashed against it and dispersed, leaving no mark.

He took a step toward her, his eyes narrowed. "You aren't a pactee."

His voice was deep and unlike anything she'd ever heard. As if magic itself reverberated within it. Her eyes skimmed past his muscular figure, toward clawed hands, and only then did she spot two humans within his grasp, a man and a woman. The demon tossed the woman to the ground. Whatever he said to her, it was too far away for Atissa to catch, but it also mattered little. If fire didn't work against him, she had to try something else.

The incantation for ice spikes was long, but no other spell surfaced in her memory, and she could either try to cast it or waste time searching for something else. With her hands trembling and breath hastened, she began.

With two quick leaps, the demon was beside her.

"Don't oppose me," he said as his claw closed around her neck. He put enough pressure to stifle the words she was uttering, but allowed her to breathe. "You aren't a pactee," he repeated. "Yet you use magic. What are you?"

Talking with her throat smashed would be difficult, so Atissa relaxed in his grip as much as instinct allowed her. The demon, in return, loosened it enough for her to take a deep breath.

A pactee must have been something to do with arcanists, so she replied, "I'm Atissa. A high mage and daughter of the former first archmage Yoreus." Surprisingly, it hurt to even mention his name, and Atissa fought the wave of emotions overwhelming her. Her relationship with her father was not one of deep love, but as long as she did his bidding without question, he'd offered enough care and protection. Yet standing eye to eye with a formidable monster was hardly the time for pondering whether she should grieve him.

The demon cocked his head. "And how did you keep your magic with Veranesh free?"

That question forced her to look closer at him. His face was almost human, but the long nose resembled a beak, all the more in the day's waning light. If he mentioned that name, he couldn't be Veranesh, and he didn't look like the other demon she'd seen in front of the High Towers. She took a deep breath. Her father's letter mentioned an old agreement between the high mages and demons... Perhaps this wasn't an enemy, but an ally. Still within his grip, she had little to lose in telling the truth.

"There are three demons captured within this building, much like Veranesh was," she replied. "My father prepared it in case... in case our enemy regained his freedom. I use them to provide me with magic."

She could swear the demon lost his murderous expression, as if he approved of trapping his brethren. "And what of your father?"

Atissa swallowed. "Killed by Arcanist Kamira, who has now claimed the High Towers for herself." Her words sounded more bitter than she'd intended, but as much as she was used to the high mages' power plays taking their toll —often in equal amounts of prestige and blood—it was hard to discard her own father's death as yet another casualty of Towers politics. That woman, Kamira, was an arcanist, and she had no right to stand against the first archmage, let alone kill him.

The demon let her go. "We have an enemy in common, so I will respect the agreement we've made with the high mages. My name is Myrkan. Serve me well, and you will be rewarded."

Atissa forced herself to bow, though her pride demanded otherwise. Without her father's power and protection, she was nothing, and her magic would fail against a demon—the short scuffle had proven it already. All she had were her wits and the meager experience of playing games in the High Towers. According to old books and teachers' warnings, demons were more beguiling than most humans, and her father himself had warned her about trusting any. But trust was the last thing on her mind. She needed the demon's strength. If it required serving him, she would.

"Now, find me something to bind those two..." He looked over his shoulder. "To bind this one."

Atissa followed his gaze. The darkness concealed the view, but it seemed that the woman must have run away and could become a problem if she alerted Kamira and her demons, but Myrkan showed no concern.

"I should have some ropes or fabric in the house." She gestured toward the building. "He'll also need water and food if you want to keep him alive."

Myrkan huffed, but gave her a nod, and Atissa rushed inside. As soon as she entered, Dynar stepped forward, and she put her finger to her lips before leading him deeper into the house.

"Find me some ropes or twine," she whispered. Without knowing the house like he did, searching for them could take longer than the demon's patience lasted. "Once I'm back outside, you'll lead everyone to the back. Sneak out through the garden door and make it for the woods. Go to a nearby village or back to your families." A thought struck her. "But don't go to Kaighal. It's going to be dangerous there."

"But my lady, that creature outside…"

"I'm a high mage. I know how to handle it," she replied with more confidence than she felt. "But to work, I need you all out of the harm's way." As much as she welcomed Dynar's unwavering loyalty, it seemed better to send him and others away. With one careless remark they could ruin her work, and their presence could make it appear like they were plenty lackeys to choose from, and Atissa was replaceable. With no one else around, Myrkan would have to rely on her.

Dynar bowed. "As you wish, my lady."

"Take enough supplies for travel, but don't burden yourself too much and keep quiet," she said. "The demon is fast, so if he hears you, I won't be able to stop him." If Myrkan's hearing was good enough to catch footsteps or any noise at the other side of the building, he would have heard this conversation as well, but Atissa didn't want the servants to waste time collecting valuables, taking away what was rightfully hers. "Go now. Find those ropes and let others know. The demon's patience only lasts so long, and so will the darkness."

～

KOSHMARNYK REGAINED consciousness soon after the unexpected attack knocked him out, but he knew better than to reveal it. The glimpse of the demon he caught made it clear that Veranesh's enemies were closer than they all had thought. At first he suspected Mayetti was in cahoots with the creature who carried him slung across his shoulder, but overhearing their conversation had proven him wrong. On the other hand, with all the information Mayetti was sharing with their captor, she might as well have been allied with him. To preserve her own life, the foolish woman was giving away everything the demons needed to see to Kaighal's fall. Yet he remained motionless and quiet. Fighting one on one with such a powerful creature was wishing for death, and while in the days of his youth Koshmarnyk would have been tempted to take the challenge and accept the risk, he needed to survive to bring news back to the city.

The journey in the demon's grip was hardly comfortable, but he doubted the demon would let him walk on his own. With Mayetti revealing to the demon all about Koshmarnyk's relationship with Kamira, he was too valuable for the demon to risk losing sight of him.

Myrkan didn't let go of him even when the fighting started. The sound of crumbled stones and a man's scream carried in the air.

Koshmarnyk chanced a glance, but the world around him was a blur of speed.

It came as no surprise that his captor disposed of his opponents quickly, but what caught Koshmarnyk's attention was the conversation that followed. A high mage, and the daughter of Yoreus himself, had survived and preserved her magic. Her alliance with Myrkan could bring all sorts of trouble both to Kaighal and Kamira. Perhaps Atissa was the one behind the attempt on Kamira's life...

His back slammed into something hard, pushing the air out of his lungs and forcing his eyes open.

"I thought you were awake," Myrkan sneered.

The demon's face was too close for Koshmarnyk's liking, but when he shifted, he did so more from the need to examine his body's reaction than to move away. No sharp pain followed, giving him hope of no broken bones or other serious injuries, but he needed to ensure Myrkan didn't toss him around much more.

"You reek of that hoyve, Veranesh." The demon's claw ran along Koshmarnyk's forearm. "And of some others."

Disgust showed on Myrkan's face as he ripped the tunic's sleeve and inspected the imbued stones blended with Koshmarnyk's skin. His claws closed around one of them, and dug deeper, piercing skin and flesh.

Koshmarnyk jerked, and a muffled groan escaped his lips as the demon ripped the stone out of his body. Myrkan didn't stop at one, and by the third one, Koshmarnyk couldn't hold his scream. Its echo bounced off the distant trees to return the sound of his pain multiplied.

"That's better, human. Do you think you could scream loud enough to call Veranesh's pawn here? Or will I have to send her those bloodied stones first?"

Koshmarnyk's stomach churned. Back in his days in the Western Kingdom's army, he'd met many wicked people, men and women finding delight in tormenting prisoners or those who were weaker. With the details of those memories still disturbingly fresh, though it'd been nearly twenty years since, he recognized the familiar note in Myrkan's voice. Like some of Koshmarnyk's past comrades, the demon reveled in torture, drinking the feeling of power that flowed from abuse. A few stones ripped had to be but a taste of what could happen to all the people in Kaighal should the city fall. Koshmarnyk had no illusions that both Veranesh and Fyertash perceived humans as little more than useful tools, but neither of them seemed quick to violence. To them, it was nothing but a possible means to an end they sought, and only when it was the best of choices. Which, given their cunning and plotting natures, it rarely was.

"Do you really think Veranesh would let her leave the city?" Koshmarnyk asked. With someone like Myrkan, it seemed better to make it look like Kamira was indeed a pawn in the other demon's hands. Mayetti might have flapped her tongue, but she also had to admit she was an outsider in the Towers, while Koshmarnyk could play the lover's card and boast intimate knowledge. If only he knew what kind of ploys would benefit Kamira...

Myrkan huffed at Veranesh's name. The demon went for another stone, and Koshmarnyk braced himself for more pain.

"If you keep doing that, he'll die before he's of any use," Atissa said.

She was standing nearby, by the building's entrance, her posture stiff and her brown skin marred with pallor. Apparently, no matter how spoiled or calculating Yoreus's daughter might be, she had no taste for torture. Perhaps Koshmarnyk could use her soft heart to drive a wedge between the freshly bound allies.

"Watch your tongue, human," Myrkan barked. "His dead body can be as much of use. And someone who thinks he can become equal to yalari with a few handfuls of our magic should be taught a lesson." His claw skimmed another stone on Koshmarnyk's forearm. "But this can wait."

"I brought the ropes you asked for." Atissa stepped closer.

The expression on Myrkan's face softened, as if he was pleased with her obedience. With a quick move, he snatched the ropes and bound Koshmarnyk so tight, the adept's arms crushed against his chest. "Guard him. I'm going after the one who got away." Once he was done tying the adept's ankles, he opened his wings and took off.

Koshmarnyk looked after the demon until he dove into the trees. "You saw what he's capable of." He moved his body enough to expose his bloodied forearm. The wounds ached, but after the initial shock, the pain was numb enough to bear. Soon, other stones would help him heal... Unless Myrkan finished what he'd started. "Do you think your petty revenge is worth the lives of everyone in Kaighal? Or their suffering?"

Atissa pouted. "You're the mage killer, aren't you?" The way she said it, it sounded like an accusation or a reminder that he was her enemy as well.

He had to smile. "I'm not him. But I did help Kamira achieve her goal."

"Then whatever happens to the city, is on your and her hands," she replied without hesitation.

"Perhaps it is." Koshmarnyk looked her in the eye without shame. "But she's there, in Kaighal, doing her best to ensure everyone is safe. She's not away, hidden in the woods, plotting with the very demon who wishes to see the city fall."

She jerked as if the words carried the strength of a punch. She gave him a nasty glare and retreated inside the building.

Hurtful words should provide enough food for thought to change her mind about allying with a ruthless demon, but once Myrkan returned, Koshmarnyk could do little more to ensure the battle between two Atissas—the spoiled young woman bound on revenge and the one who was still innocent and caring enough—ended in his favor. He shifted. With little effort, he could free himself from his binds, but Myrkan had the advantage of flight, and getting away would be difficult. He needed a better plan.

A woman screamed in the distance.

Even though it was distorted by the echo between the trees, he knew the voice belonged to Mayetti. Koshmarnyk pressed his lips together. The treacherous adept deserved death, but to suffer it at a vicious demon's hand wasn't something Koshmarnyk could cherish. Atissa stepped out, her eyes slightly widened. She was looking at the trees as if trying to see what they were concealing. Then she gave Koshmarnyk a glance.

All he did was glare back at her. If she was smart enough, she would understand what kind of creature Myrkan was, and what he did to those who were no longer of use to him... or simply when he felt like dealing pain. Any more words could destroy that hint of doubt that flashed on Atissa's face, so Koshmarnyk let the scream, faded now but likely still ringing in the young mage's ears, to do the work for him.

16

As Myrkan took flight, he couldn't help smiling. Mayetti might have thought herself cunning, but she was a fool on two accounts. The first one was running from Myrkan. The second one was not tossing the few trinkets imbued with yalari energy. She must have thought he hadn't searched her belongings earlier out of confidence, but he let her keep her belongings because they ensured he could find her easily. Their travel through the forest was enough for Myrkan to learn the flow of the energies surrounding her, and now only distance could prevent him from finding his mark. Distance a human on her weak legs couldn't cover. Mayetti would pay for her foolishness, serving as an example: no one defied Myrkan.

As wind blew from the south, carrying other energies, Myrkan flew closer to the ground. Regardless of how much he wanted to take his time with the woman, he better be quick about it. He was so close to the city that his silhouette against the sky could draw someone's attention, and the last thing he wanted was Veranesh learning of his presence. On the other hand, he'd welcome Fyertash's arrival, but the sly yalari was too cunning to leave the safety of the city, likely seeking protection within the reach of Veranesh's shadow.

Myrkan scoffed. *Another fool!* Fyertash could have had so much if he remained Arujhan's ally, but he tossed it all away in the name of some ludicrous plot. This was why he never would stand among the most powerful kanyalari, and when the time came, he'd pay for his betrayal. Myrkan furrowed his brow. If he wanted to collect the payment, he had to ensure Fyertash was caught alive, and that would be difficult. If the traitor died, he'd be reborn in Yalarethe, and Myrkan didn't intend to return there.

That was all in the future, though. First, he had to find the first of the fools who'd crossed him.

His flight wasn't long, but the woman had covered more distance than he'd expected. Fear was a powerful motivator, and Myrkan would use it to his benefit. He dove, his arm raised to protect his face from the trees' lashing, and folded his wings when he was close to Mayetti. The heavy landing shook everything and sent Mayetti to the ground. Myrkan savored the terror on her face as she scrambled backward, all too aware that her death was standing in front of her.

She was quiet, staring at him wide-eyed, but he preferred she beg. It would be amusing to learn what lies, flatteries, or secrets she could conjure to save her skin. *Pitiful.* And to think he'd intended to make her more than a tool, a subordinate ally that would carry out his will and find him a way into the city...

A new idea flashed in his mind. Perhaps he could still turn this to his benefit. Fear could serve him better than making a deal with Mayetti, as he'd planned before.

"You want to live, don't you?" he asked. The desire to dig his claws into her remained strong, and part of him wanted a daring response that would justify his urge.

Mayetti swallowed and nodded. Her eyes became more focused, and faint hope replaced terror on her face. She was smart enough to see he wanted something from her and even smarter to not say anything until the deal was made. Had she made any witty remarks, he would have disposed of her.

"You will do something for me. You will carry something for me back into the city."

Myrkan looked around, but his choice was limited in the woods. A jewel would be perfect, an intricate human trinket would do, but all he found nearby was a stone. It looked tiny in his palm, but it meant his human pawn would be able to carry it into the city without drawing any attention.

Mayetti watched him as he held it, whispering words in his own language and filling the stone with his power. It brought a sliver of satisfaction that his fellow kanyalari, often more powerful than he was, had failed to discover such a useful trick. Humans made their imbued stones, spelling the energies from Yalarethe into objects, but no other kanyalari thought to do the same—only him. If done properly, he could not only find the stone even from a great distance, but he could also observe and communicate through it. A trick that helped him win the Devanshari capital when the magical barrier held everyone else out and clueless. He smiled at the memory of the gentle whispers he'd poured into the human queen's ears, of the cunning manipulation that led her to destroy her own defenses as she greedily sated her hunger with the very magic that was supposed to protect her city. Once the barrier was weakened, it didn't take much to breach it.

This time he couldn't count on such subtlety, but he didn't have to. This human city was so divided that many would side with him to spite their opponents.

He looked at Mayetti again. "Your city doesn't have to crumble like the one across the seas did. They didn't listen and weren't willing to make peace, so they paid the highest price. Perhaps your Gildya is smarter than them. Bring this stone to whomever you think is both powerful and reasonable enough to talk to us." He passed the stone to her.

"I know of such a person," Mayetti replied. "How does it work?"

"Put what you humans call an imbued stone beside it, and you'll be able to speak with me."

Mayetti put the stone into her satchel. "I'll deliver it."

She'd regained most of her composure and confidence, and Myrkan grimaced. It seemed that the lesson of fear wasn't enough. He looked straight at her, and a shadow of doubt passed over her face. "I know you will."

Before she could do anything, he snatched her and yanked her closer. The short scream that escaped her mouth soothed some of his ire. Too bad he didn't have time to make her beg for her life... But he had enough time to teach another lesson, that of pain. With one swift move, he ran his claw against her back, tearing her clothes and the skin and flesh underneath.

This time Mayetti screamed longer and louder, her voice echoing among the trees.

If only he had time to play with her longer... But the man who carried the power of yalari within him was more important, as he had ties with Veranesh's pactee. Myrkan gave the woman one last look. "This is so that you remember what I'll do if you try to cross me again. Deliver the stone or even your city's walls won't protect you from me."

Her face, twisted with fear and pain, marked with smudges of tears, was a pleasant sight. She nodded eagerly.

Satisfied, Myrkan took off as she stumbled through the woods.

The gusts of wind during his fight cooled his instincts. Perhaps the wound he'd given her was a little too deep. If she bled out somewhere in the thicket, the stone would have been a wasted effort. *It doesn't matter.* He already had another tool, an eager and smart one. If Mayetti failed to make it back to the city, he could always send Atissa in. She would deliver another stone for him, perhaps along with—Myrkan smiled—a severed hand of the new archmage's lover. That would be an interesting way to test how loyal Veranesh's pactee really was.

Atissa rubbed her eyes in a vain attempt to chase tiredness away. Myrkan hadn't allowed her to sleep inside the building, so she spent the night on the ground, on a pile of hastily gathered blankets and throws. If that wasn't enough, the demon seemed to need no sleep and spent his waking hours torturing the adept. By the time the sun peeked out from behind the tree line, he must have already found and ripped all the imbued stones from the poor man's body. The adept didn't scream much anymore, but his huffs and groans, along with Myrkan's vicious remarks, were enough to keep Atissa awake. In the dark of the night, she couldn't help wondering whether the demon would turn on her after he was done with his other captive, because he had to realize soon enough that she was hardly useful with limited magic skills and no influence back in Kaighal.

In the morning, when the light revealed the adept's torn and bloodied clothes, her stomach churned. And the vicious expression on Myrkan's face told her he was far from done.

Atissa pressed her lips together. The demon was her only chance for revenge. To see Kamira die for what she'd done could bring satisfaction, but unless Atissa did it with her own hands or magic, nobody would care about her any more than they did when her father was alive. Just like back in the High Towers when she met her father's every wish, she would be only a tool in Myrkan's hands. Even if she claimed the archmage's title, even if she tried to assert power... no one would ever respect her, and she would be forever cowering in fear of what the demon could do to her or anyone else.

She let out a sigh, not caring anymore whether Myrkan noticed she was awake. It mattered little what she did. Others would always see her as a pawn and nothing more.

The adept threw her a compassionate, knowing glance, as if out of them two she was in the worse position. And, it struck her, perhaps she was, in a way. After all, he might have been the one suffering and he would likely die, but he endured the torment for the woman he loved and who likely loved him back. With Ryell's departure, Atissa had no one, and in the end, she would die doing someone else's bidding, never chasing her own dreams, never fulfilling her own ambitions. That gave her pause. Until now she believed to know what she was after. An archmage's position, along with power and respect, seemed like a worthy goal, but with all that had happened, Atissa had to ask herself: was it her dream or her father's? With the question came doubt, but no matter what she could wish for, she was stuck with decisions others had made for her.

Myrkan smacked the adept, bringing Atissa back to reality. Regardless of how much effort the demon might put in keeping his victim alive, any human would succumb to prolonged torture soon enough. Then she would be next, if she didn't find a way to convince the demon of her usefulness. Unless...

Unless she made a choice for herself, perhaps for the first time in her life. But rash choices often turned out to be mistakes, and for this one she could pay with her life.

Myrkan smirked at her. "I would have expected you to be more accustomed to blood and pain."

She pushed her chin up, the pity in his voice sealing her decision. "I admit, the odor is revolting," she replied with all confidence, mustering a smug expression. "But what disgusts me more is wasting a good tool." She pointed at the adept. "He might not admit it, but I bet he knows the archmage's secrets. Secrets that could be useful for us."

The demon huffed. "You're naïve if you think he'll talk."

Atissa gave him a sly smile as a plan formed in her head. "With a little help, he will. My father used to bring other mages here, treat them to good food and better drinks, all doused with a powder that made them talk... spill the secrets they didn't even know they had." After so many years playing games in the High Towers, both for gain and sheer pleasure, she could spin words into an alluring tale with ease. "If I can find it among his belongings, we could gain some insights into our enemies' steps." It didn't escape her that the adept tensed at her words.

Myrkan's narrow, almost lipless mouth stretched in a grin. "Fetch it, then."

She nodded and rushed inside the mansion, her heart beating to the rhythm of her hurried steps. All she had were her father's notes in the hidden laboratory and no certainty the powder she had in mind was still there, but if she failed to find it, Myrkan would likely find solace in more torture. Information, it seemed, was a secondary matter to him.

Her father's hidden workshop looked exactly how she

had left it. The demons trapped in the crystals were as motionless as always, and it remained unclear whether any were aware of another demon nearby. Atissa turned her eyes away from the dark shadows within the milky stones. As long as they provided her with magic, everything else was a pointless pondering, and she had no time to waste.

The thick leather pouch rested among vials and wooden boxes. Atissa weighed it in her hand. According to the notes she'd found in her father's papers, a few handfuls were enough, but she wouldn't take chances. She'd use it all.

A glance at the workshop made her long for more time and more preparation, but she couldn't risk Myrkan's anger. All she did was fasten a small dagger to her side on her way out, hiding it beneath her shirt. She'd need a blade.

Close to the mansion's front door, another scream reached her. It seemed that the demon had little patience. Taking a deep breath, she unfastened the pouch's strings. With so little time to plan, she had to improvise and rely on luck.

As she walked out, Myrkan turned his head to her, his bloodied claw still on the adept's shoulder. It seemed that with no stones left to rip out, he'd moved on to tearing the flesh itself.

"I found it," she said to pull the demon's attention away from the wounded man. At the back of her mind, she couldn't help wondering whether the adept was already on the brink of death, and if her decision would ultimately matter little.

Myrkan looked toward her, his expression shifting from cruelty to satisfaction. Atissa's heart sped up. With a calculated, well-practiced awkwardness, she tripped, like many times in her first student years in the High Towers when she wanted others to underestimate her. The feigned loss of balance was enough to send the pouch flying in an inconspicuous manner. Atissa followed its arc with hope more intense than she should have revealed if she cared for her own safety, but her blood rushed through her veins too fast to keep pretending and start apologizing like a clumsy servant would.

The demon narrowed his eyes, focused and suspicious. He caught the pouch mid-flight with a predator-like agility, and Atissa held her breath. Fortunately, the impact and loose strings were enough to release the fine powder all around Myrkan.

Even from a distance, Atissa sensed magic within the shimmering cloud.

"Foolish…" The demon took a step toward her. He collapsed to the ground before another word left his mouth.

The tremble of the ground stirred the cloud of powder, and Atissa quickly made her way around it as it settled on the demon. Under the adept's inquisitive glare, she cut his ties. "Can you walk? I don't know how long the powder will work."

Slowly, he pushed himself up along the wall, his balance too wobbly for Atissa's liking. His eyes were on the dagger. "Give it to me."

She pursed her lips. "Can you kill a demon with one strike?" If he failed, they'd both be dead. "Come, we have to hurry." Without waiting for his reply or protest, she put his arm around her shoulders. As thin as he looked, his weight still burdened her enough to make running impossible.

"You should run," he said. "The demon will come after me first, so you have a chance of getting far enough away."

"Or he'll come after me, because you can't run far," she replied. Perhaps it would have been better to hide inside her home where she could see to the adept's wounds and sneak away later when Myrkan flew away.

Silence followed. The adept must know that no matter what they did, neither of them was a match for Myrkan. She had to put her hope in the powder's strength to keep the demon asleep.

"Thank you," the adept said when they reached the tree line. "It was brave what you did."

"It will be for naught if we don't get the word to Kaighal," she replied reflexively, concealing her feelings.

That man hardly knew her. He was aware she had reasons to hate his lover. Yet his praise, in simple words and plain tone, carried more weight than any exaggerated applause from her father. Despite the fear that the demon would descend upon them any moment, and despite the bitterness that her own past carried, Atissa offered him a small smile. Perhaps, if they survived, there was a way for her to carve a path paved with her own choices, no matter where they would lead her.

17

The smell of curative herbs filled the room, but instead of bringing comfort and a feeling of safety, it refreshed Mayetti's memories of her encounter with the demon. Frustration, humiliation, anger, and fear kept overflowing in her body, and she could hardly hold still lying on her stomach while Gildya's finest physician saw to her wound.

"It's the first time I've seen an injury like that," the young woman said with too much fascination for Mayetti's liking. "How big was the claw? How curled?"

Mayetti groaned, openly expressing her annoyance. The adept was supposed to clean her wound, apply salves, and bandage it up, not consider those tasks scientific research.

"It would help to know if their claws carry poison," the woman continued as if she hadn't noticed Mayetti's reaction. "Maybe I should send word to the High Towers. The demonologists would know—"

"*No.*" Mayetti put all her authority into that one word. "Check our own records instead. I know that in the past adepts studied demonlings, and they might even have remedies developed. If we ask the Towers, we're once more putting ourselves in a pleading position. We can't weaken Gildya's authority even more."

She hoped the argument would suffice. As inquisitive as the physician was, she'd likely love the idea of digging through the piles of old documents to find an answer... and possibly use it in her other research. This would ensure that the Towers wouldn't know about what happened to Mayetti, since Alluvendran said he'd shared his plans with his lover. If the archmage learned that Mayetti survived, questions would follow, and even though, on her way back to Kaighal, Mayetti had come up with a convincing tale in which she and Adept Alluvendran were attacked by the demon, and the adept bravely gave his life to allow her escape, she'd rather not test it against a Tivarashan woman's cunning. With Alluvendran likely already dead, nobody needed to know what had transpired. Even Gildya's council was unaware of her plot.

"I'll see what I can find, though too much delay might lower the chances of treating any poison," the woman said, wrapping bandages around Mayetti's chest.

"Let me worry about that," Mayetti grumbled. "Are you done yet?"

"Almost." The adept rushed the last few moves then collected her instruments and bottles. "If you feel any change, even if it's not within the wound itself, let me know. I left some pain-relief concoction in the jug as well, should the wound give you too much trouble."

Mayetti forced herself to show some gratitude, "Thank you." Even if the woman was a nuisance, she'd done her job, and making enemies for no good reason was a recipe for trouble. Mayetti hid a grimace. There had been too much trouble already. Not only had she failed to capture

Alluvendran, but the demon encounter kept her from reaching her compatriots from the west and delivering news of what was happening in Kaighal. She'd have to find a way to contact them soon. The mere thought of leaving the safety of Kaighal's walls again brought a shiver. If Myrkan found her again, he could finish what he'd started.

"Be well, adept," he healer said.

As the woman was leaving, another head poked in through the open door.

"May I come in?" Adept Ervan asked. "I heard you were wounded. What happened?" he added once she gave him a nod.

Mayetti waited till he closed the door. "The ambush went as planned, until a demon appeared." With all her resolve, she forced her body to be still, though the memory of Myrkan's claw on her back brought shivers. Ervan didn't have to see her weakness, even if fearing such a monster was justified. "He took us both prisoner but seemed more interested in Alluvendran."

"Why is that?" Uninvited, Ervan sat down on the chair beside her bed.

She grabbed a shirt and slid into it, ignoring the pain. Usually, nudity didn't bother her, and it could be a way to distract her opponents, men and women alike, but Ervan's prying eyes irritated her. He was clearly more interested in judging the extent of her wound than admiring her curves, as he should.

"I believe that, despite what the first archmage is saying, the demons aren't here to besiege the city itself. Contrary to the Devanshari nation, we have no powerful artifact that would interest them. They're coming solely because of the two demons that now reside in the Towers." Mayetti smiled cunningly. "If Gildya was to... enter negotiations, we could avoid all the bloodshed, become saviors of the city, and get rid of the archmage's sole source of power in one swift move."

Ervan's eyes lit up, but then he shook his head. "It's too risky. Such talks would require someone high in the ranks, and no one in their right mind would abandon the safety of the city walls. Even assuming that we find a volunteer, and the demons would be willing to discuss certain matters rather than killing any messenger, we can't do it under the archmage's nose."

"Perhaps you can..." she said with a hint of mystery. The stone still rested in the pocket of her bloodied and torn outfit, and to fish it out meant the pain of both the grueling memories and of the wound, but she stretched down toward the floor and retrieved it. "The demons do want to talk, and with this stone in your hand, you don't have to risk your life. The conversation could be had within the privacy of one's quarters, or in another place where prying eyes and curious ears have no access. Using it is as simple as placing it beside another imbued stone." She handed it to him, and relief washed over her. She'd done as Myrkan asked, so he might spare her life. And not for a heartbeat did she doubt Ervan would use it: his curiosity alone would drive him to do so, and his thirst for power and knowledge would not allow any doubts.

"You're suggesting to keep it away from the council." Ervan turned the stone in his fingers.

Mayetti had been playing games for too long to give him what he wanted—clear proof that she was ready to go against other adepts. She shrugged indifferently. "You said it yourself not so long ago. The council is too focused on making agreements with the High Towers instead of finding a way to ensure our strong position in the city. But I've been traveling and away from Kaighal for years, so perhaps I'm not reading the circumstances right. I'll trust your judgment on that matter and support any decision you make, as I know you'll act in the best interest of us all. Until then, I won't mention the demon or the stone to anyone."

Ervan was an experienced player himself—at least enough to know when to stop pressing. "Very well." He stood up and offered her a slight bow. "I hope you'll recover soon, because it's always a delight to work with you, Adept Mayetti, and I'm looking forward to a long, fruitful cooperation."

The smile she offered him was genuine. "Likewise, Adept Ervan."

When he left, Mayetti carefully positioned herself against pillows. At the right angle, she could hardly feel the wound, and though it still burned, reminding her of what had transpired, she was already looking forward. Perhaps her utter failure could be still turned into a triumph. Surely Alluvendran's death was a waste, because his inventions could have brought her homeland many benefits, but since he was overly loyal to the archmage, trying to turn him could have been a fruitless endeavor, and prisoners forced to work rarely shared their true brilliance. Yet she had been hoping to bring him back west, adding another mission to the list of her many successes. *What a waste.*

On the other hand, the encounter with Myrkan, no matter how damaging to her previous plans, offered new and possibly exciting opportunities. If Ervan came to an agreement with the invaders and handed the archmage's demons over to them, Gildya would trump High Towers, reducing them to a group of insignificant demonologists. And after the demons left, Kaighal would be defenseless, because it would take time for Gildya to find ways to match the powers the mages and demonologists used to protect the city. A perfect target for her homeland to finally claim. She was certain the Western armies would be ready, since for weeks now the kingdom had been moving its troops closer to the border.

Mayetti relaxed, enjoying the thought of her future triumph. Adept Ervan would do the work needed to strip the city of its power, so she could take time to recover, avoiding drawing attention to herself. Yes, working with him was indeed a rare delight.

Pain stabbed her in the back, reminding her of what she'd suffered. If she was not a woman of science, she'd wonder whether it was Myrkan himself reaching to her somehow, to remind her that no matter what she did, he'd always have the upper hand. She shivered. Before the deal with the demons was done, she had to find a way to secretly leave Kaighal and make it back home. Only the distance and the power of the Western Kingdom could keep her safe.

With her hand shaking, she poured some of the concoction into the mug. It would take time for the wound to heal and for her to be able to move freely enough to attempt leaving the city, but at least she didn't have to suffer through it. Without hesitation, she downed the liquid and rested back against the pillow.

The strange aftertaste in her mouth tugged at her instincts. The smell and the flavor was that of the pain-relief mixture, but there had to be something more... Her eyes widened as her body flushed with sudden hotness, and the numbness in her limbs foretold of what was to come.

Ervan! That treacherous, lying bastard!

In hindsight, she should have known that he wouldn't risk leaving her alive. A witness to his unscrupulous plans and the only other person who knew of Myrkan's offer. Was it the healer who'd added the poison to the concoction on Ervan's behalf, or was it the adept himself who did the deed while she was searching for the stone? No matter. She stumbled out of bed, heading for the door. She needed to find help first—someone to administer the antidote and bring Ervan's betrayal to the council's attention.

Her hand, stretched, reached the door handle, but her numb fingers refused to wrap around it. Mayetti made one more step, letting her body crash into the door and hoping it would yield under her weight.

Instead, she collapsed on the floor, her face forever frozen in a hateful expression.

IT MIGHT HAVE BEEN her imagination, but with every step, the adept seemed to regain his strength. The wounds Atissa had expected to keep bleeding clotted, and he stopped leaning heavily on her, even if his stiffened and slow moves still reflected the torture his body had endured through the night. In comparison, her own energy was waning. As the adrenaline rush faded, the sleepless night, lack of food, and fear started weighing on her. Even rested and fed, she hardly made a good traveler, so the farther they went, the more apparent it became that it wasn't the wounded man who would slow them down.

The adept remained silent, likely focused on making it through the forest or conserving his strength, and Atissa found little reason to start a conversation herself. With nothing else to do, her mind wandered, and she couldn't help questioning the choice she'd made. The demon cared little for her, undoubtedly, but she should have chosen to do his bidding for a little longer. She should have made sure the adept stayed alive, so that the monster's cruelty would focus on him, and waited for the right moment to sneak away. If she was patient enough, perhaps she'd have even found some way to outsmart him. But to what end? She clenched her fists.

"I owe you my life," the adept said, "and I will repay my debt. But I won't help you go against Kamira."

She kept her grimace to herself. He must have thought little of her if he considered she'd helped him only because he knew the first archmage. "I wouldn't expect you to." Her voice sounded colder than she'd intended, but the remark had grated on her nerves. A bitter realization lingered in her thoughts: even though, for once, she'd done something selfless, putting her own wellbeing at risk, she was still suspected of hidden motives. Perhaps no matter what she did, it was bound to stay like that forever.

The adept regarded her in silence. The half-smile he offered her after a while was warm. "I'm Koshmarnyk. I appreciate what you did."

He already knew who she was, so no other introduction was necessary, and a quick nod sufficed for an acknowledgment. The less they talked, the better. Maybe she'd be able to forget that she'd risked her own life to help an ally of a woman who had killed her father. That again made her consider her life and choices so far, but this time she forced her thoughts in another direction. Pondering the same things without clear answers or solutions would do her no good. First, she had to stay alive. Any other decisions or resolutions would have to come later, when she had the luxury of such considerations.

The bushes thinned, and they stepped out onto a dirt road. Narrow and partially overgrown, it wasn't frequented much, but Atissa stopped anyway. "We should keep to the trees." She couldn't help a nervous glance at the skies.

"Even if the demon wakes up soon, I don't think he will come for us in the daytime," Koshmarnyk said. "It's too close to the city. He wouldn't risk being seen."

Of course—she should have remembered the other demons. Myrkan had made it clear that Veranesh was his foe. "Do you think we will make it to Kaighal before nightfall?" With the dark concealing him, Myrkan could come after them even closer to the city. The image of the cruel creature swooping down on them, along with the memory of the woman's scream she'd heard the previous night, made her shiver. Neither trees nor nightfall saved that other woman. Atissa forced herself to keep moving, though her heart sank and hiding fear seemed pointless.

"We'll get close enough to be safe," Koshmarnyk replied with confidence.

She wanted to believe him, but he might have not noticed that she was already losing her strength, and she'd be exhausted long before the sundown. Yet she offered him a smile of gratitude. Her concerns and problems didn't have to be his.

As Koshmarnyk gestured to continue down the road, two men walked out behind them.

"Mayetti and her thugs should have made it to the camp last night," one of them said.

"You know her. Some other scheme came up, and she'll arrive later."

They spoke with the heavy accent of the Western Kingdom, and at first, Atissa took them for merchant guards, but the way Koshmarnyk tensed told her of danger.

The men stopped mid-step and, without hesitation, reached for their swords. "Intruders!" one of them shouted.

The way they moved in matching motions made Atissa think of soldiers, and her heart skipped a beat. Every citizen of Kaighal knew the story of the grueling siege the Western Kingdom had laid to their city hundreds of years ago. Kaighal might have remained undefeated, but that didn't mean its far-west neighbors wouldn't try again. And the high mages' fall must have sounded like a perfect opportunity to seize control of the city.

A sneer twisted her lips. They must have missed the news of demons defending the city, and others coming to destroy it. Or perhaps they hadn't. If they waited long enough for the invaders to wear down Kaighal's defenses, their victory would be easy.

In the distance, many more voices rose, and the military-style call-outs echoing within the forest not only confirmed Atissa's guesses, but also told her they would be facing a large squad.

"I could use that knife now," Koshmarnyk said. "And you should run. Someone needs to get the news to the city."

Run? A dry laugh escaped her. She'd be out of breath before the fight even broke out. Yet she handed him the knife. "You're the one to go. I have a better chance of holding them off." Without waiting for his reply, she whispered a spell, pointing at the approaching men, and a moment after the condensation of cooling air appeared, a spike of ice darted between the trees. Their reactions were too little, too late, and the projectile buried itself in her target's sword arm. He let out a yell as he reeled backward, clutching the limb. When his back hit the large tree behind him, he rolled to the far side. Blood dripped from his fingers, and his companion took cover with all due caution.

Atissa watched them, mesmerized, a wave of unexpected satisfaction washing over her. Until now, magic was nothing but a means of advancing through the ranks, a requirement necessary to gain access to the power that came with position and influence. For the first time, it felt like magic was power in and of itself. The men still stood behind the trees, peeking out with concern on their faces. They'd likely never fought a mage, it dawned on Atissa.

"Go," she said with newfound confidence. "I'll be fine."

He hesitated, but nodded. "If you get back to the city, come to the Towers. You don't have to be an enemy."

She doubted the first archmage would be happy to see her, but thankfully Koshmarnyk didn't expect a reply. He took off, and she stood on the road, watching the two men nearby and listening to the shouts that suggested others were near.

She chanted another spell. The two men scrambled, trying to see and avoid the attack. Atissa didn't give them a chance. Flames engulfed her opponents, soaring high enough to char the lower branches hanging over the road, and soon enough, two blackened bodies fell to the ground. With no one else in sight, she considered retreating, but even if narrow, the road gave her enough space to see any danger, and if she retreated, the Westerners could go after Koshmarnyk instead.

So she stood her ground.

More men and women ran out from the bushes across the road, but the smoldered bodies gave them pause. As they fanned out, slowly encircling her, she counted at least a dozen. Her confidence faltered. If she didn't want to burn the forest down, she had to refrain from using fire, but ice spikes could be dodged by seasoned warriors. Nor could she cast them quickly enough to repel all of those approaching.

A whizzing made her jerk, and that instinctive move saved her life. An arrow grazed her arm, drawing little blood. Wide-eyed, Atissa uttered another spell, her voice so shaky, she was wondering if she'd be able to cast it. Her barrier rose around her as a few more arrows whistled in her direction. She breathed out, but the relief was fleeting, as she realized she was trapped. It was an intricacy of magic combat she was only now learning: the same magic that protected her also prevented her spells from reaching their targets.

Desperate, she searched for a solution. The archmages often weaved spells together in a skillful manner, casting two or even three at a time, but she remembered little from the lessons her father had insisted on. Battle magic was useless in peaceful Kaighal and in the High Towers, where subtle subterfuge yielded better rewards than blunt actions.

She flinched when one of the steel-clad women charged, her armor smashing against the barrier. The magic held, as expected, but as several more women and men in heavy plates approached, Atissa couldn't help wondering how long her protection would last. She'd expected to stand against a group of scouts and lightly armored rangers, not powerful warriors like the five testing her barrier.

Their repeated efforts made her resolve strengthen. Fire risk or not, once they broke through, she'd meet them with flames. If the forest burned, she'd worry about it later.

A sudden roar echoed over the trees, so strong it shook the canopies like the wind. The attackers took a step back, looking around with their weapons at the ready, but Atissa stood frozen. She knew that voice, full of cruelty and hatred. Myrkan had finally woken up and realized the extent of her treachery.

One of the men looked straight at her. "What was that?"

Her face must have already been pale, so Atissa let her fear ring within the one word: "Death." It didn't matter that

Myrkan meant death for her too. If she convinced them to run for their lives, she at least would have a chance at hiding or sneaking away.

Hushed comments rose around her, and she recognized the tone of concern that accompanied unknown threats. They all took several steps back, watching her and their surroundings in cycles and with uncertainty, but none showed any fear.

Atissa understood they would not leave, and her heart sank. No matter how well her barrier held against other humans, it would likely crumble under the demon's power. In a glimpse of a grim realization that Myrkan would not let her die easily, she regretted handing the knife over to Koshmarnyk. Resigned, she exhaled and relaxed her muscles. She'd played her hand and lost.

And then, without any warning or explanation, her barrier vanished.

THE WOODS WERE A FAMILIAR PLACE, but they did little to calm the storm in Ryell's heart. *Played, played again!* No matter how hard he tried to do what was right, to offer his aid and uphold his honor as a royal guard, the world repaid him with betrayal and cruelty.

In the fading light of the day, the forest looked more menacing than comforting, bringing back memories of the lost war and the blood spilled. With the sun already down, shadows stretched across the ground, and bushes darkened, grating at Ryell's instincts. Back in Devanshari, any tree trunk and every branch could hide a demonling, and as he made his way between trees, he flinched at every sound, unable to convince himself this was another forest on another continent. The memories were just too strong and too painful to ignore, and the backdrop of the dark woods too perfect.

He sighed. At least the shadows of the past kept him from the torment of the present... At the same time, he couldn't escape them for long. Leaving Atissa meant that he once more had no goal. At first, he meant to return to Kaighal and offer his services to King Allyv, but Ryell's involvement in the queen's death made the thought of serving her son uneasy. He was not a liar, and he wouldn't be able to keep his face straight if someone mentioned Cahala qi'Devanshari.

And then there was Kamira. Ryell's fists closed at the memory of how she'd manipulated him. How she'd used him to deceive the archmage and devise her trap, letting them think they were the ones to set it. She'd claimed she was looking for a way to escape the demon's influence, but instead, she freed him and brought him to the city. Moreover, she'd become the first archmage of the new Towers, proving that all her schemes were aimed only at getting revenge and gaining power. No, with her holding the most esteemed position in Kaighal and with demons at her side, returning to the city was out of question.

Of course, deciding where *not* to go did little to help Ryell find his direction. He pondered finding a way back home, but with demons coming across the sea, no ship would risk the journey, and even if some captain was daring or foolish enough, Ryell would only step back into the past, into the crumbled beauty of the Devanshari capital that had become a grave to many of its people. He couldn't rebuild it single-handedly, and if some people survived within its ruins and all the way to the borders, they'd be more focused on their own survival. Perhaps, one day, he could return to his homeland, but until then, he had to find a new path... a new life.

The forest offered a temporary respite, and Ryell was certain that if he wandered long enough, he'd find a settlement, but unless he wanted to become a farmer or a lowly guard, it presented no opportunities. Besides, staying so close to Kaighal meant both remaining in the shadow of Kamira's future plots and getting caught in the demons' invasion. Where could he go then? As he walked in the darkness, no aim and no direction yet, he pondered his options.

The way east, across the sea and back home, was out of the question. To the north, there was Tivarashan, and he'd rather run back straight to Kaighal than enter the lands of people who had no reservations about worshiping demons. South was a barren desert, so hardly a place of choice, and the west... He didn't know much about what waited there. From what he understood, the land all the way to the mountain range—the Spine, as the inhabitants of Tyorane called it—was under the informal control of Kaighal. Peppered with small towns and villages, it was as much of a choice as staying in the woods. But beyond the mountains, there could be possibilities.

Ryell didn't know much about the Western Kingdom, except that it had invaded Kaighal's lands some years after the Cataclysm. The city held against its forces, mostly through the combined efforts of high mages and Gildya's adepts, and the kingdom's armies withdrew, never to try to claim the city again. Centuries had passed since, and from what Ryell understood, Western merchants were as welcome in the city as the Tivarashan were, trading with the city itself and using its port to send their wares to Juamha. That meant the people of the kingdom weren't bloodthirsty invaders, but rather hardworking and ambitious men who seized opportunities—be they military or trade ones.

A glimmer of hope presented itself: the Western Kingdom was a place he could go and start a new life. Away from everything and everyone that would remind Ryell of his failures, of being betrayed, of demons... There could be a bright future waiting for him there. Yet before he set out, he needed to see to his survival first. Leaving unprepared with Atissa had taught him a harsh lesson, and storming out of her home, stopping only to pick up his belongings, was not a good start to a long and strenuous journey. He needed supplies, equipment, and a guide as well, unless he wanted to risk getting lost in the mountains... That meant accepting any work he came across. Or, perhaps, he'd find merchants heading back west and offer his services as a guard in exchange for food. Yes, that could work.

A flash of light caught his attention. He focused on it, and the first rays of the morning sun pushing their way through the canopy teased his eyes. Wrapped up in his own thoughts, he hadn't noticed the passing of time. *I must have been wandering the whole night.* Having paid no attention to the direction of his steps, he had no idea where he was, but it didn't matter. As long as he found a settlement on his way, he would know soon enough. His body demanded rest after the night of walking, but he could make it a bit farther before he had to stop.

With his heart and step lighter, Ryell almost missed the crack of a branch nearby. He froze, but no other sound followed. With hand on his sword, he made a cautious approach. It could have been an animal or even a branch falling off, but his blood was already rushing, anticipating an attack. Too many times, during his regiment's retreat from the Devanshari border toward the capital, such a sound was the only tell of an impending ambush. With each life they lost, Ryell's instincts had sharpened to the sounds, and he couldn't ignore them even in a peaceful forest in Tyorane.

"Hand off the blade," a woman said behind him.

Her heavy, unfamiliar accent made it hard to understand, but Ryell caught the meaning of the message and the threat within it. Slowly, he moved his arms away from his body.

Around him, bushes rustled, and four people stepped out, three men and another woman. The one behind him moved around, allowing Ryell to inspect her sturdy armor and the long blade she kept pointed at him. Others kept their distance but had their weapons at the ready.

She looked him up and down. "You aren't from Kaighal." Neither was she, as far as Ryell could tell. Her skin was lighter than local people's, but it didn't have the gray hue of Tivarashan, and her hair was light, almost blond.

"I'm just a traveler," he said. "I come from Juamha, the land across the sea."

The way she regarded him, with both curiosity and caution, showed no malice. Her weapon, then, was drawn out of caution and not ill intent. Ryell offered a gentle smile. Hopefully, they could come to an agreement.

A roar tore through the forest, scaring birds. The men and women around Ryell tensed, and he stood wide-eyed, as the sound was too familiar for comfort. Blood rushed through his veins but brought cold to his spine and limbs.

"What was that?" the leader said.

"A higher demon." Ryell forced the response through his clenched throat. "Perhaps one of the two that dwell in Kaighal."

"Demons? In Kaighal?" one of the men said, stirring the others.

Only at their leader's gesture did they resume their stances, telling much of their proper training. These were no thugs or a ragtag group. They had to be a real unit.

"You know of those demons?" the woman asked Ryell. "Do you know how to fight them?"

He shook his head. "There's no fighting a higher demon, not unless you're prepared to pay a high price in blood. You'd need many more men to stand a chance against it. But if you leave all the magic-infused items behind, it's easy enough to hide in the woods like this." He couldn't be sure the demon cared about the strangers any more than it cared about him, but on the other hand, those creatures loved slaughter and torture, so they didn't need a reason to go after any human.

The woman nodded and sheathed her sword. "Gather everyone you can. We're heading out immediately."

"But Mayetti..." one of the other women protested.

"Mayetti is over a day late. For all we know, that demon got her or her schemes failed her," the leader replied. "I'm not risking everyone's lives just to wait for her. And the news of a new threat is more important than her."

She made a gesture, and a man held up a piece of wood to his mouth. A shrilling sound, oddly reminding Ryell of an exotic bird, carried through the forest. It must have been a signal to others, but Ryell had a hard time guessing its nature—an alarm or a rally, perhaps.

The leader looked at Ryell. "Will you come with us? Our camp is nearby, and you seem to have a lot of knowledge of those creatures and of what's going on in Kaighal. We could use your aid."

Ryell hesitated. Her request seemed earnest, and she

cared for those under her command. And, more importantly, she needed Ryell and was openly asking him for help. She could have had him bound and coerced all the knowledge... Yet she chose to make a humble request instead. With nowhere else to go, sticking with them was as good a choice as any other, and perhaps it would be a first step toward his new goal.

"I'll go with you," he replied. "But who are you?"

She smiled, waving at her men to sheathe their weapons and head out. "We come from what people of Kaighal call the Western Kingdom."

18

The High Towers weren't a place Mizena had wanted to ever visit again, but when the first archmage called, only a fool refused. Besides, she couldn't help being curious. The news of turmoil among the high mages had reached her, of course, and she would have considered it yet another shuffle among the ambitious men and women, but the new archmage had turned out to be a surprise... and she brought demons along with her. Whenever Mizena overheard others discussing the presence of those creatures, she remembered the odd but unimposing duo she used to spy on mere weeks ago. To think that Kamira went on to become the new archmage made Mizena wonder what kind of a woman she really was. Tivarashans were considered cunning and sly, but at the same time, it didn't seem that Veelk would allow someone two-faced to be his companion. But then, love was often blind, and a simple man like him could have been smitten by a sophisticated noblewoman that Kamira might, in fact, have been.

Soon enough, she'd get a glimpse, as with every step up

the stairway, she was getting closer to finally meeting the archmage in person.

The mage—or the arcanist, if Mizena was to give in to the new titles around the Towers—who led her was a young woman with a slightly bewildered expression forever frozen on her face. It might have been caused by the demons' presence or the changes themselves, but Mizena committed her guide's face to memory nevertheless. There might have been secrets to uncover within the Towers' turmoil as power undoubtedly shifted, people left, and opportunists sought to further their goals. In such an environment, a well-informed spy could thrive and earn a year's worth of coin within days.

Mizena caught similar expressions on several other faces, but nothing else suggested that the Towers themselves had suffered through the change. Everyone still went about their business, and although the corridors seemed a bit emptier in comparison to that one time she'd gone to see Archmage Yoreus a few years earlier, everything else looked in place and in order. Not that Mizena had expected pools of blood or crumbled walls.

Yet when she and her guide finally ascended the last of many flights of stairs, and she walked into a large, circular chamber, signs of destruction presented themselves. The crystal dome above it—which on bright days reflected the sun, shimmering like a rare jewel for everyone in Kaighal to see—lay shattered in pieces, swept to the sides, but not removed. A few of the columns supporting the roof bore marks of fire. Mizena's guide pointed to the table by one of the large windows and the lone woman standing by it, studying documents, but a movement in the corner of her eye caught Mizena's attention, making her look up. Two massive creatures perched at the edges of what used to be the dome. From this distance, their shapes looked human enough, but their large wings left no doubt to their true nature, and when one of them turned his head toward her, Mizena openly stared at his face, so resemblant of a bird in its shape.

Only the sound of steps nearby made her tear her eyes away and turn toward the approaching archmage. Kamira looked exactly like Mizena remembered from those few occasions she'd followed her and Veelk, as if the woman hadn't claimed the most powerful position in Kaighal but was still a wandering demonologist with little to her name.

"You look more curious than scared," Kamira said.

Mizena shrugged. Fear was part of life, and demons from afar seemed less deadly than some people up close. "There's coin in being curious." If Kamira had made an effort to have her found, she knew well what kind of business Mizena conducted.

"Veelk said you're good. You managed to follow him unnoticed for a while. He also said that you're a bit too honest for a spy."

Mizena had no trouble imagining the muscular warrior making such a remark. "If honesty is what keeps me out of a blade's reach, I'm honest. Dead, I can't gather or sell information."

"But you haven't sold... the one for which the previous archmage would have paid generously."

"As your companion put it," Mizena replied with a grin, "I'm a bit too honest and too loyal for my own good. But something tells me this is exactly the kind of spy you seek to employ."

The archmage nodded. "I need someone to find out who is hiring Darethal's Thorns in Kaighal. It'll likely be someone from the Tivarashan, and I need to know who exactly and whether they're working with the royal envoy Queen Andalisha sent."

"You're quite certain it's them?" Mizena replied. "It could have been Gildya or even some mages... The first archmage always makes enemies." Even if Mizena wasn't sure that Kamira was their target, a little fishing could help her find her footing in the search for answers.

The expression on Kamira's face made it clear she was aware how her rise to power had stirred somewhat stagnant political waters in Kaighal, but she shook her head. "Hardly any former high mage could afford Darethal's Thorns, and Gildya... I don't think they would trust Tivarashans to pay them for such a job. At least not twice."

"Twice?" Mizena said. "Darethal's Thorns don't fail."

Kamira looked her in the eye. "Then it might not be safe for a spy to mention to anyone that they did fail their assignment twice. But I'll leave it up to you to decide how to gather the information."

Mizena swallowed. The request wasn't simple spying on rivals or gathering gossip of any unrest or subterfuge that posed little danger to the one asking questions. To get information about the Darethal's Thorns' moves meant risking her life, if she approached the wrong person in the wrong way.

"You will be paid for your services," the archmage continued. "I chose you because Veelk considers you trustworthy, not because of what you might owe him. You can always say no."

"I'll do it," Mizena replied. "Though I can't promise I'll find anything. Knowledge of their doings is dangerous, so people might not be willing to talk."

"I understand," Kamira said. "If you need coin to convince anyone hesitant, speak to the seventh archmage,

Bryoen. I instructed her to provide you with the resources you need."

Mizena gave a nod. It seemed that Kamira was willing to trust her when it came to money. The information gathering would be easier when there was enough coin for bribes and other incentives, and perhaps she could even get what was needed without putting herself too much at risk. There was little else to discuss, but before she could offer any parting words, the door swung open and a middle-aged woman walked in. She wore rather plain clothes, but her aura of authority suggested a person of power, perhaps even another archmage.

"Adept Koshmarnyk returned," the newcomer said. "He's badly wounded and exhausted, but he said something about a demon lurking nearby."

The expression on Kamira's face changed. She didn't try to conceal her concern when she looked at the bigger of the demons. The creature took off through the shattered roof, and Kamira looked back to Mizena. "I must go now. I hope you'll bring me some good news." And she rushed out with the other woman.

Left alone, Mizena looked around, more to sate her own curiosity than in search of any tidbits of information to trade later. Kamira might have made it clear that the job had nothing to do with Mizena's debt to Veelk, but with good terms and good pay, there was little reason to sell any of the archmage's secrets for meager coin. From what Mizena had seen and guessed, both Kamira shad her tribal companion valued honesty and loyalty, so she'd be a fool to turn on them.

"Come closer, human."

She flinched at that deep voice. The smaller of the demons still sat perched at the dome's edge, so motionless and silent that she'd allowed herself to forget his presence. She took cautious steps forward, though the creature's face expressed amusement, not threat. Yet Mizena didn't miss the cunning glare of slightly narrowed eyes. The demon's shrewdness could be a bigger threat than his claws.

"Spies collect and trade messages for pay, don't they?" he asked. "I have a message for you to trade, then."

"And do you have pay as well?" she couldn't help asking. "Or will I have to ask the archmage for the coin?" It might have been coincidence the demon spoke to her only when others left, but she preferred to make sure.

The demon's wide smile told her he knew why she asked the question. "I have payment." He demonstrated a shining stone in his hand. Though small in comparison to his fingers, it would be much bigger in human hands. "This is what humans call an imbued stone. I'm told it would fetch a good price. Enough for you to have your pay, and to pay someone else to deliver the message."

"Someone else?"

"The message needs to reach the most powerful yalari... the most powerful demon among those that will arrive to besiege the town. His name is Arujhan," the demon said. "Such a task might be dangerous for the messenger, and the archmage needs you, so I'd rather see you find someone else for the task."

Mizena swallowed, questions swarming her head, and possible answers lurking unpleasantly at the edge of the thoughts. "And what's the message?"

"Arujhan is to be told that Veranesh will be flying alone, southwest, through the desert, on the third day of their arrival to these lands."

A step back was her instinctive reaction. "How can you know so precisely? They aren't even here yet."

The demon looked down at her. "It's irrelevant. All that matters is that Arujhan receives the message. Can you do it?"

"Does the archmage know you're setting a trap for the other demon?" she asked, playing for time. To refuse didn't seem wise, but she couldn't agree to be the means of betrayal. She owed a debt to Veelk, and therefore to the archmage as well.

"She does not and she will not, human. The archmage has a city to defend." The demon leaned forward, looking into her eyes. "A city that will be much safer if the two most powerful yalari fight away from it, don't you think?"

She hesitated. Kamira and other arcanists claimed that the two demons were in Kaighal to help defend it, but the creature's request suggested there was some rift between them. At the same time, she couldn't deny that the demon's logic was sound. Kaighal stood a better chance with fewer demons around... unless the one called Arujhan won and returned.

The demon kept watching her with a slight but unnerving smile, as if he knew exactly what she was thinking about. "Ask your questions, human. You're too smart to refuse me openly, but I need you to do what I ask, not only promise it. So ask, and I'll give you answers."

Mizena shook her head. "I have no way to know whether you're telling the truth. If you cared for the city, you wouldn't be setting a trap for your... companion."

"How can you be sure it's not a trap for Arujhan?" the demon asked playfully. "I have no love for either of them, but I'm no match for their strength. I do want the archmage to succeed in her efforts, though, and with both Veranesh and Arujhan out of the way, we can actually defend this city.

If they fight here... their confrontation could bring about another Cataclysm."

Mizena held her breath. She'd never known Veranesh's name before the fall of the high mages, but after the announcements had been made, gossip started circling. She didn't want to believe that Kamira would bring to Kaighal the very demon who was said to have wiped out the ancient kingdom, but perhaps there was a grain of truth to such claims. "And why you don't want the archmage to know?"

"Because she won't approve of the plan," the demon replied. "She takes care of her allies even if there's a high price to pay. If you don't trust me, ask Veranesh when he returns, but do not tell her. And consider this... Whether you do it or not, Veranesh will soon be far away in the desert. Would you rather see Arujhan, the yalari who matches him in power, crushing the city's walls, or away as well?"

"I've heard enough," Mizena replied. The more she listened to the demon, the more convinced she would be, but that meant possibly betraying Kamira's trust. She turned away.

"You forgot your payment, human."

She glanced at him over his shoulder. "I didn't say I would do what you ask."

The demon grinned. "You also didn't say you wouldn't." With a gentle flick of his wrist, he tossed the shining stone.

"Payment comes after the job." Yet she caught it.

A gust of wind and the whooshing of wings filled the chamber. The other demon landed at the edge of the dome. The two creatures exchanged words in their language, and Mizena waited. The bigger one soon spread his wings again, but the smaller one stopped him with a gesture and then pointed at her.

"I have no time for you, human. I must leave immediately. But whatever Fyertash asked you to do, do it," the demon said. "And don't tell my pactee... the archmage. Her concerns are of human matters, not ours."

He took off, and Fyertash looked at Mizena. "Is that enough?"

"Hardly, but it'll do what you ask." It seemed that he told at least some truth, and Veranesh had left, though earlier than expected. Perhaps there was a trap within the trap after all. "And I will tell the archmage," she added, putting away her payment. The stone, though lighter than she'd expected, took most of the space in her coin pouch.

To her surprise, the demon smiled. "Of course you will. She wouldn't have sought your services if you weren't loyal."

A strange note in his voice caught her attention, and her eyes widened as understanding dawned on her. "You were testing me."

"If you had agreed to keep things from her, I would know I can't trust you. Nor can she, for that matter."

The message was clear: she wouldn't have left the chamber alive. Swallowing, she gave him a nod. Ever since her unfortunate encounter with the former first archmage's henchmen, she'd considered the High Towers a place too dangerous to associate herself with. There was information and money to be earned in many other ways, without getting noticed by those who were powerful and quick to dispose of anyone they found inconvenient. It seemed that with Kamira's ascension to the position, the High Towers had become even deadlier, as demons had their own games.

Yet Mizena couldn't help glancing over her shoulder again at the demon perched above the chamber. She might have been one of the best in Kaighal, but if she abandoned her careful approach to things, perhaps there was more to life than earning money from safely obtained information. A jolt of adrenaline shot through her blood. If needed, she could always back out. Until then, she'd see if her skills were truly enough to be considered one of the best spies in Kaighal.

~

WHEN KAMIRA ENTERED her private chambers and headed straight for the bedroom, two students were fussing around Koshmarnyk. One was cleaning his wounds, and the other one insisted on pouring a concoction down his throat, to which the adept adamantly objected, verbally and physically, making the other carer's work equally difficult with all the jerks and twists. She almost gasped at the state he was in. The patterns of dried blood on his ripped clothes spoke of his injuries, and his face, though calm, betrayed pain in uncontrolled tics when he moved too rapidly.

"I have to stay awake to speak with the archmage," he argued, unaware of Kamira's presence. "I'll drink it later."

"You won't speak with anyone if you die of your wounds," the young woman said. Without waiting for a reply, she made another attempt to force the mixture in.

It didn't escape Kamira that both of the students approached their duties with seriousness and dedication, despite their patient's attitude, and she made a mental note to give them due praise later. Despite the grim circumstances, it was comforting to think that truly dedicated youngsters stuck around when high magic fell and that perhaps if the city survived the demons' attack, the High Towers would become a place of true knowledge and true greatness.

Koshmarnyk tore away from the cup, and his eyes rested

on Kamira. A half-smile curled his lips. "It seems that I won't die before I speak with her."

Both students tensed at the sight of her. "Archmage."

She gave them a nod. "Thank you for your efforts. I need to speak with Adept Koshmarnyk now. I'll call for you if there's still a need for your help." She approached the bed, taking the mug from the student's hand. The other was already putting the washcloth away.

As they left, Kamira took time to inspect the extent of his injuries, and gasped at the torn flesh where his stones used to be.

"At least I still have all my limbs," he offered wryly. "Mayetti was indeed planning a trap, but we were both ambushed by a demon."

She swallowed. As much as she'd rather see to his wounds and ensure his rest, this information was more important than her personal feelings. "Veranesh will likely have to hear it too." The demon had taken off when she was leaving the chamber, so unless he was scouting, he was already nearby, but before she invited him into the conversation, she wanted to make sure there weren't things Koshmarnyk preferred not to tell her in his presence.

As soon as he gave a nod, she rushed to the window. As she expected, the demon was hovering outside.

"It's good to see you alive." Veranesh eyed Koshmarnyk with curiosity and little concern. "Have you gone against one of my kin?"

"Hardly," Koshmarnyk replied. "Myrkan ambushed me and the treacherous adept I was with. He was after knowledge. She told him that what's commonly known, but he wanted more." He indicated his wounds.

"How did you escape?" the demon asked.

Kamira grimaced at the clear distrust in Veranesh's

voice, but she couldn't blame him. A wounded man, on the brink of death, could hardly outrun a demon, which suggested Koshmarnyk had come to an agreement.

"Only by chance, I suppose," Koshmarnyk replied. "Myrkan found Yoreus's daughter, Atissa, in the woods, and even though it seemed she sided with him at first, she had a change of heart and helped me get away."

They had only met once, but the young woman's face resurfaced in Kamira's memory in an instant. "Atissa?" As much as she trusted him, the same couldn't be said about Yoreus's daughter.

Koshmarnyk became somber. "I know what you think, but I'm willing to believe her goodwill. Myrkan threatened her as well, and she risked her life to help me. They didn't have a chance to come up with such a plan in secret."

Despite the help she'd given Koshmarnyk, Atissa's actions could mean secret goals and more trouble, but that was a concern for another time. Yoreus's daughter had hardly any resources at her disposal, no magic nor allies, especially if she truly turned on Myrkan. In comparison to what else might have been waiting for Kamira, Atissa's personal revenge held little weight. At the same time, Kamira cautioned herself, the vengeful young woman's intrigues could bring unexpected outcomes that would affect the city's defense.

"And when we came across more trouble," Koshmarnyk continued, "she stayed behind to ensure I had a chance to bring news to you."

Kamira's blood ran cold. "More trouble?"

"It was only a scouting party, but I think the Western Kingdom is preparing to make their move on Kaighal. I think Mayetti was meaning to meet with them. I know we thought this was Gildya's attempt at undermining your position, but they might not even be aware of her schemes. They would want me out of the picture, but I doubt they are desperate enough to side with the Westerners. To make such an alliance, they would have to give up whatever power they have left."

She swallowed. The Western Kingdom had kept away ever since their last failed attempt to conquer Kaighal ages ago, and that they were reacting so quickly to the wave of changes in the city raised concerns. The city council, Gildya, and anyone involved in defense planning had to be made aware of it. It would be a shame to repel the demons only to see Kaighal crushed by human armies afterward.

"And what of Myrkan?" Veranesh asked.

Koshmarnyk shrugged. "We left him unconscious in the woods to the northwest of Kaighal, but I'm sure he's woken up and left by now. As far as I know, he was here alone."

"If he was after the knowledge, he's likely doing scouting for the others." Veranesh glanced back over his shoulder. "Or searching for Fyertash."

"Mayetti knew enough for Myrkan to figure out that you two are working together. By his reaction, I'd guess he was not pleased with the news. I don't think it was deception, since he didn't expect I'd live long enough to tell anyone."

Kamira waited for Veranesh's response, but he said nothing of Fyertash's trustworthiness or otherwise.

"It seems that we have less time than I had hoped for." The demon's voice revealed no emotion. "With Myrkan already here, others will follow soon enough, so I must depart immediately. Whether he wants it or not, it's time Suzhaul took a side. Until I return, prepare the city's defenses and use Fyertash as you see fit. His yalari's nature might show in his words, but he'll do as told."

She arched an eyebrow at that. A human ordering a

yalari around didn't sound plausible, but convincing Veranesh to stay would likely be a waste of time. On the other hand, if speaking to Suzhaul was so important, he should have set out much sooner.

"Don't worry, I'm not abandoning you or this city." Veranesh must have caught a change in her expression. "You have my magic at your disposal to keep asayalari from breaching the city, and Fyertash's presence will keep the powerful kanyalari at a distance, so you needn't worry too much about them."

"How..." she said, and then it dawned on her. "The binding spell." Even if other demons considered Fyertash inferior to them, the threat of being bound and destroyed would indeed make them reconsider getting too close.

"Use it yourself as well, even to its full extent if you must. You should have enough pactees to shield the city from damage, and you'll prove you are a threat to be reckoned with."

She nodded. "Anything else?"

"If needed, you can still speak with me through the nightflies." Veranesh paused and eyed Koshmarnyk. "I'd let the adept's wounds heal on their own rather than pouring magic in to hasten it, at least until the stones regrow."

"Regrow?" she said, exchanging glances with Koshmarnyk. It might just have been her impression, but the adept seemed less surprised by the idea than she was.

"That should hardly be a question, given the knowledge you already have of... different ways to bind flesh and energies from yalari's realm." Veranesh looked at Koshmarnyk. "Do take care of my pactee, adept, and of yourself as well. It seems that she's not the only one I'm going to have some interesting conversations with, should we all survive."

A slight breeze coming through the window announced his departure, as if he knew that a prolonged stay would result in a barrage of questions. With her curiosity left unsatisfied for the foreseeable future, Kamira looked at the forgotten mug still in her hand and sniffed its contents. The student who'd prepared it was quite generous with the sleepseed extract.

She offered Koshmarnyk a smile. "Is there anything else the archmage needs to know before she administers this?" she asked with a hint of playfulness. Veranesh's remark, though bringing thoughts and concerns, at least ensured her that, in time, the adept would make full recovery. If she couldn't speed it up with magic, he might as well sleep through the pain and healing.

"Is there anything *I* need to know?"

She didn't fall for his cheerful demeanor. He might have held his composure through the conversation with Veranesh, but no matter the changes in his body, he was still wounded and exhausted. As much as she'd love to indulge in spending more time with him, he needed rest, and she had to rush the preparations for the siege. "All else can wait." Even mentioning the recent assassination attempt would be pointless. In his state, he could hardly do anything to protect her, and she didn't need him to worry.

Koshmarnyk eyed her with curiosity, and she expected he knew of her avoidance—they might have spent barely a few months together, but it seemed they already knew each other well enough, and with their openness in sharing secrets, he must have caught her reluctance. Yet, without protest, he drank the concoction she gave him, and as sleepseed extract took over his body, she smiled softly, looking into his glazing eyes. Once he woke up, she'd tell him she appreciated his trust.

19

Atissa stood motionless, fighting her own terror-struck body, so that not a slightest reaction would betray the truth. Not only her barrier was gone. The faint connection to magic she'd felt since she claimed the power coming from the imprisoned demons had disappeared too. It must have been Myrkan who, unable to take his anger out on her, took away the one thing that gave her confidence. The three demons trapped in the stones under the mansion were likely no more. Come to think of that, if Myrkan went after them, her newfound home also was no more.

And soon—a thought sank in—she would be no more as well.

One of the women glanced at her inquisitively, so Atissa sent her a challenging glare worthy of an archmage's daughter with a strong resolve she wouldn't show any fear in the presence of the Westerners. Her father must have died proud, and so would she.

The warrior woman sneered, making it clear the display left little impression, and with a teasing gesture, she poked her ax at where the barrier would be. Her eyes widened as the blade went through, but surprise was quickly replaced by triumph. Her weapon rose in a menacing arc and struck down, right at Atissa.

Atissa made no attempt to dodge. To do so would only postpone the inevitable.

A loud clank of metal meeting metal rang in the air, and before Atissa focused her eyes on the wide blade of a spear that barred the ax's path, her attacker yelled and stumbled backward while the biggest man Atissa had ever seen delivered a punch that seemed to ignore the leather and chain eyelets of the woman's armor.

Others turned in an instant, their weapons at the ready. The warrior beside Atissa grinned.

She discreetly eyed his massive frame, a net of scars marking his skin, and an impressive, double-bladed spear. He wore desert nomads' clothes and looked every bit ready to take them all on, but looks could be deceiving.

"We don't have time for that, you know." A woman joined him, dressed in a similar fashion. Her voice carried a slight note of scolding, but the grin on the man's face didn't fade.

"They don't know it," he replied. "And if you care to unsheathe your weapon and look a bit more threatening, dear sister, we likely won't have to fight at all."

The woman sighed, but took a battle stance, her own spear aimed at the closest opponent. The more Atissa looked at them, the more obvious it became that they were, indeed, siblings.

The Westerners hesitated. In the distance, an eerie shrilling sound rose, stirring their ranks. Then, as if an invisible commander gave them an order, they all turned and ran.

The two warriors relaxed, but Atissa didn't dare take a

breath of relief. For all she knew, her situation hadn't improved at all if the newcomers decided she was a foe as well.

A third figure joined them, one she had missed because he was much smaller than the other two. He might have been as tall, but his shoulders were nowhere near as broad, and his body, though not sickly, lacked the sculpted, wiry muscles of his companions. He also didn't carry a spear, and the only weapon Atissa noticed was a short sword by his side. Yet he dressed as they did, and his skin had the same copper hue.

"Don't be afraid," he said with a comforting smile. "We don't kill innocent women."

"*If* she's innocent..." muttered the tall warrior, staring at the two charred bodies smoldering nearby, and then turned to her. "You do not look like an arcanist."

Atissa swallowed. "I am... I was a high mage." It seemed pointless to conceal it. "But my magic is gone now, and high mages are no more."

"The Towers fell?"

For a tribal nomad, he seemed to know enough about Kaighal, and Atissa nodded. "Arcanist Kamira defeated the first archmage and took his title for herself."

He grinned and gave his sister a friendly punch. "See? I told you she would make it."

The other man stood silent, watching everything with the curiosity of a passerby, but the woman muttered something that sounded like "That scrawny arcanist."

They clearly knew Kamira well enough to know of her plans, and Atissa froze when she realized who stood before her. "You're *the* mage killer. Her friend."

His eyes narrowed and his fingers tightened on his

weapon. Mirroring his reaction, his sister tensed. "Choose your next words carefully, mage."

Atissa lifted her hands. "I mean you no harm, and my magic is gone anyway. But you have to warn her that there is a demon nearby, and others might be coming sooner than she thinks." She looked over her shoulder, but Koshmarnyk was nowhere in sight. It seemed that as soon as he didn't have to wait for her to keep up, he could make a good pace. Unless his wounds were more severe than she thought, and the adept was lying somewhere in the woods, unconscious or dead. "There was a man with me, an adept whom the demon captured. We escaped together, but I stayed behind. I don't know if he made it, so somebody has to bring the message to Kaighal."

"Not you?"

She lifted her chin up. "My name's Atissa. Do you think she'll even receive me?"

He knew of her—his reaction told her as much. "And that's why you'd have her friend deliver the message instead?"

Atissa pressed her lips together, but she couldn't truly blame the man for his distrust. And if she cared to think about it enough, he was the mage killer who was supposed to kill her father long ago, when the whole plot seemed to have started. Perhaps two days ago she would have hated him for that. With the bitter realization of how little she'd likely mattered to her own father, she almost regretted that the man in front of her hadn't done the deed back then.

"I'm likely the last person she wants to see right now," Atissa replied. "And I'd rather not be the reason for her distraction. With the demons arriving soon, she doesn't need to wonder if she has a traitor in her midst. Go to the city, and if you don't trust my words, find the man who was with me. His name is Koshmarnyk."

All three looked at her in surprise. One expected that the archmage's friend would know her lover's name.

"Koshmarnyk, you say?" The warrior sheathed his weapon. "If he introduced himself like that, he found you trustworthy enough, and he's not one to fall for false charms."

Atissa nodded slowly. It likely wasn't the best moment to mention that Adept Koshmarnyk had witnessed her conspiring with the demon who was torturing him all night long. "Please, you should hurry. There's a demon nearby, and Kaighal needs to know."

The expression on the warrior's face suggested that he'd like to take that demon on himself, but his sister put her hand on his shoulder, pointing at the path toward Kaighal. "There will be enough demons to fight."

He sighed, then looked at Atissa. "You'll come with us." The way he said it made it clear he would not accept any refusal, but she found no threat in his voice. "The woods aren't safe for a lone woman without her magic. Besides, I'm curious what's been happening in Kaighal recently, and you seem knowledgeable enough. Then you'll tell the archmage what you know. She might have questions I wouldn't have known to ask."

Atissa hesitated. He was right about the woods. Between Myrkan and the Westerners, not to mention wild animals and any other threats, she'd have little chance of finding safety. But the thought of facing Kamira, weak and helpless, brought shivers down her spine. Not so long ago, she'd dreamed of standing in front of the arcanist as an equal. Now she would be at her mercy.

"She won't kill you for who you are," the warrior said. "But she might not believe your tale, either."

"Fair enough," Atissa replied. After all, beggars couldn't be choosers. "Have you a name to share with me, mage killer?"

He offered her a warm smile, as if by agreeing she'd proven worthy of at least a pinch of his trust. "My name is Veelk. This is my sister, Zelna, and this man here is Mawi. Come, we'll talk more on the way. If the threat is so close, we better not delay any more."

IF KAMIRA COULD, she'd stay by Koshmarnyk's side, but so many other things demanded her attention. With Myrkan close to the city and other demons arriving soon, she had to ensure everything was in place. Besides, since Veranesh had advised against using magic, she would be of no help anyway, and watching the wounds and bruises on the adept's body could lead her mind down dangerous paths. She grimaced as the thoughts came nevertheless.

People she cared about were dead or dying. Koshmarnyk should pull through, but Master Tijhran hadn't, and Veelk... Kamira put all her efforts in keeping her face neutral as she stepped into the corridor. Teachers and students shouldn't see the first archmage in distress. She closed the door to her quarters and nodded to the two students waiting nearby.

"He's asleep now. You can go," she said. "Thank you for your efforts."

They left immediately, as if years of studying in the High Towers had taught them how to act in the presence of the first archmage. Kamira sighed at the memories of Master Tijhran, still feeling the pain of loss. Their relationship wasn't built on fear and subservience, and more than once she'd engaged in discussions or even arguments with her teacher, learning and exploring possibilities. She wished for the same to happen in the Towers—for them to become a place where students were curious and eager to seek knowledge, not to please their teachers with complacency. But with the war looming over the city, Kaighal needed the archmage who instilled respect and confidence.

Kamira rubbed her temples. She had to be everything her homeland wanted her to be and everything she ran away from. If only she could hand the Towers back to Irtan... A smirk stretched her lips. The old archmage would love it, no doubt. The moment of amusement passed as quickly as it came, and Kamira resumed the role everyone expected of her, her thoughts already venturing toward the countless tasks at hand.

"Archmage Kamira!" Mizena entered the corridor. "I need to speak to you about an important matter."

The spy was clutching a large stone in her hand, and magic flowed steady and strong from it.

Kamira furrowed her brow, sensing bad news—the kind that one discussed privately. Steeling herself for what was to come, she reopened the door to her quarters and invited Mizena in.

"The demon, the smaller one... He asked a task of me," the spy said as soon as they were alone. "He wants a message sent to the demon Arujhan that Veranesh will be alone in the desert. He said it's safer if they fight away from the city."

"Did you agree?" Kamira asked, her throat clenching.

Mizena grinned. "I thought it was wise to do so. Dead spies can't bring news to archmages." She glanced at the stone in her hand. "The pay was good, too. But he did say there was a trap within a trap, and he made it look like the other demon agreed. At first, he told me not to tell you, but then he didn't seem to care. As if he was testing me."

Kamira's thoughts raced. On the surface, it sounded almost believable. Veranesh coined the plan, and Fyertash simply did his bidding. What hid below the surface, though, was more important. Words could be twisted and intentions concealed, and if Fyertash had made the plan, she had to assume hidden motives.

"The message..." Mizena said. "It might not reach its destination. It's hard to get one out with the siege in sight, and not all the thugs I could ask to deliver it are trustworthy enough to do their job. They also can't remember a thing proper, a lot of drunken and weak minds, so the words could get muddled before they reach the one they're meant for."

The spy had misread her hesitation, but Kamira still appreciated the loyalty. Veelk was lucky that he'd found such an unusual but valuable ally, and she was lucky that Mizena extended her debt to Kamira. "The other demons haven't arrived yet, so we have time," she said. "I'll have instructions left for you in the Jagged Swordsman when I know how to deal with what you've told me. Keep the stone, of course. It should fetch a good price with Gildya and pay for whatever and whomever you might need for your tasks. And get back to me as soon as you learn who's hiring Tivarashan assassins."

"Will do." With a nod, Mizena left the room.

Kamira stood undecided. With Veelk gone, Master Tijhran dead, and Koshmarnyk asleep, she had no one to confide in. Irtan had a pact with Fyertash, and for all she knew, the old man could have a hand in whatever treachery his demon might be planning. Varessa was friendly and supportive, but she knew little of demons. And Pelina... Kamira smiled at the thought of the once-high mage student who'd found enough confidence to spy on the archmages and become an arcanist. One day, Pelina could be a valuable ally, but for now she lacked both knowledge and experience. That left only one ally to discuss the matter with.

Kamira glanced at the nightflies. It was the most obvious choice, but also one that could prove her unworthy of both the title of first archmage and the demon's trust. After all, Veranesh had left dealing with Fyertash to her, and the sly demon might have told the truth, or at least a part of it. This could well be Veranesh's test to see how she'd handle the matter, as much as it could be Fyertash's veiled attempt to drive a wedge between her and Veranesh or arouse the powerful demon's ire, maybe drawing his attention away from something more important. She had to know more before speaking to Veranesh, and that meant taking a risk.

Without delay, she left her chambers once more, this time rushing to the topmost tower. The sooner she got there, the less likely her self-preservation instincts would make her reconsider.

At the back of her head, a small voice whispered that she would be lucky to make it out of such a confrontation alive.

20

When Kamira entered the initiation rite chamber, Fyertash was sitting perched on the shattered dome's edge. The wind that sneaked in when she pushed the big door open enough to squeeze through brought salt from the seaside and the faint scent of the demon's magic. He watched her with a grin.

"The little spy *did* tell you," he said, amused. "And you came to... do what exactly, pactee?"

She stared straight at him. "That's 'archmage' to you, demon."

The grin didn't fade from Fyertash's face. "I'll call you by your *other* title when you return the courtesy, and use the name for what I am, not what humans call us. Or, since we'll be spending the upcoming battles alongside each other, I could settle for my name."

He was smaller than Veranesh, without the aura of power that surrounded her demon, and the distance to the roof enhanced the false impression of his meager frame, but Kamira knew her own limits. If Fyertash lunged, no magic would save her in time.

"Alongside? Do you really think that after what I've learned I'd let you near me?" she asked. "If you're ready to betray Veranesh, you'll turn on me even faster."

"So, you've decided that I betrayed him?" Fyertash remained unmoved. "Then why speak to me at all?"

"I'm certain you have something to say to convince me otherwise." He didn't have to know that before she spoke with Veranesh, she wanted some proof.

He shrugged. "It's true that I want to send a message to other yalari. It's also true that I did so with Veranesh's approval."

"Yet he did not say anything of it to me." She couldn't resist sarcasm, though a hint of doubt set in her thoughts. After all, Veranesh had mentioned there were things they would discuss later.

Fyertash leaned forward with a sly expression. "Perhaps if you weren't so busy playing human games and played yalari games instead, he would have shared more with you." He spread his wings and left his perch, landing smoothly next to her, though far enough away for her to still look him in the eye without twisting her neck. "If you want to be treated as an equal, act like one. But if you'd rather be a human in your ways, don't complain you're not privy to our plans."

Perhaps she was indeed human in her ways, as he put it, but her Tivarashan upbringing allowed her to see a clear taunt in his words and behavior. "I suppose that's a fair way of putting it."

Fyertash didn't say anything, but the way he regarded her with narrow eyes suggested he sensed a threat.

"Veranesh said you will do as I ask," she said. "Is that true?"

"Yes." He stared at her as if expecting she'd challenge the claim.

"Then you will leave Kaighal." Kamira walked casually through the chamber. She had a spot in mind, but she wouldn't let the demon guess her destination. "If you can't be trusted, we're better off without you. And be careful. Myrkan is already nearby."

To her disappointment, he didn't react to the news of the other demon, but if Fyertash was playing Veranesh, he had to be good at hiding his emotions. Or, perhaps, the demons had already shared that knowledge.

"And if I don't do that?" Fyertash cocked his head like a curious bird inspecting a peculiar seed before devouring it.

She stopped in the right spot. With her feet firmly within the invisible circle, she turned to face him. "Then I'll kill you. You're of no use to me or Veranesh if we can't trust you."

The expression on Fyertash's face became serious. "You have his power at your disposal, but do you think it's enough against a yalari?" He inspected her. "You seem to believe so, don't you?" He spread his arms. "Make good on your threat, then, because I can't leave."

Can't, not *won't*—it didn't escape her, but after such a claim, asking for more explanations would in his eyes be a weakness or backing down, and she could likely forget getting answers or any assistance.

For the last time, she made sure her feet were right in the middle of the circle that Irtan's students had been putting around the Towers at her direction, and she summoned her barrier. She tossed a spark against it, watching the fiery lines bounce off the protective magic. The corner of Fyertash's mouth curled, and Kamira hid her own smile. Distraction was what she needed.

Under her breath, she whispered the first lines of the binding spell, while channeling more fire onto the tip of her fingers. If the demon thought she was going to fight him like any arcanist would, she had a chance.

Yet as soon as the first ties of the binding magic reached him, Fyertash jerked. For the first time since she'd walked in, his face expressed concern. He twisted, looking around, his moves rapid. Kamira almost snickered, but continued with the spell. He must have been searching for the demon who was binding him. She sped up the spell's pace. Soon, he'd realize they were the only ones around, and though she hoped her barrier would withstand his attack, she'd rather not test it. The battle with Uganel was still fresh in her memory, turning her blood ice-cold. At least this time, she wouldn't have to go as far as the destruction part of the spell...

Fyertash faced her again, and his eyes widened. Kamira's words stumbled for the heartbeat it took her to overcome the fear that the demon's fury instilled, but survival instinct took over. Any moment now, the demon would lunge.

Yet he didn't. His wings shot open, and he pushed himself off the ground.

In a rush, Kamira finished the binding, catching the demon mid-flight. Only when Fyertash fell to the ground with a loud thump that shook the nearby columns did she realize she could have let him go. After all, he was fleeing, and that was what she wanted. At the same time, his reaction, so unlike Uganel's, sparked her curiosity.

"You didn't attack me." It would be a while before he tore through the magic binding him, so she could sate her curiosity and perhaps learn a useful tidbit along the way. "Why?" Both Pardayi's and Uganel's instincts were to go after her once she started the binding.

Fyertash sighed, his posture relaxed in the binds. "I've had my moment of amusement and got perhaps more than I expected, but I promised to protect you, and to attack you, even in my own defense, would violate my agreement with Veranesh." The demon scoffed. "I should have known he would teach you..." He turned his head sharply toward her, understanding on his face. "He taught you more than just the binding, didn't he? Your threat was not an empty one. But you will not destroy me. Not here."

Kamira stood silent, not willing to admit that, indeed, she knew all three parts.

"So, are we done, archmage?" Fyertash asked, his voice ringing with the usual confidence. "Or do you intend to kill me and rid yourself of an ally?"

Kamira grimaced. Fyertash was hardly an ally, and definitely not a trustworthy one. That in a moment of instinctual fear he didn't attack her spoke in favor of his claims, and if he truly wanted to keep the information from her, he would have not chosen Mizena as his messenger. Kaighal was brimming with eager ne'er-do-wells who would betray their own parents if it brought them benefit. At the same time, it might have been a move to lull her into thinking she knew what was going on. The true message might have been sent through someone else.

Her instincts demanded she kill the demon, or at least force him to leave. Veranesh considered that sly demon an ally, but it might have been mere deception to blind his opponent. She also had to consider that if she got rid of Fyertash, she'd interfere with a plan she wasn't aware of. Her grimace deepened. In one thing, Fyertash was right. She'd foolishly not paid attention to the games the demons might have been playing.

With no other choice, she woke up the nightfly.

It uncurled from her forearm with unnatural speed, as if Veranesh was ready to react as soon as possible. As the crystal creature hovered in front of her, she pointed across the chamber. The nightfly darted across the floor, and the way it spun above Fyertash suggested a thorough inspection.

"Serves you right for playing games with my pactee," Veranesh remarked coldly. "I hope you have learned your lesson. The next one might render you useless to me, and our agreement will be no more."

Fyertash nodded with a serious expression. Whatever Veranesh had promised him, it must have been of a great value.

Veranesh flew back to Kamira. "If you're done teaching him a lesson, do release him. You only have one yalari left to defend the city."

Looking in the nightfly's crystalline and perfectly still eyes couldn't compare with looking Veranesh himself in the eye, but she still did it. "You haven't told me your true reason behind your departure."

"I do not revel in deceiving my allies, but if I had told you the truth, you would have argued or tried to stop me, likely seeing such a risk as unnecessary. And we had no time," Veranesh replied. "With Myrkan already here, I have to make sure I'm ready to face Arujhan."

She swallowed. Despite the sting that the words delivered, they carried the truth—she would have argued. And, faced with a decision already made, she had to admit that Veranesh had made the right choice. As much as she'd prefer him to stay in Kaighal, if he and Arujhan went to battle near it, the city would suffer. "What of Suzhaul, then?"

"He's a stubborn yalari. But Fyertash's presence in the mage killers' land might have changed his mind about keeping away. I'd wager he'll send aid."

She hid her disappointment. If Veranesh wasn't going to speak to Suzhaul, it meant no news of Veelk, but to ask him to head there once Arujhan was dealt with was selfish. Besides, it could put the whole city in danger if Kaighal still needed his help. Despite the demon's trust in her, she wasn't certain the defense would be successful. After all, the kingdom of Devanshari had a powerful artifact to protect it, and in the end, it had fallen anyway. On the other hand, Kamira reminded herself, the kingdom of Devanshari also had a treacherous queen.

"Since all is settled, do not call upon me anymore unless in dire need," Veranesh said. "I'd rather not have my focus diverted when I'm confronting Arujhan."

With these words, the nightfly dove and curled around her forearm, a lifeless crystal bracelet once more.

Kamira took down her barrier and stepped out of the circle. Fyertash was still lying on the floor and not making any attempts to free himself. No doubt another test whether she'd be petty enough to leave him helpless. Even if Veranesh told him to stop playing games, she suspected Fyertash would give in to his nature, this time perhaps in a less confrontational way. With a moment of focus, she removed the bind.

"I'll make sure your message is sent."

With one smooth move, Fyertash brought himself to a squat. He watched her intently, but without malice. "Uganel... It was you, wasn't it?"

She shook her head. "Veranesh was the one who destroyed him. Through a nightfly."

"But you were there, and you survived." He gave her a respectful nod. "Had I known... I might have chosen my game a little more carefully, *archmage*."

It didn't escape her that Fyertash used her chosen title. Even if in the past she loathed to partake in the manipulation dance, she knew the steps. "Kamira. Call me Kamira, if you choose so."

He burst out laughing. "A pactee worth her yalari indeed. Welcome to the games yalari play, Kamira."

Fyertash would never admit it openly, but he welcomed Kamira's departure with relief. It'd been a while since he'd experienced such a deep fear. It took all his composure to not act on his instincts and squish that pathetic human. With all her magic and support from a powerful yalari, she was still weak and vulnerable like all humans. One swipe of his claw could be her undoing. Even now, when she was already gone, the feral side of his nature kept demanding he dispose of the threat.

He ignored that urge. He'd underestimated his opponent, and it was more than her knowledge of the binding spell. The more important part was her courage and confidence in confronting him. Even if the way Kamira decided to deal with him was risky, Fyertash had pushed her into such a position, and she hadn't backed away. At the same time, he saw no foolish pride in her behavior, so she must have considered she could lose the confrontation. She didn't call upon Veranesh until she'd won, so she wasn't relying on his protection.

Such behavior was rare among humans, and even

though it posed dangers, it also sparked Fyertash's curiosity. Even his own pactee, as wise and confident as he was, never chose the path of direct confrontation, and he always acted in a way that suggested he knew he was no match for Fyertash. To meet a human who was not afraid to stand up to a yalari carried an unexpected excitement, and he'd love to test the boundaries of Kamira's courage and cunning.

He scoffed. Yet another urge he had to ignore. His little game had already gotten out of control, and could have led to Fyertash's failure. No matter how intriguing Veranesh's pactee was, he'd made too many sacrifices and waited too long to give up his revenge for fleeting enjoyment.

The door to the chamber creaked open. Fyertash looked toward it, but it wasn't Kamira returning. Instead, his own pactee walked in. Archmage Irtan had aged a lot since they'd made a pact, but his will was as strong as on the day it drew Fyertash to him.

Fyertash still remembered the first years of their pact, when they'd reluctantly shared knowledge and secrets, and built enough trust to seek a way to free Veranesh together.

"There's been quite a magical commotion here," Irtan said. "A flow of energy I've never seen before."

"The first archmage and I were working through our differences," Fyertash replied. "And she seems prone to act quickly rather than play more subtle games."

The old man's posture changed, suggesting a raised interest. "She's not usually one to play at all. You must have done something significant to raise her ire. Should I be concerned?"

"You should stop fishing. What happened is between me and the first archmage and has nothing to do with our pact."

Irtan shook his head. "You used to be more forthcoming

than that. One would think that you don't consider me your ally anymore."

"You are my pactee, and I chose you for your wisdom and your cunning. You should know by now that if you keep questioning our agreements, they will indeed be no more." Yet Fyertash knew his pactee too well. One didn't become an archmage and one didn't make a pact with the most conniving yalari there was if one settled for vague answers. Irtan was going to dig deeper and perhaps uncover secrets that weren't meant for humans. "For now, assist the archmage and ensure the city survives."

"And after it's done?" Irtan asked. "Will you share your plans with me beforehand, or should I be prepared to pursue my goals on my own?"

Fyertash grimaced. One human humiliating and outsmarting him was enough for the day. As much as he valued his pactee, perhaps it was time to act like any other yalari would. "I'll share with you what needs to be shared and aid your plans... as long as they don't involve the archmage. She's mine to play with."

The old man regarded Fyertash in silence, as if the yalari's threatening tone was something to consider. Then he nodded amiably. "Very well. For now, our agreements stand, and I'll do as you wish." As he turned away and headed for the door, he looked over his shoulder, the same jovial expression on his face. "I hope your games won't see you killed by Veranesh's hand... or by hers."

Fyertash stood motionless until the door shutting announced his pactee's departure. Then he clenched his fists. The trouble with choosing conniving allies was that they often had plans of their own and discovered secrets not meant for them. Although Fyertash was certain his pactee didn't know much about the destruction spell, Irtan's last remark made it clear he had his guesses, and suspected Kamira had some knowledge too. At least Kamira, distrustful as she was, was unlikely to share the spell, and Irtan had promised to play nice until the fighting was over. After that... The thought brought Fyertash no pleasure, but he had to consider having to kill his own pactee to make sure his promise to Veranesh was kept.

He sighed. The price for his revenge had always been high, but the further he went with his plan, the more cumbersome the payments were becoming. Yet, after decades of patience and deception, after long years of pain and humiliation, he'd never hesitate to pay what was due. No matter what would become of Fyertash after all was done, the day he got his revenge would be the sweetest in centuries.

DESPITE ALL THE changes Atissa had told Veelk about, Kaighal looked the same way it always did, but his sister and Mawi had never visited it and stared at everything around them with curiosity and amusement. The northern district was not much to look at if someone asked Veelk, with its shabby townhouses and narrow alleys, but it sufficed for his companions.

Atissa, on the other hand, walked through the street uneasily as if Kaighal hadn't been her home. Veelk couldn't blame her. With the silhouette of a demon in the skies, everything around her must have reminded her of recent events. Back in the forest, when she was facing the thugs, she seemed proud and determined, but the closer they got to the city, the more her shoulders slumped.

He had to admit: it wasn't how he'd pictured Yoreus's

daughter. He'd expected a spoiled brat, but instead, she turned out to be a smart but lost young woman. Perhaps in all this, she was a pawn to Yoreus as much as Ryell was. Veelk wouldn't put it past the archmage to use his own daughter like that, and now she had to suffer the consequences of his actions. The way she told the story of the demon Myrkan and Koshmarnyk—with hesitation and honesty, but at the same time glancing at Veelk every now and then as if she expected him to kill her at any moment— suggested that no matter what kind of person she was before, she'd changed. At the same time, for all he knew, she might have been a seasoned player, skilled at deception, and her humility and fear might have been but a mask.

Veelk smirked at that. He was willing to trust her to some extent, but if Koshmarnyk and Kamira didn't confirm her story, Atissa would have a hard time saving her life. And if she tried anything during her meeting with Kamira, she'd learn quickly that Veelk's trust didn't mean dulled reflexes.

The thought of his friends brought other concerns. At least he knew Kamira survived the insane plan she and her demon had brewed, but until he saw her with his own eyes, he worried. Survival didn't necessarily mean wellbeing, and with that scoundrel Fyertash around, she could be in danger she didn't even expect. On the other hand, if Veranesh allowed the other demon to live, there had to be some truth in Fyertash's words. Veelk grimaced at the mere memory of the demon. Undoubtedly, Fyertash had saved Veelk's life, making an effort to drag him back to his tribe across the desert and foothills, but he didn't reveal his motives even to Suzhaul, and that worried Veelk. In a way, it would have been better if Suzhaul refused to honor a life debt as not being his own and let Veelk die rather than allow Fyertash to leave. The thought that Veelk's own survival might have caused more trouble to Kamira, or even put her in danger if Fyertash's plans included getting rid of her, grated on his nerves. Things were complicated enough without demons meddling... But at least his own demonic patron had decided to join the game, if only indirectly, and that meant Veelk could ensure the sly demon didn't get in the way too much.

Veelk sent a grin to Zelna, who was eying him with growing suspicion. Even if she grumbled about being mixed up in the problems of a city she cared nothing about, he didn't miss the glint of battle lust in her eyes. She was right with what she'd said back in the forest: soon there would be plenty of demons to kill, a challenge no mage killer would pass on.

A few Devanshari women stopped and greeted Atissa warmly, paying no attention to the company she kept. "We haven't seen you in the asylum for a while," said one of them. "Will you be coming soon?"

"I'm sorry. I've been away from Kaighal," Atissa replied timidly. "I have matters to attend to in the High Towers first, but I'll try to come over soon."

The woman raised her hands. "Oh, don't worry. We're doing fine, and King Allyv has found something to help us all. We've just missed your friendly face around."

They left after Atissa reassured them once more that she'd stop by as soon as she could, and as the group continued through the streets, the smile faded from her face.

"I only helped them because my father told me so," she confessed grimly. "Yet they treat me like a friend."

"You still helped them, no matter your motives," Mawi said, matching her pace. "And your father didn't tell you to help Koshmarnyk."

Veelk fell behind to walk beside his sister and watch the exchange. Pride was clear on Zelna's face as she pointed at Mawi, and once more Veelk mused at her wisdom of choosing a small and weak man for her mate. When it came to muscles and endurance, she had enough for two already, and Mawi had other qualities that made him worthy of Veelk's sister. One of the brightest chroniclers of the tribe, he had vast knowledge of magic and demons, and he was quick to figure out problems and offer answers.

Yet Veelk couldn't help a bit of a tease. "So, should I follow our traditions and demand he stand in combat with me to prove he's worthy of you, sis?"

Zelna's glare made it clear what she thought of his suggestion, and he chuckled.

"He stood against me," she replied.

"*Stood* being the important part, I presume? You must have not hit hard enough."

A grin stretched her chiseled features. "He didn't run, neither before I hit him nor after he got back on his feet. I call it good enough."

Her tone, friendly enough but carrying a warning, made it clear she'd have no more jokes on the topic, and Veelk sighed. He missed friendly banter, but he'd rather not risk being smacked to the ground by his own sister for ignoring her wishes. At least he could hope that Kamira remained as she was, with her grumpy nature and dry wit, and she would once more welcome both his company and his teasing.

"You're heading with the mage girl straight to the Towers, aren't you?" Zelna asked.

He nodded. With all that was happening, delays could prove deadly one way or another. Once he knew that both

Kamira and Koshmarnyk were safe and learned of their plans, he'd have time for other things.

"Wait for me in..." He searched his memory for any inn other than the Jagged Swordsman. As much as he hated the idea of staying anywhere else, he couldn't arrive at his old inn without knowing what happened. Koshmarnyk was alive, but it didn't mean Lefna was as well. His throat clenched with guilt at the mere thought of the innkeeper's daughter. Veelk should have been the one to save Lefna, but at the same time, he had to admit that his friend had a better chance of getting her back home. Yet neither Fyertash, when he'd found Veelk, nor Atissa had any knowledge of what transpired, and Veelk would prefer to not walk into a grieving father.

Zelna put a hand on his shoulder. "Don't worry. We'll find somewhere and send the word to the Towers."

He looked at her with gratitude.

In front of them, Atissa livened up a bit, now fully engaged in conversation with Mawi. From the pieces Veelk caught, it was something about magic, and the interest on the woman's face was so genuine, Veelk regretted having to interrupt.

"We better get going," he told her. "The sooner we're done, the sooner we'll know what's next."

Her expression dimmed, but she didn't protest. She offered a quick word to Mawi and Zelna, who departed without delay.

"Don't worry," Veelk said. "It won't be bad if you've told me the truth."

But then, from Veelk's experience, some people rarely told the truth, so perhaps she had reason to worry. At the same time, not once since they'd entered Kaighal had she tried to run or find help. Even during the conversation with the Devanshari women, when she could have easily won their compassion and claimed she was being held against her will, Atissa seemed more interested in getting away from them than from Veelk.

She looked at Veelk without a smile, but he liked the resolve on her face and how she lifted her chin ever so slightly. "Let's go, then."

21

Jalyn paced in his room. It'd been three days since the assassination attempt, and the archmage was yet to send a message, which made him wonder whether she had changed her mind about his involvement with the defense of the city. If that was true, he couldn't blame her. With the attack he had not only witnessed, but almost fallen victim himself to, it had become clear that someone in Tivarashan wanted her dead. Kamira had no strong ties to the queendom, even with her own family, so it couldn't have been a political rival seeking revenge. As much as Jalyn hated to admit it, someone from his own family, or at least of a high position in the court, was involved. Which raised the question about Jalyn's own role in the plot. Had his own mother sent him to serve as a distraction for the archmage while she chose a more underhanded approach to deal with Kamira? Or was someone else trying to claim the success of making Kaighal accessible to Tivarashan? Either way, Jalyn couldn't blame Kamira for not trusting him anymore.

What was worse, Priestess Bayena had disappeared, and no servant of his knew where she'd gone or why. She wasn't there when Jalyn returned from the Towers, and hadn't appeared in their lodgings since. He'd demanded to be notified as soon as she appeared, but in the meantime, he had nothing to go on. Sending out servants to gather gossip would likely do no good, because if Darethal's Thorns were involved, they would have covered their tracks well enough. Tivarashans didn't pay their assassins to be sloppy and visible.

Yet... That thought gave him pause, and he stopped mid-step. The archmage had survived the assassination attempt, and judging from her conversation with another archmage, it wasn't the first try. It took extraordinary power or capabilities to achieve such a feat, and suggested that perhaps it was indeed better for Jalyn to throw his lot in with her instead of his own mother.

He swallowed bitter bile. It might have been too late for that.

At least he could heed her advice and consider his own ambitions. Throughout his life he'd been waiting for a chance to prove himself, and even challenge the centuries-old Tivarashan tradition in the process. When his mother finally burdened him with a task important enough, he'd allowed hope to blind him. Not only had he arrived in Kaighal unprepared for its local politics and for the archmage herself, but he'd also failed to foresee other possible plots, and almost paid with his life for it. Perhaps he wasn't meant to succeed at all.

He closed his fists, but with nothing or no one to punch, this gesture only emphasized his helplessness and naivety.

Kamira might be right, and his ambition might not have been his own. It would be so like Queen Andalisha to subtly nurture his desires and push them in the right direction. A word here or there, a wisely placed incentive or scorn offered at the right moment, and Jalyn wouldn't even know that he could have been dreaming of something else. But even if it was so, what else could he desire? Kaighal had no king, no ruler's position he could contend for, and he had no wealth to bring him to power in the city that cared little for lineage. To settle for some meager title that came with little influence when he was of royal Tivarashan blood seemed even more foolish than chasing the dream of the crown. At least if he fulfilled his mother's wishes, he could count on her generosity... Even if he couldn't rule the whole queendom, he could ask for lands to call his own and pretend the world outside their borders didn't exist.

A knocking on the door pulled him back to reality.

"Enter!" he called out, forcing his voice into a neutral tone.

"You wished to see me, Your Highness?" Bayena walked into the room.

The way she acted, as if he had just called for her, grated on his nerves, and her bow wasn't deep enough to appease her transgressions. "Of course I did!" he snapped. "I hope you have a good excuse for your absence when..." He hesitated. To say that he needed her would be a display of weakness and helplessness. "When our mission is at risk."

"I was at the local temple, Your Highness. Although Her Royal Majesty, your mother, requested me to accompany you in your mission, my duties as the priestess to the Four always come first," she replied. "But why would our goals be in jeopardy? Has something changed?"

Jalyn gritted his teeth, struggling to keep his composure. If he wanted to fight for the throne in the future, he couldn't allow insignificant slights to affect him, but Bayena's sly smile, enough to tell him she suspected *he* was the one to ruin their chances of winning Kaighal, was harder to endure than he'd thought. "There were two attempts on the first archmage's life, both unsuccessful."

Bayena pursed her lips. "That's a pity. Without her, the foreign demons would leave, and the city would be at Tivarashan mercy. But how does that make anything harder for us? If anything, if the archmage feels in immediate danger, she should be more open to receiving help."

Jalyn grimaced. "Darethal's Thorns were involved—both times, from what I know. I witnessed the second attempt. The archmage now knows that someone in Tivarashan is trying to kill her, and this casts a suspicion on us as well. I'm sure she'll become even more difficult."

"But all she has are suspicions?" Bayena asked. "Nothing that would point to our involvement?"

Her tone gave Jalyn pause. The concern ringing in her words was understandable, because if the archmage had doubts, any diplomatic efforts would be harder, but the way Bayena spoke, as if they actually were involved... He took a step forward, his expression firm and eyes focused. "Are *we* involved?" To think that while he worked hard on gaining the archmage's trust, his own entourage had undermined that effort made his composure shake. If he learned that Bayena was acting on her own, the queen would hear about it. Perhaps it was time to put the priests and priestesses of the Four in their place.

"My prince, I'm loyal to the crown, and I would never do anything to ruin the royal family's plans for Kaighal."

A sweet and reassuring voice delivered her reply, and Jalyn almost fell for it and the deep bow that followed. But it wasn't the false note in her words that warned him. It was the words she chose. He clenched his fists and looked her straight in the eye. "Which one of my dear sisters is meddling in here?" he asked. He ruled out his older brother, who devoted himself to the Four, advancing ranks in the Temple and making it explicit he would have nothing to do with his family... or politics, unless they were directly tied to the priesthood.

Bayena's expression changed, revealing malice. "It would have been better if you stayed oblivious to the truth, Your Highness."

"Which one?" he demanded.

She shrugged. "As soon as the first archmage dies, and the demons she cabals with leave, Princess Mefina is ready to take the city with her army. And once Kaighal is under the Four's protection, no demon invasion will happen."

Jalyn stared at her. The plan itself was brilliant in its simplicity, and so fitting for his abrupt sister, who met most of her problems head-on. What worried him was Bayena's eagerness to share it with him, as if he couldn't do anything about it... That meant another assassination attempt underway, and it must have been one she expected to not fail. At the same time, it presented an opportunity to Jalyn. If he exposed the plot to the archmage and warned her, she would likely finally start trusting him. Even his own mother might give a nod to his discovering a conspiracy by someone from his own entourage.

"Priestess Bayena," he said with all the authority he could muster, "you are hereby relieved of your duties. You will return to Kaighal's temple and await the queen's decision as to your future while I inform them of your actions and make the archmage aware that they were, by no means, a reflection of the Tivarashan approach toward Kaighal."

"I'm afraid, Your Highness, that the only thing you'll do is give sufficient reason for Tivarashan forces to attack Kaighal," the priestess replied.

With a move that he almost missed, she flung something in the air. A sharp pain tore through Jalyn's chest. He tried to look down, but his own body was refusing to obey him. His vision dimmed as he fell to his knees and collapsed on the floor moments later.

Bayena leaned over him, and whatever blade she'd used, she was now retrieving it. "A member of the royal family murdered in Kaighal will make an excellent argument to finally conquer the city, don't you think?"

Jalyn reached out to grab her, but his fingers slipped off her robe. His body was getting colder despite the warm liquid covering it... his own blood? He needed to stop the bleeding, warn the archmage, and ensure that his treacherous sister didn't get what she wanted. His arms only jerked weakly when he tried to move. He'd have to rest for a moment, gathering his strength, and then try again. If he wanted to be a king, he needed to show strength and resolve, and he would, despite his heart's fading beat trying to claim otherwise. He would show them all that Prince Jalyn of Tivarashan was worthy of his royal lineage.

The last thing he saw before consciousness left him was a shadowy figure just outside the window.

As Kamira had expected, Fyertash didn't try anything openly, but the two days after their confrontation were trying nonetheless. The demon was present whenever she worked in the initiation rite chamber, and although he only watched her from afar, his constant observation grated on Kamira's nerves. Yet to choose to do her work elsewhere would give the demon what he likely sought: proof of her weakness.

A gust of wind and a quiet thump of the demon landing behind her made her turn around.

"Archmage," Fyertash said without sarcasm. "Can you spare some of your time?"

She gave a hesitant nod. For a while now, she'd felt like she had already found the best solution to protecting the city, but in her stubbornness, she refused to stop searching for something better, and going over her own sketches and designs was surely a better use of her time than engaging in whatever game Fyertash might have conceived.

"I'd like you to take the time to learn the names and appearances of the ones we'll be facing," the demon said. "If they learn of Veranesh's departure, they will expect only one yalari capable of binding them."

"Will they even risk getting close when you're around?" she asked. "With the barrier around the city, they won't be able to get to you before you finish the binding."

Fyertash shrugged. "Any other time, perhaps they wouldn't. But what Veranesh did to Uganel... It might have made them desperate. Besides," he said with a grimace, "there will be at least two of them against one yalari they consider insignificant. If they can overcome the fear of being the one bound, I will lose."

"But can they work together like that?" Kamira asked. "From what I understand, your kind is not quick to unite."

Fyertash rubbed his chin, and his thoughtful expression made him look almost humanlike. "There will be some mistrust, that's for certain. This covenant has been falling apart since the last days of the overseas kingdom. With me gone, and Myrkan away from the others, suspicions between the other two will only grow. And if more kanyalari join them in this realm, the conflicts are even more likely."

"More?" Kamira said. Two were already challenge

enough, and that was assuming Veranesh would draw Arujhan away. "How easy it is to summon a higher de... yalari into this world? Should we expect an army?" The question she really wanted to ask was how they did that in the first place, but she suspected Fyertash wouldn't share such secrets willingly. Ever since Veranesh's summoning and Zemarion's destruction in the Cataclysm, the pursuit of summoning higher demons into the world had been forbidden on Tyorane, but since the other continent hadn't directly suffered the outcome of those events, people living there might have been more than lenient in overseeing ambitious arcanists.

"I know not how pactees perform their summonings, but the passage of our six required a dozen or so of them. You needn't worry too much, though." Fyertash's face resembled that of a hungry bird of prey. "Some of them were foolish enough to conspire against us, so there's fewer of them now. I'd wager they won't be able to bring one or two more kanyalari, and even if they could, there might not be any willing to make such a journey."

"Six of you..." Kamira narrowed her eyes, putting together all the names she was aware of. "You, Uganel, Arujhan, Myrkan, Derazin, and Trupyad. Uganel is destroyed, and you are here, yet you say only three are coming."

"Inquisitive one, just like Veranesh said you are. The six became five, as Myrkan killed Trupyad before I set out across the sea. As for the others... Come. These are the yalari coming: Arujhan, Derazin, Myrkan." With his claw, he scraped at the paint and stone, etching rough shapes. First was a demon with large wings and claws, its silhouette resemblant of Veranesh's. "Arujhan is the most powerful among them, and if we're lucky, he'll fall into Veranesh's trap. But if he doesn't..." Fyertash hesitated. "If you try to bind him, he's more likely to go for the kill than retreat, but he's also the last one to get close enough. He likes to make others work for his own goals."

Fyertash paused and etched another demon. He was massive in size, but with smaller wings, and he looked like a flying maggot. "Derazin is powerful, but a coward. Try to bind him once, and he'll never get close to the city again. Do not take it as foolishness, though. He can use his own cowardice to try to draw you out or reveal any weakness."

He made a third etching, of a demon smaller than the other two, with smaller wings and claws, but a longer, beaklike nose. He inspected it. "Myrkan... He's the weakest of them all, but that makes him all the more dangerous. He's sly and cunning, and not beyond using humans as his tools. But he's also prone to giving in his nature." He gave Kamira a knowing glance. "Much like Uganel. Make him angry or make him feel in power, and he'll forget all his wits."

The very mention of that name brought back Kamira's memories of the battle she and Veelk had endured. "I'd rather not confront any of them in person."

"That makes two of us," Fyertash replied.

She looked at him with renewed interest. It was the first time she'd heard a demon admit to their own weakness or fear, and Fyertash sounded so genuine, she almost discarded the possibility of it being a game. Of course, she'd rather hear how those coming were of no concern to him, but truth was always better than empty reassurances.

"Then why did you turn on them?" she couldn't help asking. "You mentioned revenge, but wouldn't it be better to wait safely until your enemies die by Veranesh's hand? By siding openly with him, you've made yourself a target."

If he had any reply for her, she didn't get to hear it, as the door swung open and two people rushed in.

Kamira tensed, ready to raise her barrier in an instant. It didn't escape her that Fyertash took a step forward, battle-ready and shielding her with his wing... at the same time blocking her view. She'd have to speak to him about it later. As appreciative as she was for the protection he offered without hesitation, it made her useless in any battle. Throwing magic blindly rarely brought desired effects.

"Archmage!" Mizena called out. She was running across the chamber, ignoring Fyertash's imposing posture. "I bring important news!"

Not far behind her was Archmage Irtan, his chest heaving. It must have taken a lot of effort for his old body to keep up with the nimble spy.

Kamira stepped forward without hesitation, which earned her Fyertash's grunt of disapproval. He didn't relax even at the approach of Archmage Irtan, which made her wonder how much the demon trusted the very arcanist he had a pact with.

"I thought spies were supposed to be unseen," Irtan said as he and Mizena met Kamira halfway across the chamber. "She barged in through the main entrance, startling the guards." He smirked. "She also managed to make it halfway up through the Towers before anyone caught up with her," he added with a hint of appreciation.

Mizena sent him a mean glare. "It's not the time for sneaking. The Tivarashan priestess is behind the assassinations, and she's working for the northern princess, Mefina." She looked at Kamira. "She killed the young Tivarashan noble... Jalyn. And she's likely on her way here. When she was retrieving the blade, I saw armor strengthened with imbued stones under her robes. They have an army ready to attack Kaighal once you're dead."

Kamira resisted the urge to mutter obscenities under her breath. The last thing they needed was another threat to the city, but that had to wait. First, she needed to find a way to deal with Bayena. To fight the priestess meant to fight an arcanist who had the magic of four higher demons at her disposal, and the imbued stones in her armor suggested Bayena would be able to control the magic her demons provided. Even with the magic scars and Veranesh's power to aid her, Kamira would not be a match for her. Yet she had to be. She took a deep breath.

"Archmage Irtan, make sure that the priestess makes it to this chamber undisturbed," she said. "You'll be also tasked with the safety of all the students and teachers. Move them to the lower levels of the Towers once the priestess have entered. Do not come here to help me. For the sake of the city, we can't risk both of our lives." It didn't escape her that Irtan wasn't happy with her order, but he nodded nonetheless. "And get someone to pay this woman her fair coin." She glanced at Mizena. "Come see me once all is done. I'll have more questions about what happened." No matter the outcome of her duel with the priestess, the dead prince would be a reason enough for Tivarashan to attack. She discarded that thought. Either she'd win against Bayena and have time to worry about it, or it would be someone else's problem.

Both Irtan and Mizena left without a word, and she turned to Fyertash.

"I won't be much of help," he said. "I'm no match for any of the Four alone, and if they decide one pactee's life is worth killing you, they could bind me and destroy me."

Kamira gave him a solemn nod. Fyertash's destruction

would bring death to many in the city and shatter a lot of structures, but she doubted the Four cared much about Kaighal's state after they were done, and upon a successful conquering, Tivarashan would bring their own people and materials to rebuild and resettle.

"Can you buy me some time, though?" she asked. "I need to prepare."

"That I can do." He spread his wings. "Good luck... Kamira."

She watched his departure with a grim mood. Luck was indeed something she would need in abundance, but she had no time to dwell on it. Before the demon disappeared through the shattered dome, she was already at her table, sketching out a circle.

WIND HOWLED in Fyertash's ears, but even its noise, so unfamiliar in comparison to his home world, couldn't drown out the beating of his own heart. After decades of careful planning and ensuring nobody ever suspected him of anything, his instincts rebelled against open actions and putting himself in danger. When he threw his lot in with Veranesh, he had hoped to find an ally in a yalari perhaps even more determined than he... but in his wildest plans he didn't expect they would have to face the Four. Even thinking about them made his skin crawl, and he smiled. Down below him, a mere human pactee was making her plans to stand against them, and it wasn't foolishness that fueled her composure. In a way, they were similar, both not powerful enough to face their enemies without concern but trying nonetheless.

Yet, if he truly wanted to buy that unyielding pactee some time, trying wasn't enough.

He hovered over the city, weighing his options. Finding the priestess would be easy enough, as even from this distance he could sense the powerful energy surrounding her, and continuous attacks would stop her in her tracks, but only until she called upon the Four themselves. He was no match for their power, and allowing himself to be bound and killed would help the archmage little. He needed a distraction or a cunning plan.

Energies in a magicless world stood out, and over his time in the city he'd learned to ignore the many stones imbued with asayalari power—flickers of his home but nothing to concern himself about, and the pactees around the Towers each had their own distinct aura. The human stirring the flow within the city wasn't one of them, and Fyertash grimaced when he recognized it. Meeting Suzhaul's servants was second only to facing the Four, but if he played it right, perhaps therein lay the distraction he needed. Sadly, the only mage killer who would be keen on agreeing to help him, if not for Fyertash himself then for Kamira's benefit, was likely already dead, and no one else would bother entering any agreements after Suzhaul had made it clear the tribe did not owe Fyertash anything. His grimace deepened. He had hoped that bringing a wounded mage killer back to his kin would make Suzhaul open to negotiations, but such goodwill met only with the usual adamant refusal the lone and powerful kanyalari had for everyone but the humans he chose.

Still, Fyertash had time before the Four's pactee made it through the city, so he could have a short conversation. Even if Suzhaul wasn't willing to negotiate, it seemed he had sent someone to Kaighal, and that was a good sign. Without delay, Fyertash headed where the energy was coming from.

He recognized the duo from a distance, even with the evening already darkening the streets. The woman was a mage killer and a pactee to Suzhaul, though for a reason Fyertash didn't understand, his pactees never took the gift of Suzhaul's magic. The weak man beside her was her mate. A wise man of sorts, if Fyertash recalled correctly. The sight of the duo made him smile. Were Fyertash much younger, he'd likely wonder what a powerful woman like her saw in a wimp like the one accompanying her, but the memory of how Renalea had picked Fyertash as her accomplice was enough to remind him not all the choices were the obvious ones. Renalea wanted Fyertash's wits more than the strength any other yalari could offer her, so the mage killer woman could have wanted something similar from her mate.

They saw him from afar, and the woman unstrapped her weapon, taking a battle stance. The man reached for the blade at his side, but at the same time backed away, allowing his partner space for wide swings and dodges. Wimpy or not, he must have had enough battle training.

"Fyertash," she said without any warmth. "Haven't you meddled enough already?"

At least she remembered his name, but her stance made it clear he should expect no other courtesy from her. "I'm not here to fight," he said. "But your weapon could come in handy should you be willing to kill a pactee, and help Archmage Kamira at the same time." They showed no surprise when he mentioned Kamira's title. Good. They hadn't walked into the city clueless. At the same time, he wouldn't mind learning where they got that knowledge from... but it could wait. Before the woman could turn him down, he threw more bait: "Unless, of course, Suzhaul's finest warrior is not allowed to play with the Four's pactee."

Her hearty laughter echoed within the empty street. Fyertash couldn't help wondering how many humans were watching from behind windows or hidden in the small alleys along the street. And time was running short. If he didn't strike the deal soon enough, he'd fail at his task.

"Don't try to play games, demon," she said. "Teasing me with a powerful opponent or calling me a coward will not work."

"So, will you help me?" he asked. "Kamira needs time, and I can't buy it for her alone."

Surprise flashed on her face, as if she hadn't expected a polite question and an admission of weakness. After a moment of silence, she gave a slow nod. "But if I learn you're deceiving me, I'll kill you."

Mere days ago, he would have laughed off the threat, but his recent confrontation with Kamira had made him wiser. Just like he'd learned that the confidence in Kamira's promise of killing him carried weight, he sensed the woman wasn't bluffing. He regarded her with narrowed eyes. The power of Suzhaul surrounded her like a shield, but there was something more, something stronger... His eyes focused on the blades of her weapon, and he smiled. It seemed that Suzhaul, no matter how uninterested he might be in other yalari's affairs, equipped his chosen with the means to stand against his own kin.

"Fair enough, mage killer," he replied with careful respect in his voice. Since the woman had agreed, appeasing her seemed a better choice than risking she'd turn away.

"The name's Zelna, if you bother to remember it," the woman said. "And one more thing: I help you, and you forget about any obligations that you might have convinced yourself my brother has to you."

The way she said it made it clear Veelk was still alive, and Fyertash nodded. Suzhaul would not let him collect any debt anyway, considering letting Fyertash leave alive repayment enough. It was no loss to him to agree. "This way."

He didn't have to look over his shoulder to know she followed. Suzhaul's power behind him felt like the yalari's breath on his back, and he smiled despite himself. The Four might have been unconquerable, but with the mage killer by his side, he could give Kamira the time she needed, and he had to trust she'd use it well. A woman who was capable of tricking Uganel and surviving his destruction, a woman who'd caught the eye of Veranesh himself, must have had a plan.

As he led the mage killer to where the Four's power emanated from the most, his smile shifted into a grin. It seemed that the times when yalari treated humans as inferior tools were coming to an end. Those of his kin who would not see the opportunities that came with those new potential allies could find themselves in a losing position.

And Fyertash was definitely not going to be one of them.

22

Fyertash was against letting the Four's servant anywhere near the High Towers, but disregarding the lives of humans dwelling in the city would cause friction with Kamira, and he couldn't afford losing what little trust she'd bestowed on him. So he had to allow the priestess, as the Four's pactees called themselves, to make her way through most of Kaighal first, choosing the wide street leading up to the hill on which the Towers stood as the place for confrontation.

Nearby, Suzhaul's warrior lurked, but Fyertash couldn't help wondering whether the woman would truly join the fight or would rather use the commotion to head to the Towers. Humans were frustrating in the way they formed alliances, often based on emotions rather than expected gains. Yet if he wanted to have *his* gains, he had to play by their rules.

He kept high enough in the night sky to avoid drawing attention. Once the Four's pactee appeared, he'd have one chance to finish it all before it started. If he landed a killing blow, the Four wouldn't even know what happened. He almost snickered to himself. He'd been at the game too long to hope for such a fruitful outcome.

His eyes narrowed, he watched the street and every shadow that dared to move in the light of city lanterns fueled by magic stones. When a woman took a turn into the street, walking straight toward the High Towers, he dove before his instincts recognized the Four's power and halted his approach.

The whoosh of wind accompanying his descent must have warned her. Magic condensed around the woman, barring his way, and though his claw dug deep into it, he failed to crack it. Yet she'd had to stop to protect herself, and that was good enough.

"Leave, demon," the woman said. "Unless you seek to anger those whom I serve."

"It's not their city." Fyertash pressed his claw against the barrier. Even with the energy of his own world supporting his body, he wouldn't be able to break through, but trying couldn't hurt. No matter how much the woman believed in the Four's protection, he was right here in the flesh. Even among yalari, fear always gripped stronger in the presence of an immediate danger than a distant one, and humans were even more prone to such instincts.

The woman flinched, and fear crawled under the mask of her confidence.

"It *will* be theirs when we take it." Her voice wavered only on the first words. "Now leave."

"But we're just starting." He moved ever so slightly, shifting his weight.

The woman scowled, and her muscles tensed. The flow of magic intensified, and she pushed it into the space between them. Under Fyertash's claw, the barrier swelled, but he never faltered. All the power at the Four's disposal, a whole nation of humans to choose from, and the one sent into battle had no experience at all.

She gave him a vile glare. "You'll stop being so confident when—"

She was so busy proving her superiority, she missed the trap Fyertash had set. The attack came from behind. A thin, long blade pierced the layers of protective magic with grace and force at the same time, proving that—contrary to the Four—Suzhaul only sent his best.

As the priestess turned to meet the new threat, her confident expression lost to primal fear. She twisted to avoid the mage killer's spear, but its tip still caught on her forearm, tearing the sleeve and clanking against metal beneath. Magic sparked when the blade slid off an imbued stone.

"Impressive," Fyertash muttered. A human capable of a deed Fyertash himself had failed at deserved recognition— even if her strength came from Suzhaul, and the spear's tip held the same power.

The priestess yelled out in pain and shock, but before another thrust disposed of her, she gathered more magic around her. The barrier, so close to her body, seemed to almost crush the priestess, but it dulled what would have been a killing blow. With a growl, she pushed the magic away, driving Zelna and Fyertash back. Fyertash pushed back, pounding his fist against her magic as Zelna hopped backward and resumed her assault.

Zelna kept attacking, and most of her swift thrusts pierced the barrier. Even if they fell short of reaching the priestess's flesh, they made any counterattack impossible. Between Fyertash and Zelna, the priestess was trapped, and they would be able to keep her away from the Towers for as long as the mage killer's strength lasted.

Or, Fyertash thought, *for as long as the priestess doesn't call upon the Four.*

"You will both pay for this," the priestess huffed. "The whole city will pay!" Magic burst from her barrier.

The energy did little to hurt Fyertash, and Zelna seemed unaffected as well, but the sheer power of the explosion drove both back. Instantly after recovering, Fyertash lunged forward, but the barrier was now farther away from the priestess. He grimaced, studying the woman within. Space itself gained her nothing, as she still couldn't move from her spot without risking the protection of her barrier, so there had to be some other reason...

As the priestess squatted down with a piece of chalk in her hand, he understood.

Zelna must as well, because her attacks became heavier and faster. Each time her spear pierced the barrier, Fyertash allowed himself a glimmer of hope. And each time it died when the new barrier appeared to push the blade away. When the priestess finished her circle, he took a step back. Their diversion was coming to an end, and he had to be ready to flee. He could only count on Zelna having the wits to do likewise.

The priestess moved away, and the barrier flickered. Zelna took the opportunity, and so did Fyertash, but their attacks failed to breach before the magic solidified again, and he had to give a nod to the combined power of the Four. The priestess would die sooner of old age than the magic at her disposal would dry up.

The chalk circle was now more than half outside the barrier, and Zelna struck at it without hesitation. Sparks flew to the sides along the blade's path, but the circle itself remained intact despite its feeble appearance. Fyertash narrowed his eyes. With all the energy around, he couldn't be certain, but it seemed that the chalk lines were now a part of the barrier, allowing the priestess to summon outside of her protection and at the same time ensure the circle remained undamaged for as long as she needed. Back in the kingdom of Devanshari, Fyertash had watched pactees perform summonings, but none had used a trick like that. This could be a piece of knowledge the archmage would appreciate, should she survive the impending confrontation.

The priestess smiled with triumph as she began summoning. Yet, contrary to Fyertash's expectations, these weren't the Four's ghastly apparitions that came forth, but an insignificant asayalari. The pitiful creature looked around confused, and then lunged at Zelna. One swipe of the spear disposed of it, but there were already more coming.

Fyertash forced his will over the two that appeared next, and they promptly attacked the third and fourth. The fifth, though, sneaked out, and instead of attacking Zelna, it ran past Fyertash. It took a heartbeat to kill it... Too slow, if they were to curb the incoming flow. The priestess didn't try to control the asayalari, which meant she could summon them all night long, and Zelna wouldn't be able to keep up her attacks on the barrier.

A shadow peeled off the wall, revealing Zelna's companion with his short blade. Fyertash gave him a nod, but he didn't expect the small man to take on the horde of asayalari.

"Suzhaul's blood!" Zelna growled as she killed three asayalari while four others ran into the dark. More were already scrambling outside of the circle, over their kin's corpses, and scattering into the streets. It seemed that the priestess, after all, had some battle wits.

"Go," Fyertash said without hesitation. "Make sure no one dies."

Both warriors took off, chasing the creatures. The screeches and howls in the distance suggested they caught up with their quarry, but Fyertash knew the priestess could always summon more.

She looked at him. "You lost. Now leave, and the Four might never know of your involvement."

Fyertash doubted that, but it was time to go nevertheless. He could stay a little longer and taunt her into calling upon the Four, but their confrontation could only end one way: with him bound. A blow to his pride was nothing, but if it led to his death, it would make keeping his word to Veranesh difficult, and if the Four decided to destroy him, no human would be left in Kaighal... perhaps maybe except the archmage herself.

For a heartbeat, he entertained the thought. From what he'd gathered, Kamira had survived Uganel's destruction, so she would likely be able to shield herself once more, but Veranesh could still see the city's fall as Fyertash's failure. Besides, revenge tasted best when one was alive enough to enjoy its outcome. To perish before Arujhan and Derazin would be to perish without fulfilling his goal.

"I have indeed lost," he said. Centuries of servile attitude, hiding his pride and cunning, made such an admission trivial, and it could serve well to dull the priestess's instincts. He wanted her to believe that if she could stand her ground against a mage killer trained to kill pactees and a kanyalari, one woman with her inferior magic would not be a worthy opponent. Overconfident, the priestess would be bound to make mistakes, and Fyertash had no doubt this was something Kamira would use to her advantage. But if he wanted his opponent to believe in the concession, he had to show the pride she might have expected from a yalari. "I have lost," he repeated, allowing a hint of bitterness into his voice, and a sly smile to make it look like he was trying to hide his sour feelings, "and the Four are as unconquered and insightful as always. I bow to their ability to pick the right tool for the task."

The priestess's eyes lit up with magic and anger, and Fyertash took off, allowing himself a vicious laugh. He had not expected his words to hit the mark so easily, but on the other hand, if what the little spy had told them earlier was true, the Four might have known nothing of their pactee's doings in Kaighal. If the priestess wanted to keep her secret, it gave Kamira a fighting chance. A human, no matter how immense the power she wielded, was an easier opponent than four powerful kanyalari.

He lifted higher into the air, looking at the shattered dome in the distance where Kamira was likely preparing for the confrontation. It was true that he wouldn't be of help in the battle to come, but if all else failed, he could still swoop down and take her to safety as long as the priestess remained unaware of his presence.

With that thought, he headed back to the Towers.

Despite years spent in Kaighal, Veelk had never seen the High Towers up close. Kamira loathed the place, and he had no reason to approach the building on top of the hill. Even if most of the tales of mage killers' deeds were long forgotten, some overzealous scribe could still recognize him. And as much as he liked to entertain the thought of going against the archmages, he'd rather not be chased away from Kaighal as a murderer.

As he climbed the winding road up the hill overlooking the city, the massive structure looked more and more like a maze built upward by a blind madman, reinforcing Veelk's views on high mages' pride that had them cling to the one spot in the city that made their prestige all the more apparent. He had to remind himself that high mages were no more, though he didn't like the idea that Kamira had chosen their dwelling for herself and other arcanists. On the other hand, his friend cared little about appearances, and with the looming siege, she had more important things to do than find a new seat for the new school of magic. Maybe once they drove away the demons, she would use her powers to level the old structure so that it could be rebuilt, with more architectural common sense and practicality in mind.

Beside him, Atissa walked in silence, her head and shoulders slumping as they got closer to the Towers. Veelk sent her a comforting smile. It must have been hard for her, not only because of the prospect of facing Kamira, but also everyone else. As Yoreus's daughter, she likely had many enemies among the high mages, and others might have been jealous of her position and would love to see her defeated and humiliated. Yet she kept going with no complaints or attempts to change his mind, and behind her apparent resignation, Veelk sensed growing resolve. Whomever she was before, it seemed she was maturing fast, and perhaps one day, she would be a worthy ally... if she'd told the truth to begin with. As much as he trusted his capabilities in seeing through deception, he still couldn't discard the thought that Atissa had played him.

A distant echo of a woman's scream drew his attention. It seemed to have come from the topmost tower, but with the sound bouncing off the countless walls and turrets of the structure, Veelk couldn't be certain. At least it wasn't Kamira's voice, but it didn't mean she wasn't involved.

Atissa paled. "That's not normal."

Veelk picked up his pace and made it over the last stretch to the open doors, where two guards barred his way. They wore leather armors and carried halberds, and their relaxed postures suggested neither was a seasoned warrior. No wonder—the mages relied on their magic to protect them, and the two men were likely standing guard to prevent common rabble from roaming the Towers freely.

Yet both men looked down at Veelk, their scowls expressing disgust at his unrefined looks, and his hands itched for the keshal. He stifled the urge for confrontation. There would be plenty of opportunities to fight in the future, and to dispose of them would cause more delay if after that he had to fight his way through the Towers. "I'm here to see the first archmage," he said in a neutral tone.

The guards didn't move, but an old man approached from inside the building. He wore an expensive outfit, and an aura of authority surrounded him. "The first archmage is not receiving visitors at the moment, but perhaps I can be of help."

"I doubt it," Veelk replied. "I'm sure she'll receive me as soon as she learns I'm here. I'm Veelk."

The old man scrutinized him with narrowed eyes. "Anyone could invoke the name of her friend to gain her audience." He looked to Veelk's side, where Atissa stood. "But I doubt her real friend would come in the company of the former archmage's daughter. Is this your doing, Atissa? Bringing in an assassin?"

"I brought her along so Kamira can question her about certain events," Veelk replied before Atissa could. "If you doubt who I am, go tell the archmage what I look like and she'll decide."

The old man grimaced. "Very well. You may enter and wait here. I'll go and speak with her."

He gestured at one of the guards, who led Veelk through the hallway and into a small area filled with cushioned seats. Expensive tapestries covered the walls, but the room lacked any other decorations. This must have been a place to make the commoners wait, furbished enough to make them gape and admire the mages' wealth, and nothing more. Veelk wouldn't be surprised if there were luxurious rooms as well, if those holding influence in Kaighal even had to wait at all to meet with the archmages.

Veelk didn't take a seat, but indicated for Atissa to make herself comfortable... Except she wasn't by his side anymore. *That little weasel!* It was the first time in the long time Veelk had made a mistake in judging character. Atissa must have been trained well by her father. She'd deceived Veelk with her passiveness and resignation, not taking any opportunities to flee until she was certain she could get away. He shook his head. At least she had just made it clear that he shouldn't trust anything she'd told him so far.

With nothing else to do, he waited. It didn't escape him that the guard who'd brought him here took a post outside. As if one guard would be any challenge!

The Towers were filled with strange magic that grated on his nerves. Perhaps some of the high magic lingered within its walls, or the presence of many arcanists in the same place caused it. The memory of the scream he'd heard haunted him, and he paced around the area to ease his frustration. He'd been away from Kaighal long enough, and every moment of delay could mean he wasn't there to protect Kamira.

Movement at the entrance drew his attention. The guard was barring the way to—Veelk arched his eyebrows ever so slightly—Atissa.

She pointed at Veelk. "I'm with him," she said. "You wouldn't want to explain to Archmage Irtan why I'm *outside* the waiting room instead of *inside*, would you now?"

Reluctantly, the man lifted his halberd and let her through. As soon as she passed him, the sweet, innocent act was gone, replaced by a serious expression. It seemed that, after all, her deception might not have been meant for him, so Veelk waited before making his final judgment.

"Archmage Irtan didn't go to speak with Kamira," she whispered. "Instead, he's ordering everyone to keep to the lower levels of the Towers. I heard he ordered everyone to stay away from the initiation rite chamber."

"Irtan?" Veelk said. "I know that name."

"He was the first archmage before my father. When Kamira... When the high mages fell, he declared himself an arcanist, but that old fox would say anything to save his skin and keep his power." Atissa shifted, her unease clear. "If you get us out of here, I could lead you to the chamber."

Veelk weighed his choices. Atissa could have been deceiving him, but the conversation with Irtan confirmed that Kamira was indeed the first archmage, and the old man knew of Veelk's name and his friendship with her. The memory of the woman's scream and the gripping fear that Kamira could be facing danger alone made the decision for him.

"Keep whispering as if you are still talking to me," he said.

Atissa's confusion lasted only a heartbeat, and then she nodded. She started whispering, and the odd language suggested a spell, but she made pauses and changed the pacing of her words, so it sounded like part of a conversation. Veelk smiled. She had quite a talent, and though these kinds of skills didn't encourage trust in her, her actions so far had made him think she deserved a chance.

He moved along the wall separating the waiting area from other rooms and corridors. The guard stood motionless, uninterested in what was happening inside. With one swift move, Veelk pulled the unsuspecting man inside, knocking him out. The halberd fell out from the guard's hand, but Atissa was already there. She stumbled under its weight but kept the weapon from hitting the ground. As soon as Veelk set the guard in one of the seats, he took it from her and placed it out of sight.

Excitement rushed the blood in his veins. Perhaps there was nothing to Irtan's behavior, and Kamira would know soon enough of Veelk's arrival, but he was tired of delays and waiting. He turned to Atissa. "Lead the way."

23

Kamira wasn't in the habit of pacing, but the prospect of the upcoming confrontation made it hard to keep still, and the uncertainty of when her opponent would arrive only added to her uneasiness. When she'd asked Fyertash to buy her some time, she expected mere moments, enough for her to design and draw a circle, but it seemed the demon was cunning enough to keep Bayena busy for longer. As much as she appreciated the effort, she hoped Fyertash was smart enough to not get himself destroyed... along with the city. If she had a way to send a message, she'd tell him to withdraw and let the priestess continue to the Towers. With everything done and nothing else to prepare, time was not her ally.

When the door opened and Bayena walked in, her confidence like a barrier of magic around her, it was almost a relief. The wait was over. The battle of magic and wits was about to start, and Kamira might have been at a disadvantage with the former, but she would prevail at the latter.

After Bayena's confrontation with Fyertash, it would be clear to the priestess that Kamira knew enough to be a threat, so pretending to be oblivious wouldn't work. She looked at the circle halfway through the chamber, aware that Bayena must have been following her gaze. There would be no talking until one of them established dominance... provided either of them wanted a conversation to begin with.

A jerk was enough to set things in motion, and when Bayena channeled her magic into a fiery beam, Kamira almost breathed out with relief. The priestess's reaction turned out predictable, and that meant weaknesses and mistakes to exploit during the fight.

The fire magic wasn't enough to shatter any protection Kamira might summon, but it was enough to force her on the defensive. With a vicious smile, Bayena dashed through the chamber while Kamira brought up her barrier before the flames reached her. She was safe, but she couldn't move, and that must have been the priestess's goal.

Bayena reached the circle and relaxed. "If you already knew that I was coming, you should have been waiting in this circle," she said. "Any half-skilled arcanist would have known that."

Kamira ignored the jab. "You haven't won yet," she replied. Obedient to her will, magic flowed smoothly and formed into ice spikes that whipped through the air toward the priestess.

The response was immediate. Kamira had to admire the sudden surge of power around Bayena, in a perfect flow and under flawless control. Nested in the circle the priestess was standing within, the barrier that rose was much stronger than necessary for Kamira's lousy attack.

"Pitiful," Bayena said. "I thought your demon had more power." She lifted her arms, channeling energy.

Magic condensed around the priestess like a flaming mist, tongues of fire blooming outward from her body. Such immense power might be impressive, but showing one's intentions so clearly never paid off in a battle. Especially not when the opponent was another Tivarashan woman. Kamira scoffed whenever her heritage came up, but it didn't mean she was beyond using the Tivarashan skills she'd inherited and had been schooled in when her own life was at stake.

They both knew that the priestess would have to lower the barrier to send the flames forth, and the priestess's sneer was an invitation for Kamira to try something, so she channeled enough energy to make it look like she'd fallen for the bait.

Bayena pushed the fire forward. The flames swirled inside her barrier, trapped and deadly, and a long scream tore through the chamber.

Within heartbeats, the fire died out, revealing smoldering clothes and burned skin. To Kamira's slight disappointment, it wasn't enough to kill the priestess. She would have expected her opponent to use her full power, but perhaps she thought it unnecessary against someone that had a pact with only one demon.

"Any half-skilled arcanist would have known better than to trust a circle she didn't draw," Kamira said, returning the jab. Of course, making circles into traps was not exactly an arcanist skill. Kamira got the idea from how high mages had trapped both Veranesh and her, and using Hauhan's Graver to conceal some of the symbols was child's play. But the scathing remarks served another purpose. The more she managed to unsettle Bayena into thinking there was more to pacts and arcane magic, the better. Priests and priestesses of the Four were set in their ways and too absorbed in politics to explore the boundaries of the Four's immense power.

The priestess looked around frantically, her face betraying traces of confusion and panic, though she didn't show much pain from her injuries. She threw around sparks and wind, testing the barrier around her. "It's impossible." All the magic she conjured bounced back. "Either way, you can't keep me in here forever."

Kamira sneered. "Only until you're dead." It would take Bayena a little while to realize that her own magic fed the circle and the barrier grounded in it, but eventually, she'd figure it out. As much as trapping the priestess gave Kamira the upper hand, it didn't resolve the battle. All Kamira could count on was exhausting Bayena—even if her power was near unending, her human body had to tire at some point. The more time she spent fighting the trap, the less likely she'd be in good shape to continue the real battle.

Bayena's abrupt change in body language caught Kamira's attention. Under the burned outfit shone metal and stone, much like the adornments Darethal's Thorns wore, confirming the information Mizena had brought.

Bayena fell to her knees.

Kamira cursed under her breath. She'd hoped that the priestess wasn't following the Temple's orders, instead serving the one she wanted to see as the future queen, and thus she'd refrain from asking the Four for help directly. It seemed that Bayena was finally taking Kamira seriously if she was willing to risk her demons' wrath. On the other hand, with the way the Temple favored Tivarashan ways of solving problems, in a secretive and underhanded manner, the Four could even praise their servant for taking the initiative.

While the priestess prayed, Kamira channeled magic into her own circle, the one that had already served her well in the confrontation with Fyertash. But the sly demon had never truly tested his strength against it, so she couldn't easily measure whether its defenses would suffice for the Four's power.

A barrier rose around Kamira at the same time ghastly apparitions formed around Bayena. The priestess must have been truly desperate if she'd summoned all four of them.

"Protectors of Tivarashan," Bayena said in a melodic voice, as if it was part of an incantation, "I'm in need of your aid. This traitor to your faithful nation has trapped me here. She needs to suffer punishment for her transgression."

The four immaterial images shifted when the demons' attentions turned to Kamira. She knew their names, every Tivarashan did, but with their misty silhouettes overlapping and their wings moving constantly, she couldn't make out which was which.

"You," said one of them. "You bow to another."

Kamira should have expected it. It didn't matter what the priestess had done and whether she acted with their approval or not, so long as she bent her head to them. On the other hand, a stray follower like Kamira was always a perfect lesson in the making for all those Tivarashan who were wavering in their devotion to the Four. Politics and Bayena's plots mattered little—Kamira would be punished to serve as an example for the Four's worshipers.

An apparition lunged forward, its immaterial claw swinging at Kamira's barrier... and beyond it.

It took a frantic flow of magic to reinforce it enough to push the demonic attacker back. But another of the Four was already lunging. She might have been prepared this time, but to keep them from breaching, she'd have to channel more and more. Even with the scars on her body and the time she'd spent in the crystal, there was a limit to the magic she could endure. Eventually, she would tire, while the demons would not.

"One way or another, we will see you on your knees," said the demon that attacked.

"Submit now, and you might live." One slash and the next apparition withdrew, pushed away by her thickening barrier.

The priestess said nothing, still trapped in her circle, but her eyes shone with satisfaction, and Kamira had no doubt that Bayena would have her killed no matter what agreement Kamira could make with the Four.

"You could do well serving us," another demon promised in an alluring voice, even as its claw tested Kamira's barrier again.

It was as if they each wanted their own turn at Kamira's barrier, or perhaps bragging rights for the one who triumphed. But that would mean they already considered Kamira an opponent worth bragging over. Kamira threw more magic to shield from their repeated attacks. She had to give a nod to their generosity, if they were truly offering her a pact in exchange for her obedience. They must have seen enough potential in her. Perhaps, in another life and other circumstances, she would have even considered what they were giving...

No, never, she realized with a hint of amusement. She was Tivarashan through and through, and her Tivarashan pride would rather see her die than yield.

Unless she found a way to win.

Her thoughts raced. It was one thing to face a more

powerful arcanist and another to stand against the demons of that arcanist's pact. For as long as the Four lingered in the chamber, losing was a matter of time, but to get rid of them, she'd have to reach the priestess, who might have been trapped in her circle, but was at the same time protected by it. The beneficial trap that Kamira set had backfired as soon as Bayena summoned the demons.

The flash of a distant memory, of conversations with Veranesh, sparked a wild idea. The chances were slim, but in the end, she wouldn't have to actually succeed... She simply had to convince the demons she *could* succeed, and that was doable, but first she had to find a way to keep the Four away for longer than a few moments. With their repeated attacks, she couldn't both maintain the wavering protection of her barrier and focus on her new plan.

The door swung open, and Kamira cursed under her breath. *Irtan was supposed to keep everyone away!* She needed a distraction for the demons, not herself, and anyone who was fool enough to enter the chamber risked their life and possibly hers as well, if she tried to protect the newcomer.

The sight of the man who entered almost cost Kamira her focus. Veelk stood in the doorway, his keshal at the ready. And when the next apparition took its swing, he lunged.

He was faster than she remembered, and the weapon he carried wasn't the same spear. Its dual blades emanated strong magic, and Suzhaul's aura surrounded Veelk's body as well.

The spear pierced the ghastly demon. It made no visible damage, but the apparition shrieked and dispersed, only to reappear closer to the priestess, and the other demons growled.

"Suzhaul's dog!"

"Go meddle somewhere else!"

He grinned at them.

That wide smile, full of confidence and playfulness, was all she needed to regain her spirit. Veelk was by her side again, and that meant they would get through any and all challenges. She took a deep breath as her plans adapted for the better, the more likely to succeed. "Can you keep them off me for a while?"

He arched an eyebrow. "I came here to fight demons, not mists."

Kamira smirked, but movement by the entrance caught her attention. A young woman was standing by the wall, wide-eyed. She seemed familiar, but Kamira had no time to figure out where she'd seen her. Veelk glanced over his shoulder. "Leave and close the door," he called out as he faced the immaterial demons.

They lunged again at her barrier, this time two, but Veelk was faster. His momentum and new keshal sent him flying straight through the shadowy figures, sending the demons back to Bayena, and reminding Veelk of many hours practicing combat alone. The other two lunged at Veelk in the same pattern of assault, each with one focused attack, but to Kamira's surprise, Veelk didn't dodge. She tensed as their claws struck. Even immaterial, demons could affect the human world, and if they were powerful enough, their ghastly claws could rend flesh and bone.

But the demons' attacks recoiled from Suzhaul's energy emanating from Veelk as if it were a barrier. Kamira breathed out with relief. Questions swarmed her, but they could wait. If she didn't have to worry about Veelk's survival, and he would keep the Four away, she finally had the distraction she needed.

With all the magic flowing and condensing within the

chamber, following its string proved challenging, and Veelk's dance with the demons causing random eruptions of power wasn't helping, but if she focused on Bayena, she could find the right streams of energy. The priestess stood in her circle, observing the battle in front of her with slight amusement, as if she was certain Veelk would eventually fail. Kamira watched the flow of magic around Bayena, searching for what passed through the barrier. Only the demons in their immaterial form could breach the trap circle, so those streams of energy had to belong to the Four. If she channeled energy straight at them, she could interweave her own magic with theirs to form a stable connection that would obviate Kamira needing to get close. A risky plan in all ways if they figured out what she was doing. Even if Veelk could hold their adversaries off forever, it would bring them no win unless she took chances.

Remarade, Zyreshi, Dimayatta, Periwen—the names of the Four demons had been engraved in her memory since she was old enough to repeat the words of prayers all Tivarashans chanted. She'd stopped calling upon them a long time ago, but their names never faded from her mind, and today she would finally use them... against them.

She picked Remarade out of habit: every invocation to the Four started with his name.

Under her breath, she started the incantation. Her energy slithered across the room quickly, and her chanting was quick enough to instill a sense of threat in the one being bound.

The roar that tore through the chamber was as strong as if it came from a demon present in the flesh, and the tall windows' crystal panes trembled in response. And then it died as if cut by Veelk's keshal. The magic link vanished, suggesting Remarade had broken his pact. Kamira stopped her incantation, hiding a smile at the sight of Bayena's confusion and the pause in the other demons' attacks. Then she started over. There were three left, and Zyreshi was next.

No human knew for sure, but Kamira was convinced the Four's alliance was something more than a mere agreement, and they stayed close in their own world too. And that meant Remarade must have told the others what was going on, because as soon as Kamira attempted to bind Zyreshi, the demoness shrieked and headed straight for Kamira. Veelk's spear tore through Zyreshi's immaterial silhouette, forcing her to re-form close to Bayena's circle. Kamira continued her incantation, trusting Veelk would keep the others away as well.

The link to the demoness vanished, announcing Zyreshi's departure. The other two demons circled Veelk, but their eyes were on Kamira.

Then, without a warning, both apparitions vanished.

Bayena stared at Kamira with a bewildered expression. "What did you do?" No magic of the Four flowed through the chamber, though it still lingered around the priestess, making Kamira watchful of Bayena's imbued stones. She straightened her back and lifted her chin up. "No matter. If you don't let me leave, none of us will live long enough to indulge in explanations." With a swift move, she displayed a metal orb adorned with imbued stones. "Stay away, tribal," she said as soon as Veelk tensed, "or I'll drop it, and even magic won't save you."

Veelk relaxed and took several steps back. It didn't escape Kamira that even though he didn't obscure her line of sight, he'd positioned himself between her and the priestess. His eyes were sharp, and his expression suggested he'd seen a device like that before. It looked similar to the poison orb Darethal's Thorns used, but the pattern of stones and the magic emanating from it was different... Perhaps something containing fire, similar to the device the last assassin had.

Kamira hesitated. Instincts told her that a man-made item couldn't be more dangerous than four demonic apparitions, and she was on the verge of taking the risk. If she allowed Veelk in the circle, they both would be protected, but his cautious posture made her wonder if she was underestimating the power of whatever Bayena was holding.

A shadow passed across the chamber, but Kamira didn't look up. If Fyertash sensed the Four's departure and was nearby, it would be unwise to lose the advantage by making the priestess aware of his presence.

Silence lingered. Kamira knew better than to taunt a Tivarashan woman who had suffered defeat, but to allow her to go meant risking she'd look for payback later. Even if Kamira had already angered the Four and could count on retaliation in the future, she'd worry about it after the siege.

"I'll allow you to leave the city," she said. "You will not stop at the temple or anywhere else."

Bayena grimaced. "You won't decide what I do or where I go. All you should care about is that I don't drop the device while I'm still in the Towers."

Only a fool would think it was a bluff. Cornered, the priestess would likely give up her own life to make Kamira lose hers as well, along with others in the Towers. It seemed better to make her think she could escape. With a heavy heart, Kamira nodded and indicated the door.

Bayena looked at her with satisfaction. "Wise decision... archmage."

The priestess took a step toward the exit, and then stopped, shock frozen on her face. As she collapsed, behind her emerged a woman holding a sharp piece of crystal, its tip covered in blood.

∼

WHEN VEELK TOLD her to leave, Atissa froze, unable to even nod. Even though until recently she had lived a sheltered life, it didn't take much to recognize a battle of magic—and one fought to death not to simply prove superiority over the opponent. It wasn't a place for someone like her, magicless and helpless. At best, she would be a distraction; at worst, she could be the reason Veelk failed. Yet she couldn't leave. Two Tivarashan women stood in their circles, calling upon immense powers Atissa had never bothered herself with, focused on the more political side of life in the Towers.

One of the women commanded ethereal apparitions, and the other one... Atissa had seen her only once, and even back then, imprisoned in the stone, Kamira had all her composure and confidence about her. This time her expression was even more focused, but—Atissa couldn't be sure—she was concerned. Whoever the other woman was, she posed a threat even to the first archmage herself.

That brought a bitter grimace and even more bitter thoughts. Too many memories lingered within the Towers, reminding Atissa of all the reasons she shouldn't have come back, and the last thing she needed was facing her feelings toward Kamira. In the past, she would have sided with the other woman without a second thought, choosing the one who could help her get revenge and the one who was more powerful. She almost laughed at herself. It had taken the death of her father and facing a demon to teach her that she was nothing but a pawn to those with power, and they cared little for her support.

Jealousy washed over her as she watched how Veelk fought the apparitions, glancing back at Kamira as if to reassure her he was doing fine. *Such friendship...* A sigh escaped her mouth. She'd never experienced one like that. Ryell had walked out on her, and others weren't even worth remembering, all of them seeking her favor only to get to her father.

At the same time, Veelk came to Atissa's aid the same way he did to Kamira's, and his attitude didn't change much once he'd learned who she really was. Perhaps there was a way for her to have his friendship as well.

Her hope wilted as quickly as it blossomed. With no magic nor skill, she'd never prove her worth, and with the past that linked her to Kamira's enemies, she could never earn his trust.

Yet she couldn't simply leave. Even if she wasn't help in a battle, she could keep an eye at the door. Archmage Irtan was still around, and Atissa had always thought he wasn't as senile as he appeared. After all, he'd kept her and Veelk waiting downstairs while Kamira was facing a dangerous opponent. Perhaps Irtan was truly acting on Kamira's orders, but Atissa couldn't discard the thought that he was playing his own game. With Kamira's death, the title of the first archmage would be his again. If she waited, perhaps she could thwart whatever plans the old man was weaving, and it would be a way for her to prove to Veelk that she was worth a chance.

The shrieks that tore through the chamber were inhuman. Atissa shrank. Their sound echoed with rage that surpassed that of Myrkan, and her first instinct was to run. Yet neither Kamira nor Veelk cowered, both in their battle stances and focused.

And then all the apparitions disappeared, bringing unexpected silence.

The three people stood motionless. The Tivarashan woman spoke. Atissa didn't quite catch the words, but her voice sounded confident and full of satisfaction, and once Atissa caught a glimpse of an object in the woman's hand, she understood why. Even from this distance, the imbued stones shone with powerful magic. She'd seen a similar device once, when a Gildya woman was explaining its workings to her father. Back then—and it felt like a lifetime since then—he was preparing an expedition to seal the demon in his desert prison, and his Gildya contact was reassuring him of the device's destructive power. Once dropped or thrown, it produced a fiery explosion that dwarfed even powerful magical flames. If the Tivarashan woman used it, Veelk would undoubtedly die.

Her heartbeat raced. Even if she had her magic, she would be useless in such a confrontation, but she had the element of surprise on her side. The Tivarashan woman was so focused on Kamira and Veelk that it seemed she'd entirely missed Atissa's presence. With that thought, Atissa moved along the walls, swiftly making her way from column to column supporting the chamber in the hope they would conceal her passage. Deeper within, there was a pile of shattered crystals, and while she was circling the woman, Atissa picked up a long shard.

She couldn't help a bitter thought that one of the skills she'd picked up as an archmage's daughter was not the mastery of magic, but moving swiftly and silently. Countless were the times her own father had used her to spy on others or move around the Towers inconspicuously delivering messages or discreetly picking up items. At least this time, it would be of use to her, not anyone else.

"Wise decision... archmage," the woman said.

Atissa caught malice and cunning in those words. The woman facing Kamira had a hidden plan, one that would secure her victory. One that would see both Kamira and Veelk dead.

The woman moved. With no time for doubts, Atissa jammed the crystal shard in her back.

24

The vast plains of sand and little else that humans called a desert soothed Myrkan's mood. The sight didn't have any particular appeal to him, but the barren land was devoid of everything that would remind him of his grand defeat. Not only had he allowed a weak human to outsmart him, but he'd also failed to catch her and teach her a lesson she wouldn't forget till the end of her life... Which would be short and miserable, if Myrkan had a say.

At least he'd ensured the little gaharra had no magic anymore, and slaying the three minor yalari trapped in the bowels of her home sated his immediate blood lust. Later, when the other yalari took the city, he'd find her and exact a more fitting revenge for her betrayal. Myrkan allowed himself to revel in that feeling of satisfaction. He'd take time and ensure she suffered for days before he ended her pitiful existence, and he'd let other humans witness what happened to those who opposed him.

A salty breeze carried from the sea, and Myrkan turned his head toward it, inhaling the faint scents within. Dark shapes marked the horizon and the sky above it, making it clear that his days of waiting were coming to an end. Soon, instead of comforting himself with thoughts of future victories, he would actually get to live through them.

He itched to take off and meet with his comrades, but such behavior would be that of an eager servant, not a confident kanyalari. Myrkan stretched his body, adjusting his posture. He'd show Arujhan and Derazin only what they needed to see. No one would know of his shortcomings when it came to dealing with humans.

He squinted. The silhouettes of both kanyalari were clear on the horizon, but Myrkan couldn't make out anyone else. Perhaps their reinforcements were farther away, delayed by whatever plot the pactees from the other continent concocted...

No. He shook his head. *They wouldn't try again.* There was an attempt at treachery when Myrkan and others had arrived in this world, but a swift and merciless reaction disposed of those who looked to control yalari rather than serve them, and other pactees knew their place. If Arujhan and Derazin were the only ones coming, something else must have transpired. Myrkan pushed concerns away. He'd know soon enough.

One silhouette tore away from the others and made for the shore at a fast pace. Myrkan sneered as the sense of superiority washed over him. Even a powerful kanyalari like Arujhan couldn't exercise patience and self-control enough to wait for the news.

Myrkan didn't move from his spot, and waited.

It took Arujhan a while to make it across the remaining stretch of the sea. Perhaps he wasn't as impatient as Myrkan had hoped. Or, perhaps, he was being cautious. With all the betrayal and death among their ranks, it seemed wise not to rush toward a yalari that could be a foe.

Uneasiness crawled across Myrkan's skin. Arujhan was coming first to determine whether Myrkan could be trusted. There would be questions and doubts, and no matter how confident he wanted to appear, he'd have to once more count on Arujhan's benevolence. At least if other yalari weren't coming yet, it meant that Arujhan needed Myrkan's help in dealing with Derazin. *Humiliation after humiliation... I've had enough of being treated like an inferior tool.*

Myrkan's lips twisted and curled as he attempted to conceal the nasty grimace that tried to make its way to his face. For now, he had to play his part. Later, he'd be the sole and unquestioned ruler of the human realm. He clung to this thought in desperation to keep his expression neutral, as Arujhan was getting close enough to make out the details of his face.

When Arujhan landed, nothing in his moves or posture suggested a long journey except for the dried-up salt in the creases of his outfit. Myrkan avoided glancing at the other yalari's massive wings and powerful claws. It could be taken as a sign of fear and feed suspicion.

"Were you successful in learning anything?" Arujhan asked.

"You were right. Fyertash betrayed us. There's little doubt that he has allied himself with Veranesh." Myrkan paused enough for the other yalari to think about it, but not enough for him to speak and take control of the conversation. "But I've learned so much more. The city in which Veranesh dwells is divided. It will be much easier to find traitors and allies within."

Arujhan gave him a nod. "You'll tell me more once Derazin and the pactees arrive."

"What about others? Are they far behind?"

The powerful kanyalari shifted, and uncertainty passed over his face before his usual mask of confidence returned. "We don't know. Some were supposed to join us, but Veranesh's regaining his freedom and Uganel's destruction might have made them change their minds. Or perhaps it's taking longer to bring them into this world."

Disposing of those pactees who sought to gain control over the yalari who had crossed to the human world should have dealt with any disobedience, but the ones that were left alive might have not been powerful enough to perform the summonings as fast as their predecessors did.

Movement in the skies to the northeast caught his eye. Myrkan tensed as soon as he recognized the all-too-familiar shape, and Arujhan turned with caution to follow his gaze.

Far from them, Fyertash hovered over the sea, carrying a burden that looked like a human. He dropped it before Myrkan had time to have a closer look, and as the body hit the water, it erupted into an explosion so fierce that steam rose at the edges of the fiery storm, and its flames almost reached Fyertash's feet.

The sly yalari watched it die out, and only then did he look toward Myrkan and Arujhan. Then he threw a glance toward the sea, as if confirming that Derazin and the asayalari army were also coming. He did nothing else, hanging in the air and watching.

Myrkan took a step forward, but Arujhan barred the way with his forearm.

"Don't be a fool," Arujhan said. "This might be a trap to draw us out."

To argue with a powerful kanyalari like him was pointless, so Myrkan gave his companion a reluctant nod, reserving his doubts. This might have been their best opportunity to not only capture Fyertash, but also take away some of Veranesh's resources. The odds of the three of them fighting Veranesh alone were already not favorable enough for Myrkan's liking, and to allow their opponent to keep his ally meant making those odds even less appealing.

Fyertash was already making his way back to the city, his flight slow enough to be considered a tease, but Arujhan stood in place. With narrow eyes, he followed the other yalari, and Myrkan could swear there was a genuine concern sneaking into Arujhan's expression.

If Arujhan worried about Fyertash so much, they should have gone after him. Myrkan hid his displeasure. They still had an advantage over Veranesh, and with the information Myrkan had gathered, there could be ways of tipping the scales of the upcoming battle significantly in their favor.

Just a little longer, he reminded himself. Soon, all other yalari would be gone, having either killed each other or returned to Yalarethe, and the human domain would be his. All he had to do was to ensure he was the last one alive. And that should be a task easy enough.

KAMIRA'S first instinctive reaction was to bring up her barrier, but Veelk dashed forward. Before Bayena's body hit the floor, he closed his fist around her hand and the device. Whatever the contraption was meant to do, he must have stopped it, and Kamira let her magic disperse once more.

The young woman behind the body looked at him. "Does this make us even?" she asked with somber seriousness.

His expression softening, Veelk nodded.

The sound of the young woman's voice allowed Kamira

to finally place her among many memories. Her features were gentler than those of her father, but when she spoke, Atissa sounded much like Yoreus did. Their eyes met.

"Koshmarnyk made it back," Kamira said without hostility. No matter what Atissa's goals were, her help deserved acknowledging. "He told me what happened."

Atissa breathed out with relief.

"This conversation will have to wait until we deal with the device," Veelk said. "Those things are nasty when they explode."

Kamira looked up the ceiling, and sure enough, Fyertash was squatting at the edge of what once was the crystal dome, in a spot in which the priestess wouldn't have been able to notice his presence. "Do you think you can dispose of it? Drop it in the sea, perhaps?"

Fyertash flew down, landing softly near Veelk, but his presence still sent Atissa back-pedaling with horror on her face. It seemed that the encounter with Myrkan had instilled a fear of demons in her, and rightly so. It also lent truth to what Koshmarnyk had said about Atissa's change of heart. Even the most deceptive person wouldn't be able to feign such an instinctive reaction of terror.

"If I take her body as well, it should be safe," Fyertash said.

Veelk shifted, his expression demonstrating distrust, but in the end he moved, allowing the demon closer to the dead priestess. Fyertash pushed the hand holding the device over her torso. Kamira grimaced when the sound of crushed bones filled the chamber, blood splashing from the mutilated body as the demon forced it into a mangled ball of flesh. He took off as soon as he ensured the device was safe within.

Atissa put down the crystal shard she was holding and

took a step back. "Koshmarnyk already told you everything I could tell you, so with your permission, I'll leave now."

It didn't escape Kamira that Atissa sounded grim and resigned. "And where will you go?" she asked softly. "Myrkan's likely still lurking outside the city, and you have no home in Kaighal other than the Towers, have you?"

Atissa hesitated, looking between Veelk and Kamira, her lips trembling but chin high. No matter what she'd been through, Yoreus's daughter still had pride left. At the same time, no anger or hate showed on her face, only surrender.

"Why don't you take your old room for now?" Kamira offered. "You can rest and gather your thoughts. If you decide to leave, no one will stop you."

"And if I decide to stay?"

Kamira couldn't resist a smile at the challenge in the other woman's voice. "With the invasion coming, we can use all the help we can get, even if you don't make a pact." She looked Atissa in the eye. "As to whether I should consider you a threat... You know firsthand what demons are capable of. If it's revenge that you really want, I think you are smart enough to wait till the city is safe."

Atissa swallowed and gave a stiff nod.

"But I don't think you really want it, do you?" Kamira asked. Of course, the answer to that question could still be a lie, but she couldn't help her curiosity. Koshmarnyk had spoken of Atissa as if she'd become someone more than just Yoreus's pawn, and Veelk had brought her to the Towers, so she couldn't have been manipulative with him. Had she tried to play him, she'd be lying dead somewhere where no one would find the body.

"I want... I want something for myself." Atissa glanced at Veelk and then back at Kamira. "I think I want... friendship. If I can earn it."

Kamira knew better than to ask what had happened with Ryell, or even where Ryell was. It seemed that no matter what might have bound them together in the past, it wasn't genuine enough to satisfy whatever Atissa was seeking. "Find Archmage Irtan. Tell him you'll be staying in your father's quarters. When you're ready, he'll give you tasks to do."

Atissa regarded her with curiosity. "Do you trust him?"

It might have been an odd question coming from someone who must have been aware that her own trustworthiness was in question, but Kamira saw wisdom in it. Atissa had been around the Towers for much longer than Kamira, and *she* didn't trust Irtan. Perhaps it was an offer to keep an eye at him as well.

"For now, our goals align. Irtan wants this city saved as much as I do," Kamira replied. "After that... I suppose those who are still alive will have to sort out their friends and foes, won't they?"

A warm smile flashed over Atissa's face. "You find yourself strange allies. But I can see why they follow you." She hesitated. "Thank you... for the chance." She gave Veelk a nod and left the chamber.

As soon as Atissa closed the door behind her, Kamira enclosed Veelk in a tight embrace. Strange magic still pulsated around and within him, but she didn't care. "Fyertash told me what happened." She wanted to share all her fears and thoughts with him: that she'd never see him again, that she'd sent him to his death, that she wasn't there to aid him... And the guilt that she hadn't sought him out, choosing the city instead.

He reciprocated the hug, his arms as strong and reassuring as ever. "I'm sure he made it look worse than it was... That sly demon can't be trusted with his words. I had hoped that after Suzhaul gave him a warning, Fyertash would stop getting involved."

She didn't fall for his jovial tone. "You survived. But you've changed," she whispered.

"So did you." Seriousness lingered in his words, but the smile didn't left his face. "We do what we must to survive. At least now I'm here, so you won't be free to do any foolish things, like sacrificing yourself or fighting Tivarashan priestesses. I thought we were going to fight the demons from overseas, not the ones in the north."

She appreciated the opening he gave her, likely one he wanted her to take, as always when he offered her easy wins in hopes of remedying her mood. "Suzhaul wouldn't have sent you if he feared the Four," she said, teasing enough to reassure him her grim thoughts were leaving. "Come. Koshmarnyk will be happy to know you've made it. And Lefna's alive as well." Undoubtedly, he could use some good news for a change.

The beating of wings sounded above them. They split in an instant, their long-honed instincts preparing for a possible threat. Fyertash landed softly, at a distance, and Kamira relaxed. Veelk still held his battle stance.

"Good. You're eager to fight," Fyertash said. "You'll have quarry soon enough." He looked at Kamira. "I hope your defenses are ready. Arujhan and others are arriving."

Kamira's heart went still for a beat. She'd known that day would come, but she'd been hoping for more time and better preparations. So many things were still unresolved, so many other still unknown...

Veelk shifted, abandoning his fighting stance, and Kamira smiled despite herself. With him back at her side, she could face all the demon race if needed, and there were others too. Koshmarnyk was already recovering, eager to finish the devices that were to protect the city, and no matter what hidden goals Archmage Irtan might have had, she could count on his wisdom and magic. She looked Fyertash up and down. Even if he couldn't resist playing games, the demon was still on their side.

"We're ready," she said with full confidence.

THANK YOU FOR READING

Thank you for reading! If you enjoyed the book, please consider leaving a review.
Kamira's and Veelk's adventures continue in

Demon Siege

If you'd like to know how Kamira and Veelk met, sign up for the author's newsletter and receive your complimentary copy of Scourges, Spells, and Serenades – a collection that contains two stories featuring Kamira and Veelk as well as other short stories:
authorjm.com

ABOUT THE AUTHOR

Joanna might be a bit too cautious to do anything even remotely daring or dangerous herself, so she writes about daring adventures and dangerous magic instead. Yet, she found enough courage to abandon her life in Poland and move to Ireland, and then some years later, she abandoned her life in Ireland to move over to the US. She's determined to settle there, once she finally chooses which state to reside in.

When she's not writing or thinking about writing, she plays video games or makes amateur art. She lives the happy life of a recluse, surrounded by her husband, a stuffed red monkey, and a small collection of books she insisted on hauling across two continents.

You can find the full list of her publications and more about her at:

http://authorjm.com

and connect with her via social media:

facebook.com/AuthorJMac

instagram.com/authorjmac

indiepocalypse.social/@AuthorJMac

bsky.app/profile/authorjmac.bsky.social

threads.net/@authorjmac

x.com/AuthorJMac

goodreads.com/authorjmac

bookbub.com/authors/joanna-maciejewska

ACKNOWLEDGMENTS

As always, this book wouldn't see its completion if not for the help of wonderful friends who supported me through all the stages of its creation.

My husband, Inq, believed in me even when I doubted myself, at the same time dispensing a solid kick in the backside whenever I needed one. He listened to my ideas, helped solve plot issues, and had a hand in some on-page deaths.

Piotr Schmidtke who—once again—had read the book multiple times, giving me impromptu brainstorming sessions, which helped to enhance those parts of the book I initially overlooked.

There are also beta readers: Mariusz Kubiński and Kamil Jach who stuck with me until now and donated their time and insights to make Shadows Over Kaighal better, and Mattheus who became a fan of the series and volunteered to become a beta reader for book 3.

My writing friends were also there for me—J. Morgyn White, L.A. McGinnis, Chesley Cox, and Sara Marschand motivated me to keep going, especially at the times when I'd rather do anything but write.

Last but not least, a huge thanks to Jake whose cover designs for the series make me smile whenever I look at them, and to Arran McNikol who tirelessly tracked all my second-language English mishaps.

www.ingramcontent.com/pod-product-compliance
Lightning Source LLC
Chambersburg PA
CBHW061301190726
48288CB00002B/301